Dear Reader:

Scotland Yard's Detective Chief Inspector Nicholas Drummond is on the first flight to New York when he learns that his colleague Elaine York, the "minder" of the crown jewels for the *Jewel of the Lion* exhibit at the Metropolitan Museum of Art, was murdered. Not only that, but the centerpiece of the exhibit, the infamous Koh-i-Noor diamond, was stolen from the queen mother's crown. Drummond, American born but raised in the UK, is a dark, dangerous, fast-rising star in the Yard who never backs down. And this case is no exception.

Special Agents Lacey Sherlock and Dillon Savich (from my FBI series) don't hesitate to help Drummond find the cunning international thief known as the Fox. Nonstop action and high stakes intensify as the chase gets deadly. The Fox will stop at nothing to deliver the Koh-i-Noor to the man who believes in its deadly prophecy. Nicholas Drummond, along with his partner, FBI Special Agent Mike Caine, lays it on the line to retrieve the diamond for queen and country.

I hope you enjoy *The Final Cut*, the first international thriller in my new series, A Brit in the FBI. Do let me know what you think by emailing me at readmoi@gmail.com or visiting me at facebook.com/catherinecoulterbooks.

Catherine Coulter

continued . . .

TITLES BY CATHERINE COULTER

THE FBI THRILLERS

A BRIT IN THE FBI SERIES
(WITH J. T. ELLISON)

THE FINAL CUT

CATHERINE COULTER

and J. T. ELLISON

J JOVE BOOKS | *New York*

THE BERKLEY PUBLISHING GROUP
Published by the Penguin Group
Penguin Group (USA) LLC
375 Hudson Street, New York, New York 10014

USA • Canada • UK • Ireland • Australia • New Zealand • India • South Africa • China

penguin.com

A Penguin Random House Company

THE FINAL CUT

A Jove Book / published by arrangement with the author

Jove Books are published by The Berkley Publishing Group.
JOVE® is a registered trademark of Penguin Group (USA) LLC.
The "J" design is a trademark of Penguin Group (USA) LLC.

For information, address: The Berkley Publishing Group,
a division of Penguin Group (USA) LLC,
375 Hudson Street, New York, New York 10014.

ISBN: 978-0-515-15452-8

PUBLISHING HISTORY
G. P. Putnam's Sons hardcover edition / September 2013
Jove premium edition / September 2014

PRINTED IN THE UNITED STATES OF AMERICA

10 9 8 7 6 5 4 3 2 1

Cover design by Nellys Liang.

To J. T. Ellison for accompanying me on this wonderful new journey. You're one of the very best decisions I ever made. I'm sure Nicholas Drummond will take us on another super adventure.

To Karen Evans, my right hand and left hand and half my brain, whose oar is always rowing the boat smartly forward.

Thank you both for your great dedication to this special project and your enthusiasm and constant good humor.

To Angela Bell, FBI, thank you for your continued assistance. You're such a treasure. Imagine, Nicholas Drummond is indeed the very first Brit in the FBI (verified by the FBI).

—CATHERINE COULTER

For Randy, who stands by my side and keeps me strong; and Catherine, who took a chance.

—J. T. ELLISON

PROLOGUE

Saleem drummed his long fingers on the table, giving only a cursory glance out the window to the clear Parisian night, and wondered yet again—*Where is he?* Ten minutes late. No one kept him waiting, no one. The Fox had set this meeting at the Ritz. The least he could do was be on time.

He caught his reflection in the glass and was pleased with what he saw. His dinner jacket fit like a dream, and he looked important, a man to be respected and feared, the way his father had always taught him.

Yet the Fox, this common *thief*, was keeping him waiting.

He sensed heads turning, and looked up. An incredible woman was strolling across the bar in a skintight black dress and tall, sharp stilettos, her sleek black hair pulled back in a twist, showing the fine bones of her face. She was lithe and moved like a dancer. She looked expensive and mysterious, and maybe there was a hint of danger in that arrogant tilt of her head? Like every other breathing man in the bar, he felt a kick of lust. He enjoyed the show for a moment, then dismissed her. He had bigger fish to fry tonight.

He looked at his watch again. Annoyed, he shot his cuffs and sat back, staring out into the star-studded Parisian sky. Five more minutes, then he would leave. They could set another meeting, on his terms this time, and the Fox would be clear as to who was in control.

He glanced back at the woman and saw she was staring at him as she walked slowly toward him. She didn't pause, didn't look at anyone else, only him. He didn't need this now. He only wanted his thief to show up and get this job settled.

She stopped at his table and said, "You are Saleem. I am here to do business with you."

A waiter hovered behind her, a bottle of Dom Pérignon in his hands. She nodded. He pulled out her chair and she sat down.

Saleem stared, his mind scrambling. What was going on here? Had the Fox sent this exotic creature to do his business for him? Was she his mistress? What?

As if she could read his mind, she said with a small smile, "I am who you seek, Saleem."

He'd searched for three months before he'd finally found the Fox. He would have never guessed the master thief was this woman who looked more like a rich man's mistress than the most successful thief in the world. She was stunning, true, but it was her eyes that knocked a man on his heels—they were a clear, icy blue, the irises rimmed in black, imperceptibly slanted at the corners. And she was looking at him straight on, amused at his surprise, waiting for him to speak. He realized in that moment the fact that she was a woman served his purposes very well indeed. Yes, this was perfect.

The skill set the Fox provided was unparalleled. Legendary, even. The best—he'd heard it from his father and several trusted men of his acquaintance.

He wondered dispassionately if in addition to stealing she was any good in bed. After they finished their business, would she want to go upstairs to his suite? He supposed he wouldn't mind, but first things first.

He watched the waiter fill her flute with champagne. She raised the flute, tipped it toward him for a moment. No smile, only a rather bored assessment in her clear blue eyes. It shocked him. She found him boring? He watched her drink the champagne straight down, never taking her eyes off him, fully aware he was watching her every move. She slowly licked her lips. A signal?

He still said nothing, merely signaled to the waiter to pour her another. She drank again, still silent. He knew all the men in the bar were looking at them, wondering what she was to him. How their expressions would change if he announced to the bar who and what she was.

He sipped his Macallan, felt the smooth fire of the sixty-four-year-old whiskey slide down his throat.

When he'd finally found the Fox, they'd corresponded through a coded email account utilizing a simple and elegant system of protection—they both had passwords to the account. Saleem would write an email and save it as a draft, and the Fox would log in, read the mail in the drafts folder, delete it, then write a response and save it to drafts. They'd been writing for weeks now, the messages short, direct. They'd scheduled this, their first and only meeting, last week, and the account had been dormant since. He'd believed he knew women, knew how they thought, knew how they negotiated to get what they wanted, but never had he gotten the slightest hint the Fox was a woman. Amazing.

He set his glass on the table. "Are you really the person I seek?"

She only nodded again, that slight smile playing around her mouth. She never looked away from him.

Saleem said slowly, "Very well. Let us begin."

She slid a piece of paper across the table. Her hands were slim and elegant, nails short and polished the palest pink. Her forearm slid briefly from the edge of her sleeve with a graceful whisper of fabric, and her delicate wrist turned slightly. He saw generations of her ancestors in the sleek, unconscious movement. Like a geisha serving him tea before she robbed him blind and slipped a knife between his ribs.

He opened the slip of paper and kept his face still, not reacting to the number she'd written. Never in their emails had they discussed her price.

He looked up to see her watching him, her eyes so blue he would swear that if he looked long enough, he would see the azure skies of his homeland, except he realized in that moment her eyes were blank and empty and devoid of anything but shrewd amusement. A chill moved down his spine. He'd never felt this sort of fear before in his life, of anyone, particularly a woman. He hated it, yet it was there deep inside him, this knowledge of her, and with it was a corrosive fear.

Her voice was deep and soft, and he leaned forward automatically when she spoke, though he could hear her clearly above the conversations in the bar.

"You are surprised."

"Yes."

"That is nothing for something so priceless." She snapped her fingers and looked away, but not before he saw the indifference in her eyes, and it enraged him. She knew he would pay the amount she'd written on the paper, doubtless guessed he'd pay double her price, triple if necessary, his need was so great. He realized there was no real negotiating here. And they both knew it.

He sat back in his chair and watched her finish her champagne, her every move elegant, studied. He'd take the deal she offered because he couldn't trust this job to anyone else. He needed the very best. So much money, but he knew she'd earn every penny.

She looked calm, sure of herself, and he wanted to hurt her.

Before his father had died, he'd told Saleem of this thief called the Fox, and there had been admiration in his voice. But his father had never told him the Fox was a woman. Had he known? Of course he'd known. His father had also told him the Fox was Saleem's age, no older, and when he'd seen her strolling toward him, he'd believed her younger. *The Fox is the very best, my son, the very best. I only knew of one failure, and it was an impossible task.* But his father wouldn't tell him about the failure, merely looked through him, beyond him, when he'd asked.

Looking at her now, Saleem wondered if this job was to be her final curtain. Well, why not? With the amount of money he was paying her, she could retire, take no more chances of getting caught and hung. She could disappear permanently, settle down. No more looking over her shoulder. The world would be her oyster and he would give her the pearl.

The waiter arrived with more champagne. When her glass was full, she lifted it, hovering over the midpoint of the table. "Half now. Do we have an agreement?"

Saleem met her eyes and raised his whiskey.

"We do. Yes, I believe we do."

For the first time, she clinked her glass to his, took a small sip to seal the bargain, and placed the flute on the table. She stood.

So she didn't want to go upstairs with him. Too bad. The words spilled from his mouth anyway, even though he didn't mean it, a stupid knee-jerk man's reaction to a beautiful woman.

"You should stay tonight. With me."

She didn't laugh, but he thought she wanted to. She said in a low, smooth voice, a brow arched, "I already know where you sleep, Saleem Singh Lanighan. I don't believe I care to join you."

Surprise hit him like a fist. He'd taken all possible

measures to be anonymous, to hide himself thoroughly. But she'd found his true identity. But how?

"You know my full name?"

A predator's contempt flashed in her cool blue eyes. "Of course I know your name. I know everything about you."

Everything? She knew he was his father's son?

In his business dealings he'd always held the upper hand, always wielded the final power over his opponents. He knew it was whispered he was the Devil, and he liked that. All recognized he was cunning, confident of his own worth, the one to be placated, the one who was feared. No longer.

He'd met the real Devil tonight, and she drank champagne. Was his father watching him? And laughing?

The Fox said, "I will email the information, then you will close the account. When half the money—a full twenty-five million—is wired to my account, I will begin. Not a moment before. You will not hear from me again. I will come to you when the job is finished. It is a pleasure doing business with you."

"Wait." He stood as well. He cleared his throat, spoke quietly because he knew well the effect of his voice, knew the arrogance of his breeding and background came clearly through.

"I know your reputation, so I am not surprised you managed to discover who I am. However, I only know you as the Fox. Give me your real name. For fifty million dollars, I am owed at least that."

The Devil smiled from the Fox's beautiful face, and that cold, cold smile froze his blood.

"You are owed nothing but your prize, lion cub. Or should I call you the Lion now? Your father's untimely death places you in control. Will you be as interesting as your father, lion cub? Will you show yourself cunning and ripe, ready for plunder?"

She fell silent for a moment, assessing him yet again, then dismissed him with a nod, and he knew to his gut she didn't fear him, not at all. But if she failed in this, she would regret her mistake. He would kill her himself.

His voice rose. "If you're going to work for me, you'll do as I say. Now tell me your name."

He would swear she looked into his very soul then and found him wanting. Quiet and calm, she said, "Be patient and you will be rewarded."

He wouldn't allow this, not from a criminal who believed herself above him, above the Lion. She would heed this demand. He caught her arm and drew her near.

Her voice was perfectly pleasant. "Let go of me this instant."

He squeezed her arm, hard. He wasn't going to let her believe he was of little or no account except for his huge riches. She needed to understand who he was, what he was, what he could do to her. He was the Lion now, and what he wanted he got.

"Your real name," he said. "I insist."

The patrons were beginning to notice their standoff. Saleem knew the last thing she'd want was to be remembered, so he was pleased when she smiled and leaned in close as if she were kissing him good-bye. She whispered in his ear as she stroked her palm across his neck, and he dropped her arm with a gasp.

With an ice-cold smile, she said, "Do not look for me, Saleem Singh Lanighan. I will find you."

She walked away. He felt the other men's eyes follow her every step through the lounge. Then she was gone, disappeared out to the street into the Paris night.

Saleem sat back down and pressed his napkin to the side of his neck against the sting. He didn't know where she'd had the knife hidden, but she'd managed to bring it to his throat without anyone noticing. He felt the thin gash throb, and with it, he tasted fear, fear of the Devil.

She'd left him with three words, words that would settle in his belly and sigh in his brain for months to come. He realized he'd heard the name before, not from his father but from other men, whispered in the darkest corners, but he'd never realized, never known, and now he was left to wonder how long he would feel her cold lips trailing down his throat, following the thin stream of blood as she whispered her name.

"I am Kitsune."

1

London
Present
Thursday, before dawn

Nicholas Drummond lived for these moments. His shoulders were relaxed, his hands loose, warm, and ready inside thin leather gloves. He could feel his heart beat a slow, steady cadence, feel the adrenaline shooting so high he could fly. His breath puffed white in the frigid morning air, not unexpected on an early January morning in London. There was nothing like a hostage situation to get one's blood pumping, and he was ready.

He took in the scene as he'd been trained to do, complemented by years of experience: shooters positioned on the roofs in a three-block triangular radius, sirens wailing behind shouts and screams, and a single semiautomatic weapon bursting out an occasional staccato drumbeat. The streets were shut down in all directions. A helicopter's rotors whumped overhead. His team was lined up behind him, waiting for the go signal.

His suspect was thirty yards away, tucked out of sight, ten feet from the left of the entrance to the Victoria Street Underground, and not shy about letting them know his position. He'd been told the guy was a nutter—not a surprise, given he'd been wild-eyed in his demands for money from a second-rate kiosk before dawn. Instead of making a run for it, he'd grabbed a woman and was now holed up, shooting away. Where he had found a semi-automatic weapon, plus enough ammunition to take out Khartoum, Nicholas didn't know. He didn't care about the answer, only wanted this to end peaceably.

At least the hostage hadn't been killed yet. She was a middle-aged woman, now lying on her side maybe six feet from the shooter, trussed up with duct tape. They could see her face, leached of color and terrified. He could imagine her screams of terror if her mouth weren't taped.

No, she wasn't dead. Yet. Which presented a problem—one wrong move and a bullet would go into her head.

Nicholas glanced over his shoulder at his second, Detective Inspector Gareth Scott, tucked against the curb, his expression edgy, a flash of excitement in his eyes. He clutched his Heckler & Koch MP5 against his chest. His Glock 17 was in its shoulder holster.

The suspect stopped firing his weapon, and there was sudden blessed silence. Nicholas didn't think the guy had run out of bullets. Had the gun jammed? They should be so lucky. What was he thinking? Planning?

Nicholas dropped down beside Gareth. "We have ourselves a crazy. Brief me on the rest."

"We have a photo, taken from the eastern rooftop. It's

blurred, but Facial Recognition did their magic. The guy's name is Esposito, out of prison only a month. I guess he woke up real early and decided he needed some excitement in his life and went on this little rampage."

"What set him off?"

"We don't know. He took four quid out of the kiosk till, all the guy had at this hour of the morning, and grabbed the woman when the police showed up."

Esposito raised his weapon again and blasted half a dozen bullets into the foggy morning air.

Nicholas saw a brief glimpse of the man's head, but the angle made it impossible for the snipers to take him out. He wouldn't give them permission to fire anyway, not if there was a chance of hitting the woman. He had to make a decision—time was running short.

Nicholas glanced at his watch—5:16 a.m., an ungodly hour in winter, barely light enough to see. At least it wasn't raining, but clouds were fat and black overhead, all they needed to make this a real party.

Esposito continued shooting, then stopped mid-blast and shouted, "You stupid coppers back off or she's dead, you hear me? I'll let her go as soon as I'm clear!"

There was return gunfire, and Esposito screamed, "Shoot at me again and I swear I'll kill her. Back off. Back off!"

Nicholas shouted, "We'll back off. Don't hurt the woman."

Esposito's answer was a bullet that flew a couple of feet over Nicholas's head. "Enough," Nicholas said. "Let's get him."

"You want him alive?"

"We'll see," Nicholas said. "We need a better angle. Follow me."

They duck-walked across the street, then flattened, faces to the ground, just before a fusillade of bullets kicked up gravel two feet away from their earlier position. Gareth cursed. "At least the guy's a lousy shot."

Silence again, except for their fast breaths. Nicholas didn't think Esposito had seen them move. "Keep still and stay down," he whispered. They were only twenty yards downwind now, sheltered by the construction in front of the station's façade. A good spot, though if Esposito moved, turned, he might very well see them and they'd be dead.

Almost as if he knew what they were doing, Esposito grabbed the woman, held her in front of him as a shield, and dragged her fifteen feet before pulling her down behind a big metal construction bin. Now Esposito was facing away from them, a good thirty feet from their position. He was squatted down behind the bin, leaning around the side to check for threats, ready to fire.

And Nicholas thought, *This is surely a gift from the Almighty.* He was staring at the bottom of the construction bin. Its base was at least three inches off the ground. He smiled as he smoothly rolled onto his belly and pulled his Glock 17 from his shoulder holster. He aimed at those three precious inches on the underside of the bin, sighting carefully. The guy had big feet in shiny white Nikes, a bull's-eye target if there ever was one.

Nicholas squeezed the trigger. The man yelped and

hopped away from the bin, stumbled, and went down hard on the pavement.

"Take him now!" Nicholas yelled into his shoulder radio. He jumped to his feet as he spoke. "And do mind his weapon, people."

His team rushed to surround Esposito, who'd fallen five feet from his hiding place behind the bin. He saw them running at him and slammed his weapon to the ground, threw his arms up in surrender, and the standoff was over. And no one was dead, or even badly hurt.

A metallic horn rang out signaling the engagement was over.

Gareth clapped his boss on the shoulder. "Nice one," he said, then called out, "A-Team, to me."

A smattering of applause made Nicholas turn, but before he could holster his Glock, a voice boomed over the loudspeaker. "Detective Chief Inspector Drummond. You have broken the rules of engagement, and are hereby disqualified. Report to me immediately."

2

Gareth shook his head. "Penderley does not sound happy, Nicholas. And all you've done is show some above-average imagination."

Esposito limped over, his face twisted, so mad Nicholas wondered if he would throw a punch. But he simply squared off; his thick finger stabbed the air for emphasis. "You shot me in the bloody foot, you bloody sod!"

Nicholas couldn't help it, he grinned. "You were so scrunched together I could have gotten you in the arse, but those big Nikes of yours were waving flags at me."

"Yeah, have a big laugh. I'm serious, Drummond. I'm going to limp for a week. You weren't supposed to shoot me; you were supposed to capture me unharmed. Those were the rules, but no, you had to show off. Those rubber bullets hurt."

Nicholas rolled his eyes. "A woman's life was in the balance. I had to act, not negotiate. You shouldn't have made yourself such a target. Next time, pick a bin that hugs the tarmac."

Gareth laughed and Esposito turned on him, gave both men a fist shake and limped off. Nicholas didn't doubt there'd be payback at some point—the rubber bullets did hurt, he knew that firsthand—and Esposito was tough and smart; he'd come up with something that would make Nicholas want to weep, but that would be tomorrow or next week. Penderley was now.

"He'll get over it," Gareth said. "Buy him a pint at The Feathers tonight and he'll soon forgive you."

Not a chance, Nicholas thought, and went to see his boss, Hamish Penderley, detective chief superintendent of the Metropolitan Police's Operational Command Unit, a stiff-necked old buzzard in his early sixties who'd played by the same set of rules for forty years, and would take those same rules to the grave with him. Penderley was self-made, state educated, the third son of a bartender in Coventry, and proud of it.

Nicholas came from wealth and an old name, and that rankled and galled some people he worked with. Thankfully, Penderley wasn't one of them. His issue was Nicholas's dual citizenship; he'd been born in the United States, making him less of a Brit in Penderley's eyes.

Nicholas wound his way through the obstacle course to Penderley's position on the grandstand, thinking about the newly instituted mandatory training exercises.

Everyone was on edge. Actionable terrorist threats had been made against London—again—and the Metropolitan Police felt it necessary to refresh the training all their officers received. Nicholas and his team had been to Hendon for surprise tactical weapons drills four times in the last six months. Requalifying with weapons, being dragged out of bed for real response exercises, like this dawn's kidnap-and-hostage scenario, anything and everything; it didn't matter, Penderley threw all of it at them.

Nicholas had argued, as he always did, that his homicide team knew their stuff cold, would be better utilized brushing up their profiling skills and forensic accounting, but might equaled right in Penderley's world. Penderley's *old* world.

Disapproval clung to the man like a second skin. He was tall and skinny as a pole, standing on a dais with his hands on his hips, legs spread in a triangle, binoculars around his neck, a great view of the action. All he needed were jackboots. Safari leader or ranking copper? Close call. Nicholas kept his mouth shut. He knew he could push only so far before Penderley blew, and by the look on his face, Nicholas could tell the man was hovering at the edge.

"Sir." Nicholas stood at attention in front of his boss, who, no dummy, had angled himself so the rising sun poured over his shoulder right into Nicholas's eyes.

"Drummond." His name came out in an exasperated warning, the tone he so often used when addressing

Nicholas. "You were not authorized to shoot Inspector Esposito."

"No, sir." He avoided continuing his statement. If a "But sir" came out of his mouth, it would only send Penderley into hyperspace.

"Is that all you have to say for yourself?"

No, there's a whole lot I have to say, but I didn't wake up stupid this morning; I took this training exercise seriously, and I didn't want to see the hostage dead, so I found the answer and brought down the nutter.

Penderley wanted him to protest, Nicholas saw it in his eyes, and he was tempted to say something to make the old bugger huff and puff, but he didn't.

"Yes, sir."

Penderley drew himself up straighter, if that were possible, and pronounced from on high, "Then you are disqualified."

"But sir—"

Well, he'd done it now. The blow was coming.

Penderley's body shifted, blocking the sun from Nicholas's eyes. He blinked the older man into focus.

"I've told you a hundred times, Drummond. There are rules in this world. And when I delineate rules of engagement, you are expected to follow them. You will return to Hendon tomorrow morning, with your team, and try it again. And this time, you will do it my way. Do you understand?"

Back and forth. Every day it was the same with them, back and forth, Penderley pushing, Nicholas pulling, never seeing eye to eye unless the threat was real and Nicholas was needed to break the rules.

"I believe the object of the exercise was to neutralize the threat."

He heard a hiss behind him and turned to see Esposito glaring at him, leaning against the edge of the dais, still rubbing his sore foot.

Nicholas ignored Esposito and returned his eyes to his boss. "I neutralized the threat, and the hostage is safe. This is the outcome we all wanted."

Penderley's face turned red. Nicholas braced himself for the hammer, but it didn't fall. Instead Penderley sighed, shook his head. "You try my patience, lad. Tomorrow morning. Five o'clock sharp." He smiled, a wolf with lots of sharp teeth, and added, his voice very precise, "Don't be late or you'll do it again the next day." Penderley's phone rang. "You're excused."

Nicholas stalked off, frustrated, wanting to kick something, but he headed straight for his car. One sore foot— surely that didn't qualify as a bad outcome. What was the point of an exercise that didn't accomplish the goal? In a real situation, his actions would get him more than a pat on the back.

Up at four o'clock tomorrow morning again. *Thank you, sir.*

He'd just put his hand on the gearshift when Penderley came rushing toward the car, waving his hands wildly to get Nicholas's attention.

Nicholas stepped out of the BMW. "What is it? What's wrong?"

Penderley was out of breath, or choked up, Nicholas couldn't be certain which. He soon realized it was both.

"Nicholas," Penderley said, laying a hand on his shoulder. "Terrible news. It's Inspector Elaine York. She's been murdered."

3

The security was amazing, which didn't matter a bit, since she knew every single bell and whistle in place to protect the star of the *Jewel of the Lion* exhibit—the famous and infamous Koh-i-Noor diamond—currently nesting in the center of the queen mother's crown. As for all the boots on the ground, she knew their schedules, knew where they'd be each moment for the next hour.

She was whistling "Born to Be Wild" as she strolled into the museum café to order a cappuccino. She turned her face to the camera for a good look. She waved to the half-dozen staff she recognized, smiled, chatted, even nodded at a couple of museum visitors seated at the small tables.

Once she had her cappuccino in hand, she was careful to give the camera an excellent profile, establishing her whereabouts in the café. Once she paid for the drink, she continued toward the first-floor restrooms and walked directly through to the connecting staff door.

At the back of the hallway was a staircase to the basement. She set down her cappuccino, pulled on gloves, and slipped through the unlatched door to the basement. She ran down the three flights to the outer room of the museum's electrical grid. She paused a moment, listening. No one was about, not a single sound coming from anywhere.

She pulled a lovely bit of technology she'd borrowed from an IRA bomber out of her jacket pocket, a time-delayed electromagnetic pulse that coursed through a relay capacitor. She hummed as she placed the small device behind the bank of computers and set the timer. No permanent damage, but when it blew, the computers would shut down, the cameras would go blank, and the alarm systems would go offline. For five minutes, the entire museum would be off the grid—and that would be enough.

She went back to the fifth floor. And waited.

Three minutes to go.

Two.

One.

There was a small grinding noise, boom, boom, boom, and out went the lights.

Now the fun would begin.

4

Nicholas no longer felt the cold. Memories flooded through him: Elaine's infectious laugh, her excellent mind, the touch of whimsy that colored her view of the world, and that need of hers to search out what hovered beyond what couldn't be seen, and of course there was more, much more. He thought of her lying against him in the night, her head nestling against his shoulder, her breathing soft and slow, the occasional whisper about her mother, who'd been diagnosed with Alzheimer's, her ex-husband's latest antics. But that was before she'd come to work for him. They hadn't lost each other, though. The gentler memories morphed smoothly into the Elaine he knew now, a smart, focused cop striding beside him, doing whatever was asked and some that wasn't. But no more whispers in the night, no more confidences.

He'd cared for her deeply, and now she was gone,

simply gone in the blink of an eye. He remembered the night before she'd left for New York four months ago. A dozen coppers crowded at a table at The Feathers, all toasting her, wishing her luck with the queen mum's crown, warning her about horny Yanks.

This was impossible. A searing pain began in his chest.

"How?"

Penderley said, "Shot and dumped. Her body was found by two schoolchildren on the bank of the East River. We are waiting to hear from the New York FBI for the autopsy results. They will be heading the investigation into her death."

Nicholas was silent, and Penderley gave him a moment to absorb the reality. He knew the two worked very well together, knew they'd been closer before Elaine York had joined his unit last year. He rubbed his hand across his face, feeling very old. It shouldn't have happened, and it made no sense that it had happened. She was in New York as a minder for the crown jewels, not a bodyguard or a copper. Penderley felt the loss of her like a fist to the gut.

Nicholas was still trying to wrap his head around the impossible reality. "I don't understand. She was shot? Murdered? But that's impossible, isn't it? How could she have made enemies in New York working with the Metropolitan Museum of Art? I must go to New York. Immediately." He turned back to the car, and Penderley grabbed his arm.

"Slow down. It's a terrible thing, but you know she wanted this assignment, practically begged me to send her to New York with the crown jewels. Imagine, our precious jewels leaving England, what a bloody mistake they're making—"

Nicholas interrupted him. "I must go to New York, sir. Right now. I can catch the first flight."

Penderley dropped Nicholas's arm. "You think you can somehow get the FBI to accept you enough to fold you into their ranks, let you be involved in solving her murder? This is the *Americans* we're talking about here, Nicholas. Believe me, the FBI in New York have this well in hand. They don't want or need you."

Nicholas couldn't stand here, his breath making clouds in the morning mist, knowing someone had shot Elaine, killed her, and wasn't already being punished for the crime. He had to act. One more try. "Sir, she was valuable—as a cop, as a person. I owe it to her. I'd owe it to any member of my team."

"You will stay right here. That's a direct order, Chief Inspector Drummond. Don't forget, you have training in the morning back here."

Training? When Elaine was dead? Was the old bugger nuts?

"Look, take the day. I must call her mother now. The good Lord knows if she'll even be able to understand me, what with the Alzheimer's. For heaven's sake, *stand down.*"

Penderley marched toward his ancient green Jaguar; the car was so old that Penderley's own son had learned to drive with it. Nicholas slid behind the wheel of his car, closed his eyes.

Elaine, dead. Maybe they'd misidentified the body.

Surely that was possible. She was a foreigner, maybe—but when was the last time that had happened?

He put the car in gear and whipped it around, gravel spitting out from under the tires, glad he hadn't mentioned his uncle Bo, recently retired FBI special agent in charge of the New York Field Office, now the head of security for the *Jewel of the Lion* exhibit at the Metropolitan Museum. Bo liked Elaine. He would be happy for Nicholas's help. Especially if Nicholas talked to him before Penderley could shut him down.

The drive from the Peel Center, where Hendon Police College was housed, to Nicholas's home, Drummond House in Westminster, London, took twenty-five minutes. He left his BMW on the street, double-stepped the stairs, and was at the point of sticking his key in the door when his butler, Nigel, opened it and, seeing his master coming through the door like a Pamplona bull, quickly stepped aside.

"Sir? I wasn't expecting you home so soon. Is everything all right?"

Nicholas shouted over his shoulder as he ran up the stairs to change, "Everything is completely wrong, Nigel. Grab my go bag. I'm going to New York."

5

Special Agent Michaela Caine watched the crime scene techs zip Inspector Elaine York's body in its black cocoon and line it up on the stretcher. She'd been called to the scene because York, a foreign national and therefore under the FBI's purview, had been found shot in the chest, washed up on the shore of the East River. She was an inspector with New Scotland Yard, and now she was dead on American soil. This was about as bad as it got.

Mike was freezing, the winter sunset a memory. The crime scene, now lit by four portable klieg lights, cast an unearthly glow and added exactly zero heat. More crime scene techs moved back and forth along the shoreline, searching for anything to explain how and why Inspector York's body had washed up on shore in this particular spot.

"This is a hell of a thing," said her boss Milo Zachery,

the brand-new SAC of the New York Field Office Criminal Division. He looked miserable, and she couldn't blame him. He was right, this was a humongous mess, which was why she'd called to alert him as soon as she'd gotten a firm confirmation on the ID, and now he was here to assess the situation. Zachery was in his late forties, trim and fit, the quintessential FBI SAC. Looking at him made Mike stand up straighter.

"Everyone's going to be bloodied before this is over," he said. "Our Brit counterparts will go on the warpath if we don't handle this perfectly." He waved his hand toward the medical examiner's van. "York came over from Scotland Yard as a special attaché for the *Jewel of the Lion* exhibit at the Met before I was made SAC, so I'm not familiar with everything she was doing. An inspector with Scotland Yard, killed on our turf? Our butts are going to be shining in the spotlight. Run me through it; I'll need to be prepared when the wolves descend, and descend they will, big-time."

Mike said, "She was partnered up with Ben Houston, from Art Crimes; I called him right after I called you. He should be here any minute. He can give us all the details. He was really upset. He liked her, said she was sharper than his daddy's stiletto, and pretty as a Viking sunset, whatever that means." *But she's not pretty now,* and for a moment, Mike was so pissed she couldn't speak.

She continued, her voice steady. "We don't have much, sir. She was shot in the upper-left chest, small caliber, no exit. Might not be the actual cause of death. Outside of her badge clipped to her skirt, no personal effects have been found. I'd say she hasn't been in the water long, but with the temperatures, the water preserves the body, so it could be longer. We're going to have to wait for the autopsy to get the full story. We'll have to see who saw her last, figure up a timeline from there."

"Who found her?"

"Two kids sneaking some pot. They saw her tangled in garbage near the shore and called it in. We've got impressions of the footprints around the water's edge, but I'm willing to bet this week's salary they belong to the kids who found the body. I've seen no other viable impressions outside of theirs."

Special Agent Ben Houston appeared at her right elbow and shook hands with both Mike and Zachery. He looked shocked and angry, and hurting, she thought, and Mike wondered how close he'd been to Inspector York.

Zachery said, "Ben, give me your input on her, anything that could help us figure this out."

Mike saw he was trying to get it together, trying to clamp down on his anger, his grief. "Ben, yes, please," Mike said, "can you tell me about her? I need everything so I can start looking into her world."

Ben swallowed hard. "She's been with the Metropolitan Police in London her whole career. The people she was working with at the Met will have her personal details. I do know she thought her people were absolutely crazy for bringing the jewels out of the Tower of London."

Zachery said, "Was she doing anything hinky, anything to draw unwanted attention or make herself a victim? Any affairs? Pissed-off lovers?"

Ben shook his head. "She liked her job, did it to the best of her ability. Lovers, no, none I've heard about. She is—was—a really pretty girl, but very focused, very determined. She's a runner; she ran the upstate marathon with me last November when the New York Marathon was canceled. I got a calf cramp, and she insisted on staying with me. I ruined her time." He swallowed, turning to see the proof of her death in the medical examiner's van, idling quietly ten yards away. "She didn't drink, smoke, nothing to harm her innards, although she loved our American coffee. We had lunch and dinner a few times. She was a vegetarian. She was—well, fun to be with, and kind. Yes, she was kind. I can't imagine why anyone would kill her, it doesn't make sense. I mean, why? This—this is bad."

Zachery said, "So she was responsible for the safety of the crown jewels for the exhibit that's starting at the Met?"

Ben nodded. "She was sent here as a legal attaché to oversee the arrival, display, and departure of the *Jewel of the Lion* exhibit from London. She's been here about four months now. She's got a place over in Murray Hill, a rental." He stared at the rocky shoreline, and his jaw tightened. "Did you know the Brits are so protective of their crown jewels it took an act of Parliament to allow this exhibit to happen?"

Mike said, "An act of Parliament? So this exhibit is a pretty big deal. Ben, do you think whoever shot her could be an over-the-top Brit, really upset at the idea of the crown jewels coming to the U.S.?"

"Anything's possible, but murdering the minder to stop the exhibit, which it wouldn't? She had no say about the exhibit itself. Those issues were between the Met and the Brits and the insurance companies."

Zachery said, "I didn't know about the act of Parliament, either. I did know the Met was hosting this once-in-a-lifetime exhibit to coincide with Prince William and Duchess Kate's state trip here next week."

Ben said, "Yeah, it's been crazy with all the legal mumbo jumbo. The centerpiece of the exhibit is the queen mother's crown, which holds the Koh-i-Noor diamond, the Jewel of the Lion itself. The way they set up the transfer of the jewels to America technically keeps them on sovereign soil until they hit the floor of the Met. Elaine had a lot of pressure on her. The jewels have been in the museum for two days now. She was also in charge of the gala at the Met tomorrow night—wait, I guess we're talking tonight now—to debut the exhibit. Private affair. Very pricey. Elaine asked me if I—"

He trailed off, and Mike realized that Ben had been attending the gala as Elaine's guest. She touched her hand to his arm again. "I'm so sorry, Ben."

Anger sheened his eyes, and he swallowed. "I'll go back to Federal Plaza and put together as much information for you as I can so you can get briefed on her role and what—" It was as if Ben had run out of words. He stared at the sluggishly moving East River, cold and black beneath a sliver of moon.

The techs whistled and the medical examiner's van

pulled away. They watched until the van was out of sight, a silent tribute to their fallen comrade.

Zachery pulled his watch cap over his ears. "It's too cold to stand out here much longer. Someone wanted the inspector out of the way. The question is why? It's got to have something to do with the exhibit. Do you know what's going to happen now, Ben, over the pond?"

Ben's cop eyes were colder than the river. He said, "Scotland Yard has to assess what's happened and how to react. As for the folks at the Met, I'll speak to Dr. Browning, the curator of the exhibit, see what she's going to do now that Inspector York is dead. The NYPD isn't going to horn in on this, are they?"

Mike said, "I already spoke to Captain Slaughter of the Seventeenth Precinct. They'll cooperate, anything we need. I promised to keep him in the loop, but he won't interfere. This exhibit is important for the city; there's tons of tourist dollars at stake. Adding a high-profile murder to its coverage? My feeling is NYPD will want to stay a continent away from this."

Zachery breathed out a sigh of relief. "That's good. Even though no one wants this kind of press attached to the big event at the Met, it's going to blow up, you all know that. I've got to brief our media reps. They'll want to think about how they're going to spin it to the world." He looked at his watch.

"Speaking of which, I've gotta run. I'll be on my cell. If you need anything, text me. Keep me updated, Mike." He nodded to Ben and strode off into the darkness, his shoulders not so straight now since the weight of Inspector York's vicious murder was his responsibility to carry.

Mike huddled deeper in her jacket as a sudden blast of winter air whipped off the river. She wondered, yet again, *What did you find out, Elaine, that scared someone so badly they had to murder you?*

6

Nicholas barely made the 8:30 a.m. nonstop to New York. Flashing his Metropolitan Police credentials helped him jump the ridiculously long security line. Now he was on board and the plane was hurtling westward, the rows around him eerily empty.

The moment the flight attendants announced electronic devices were allowed, Nicholas had his laptop open and hooked into the plane's wireless system. First stop was his email. There were three messages from Penderley, subject lines increasingly angry. Nicholas had hoped for more time before Penderley found out where he was headed. He deleted the messages; they could duke it out later, after Nicholas was up to speed on Elaine's murder. Maybe.

An icon began flashing on his screen, a private instant message from his uncle, Bo Horsley, the American cowboy

FBI agent Nicholas had spent his childhood idolizing. Now, as a man, and a law enforcement officer in his own right, Nicholas's respect for his uncle had only grown. Bo was one of the smartest men he knew, one of the best men he knew. He also excelled at bowling, a particular American pastime he'd tried to teach Nicholas as a boy. Nicholas remembered his bowling balls usually ended up in the gutter. Was that the right word? He shook his head. He felt relief seeing the instant message. Bo would understand his motive for coming, and would help.

Nicholas clicked on the instant message.

Dear Nick,

    I'm so sorry about Elaine. As soon as you can, Skype me at this number. Try for secure, too, because we have a problem.

Love, Uncle Bo

More problems. Elaine's death wasn't enough? He felt the now familiar punch of grief, the hard emptiness of it, and turned it off. He'd never see her down another Guinness, leaving a foam mustache on her upper lip, never tease her again about her tarot card readings, a weekly mainstay in her life. All he could do was find out who'd killed her, and why. Since Penderley had told him, he'd sworn to her over and over he would. But it wouldn't bring her back.

He asked for a cup of tea from a redheaded flight attendant. His uncle Bo would smooth things between him and the FBI in New York so they'd let him work with them. He wondered when he got back to London if he'd still have a job with New Scotland Yard. He saw Penderley in his mind's eye demanding his execution. The way he felt right now, he simply didn't care.

He broke out his headphones, opened Skype, and dialed up Bo, who answered on the first ring. His face filled the screen, so similar to Nicholas's mother's. Bo looked tired. No, more than that, he looked beaten down.

"Nick, it's good to see your face. I'm very sorry about your friend Elaine. She was smart and kind and worked well with all of us savage Americans. I remember she was wide eyed at my office view of the city and the East River. I sent her right over to the Empire State Building to see the whole city. Everyone at the Met misses her."

"Thank you, Uncle Bo. Elaine always wanted to travel to New York. She even spoke a couple of times of making a permanent move. She loved her time working there." He paused, got hold of himself. "I can't believe she's really gone. Uncle Bo, do you know what she got herself into over there?"

"I'm sorry, but I don't know anything about her murder yet, Nick. Unfortunately, this isn't only about Elaine anymore. Like I messaged you, we got another problem. Are you secure?"

"Hold on a moment." Nicholas tapped at the keyboard, and a program he'd written several years earlier, a simple and elegant mobile encryption, kicked in. He gave it a second to overwrite the public wireless system he was using.

"Uncle Bo, I forgot to tell you. I'm midway over the Atlantic on my way to you."

Uncle Bo merely smiled at him. "Your mom called me, told me what happened, that you were on your way. No surprise. I knew you wouldn't be content to wait in London. Now, how secure are you?"

"I'm as secure as I can be without hurting the plane's radio integrity. I have the row to myself and no one's behind me; not many people are traveling after the Christmas and New Year's rush."

"Understandable. Now, I'm not at the Met, Nick, I'm here in Chelsea with FBI agents Savich and Sherlock. They came to New York for two things, the gala tonight and to speak to a very convivial Russian art-loving mobster about a painting they think he stole. Savich, come front and center and meet my nephew."

Nicholas knew the man's face, had seen it in articles, in newspapers, on the Internet. It was a hard face, unsmiling at the moment. Who would imagine this big, muscular man was a computer genius? He had a swarthy complexion and cheekbones to cut ice, and nearly black eyes that could nail you to the spot. His dark hair looked damp, as though he hadn't been long out of the shower. Nicholas decided Savich could face down both Nicholas's grandfather and the Devil, and maybe win. No, not his grandfather, the old curmudgeon. He said, "I've heard a lot about you, Agent Savich. It's a pleasure."

Savich nodded at a man who could be his younger brother, and wasn't that a kick? "And you're Bo's nephew. It's good to meet you finally. This is my wife, Agent Lacey Sherlock."

Nicholas looked into the face of a young woman with

beautiful red curly hair, no, not really red, but for the life of him, he couldn't place the color. Titian, maybe? White skin, summer blue eyes. It was like the Devil had captured his perfect opposite.

"A pleasure, Nicholas. Call me Sherlock, and let me tell you, Bo talks about you nonstop. He even claims you could be as good as Dillon in the next decade or so."

Nicholas laughed. "It's a pleasure to meet both of you." And then he waited for Bo to tell him what was going on.

Bo leaned forward and said quietly, "We're trying to keep this hush-hush for the moment. Both Savich and Sherlock are in on this, so you don't have to hold anything back." Bo took a deep breath. "Here's the thing, Nick, the Koh-i-Noor diamond's been stolen from the *Jewel of the Lion* exhibit."

7

New York, New York
201 East 36th Street
Inspector Elaine York's apartment
Thursday, 2:00 a.m.

Inspector Elaine York's apartment building in Murray Hill was nineteen stories of sturdy, well-maintained red brick in the middle of a good solid neighborhood for young professionals.

But not good enough.

Agent Paulie Jernigan of the crime scene unit was waiting for Mike when she arrived, standing in front of the building with the slightly bored, seen-it-all, *Let's get to work, I'm hungry for dinner* look all techs had nailed, probably taught in tech classes.

"You ready?"

"Ready as I'll ever be. Glad they have an elevator. Vic's apartment is on the fifth floor; it would be a pain to drag all my equipment up five flights of stairs this late at night."

Mike put a hand on her hip. "Hey, I could carry one of those little toothpick brushes you have stashed in your kit. Surely that would lighten your load."

He laughed, and she followed him into the building. It was quiet, eerily so at this hour, and Mike had to resist the urge to whisper.

The elevator doors closed behind them with a metallic whoosh.

"You adjusting to the new SAC, Mike?"

"Yeah. I like him. Zachery's a straight shooter. I miss Bo Horsley, of course. How could I not? But I've worked with Zachery before, in Omaha. He's good people. He and my dad got along well."

Paulie said, "That's right, your dad is the Omaha chief of police. Zachery didn't bigfoot him?"

"Not that Dad ever said. He did mention a couple of the local agents started to give him trouble, but once he gave them his patented 'don't make me hurt you' look, they minded their manners."

Paulie said, "Even so, I'll bet the transition's gonna be tough. Horsley trusted all of us implicitly."

"Zachery will, too. Give him a little time to get settled and learn his way around. The New York Field Office is a different zoo than he's used to."

The elevator dinged and they stepped out into a wide hallway, silent as a tomb in the dead of night. No insomniacs on this floor. Elaine York had the end apartment.

Paulie unlocked the door. "I got the keys from the

super while I was waiting. He went back to bed, no show of curiosity at all—a real New Yorker."

She edged into the dark apartment, and the smell hit her in the face—the heavy, dead air, the beginnings of rot. Her hand went to her Glock.

"Step back, Paulie. We got trouble."

8

British Airways Flight 117
Over the Atlantic Ocean
Thursday, 9:00 a.m.

Nicholas stared at his uncle. "Stolen? The Koh-i-Noor? I can't believe it. That bloody stone is impossible to steal. And your security has to be unbeatable. So what happened?"

Bo shook his head. "I thought stealing the diamond would be impossible, too, but the fact is it's gone. It's been replaced with one of the two cubic zirconia replicas the palace allowed made some ten years ago. The good thing is we're pretty sure we know when it was stolen—yesterday we had a power outage. All computers, all video feeds, all communications, everything was off-line for five whole minutes, then just as suddenly it came back on. There was a thorough check of every treasure in the Met, and I personally checked the *Jewel of the Lion* exhibit room, but the crown jewels looked untouched. Everything was where it was supposed to be throughout the museum, so we chalked it up to a glitch somewhere in the system, nothing nefarious.

"Then the curator of the *Jewel of the Lion* exhibit, Dr. Browning, received a call from Arizona, a man named Peter Grisley, who owns the two cubic zirconia replicas of the Koh-i-Noor. The replicas had been stolen. Dr. Browning came to me right away, quietly, worried something was wrong. It was her idea to test the diamond, and sure enough, the tester showed the Koh-i-Noor to be a fake.

"Talk about a hit to the chops. We're doing all we can, but to have this happen on American soil, during a once-in-a-lifetime exhibit? It's more than a disaster. It might start another Revolutionary War."

Not an understatement.

"Uncle Bo, worse than a war, the world media will crucify the U.S. Of course you know that no one on the outside could have done this. Have you pinned down possible staff not accounted for during the power outage?"

"First thing we did. They were all accounted for. There aren't that many involved—only designated museum staff and the insurance people have access to the exhibit space where all the crown jewels are displayed. In addition, you know we vetted everyone and their pets three ways to Sunday, over and above the designated staff." He paused, then said quietly, his voice heavy, "There was only one person we couldn't account for during the power outage: Inspector Elaine York. And now she's dead."

Nicholas spoke carefully, seeing now where his uncle

was headed. "Perhaps the diamond wasn't stolen from the museum at all. Perhaps it was taken before it left England, or maybe during transit."

"I wish. Dr. Browning and Inspector York and the indemnity insurance expert tested the Koh-i-Noor when it arrived at the museum. It was definitely stolen post–arrival at the Met."

Savich said, "Whoever managed to switch out the diamond was very good and very fast. There is simply no sign of a break-in, no sign that anyone was even in the exhibit room, which means it was meant to go unnoticed. And it very nearly did, if not for the call to Dr. Browning from Peter Grisley reporting his missing replicas, one of which now sits proudly in the center of the queen mother's crown."

Nicholas asked, "Is it possible the power outage was for real and the switch was made at another time and not during the five-minute period?"

Bo said, "I can't imagine how, Nick."

"You all know how sophisticated the security is on the crown jewels in the Tower of London, the beefeaters are all ex-military and tough as nuts, so there's no chance to steal the diamond there."

"My security is like a police force, too. They're all armed, and we've upgraded our measures even further since the jewels arrived on-site. We're a well-oiled machine. I know these people, Nick, and I'm sure as I can be that no one on my security staff could have anything to do with this. But regardless, we're checking again, going even deeper, if that's possible, eliminating my people first, then their lovers and friends, and the remaining museum staff, any- and everyone we can think of to look at. Everyone. But bottom line—this was a master thief."

Nicholas said, "Tell me about your security, Uncle Bo."

It was Savich who said, "I consulted with Bo's team on the installation of the biometric security systems. You need a palm print and two different pass cards to even access the exhibit room, and the cases have a rotating binary lock."

Sherlock said, "Add in the incredible physical security, the fact no one was out of place during the power outage, and no one Bo knows of could do this, and the theft and switch seems, well, if not impossible, then almost magical. But—"

Bo nodded. "Yes, but— Look, Nick, I don't know if Inspector York had the expertise to pull this theft off, but she's the only one of the primaries not accounted for."

"I knew Inspector York very well," Nicholas said, "her strengths, weaknesses, her talents. As far as I know, she doesn't have the necessary skills."

Savich said, "Nicholas, how much would you have to know to pull this off? She knew the setup, knew the diamond, certainly could figure out what tools she would need to make the switch."

Nicholas was shaking his head as he said, "So she also flew to Arizona and stole the two replicas? Have you checked the airlines, Uncle Bo?"

"Yes. Elaine hasn't left New York City, at least by commercial airline."

Sherlock said, "She either flew to Arizona under the

radar and we haven't found out how yet, or she had someone to help her, inside the Met. Sorry, Nicholas, but I can't see it coming down any other way. But the big question in my mind is why Inspector York was killed. A falling-out among thieves? What else could it be? You say you knew her very well. You say she couldn't do this. How certain are you?"

"I doubt Elaine could bring herself to shoplift from Harrods on a bet. You know I wouldn't have had her on my staff if she weren't top-notch. She was there to mind the Koh-i-Noor, to make sure nothing happened, to protect the diamond, not to steal it. The idea is simply ridiculous." Nicholas paused for a moment, then said flatly, "I trusted her with my life."

No one said anything to that.

Nicholas said, "Maybe Elaine was murdered because she found out something about the theft."

"Then she should have come to me immediately," Bo said. "If she wasn't involved in the theft, and she discovered something? Nick, think about it. She never came to me."

Nicholas hated it, simply hated it, but still the arguments were solid. How could he convince them Elaine hadn't been part of it? He looked closely at his uncle and thought Bo suddenly looked old and tired. All of them knew he would be the scapegoat, no matter who was responsible. Even if the diamond was found unharmed, Bo's security firm would go down in history as the one who let the Koh-i-Noor slip away in the first place. Elaine and his uncle, both their names would be ruined.

Bo said, "Understand me, Nick, I don't like throwing accusations at dead people. But there's another thing. Yesterday morning, fifteen minutes after the electricity came back on, Elaine came to my office to tell me she was going home sick. It was a very out-of-character move for her."

He could only try. Nicholas said, "Uncle Bo, there has to be a different scenario we haven't thought of, with different players."

"Nick, I promise we'll keep considering anything that even sounds plausible. Look, I haven't known Elaine all that long, but I can't imagine her stealing the diamond any more than you can. Unfortunately, she's the only one who can't speak for herself. The insurance people are going to dive that way, and I can't stop it. And you know as well as I do that you never really know another person."

Nicholas nodded, feeling a bit defeated himself. "Is the New York FBI investigating both Elaine's murder and the missing diamond?"

Bo smiled, a smile Nicholas recognized from his childhood. Naughty, that smile, and sly.

"What are you planning, Uncle Bo?"

"Well, you see, Nick, here's the thing. We haven't officially told anyone the jewel is missing yet."

9

Nicholas stared at the three grinning faces on his laptop screen. "What? No one's been informed of the theft? Uncle Bo, are you mad?"

"Maybe. Here's the thing: the moment I tell the director of the Met the Koh-i-Noor is gone, he'll order an immediate lockdown—that means no exhibit and no gala, the media will be loosed, and they'll swarm all over us. The whole thing will go viral in thirty minutes."

Sherlock said, "The moment word gets out, we lose our advantage and have much less chance of identifying our thief."

Bo continued. "I want time, Nick, without having to worry that paparazzi will show up in the men's room with cameras and recorders, time without the overwhelming media distractions. I want time so we can catch whoever did this and get the Koh-i-Noor back. I don't want to tell the director anything, not until—well, until I've had my shot at resolving this."

It was a disaster waiting to happen. No, the disaster had already happened.

Savich said, "We've come up with a plan, and we want you on board. I've seen the real Koh-i-Noor. It's a massive diamond, over one hundred carats. It's so big it looks fake anyway."

Nicholas said, "I've seen it as well. Many times."

Bo said, "This replacement diamond? It's an exact replica. Honestly, I couldn't tell the difference. The size of it makes it look surreal."

Sherlock continued. "Here's the plan, Nicholas: we carry on with the big gala as planned. All the guests can ooh and aah over the fake Koh-i-Noor and not know the difference, and all will be well in the kingdom, at least for tonight."

Bo said, "We believe it's audacious, but doable. What do you think, Nick?"

Audacious was an understatement. Nicholas said, "I like it, but there's one thing. Uncle Bo. You've got to tell the director, and you've got to sell him on what we're doing, tell him we're the ones who need to control the situation, not let the media grab it and run with it to the good Lord knows where. Your biggest selling point? His bloody job."

Savich said, "He'll go along when you remind him the Met will have to pony up the indemnity the museum paid for."

Bo said, "I may be able to sell it to the director, but

I'll have to swear on the head of my sainted mother that I'll get the Koh-i-Noor back. He'll buy keeping it quiet for the time being; he'll realize it would ruin him as well as the rest of us. And if Elaine wasn't involved, the thief could possibly show up tonight. If we manage to keep it quiet, he won't know we're aware the diamond's missing."

Sherlock said, "The thief has to be someone intimate with all the security systems you have in place, Bo, who knows any inherent weaknesses, the triggers, everything. Someone close to the exhibit, and close to you. Someone you trust. Will he show up tonight? Very possibly. To deflect any suspicion, to give him more time to do whatever it is he plans to do with the Koh-i-Noor. Or he's long gone as we speak."

Savich said, "And if Elaine York was murdered for her involvement, then there is indeed someone else involved, someone dangerous, someone who's already committed murder."

They all took that in, then Bo said, "We don't want to tip our hand too early. I'll need something to explain why all three of you are here."

"Uncle Bo, you can tell the Met staff and your people that you've been surprised with a new foreign dignitary coming to the gala tonight. That will explain the FBI's presence. You can explain my presence with the truth: I'm here to find out who murdered my inspector."

Bo rubbed his square jaw for a moment. "That will work. The key to this is to watch everyone close to the exhibit who shows tonight at the gala. If anyone doesn't show, then we'll know they're involved, and can take immediate action. I'll tell you, I'm ready to track the guy to the ends of the earth."

Sherlock said, "Either our thief is also a murderer or he isn't. Either he's long gone and doesn't show for work or he thinks we're idiots and wants to come see the show."

Bo no longer looked like he wanted to shoot himself. He was rubbing his hands together. "We can do this. Nick, I'll have someone at the airport to meet you and bring you directly to the Met."

Nicholas closed down the call and shut his eyes. How much time could they buy? Things like this got out even when you'd swear they wouldn't.

One of his uncle's phrases stuck in his mind, replaying itself on a loop. *It was a master thief.*

A master thief who'd managed to get through Uncle Bo's security checks. Elaine as a suspect was ridiculous. He'd never believe it, never, but a master thief, someone either hired to pull off a theft of this magnitude or acting of their own accord to try and sell the diamond on the black market, yes, that made more sense. No run-of-the-mill sort of thief, either. This was the work of a pro. A legend.

He had a place to start. Find the thief, clear Elaine. It became his mantra.

He was due to land at JFK at 11:10 a.m. He reset his vintage Breitling to eastern time, calculated that the flight had several hours left. Plenty of time to develop a list of the top thieves in the world.

10

New York, New York
201 East 36th Street
Inspector Elaine York's apartment
Thursday, 2:00 a.m.

Mike pulled her Glock from its holster and flipped on the light switch beside the door. She cleared the corners, Glock swinging in a careful arc, as she made her way through the entry hall and right into the living room.

Paulie said from behind her, "Oh, not good."

Mike edged farther into the room, gun still at the ready, saw a dead man, face congested with blood, his body half on, half off the couch. She didn't see any blood, or wounds. *What happened, Elaine? Did you and this guy fight and you both lost? But how did you get in the East River?*

"Dude is seriously dead," Paulie said, coming forward to look at the body with the detached curiosity Mike had become accustomed to from crime scene techs. "Check it out. There's a syringe in his thigh."

"Stay with the dead guy. I need to make sure there's

no one here." She cleared the small dining room, the modern efficiency kitchen, down the hall into the one bedroom, her breathing steady, her Glock at the ready. She took only a quick look. The bedroom seemed undisturbed, nothing messy lying around. Nothing obvious had happened in here. She walked into the decent-size single bathroom—it was wrecked.

A lacquer painting of brilliant red poppies hung drunkenly on the wall, and the contents of York's makeup bag were spilled on the countertop. Bottles were tipped over on the vanity. The blue bathroom rug was shoved into a corner, and a bottle of room spray was on the floor. The shower curtain was open wide. This was clearly where the struggle with her murderer began.

She called the ME and more CSU people. They were in for a long night.

Mike remembered Elaine had been dressed in business clothes but no shoes. She tried to work up the scene in her head: Elaine returning home from a long day's work, leaving the man in the living room to take it easy, slipping off her shoes, rubbing her feet a bit, then heading for the shower. Or the man was hiding in the bathroom, leaping out at her. She fought for her life; they struggled back into the living room. She somehow turned the needle back on him, and he got her gun from her and shot her with it. That didn't work. The dead guy was big, didn't look at all helpless. Elaine was only five-foot-six or so; he would have overpowered her in a second.

There had to have been a third person involved. A person who murdered them both. She was sure of it.

Mike walked backward from the bathroom to the living room, eyeing the overturned chair, sofa pillows on the floor, a broken glass near the ottoman. The struggle ended here, with the body. So the man had fought the murderer. He'd died, and Elaine had ended up in the river. Whatever the actual scenario, the murderer had been smart and strong and fast. He'd murdered both a big man and a trained cop. He must have left believing Elaine York dead, only she hadn't been dead, not yet, not until she'd wandered into the East River.

Paulie stood over the victim. "Find anything?"

"A trail of broken and overturned stuff. Bathroom's totaled."

"Come look at this, Mike."

"What do you have?"

"Initially I thought his face was just congested, but look at how red his skin is. And look at the corners of his mouth, that black stuff." Paulie bent close to the body and sniffed. "Hmm. You try."

Smelling a dead guy's breath didn't rank high on her list of fun things to do, but she leaned down and breathed in. Patchouli. Garlic, maybe onions. And death, the smell of death.

"Am I supposed to smell something special?"

"Almonds."

Her head jerked up. "You're thinking cyanide?"

"Yeah. Whatever, I'd still steer clear if I were you. I've seen a cyanide poisoning before; it looked like this."

Mike said, "Rigor has passed. I'd say he's been dead awhile, maybe a day." She slipped on nitrile gloves and pulled the dead man's wallet out of his back pocket. "According to the driver's license, this is Vladimir Kochen, and he lives in Brighton Beach."

Paulie scratched his neck. "Not to make assumptions, but you know a lot of the Russians out there are mobbed up."

"Tell me, then, what would a Scotland Yard inspector be doing with a Russian mobster in her apartment? Maybe he's a friend who showed up at the wrong time?" Yeah, like she believed that for a second. Mike rubbed her hand over her forehead where a headache was beginning to brew. "Zachery's going to love this. No choice, time to wake him up." She dialed his cell phone. He answered on the first ring, sounding wide awake.

"Hey, boss. We've got another body in York's apartment. Russian from Brighton. There's no sign of a break-in, no sign someone tossed the place, but there was a struggle. The dead Russian has a syringe sticking out of his leg. Paulie thinks it's cyanide. We'll process the scene and let you know if we find anything else."

Zachery groaned. "What did this woman get herself into? Don't mind me, rhetorical question. Do what you need to. Thanks for the heads-up. Call Captain Slaughter from NYPD, let him know what's going on, see if he wants to send some people, or not, since the FBI's dealing with it."

She called Captain Slaughter, woke him from a dead sleep, told him what they'd found. Slaughter told her to keep him in the loop and volunteered to send over a couple of officers to interview neighbors, check out the neighborhood. He sounded relieved it was her problem.

They heard sirens. Their crew was here. And weren't the neighbors going to love this disturbance in the middle of the night.

Five minutes later, the new medical examiner lumbered into the apartment. Janovich was heavyset and tired, with hangdog eyes and a graying beard. Another dragged from the warmth of his bed.

"Special Agent Mike Caine," she said, and held out her hand. "We met—"

"At the Kirkland crime scene. I remember. Those crazies ever get caught?"

"We got them, yes."

"So why are we here?"

"Inspector Elaine York from Scotland Yard was murdered; this is her place. I got here and found a dead Russian."

"She's the one pulled from the river earlier?"

Mike nodded. "That's her. I think you're going to find this guy interesting, too." She pointed to the body. "There's a needle sticking out of his right thigh."

Janovich stroked long fingers through his graying beard. "Gotta admit, don't see that every day."

"I'll let you get to it. Please let me know if you find anything of interest."

Mike walked through the apartment again, going over different scenarios this time, trying to figure out how it had all gone down. She said aloud, "It doesn't make sense."

"What doesn't?"

She jumped. Ben had snuck up on her.

"What are you doing here?"

"Couldn't sleep, so when Zachery texted me and asked me to come over and help you, I already had one foot out the door."

"Okay, I'm glad you're here. Would you check nine-one-one, see if York made any distress calls? I'm going to scope out the rest of the building, go across the street to fetch the feed from a video camera I saw. York might be on it. Maybe our Russian, too. And the killer."

She'd pressed the elevator button for the lobby when her cell rang. She hadn't received a middle-of-the-night call from her former SAC Bo Horsley in several weeks, not since he'd retired. She knew immediately something was very wrong.

"Sir? What's happened?"

"Mike, good to hear your voice, even though it's the middle of the night. Zachery called me to let me know there's more to Elaine's case than we first thought, wanted me to know right away. Talk to me, Mike."

And so she told him what she saw, some of her theories, ending with, "There was clearly a third person here. Though how he pulled it off, I don't know."

He paused for a moment, and she heard him talking to someone in the background. Then he said, "Have I got a nice surprise for you, Mike. You've heard of Savich and Sherlock, right?"

"Of course. I worked with Dillon Savich on breaking a Chinese cyber-crime syndicate. He's incredible."

"He's not the only incredible one. Sherlock has this gift. She walks into a crime scene and can tell you exactly what happened. Both Savich and Sherlock are here with me. And we're all still wide awake. You want me to send them to you? Sherlock's up for it, if you are."

I must really be stupid tired to need help on a crime scene like this, Mike thought, but she agreed instantly. Why should other agents sleep when she couldn't? "Send them over."

"Okay," Bo said, "they're on their way. Now, Mike, I need a favor. Milo said that since you were the lead on this case, you were the one to do it. My nephew, who is also Elaine's boss, is on a plane from London as we speak. He lands at eleven ten a.m., British Airways coming into JFK. Can you pick him up and fill him in on what's happening?"

Bo's nephew? Great, just wonderful. She knew all about Bo's nephew, the only offspring of Bo's sister and a Brit father who was some damned aristocrat. She knew more about him than she wanted to know, since Bo spoke of him as often as he did his own four girls. He was supposed to be this frigging super-spy who'd given it all up for a reason Bo had never mentioned and joined Scotland Yard. And now he was coming to stick his nose under the tent, probably stick in his whole big foot. No, that was wrong. He'd want to barge right into the tent and take charge. She could see this guy throwing his weight around. She didn't need this, she really didn't.

"What's his name again, sir?"

"I thought you'd remember, Mike. Well, no matter, his name is Nicholas Drummond. Detective Chief Inspector Drummond of New Scotland Yard."

Detective chief inspector—it figured. She glanced at her watch. It was nearly 3:00 a.m. So much for getting some sleep.

"Okay, I'll fetch him."

"Thanks, Mike." Bo's voice was jazzed, full of manic energy, and she frowned into her cell.

"All right, sir. I know you. You haven't told me everything. Why'd you really call?"

"Always so sharp. Mike, I need your absolute discretion."

"Certainly, sir. What's wrong?"

He lowered his voice and dropped a bombshell.

"The Koh-i-Noor's been stolen."

11

Savich and Sherlock arrived at Elaine York's apartment building twenty minutes later. In the elevator, Savich pulled Sherlock close. "You sure you're up for this, sweetheart? It's late, we're both pretty wiped."

She leaned up and laid her hand on his cheek. "I've got a call in for my second wind. It should be here momentarily. Believe me, Dillon, we'll sleep late tomorrow. And this is important."

The doors opened, and there was a beehive of activity at the end of the hall. They walked through the door to Elaine York's apartment and were met by a young woman who looked pissed, impatient, and bone tired.

Savich said, "Agent Caine? It's good to see you again."

"Agent Savich." A smile bloomed and she grabbed his hand, pumped it up and down. "We've got ourselves a real puzzle here. I can't believe you guys came out in the middle of the night. Thanks for coming by to take a look."

"It's a strange night, all the way around," he said, and introduced her to Sherlock.

Sherlock found herself at Mike Caine's eye level. "Let's get to it, then maybe we can all get some sleep."

"I don't know about this," Mike said, after she'd released Sherlock's hand. "It's so bizarre, the whole deal. I mean, there's a dead guy on the sofa with a needle in his thigh and Elaine York was in the East River—"

Savich cut her off. "Bo told us about everything, Agent Caine—"

"Please call me Mike."

He nodded. "Mike. Call me Dillon."

"And you can call me Sherlock."

"I always wanted to meet Sherlock," Mike said. "I do hope you don't smoke a pipe. Oh, dear, sorry for that. I'm punchy."

They all paused in the small entryway to see four people watching them. More introductions, then Mike said, "Everyone, take a break, okay? Five minutes."

Savich said, "Let's let Sherlock walk through the scene, see what she thinks. Have you identified the dead guy?"

"Yeah, his name's Vladimir Kochen, a Russian from Brighton Beach. That's Mob territory."

Savich helped Sherlock out of her coat. "Go to it, and I'll see what MAX can find out about Kochen."

When the apartment was quiet, Sherlock walked into the living room. She said nothing at all, simply looked at the dead man, at the needle sticking out of his leg. She studied the living room, studied him again, then walked down the hall to the bathroom.

Sherlock came back in a few minutes, smiled at Mike. "Please understand, Mike, what I think isn't necessarily what happened, okay?"

"Yes, of course I understand."

Sherlock sighed. "It's all so sad and so very brutal."

Mike said, "I agree, Sherlock, and I appreciate your coming out in the middle of the night to give it a try, but it's okay. I'm sorry you've gone to so much trouble—"

"No, you misunderstand me." Sherlock walked to stand over the dead Russian. "He's a soldier, a big man, muscular, hard. He wasn't taken by force but by cunning."

Mike said, "A soldier? He's not military that we know of, but we're still running his records."

Savich looked up from where he sat with MAX open on his legs. "That isn't what Sherlock meant. Vladimir Kochen is a foot soldier for a Russian Mob boss. Do you know the Anatoly crime family?"

Sherlock whirled around so fast she nearly fell over. "You've got to be kidding me, Dillon. Anatoly, really?"

Savich laughed. "Yep, and that makes it one very small world."

Mike said, "I do know Anatoly, and his less-than-savory connections. Anatoly's an art lover and collector, a big supporter of the Met. He's got to be in this somehow. I have no idea how all this ties together, but it must, somehow. Is that what you mean by it being a small world?" Mike cocked her head to the side.

"Sherlock and I are up here not only to see the *Jewel of the Lion* exhibit, but also to speak to Andrei Anatoly about one of my grandmother's paintings. An expert on her work was visiting the Prado Museum and spotted the fake, told the director and called me. We don't think it had been switched that long ago, because one of our art-crimes agents told me he'd heard buzz about Anatoly bragging about a new acquisition, *The Night Tower*."

Mike was astounded. "*The Night Tower*? The world just got microscopic. *The Night Tower*, it's one of my favorite paintings. I've never been to Europe, but I always wanted my first trip to be to Madrid, to see that painting at the Prado. Your grandmother is really Sarah Elliott?"

He nodded. "So back to our small world. What the devil is one of Anatoly's men doing here with the minder of the Koh-i-Noor diamond?"

No answer to that question. Savich said to Sherlock, "Tell us what happened here."

Sherlock looked like her second wind had finally arrived. She walked over to the dead man and spoke quickly, moving around the room to illustrate her thoughts. "The killer, and I'll bet it is a man, knocked on the door; Kochen answered it and got shot immediately with a tranquilizer." She picked up his arm. "Look at the stain on his jacket, right here. I'll bet that's where the killer shot him—in the arm. You wouldn't want to go one-on-one with this guy, he's too big, too strong, probably well trained and vicious. Too many variables, particularly with another trained cop in the apartment. The killer probably expected her to be in the living room as well, and planned to shoot them both with the tranquilizers, but she was in the bathroom, getting ready to take a shower.

"Once Kochen was stunned, the murderer dragged him to the sofa, then shot him full of cyanide before he had a chance to recover. And it is cyanide. I can smell it."

She gestured toward the hall. "York heard the scuffle and grabbed her gun. The killer attacked her, wrestled the gun from her, and shot her with it. The autopsy will probably show she had cyanide in her system, too; the killer would have had another plunger full to use on her. Whether he got a full load into her or not, we'll have to see. She fought him, though, hard. And he left her for dead, a bullet in the chest. That's my best guess."

Mike was staring at her. "Yes," she said, "yes, I can see that now. It's very clear. Thank you."

Sherlock said, "Are her things still here, Mike?"

"Her computer is missing; the power cord is on the desk. Her bag was rifled through, though her money and cards are still there. It's impossible to know if anything else was taken. We've even got her cell phone. So why did the murderer take her computer? Something was on it that either worried him or—or what? We'll find out. You know, Sherlock, the tranquilizer—that hadn't occurred to me—"

Savich said, "Your ME would have found traces in their systems, seen the injection sites. Sherlock just found it a bit faster."

Mike didn't say another word. It was odd, but she felt both punchy with fatigue and buzzed. She hugged

Sherlock right there with the dead Russian on the sofa and Dr. Janovich now back in the living room, pulling off the man's coat to see if he could visually identify an injection site for the tranquilizer. He found it and gave Sherlock a puzzled look.

Sherlock yawned. "Oh, sorry about that. It's been a long day. If that's all, Mike, we'll see you—well, tonight, I guess, at the gala. I know this is tough, but we'll figure it all out. Try to catch some sleep, okay?"

"And keep us posted," Savich said, and shook her hand, nodded to Dr. Janovich, and they left. The taxi they'd asked to wait downstairs thankfully hadn't taken off, and they were back to Chelsea in twenty minutes.

Savich never thought a bed could feel like heaven, but this one did.

12

Nicholas hadn't been to New York in a couple of years, since a visit with his mother to see Uncle Bo, Aunt Emily, and his four female cousins, all of whom worshipped his mother. Regardless of the circumstances, the energy of the place gave him an instant buzz. If only he could share this with Elaine, instead of bringing her home in a box.

When they landed, he turned on his phone, saw a text from Uncle Bo.

> Agent Mike Caine will meet you at the gate. See you
> soon.

He gathered his bag and left the plane. His eyes scanned the crowd—Mike Caine—that was the agent's real name? Wouldn't it be a hoot if the actor strolled up and said hullo?

He entered the main terminal and immediately noticed a tall, lean blonde with her hair in a ponytail and dark glasses tucked into her shirt alter course to intercept him, no hesitation, a guided missile. He took note of the bulge under the left corner of her black leather jacket; she had a gun strapped to her hip. She stopped two feet short, ignored all the travelers parting to flow around them, and said, "I'm Special Agent Michaela Caine with the New York Field Office. Glad to meet you," and she opened a black leather case to show him a blue-and-white card stamped "FBI." She stuck out her hand. "You must be Bo's nephew."

He shook her hand. "Yes. I was expecting someone older. And more male."

"Ah, yes. People do. And trust me, I've heard all the jokes."

"I daresay. I'm Drummond. Nicholas Drummond. Thank you for coming to gather me."

Her idiot mind said, *Bond, James Bond*. So this was Bo's super-spy nephew. And didn't Drummond look the part, dark hair and eyes and, Lord above, was that a cleft in his chin? He'd probably shaved long before he boarded the plane to come to New York, and he had a five-o'clock shadow, or whatever o'clock it was in England. It made him look dangerous. She bet he was stubborn as a mule, and a player. The way he eyed her, sizing her up, yes, definitely a player.

"It's no problem. Do you have luggage?"

He looked down at a soft-as-butter dark brown leather carry-on bag that looked like it cost one of her paychecks.

"Only this overnight bag. I took the first flight from London practically the minute I heard."

She nodded, saying only, "My car's this way," since she couldn't very well lead off with *Hey, Mr. Aren't I Great, I hear you are a super-spy.* He stepped ahead of her to open the door, and she saw Mr. Super-Spy had a very nice butt. So did James Bond. Well, since he was going to horn in, it balanced the scales a bit that he wasn't hard to look at.

As they walked to the car, Nicholas noticed Agent Caine had a long stride that matched his own quite well. Her blond ponytail swung back and forth like a metronome as she walked. She wore black leather motorcycle boots—low-heeled—dark jeans, and a scoop-neck black sweater over a white button-down. The black leather jacket completed the biker-chic look.

She didn't look like any FBI agent he'd met before, not that he'd met all that many. Actually, he thought she looked like a motorbike-riding librarian. She looked like she'd shush him if he made any noise, then maybe smack him with her riding gloves.

When they reached the escalator, he gestured for her to go first. A brow shot up, and she said, "Thank you. It's a pleasure to finally meet you. I worked for your uncle Bo for years. He was always bragging about you, not that any of us believed a single word he said or even listened much, for that matter. I do know he takes full credit for influencing you to become a cop."

Her voice was nice, like honey, smooth and deep, no discernible accent. Midwest, then. She was young, too, late twenties, maybe thirty. Since he wasn't deaf, he'd heard the edge, loud and clear. She didn't trust him, didn't want him here, but she was being forced to let him in. Well, too bad, because he was in, all the way in.

He said, his voice so upper-class-Brit sharp it could cut glass, "My uncle only partially exaggerates, Special Agent Caine. My father was all for me joining Scotland Yard, though he didn't say it out loud. My grandfather, though, he'd just as soon my most dangerous activity would be climbing trees."

She couldn't help herself, she grinned, because her own mom felt exactly the same way about her, and the serious librarian transformed into a sweet girl with dimples. Nicholas doubted that impression would last for more than a couple seconds. But it broke the ice, finally.

She said, "We've got a long slog ahead of us. Call me Mike."

"I'm Nicholas."

"Very well, then, Nicholas. I'm sorry about the circumstances that brought you here. I've heard Elaine York was a good cop, a lovely woman. We're all sick about her death."

While the words were rote—he'd spoken them himself too many times to know otherwise—there was genuine feeling behind them. No cop wanted to see another go down; it hit too close to home.

He nodded. "She meant a great deal to me, to all of us. She will be sorely missed. I want to get to the bottom of what she got herself into, and why she was killed."

When they stepped out of the terminal into the

freezing New York winter, Nicholas hoped Nigel hadn't forgotten to add his gloves to the bag.

When the Crown Vic slid away from the curb, the man pulled out his disposable cell, punched a single button. The call was answered on the first ring.

"Yes?"

"He's here. Nicholas Drummond."

"Give me your impression of him."

"He's a big guy, looks hard, tough, but he's a pretty boy. Like all Brit cops, he's not carrying. I can take him."

"You know your job here. Follow him and the FBI agent, and report back to me everything they do. Do not engage them. Do not let them see you. If we need to take strong action, I will tell you."

"Yes, sir."

He hung up the phone and revved the engine of the Harley. Such a sweet ride. It took him only a minute to catch up to the cop car. The chick was driving, and she wasn't all that bad. They were talking. He liked the blond hair. Was it natural? He wouldn't mind verifying that himself. Even though she was an FBI agent, he didn't think she'd be much of a problem. She looked like the girl next door playing tough grown-up. But the big guy? He'd see.

His boss's voice rang loud in his head. *Stay away from her, you goon.*

He felt a quick spurt of rage—he wasn't a goon. If the

guy weren't paying so well, there were a lot of things he wouldn't mind doing to the pretty blond, and to him, but he was paying him really big bucks. And he knew in the deepest part of him, the part that recognized blackness and brutal violence, this was a man you didn't cross. Ever.

13

Before the passenger door of Mike's black Crown Vic was even closed, Nicholas got right to it. "Has the autopsy on Inspector York been completed?"

"Yes. The ME called while I was waiting for your plane to land. Her initial cause of death is drowning."

He felt a punch of surprise. *Drowning*? "I was led to believe she'd been shot."

"She was, but it wasn't a fatal wound. The ME said he'd heard from Toxicology. She'd also been injected with a small amount of potassium cyanide. Just like Sherlock said—you'll meet her and Agent Dillon Savich later, at the gala tonight."

"My uncle is always talking about Agent Savich this, Agent Sherlock that."

She shot him a look. A bit of resentment there, maybe?

Fascinating, coming from Super-Spy James Bond. Well, maybe not; now he was smiling.

Mike said, "The gunshot and the cyanide incapacitated her to the point that she was probably unconscious when she went in the water. We found a videotape from her neighborhood bodega; it shows her stumbling out of her apartment building and heading toward the river. We think she was following her regular running route out of habit. She was clearly not in her right mind, staggering and weaving toward the water. The fence there is about waist high, and she went right over the top of it.

"Another camera near the dock shows her eyes are closed as she goes over the edge. I think it's entirely possible she passed out and fell in."

All he heard was *probably unconscious* and prayed it was true.

Mike jockeyed around three cabs that honked and threw her the finger, smoothly slid out into the Van Wyck. She said, "There was a Russian found dead at her apartment, a Vladimir Kochen, a foot soldier for the Anatoly crime family. Agent Sherlock thinks he was shot with a tranquilizer gun when he opened the door, then the killer injected him with a massive dose of potassium cyanide as well. The ME hasn't verified it yet, but he thinks Sherlock's right."

"Excuse me? A Russian? Why was a Russian Mob guy at Elaine's apartment?"

Mike glanced over at him. "Don't know yet. Savich and Sherlock looked over the scene last night. She has a gift, could tell immediately what happened. I was impressed." And she told him everything Sherlock had said.

Her cell rang. The ME, Dr. Janovich, was calling. "Caine here. What have you got for me?"

She listened, then punched off. "Sherlock was right on the money. The ME found traces of a tranquilizer called fentanyl in the Russian's blood; it's an anesthetic that acts immediately. Answers that question. Tell me, do you know if Inspector York carried personal protection?"

Nicholas thought for a moment. "Yes. A SIG Sauer P226. But she didn't bring it with her to New York."

Mike said, "Did she mention buying a .22? A Taurus PT-22, to be exact?"

"Not to me, no. Why?"

"We found a .22 in her apartment under the Russian's body. The gun was bought off the street, illegally, a week ago. We think the killer put it under the body to cover his tracks, make it look like Elaine and Kochen killed one another."

"This was a well-orchestrated crime scene, then."

"Yes. We know the .22 was Elaine's because she'd written herself a receipt, stashed it in her wallet. The ballistics match the bullet the ME took out of Elaine's chest. The prints on the weapon are smudged, so the killer was wearing gloves. Her fingerprints are on the bullets.

"As for her cell phone, the only recent calls were back and forth between the staff at the Met and several calls to her mother in England. We have a warrant in for the full records, cell and home, but her complete cell records will take a few days because she was using an international phone. Lots of red tape."

"The gun purchase receipt could have been planted, then, and her signature forged."

"I suppose so," but he knew she didn't believe it. He really didn't, either. But what did that prove?

He asked, "What about her laptop? Have you started the examination yet? Elaine was a compulsive journaler. Surely there's some indication of what was happening in them."

"There wasn't a laptop, and we assumed the killer took it. Either he was covering all the bases, or there was something on it he wanted."

Nicholas tapped his fingertips on the dash, tap, tap, tap, then said, "In addition to journaling, she kept most of her work in an online cloud because she disliked carrying a laptop everywhere. She'd devised a system where she could access her files on the fly from any computer, tablet, or smartphone. Once upon a time she shared her password to the account with me. With any luck, she hasn't changed it. If she has, I have a few tricks up my sleeve that won't leave a trace. I should be able to break into her account remotely."

"You're a hacker?"

"One of my many skills," he said without expression, and Mike shot him a look that almost made him laugh. She wasn't happy about that, but then again, he didn't expect her to be. Working with the American FBI was going to be an experience, for both sides.

"Good to know, but I have some of the best computer

minds in the Bureau on my staff. I want one of them to try to access Inspector York's files. We wouldn't want the case against her murderer to be thrown out on a technicality." Even though her tone was pleasant, he heard the warning loud and clear.

Touché. He said easily, "Certainly. Of course. I understand completely," and thought jurisdiction and justice be damned, this was Elaine. No way was he going to sit back and wait for some FBI hack to do the job for him.

14

The New York skyline peeked above the concrete barriers, cold and forbidding. Traffic was backing up, and Mike took out her flasher and put it on the dash. "Sorry for the noise, but we need to get uptown, fast." The slower cars moved to the side of the road, and she gunned it.

He said, "If my uncle sent you to pick me up, can I assume you're in the loop on the other small issue?"

And of course he was involved up to his eyebrows, too, and she didn't like it. On the other hand, maybe his brain was as fine as his butt and she could use him. Maybe. She saw herself as a trainer and him as a stubborn, bullheaded Rottweiler.

"The diamond being stolen, you mean? Yes, I'm well aware of the situation, through SAC Horsley, ugh, I can't stop calling him that. He keeps insisting I call him Bo, but it's tough, since he was my SAC for years—anyway, he told me you would fill me in. We're headed directly for the Met right now to meet with your uncle Bo and the curator of the exhibit. Find out exactly what everyone knows."

"I'll tell you everything Uncle Bo told me," and he did.

She listened, never said a word until he'd finished. She was quiet, and he sensed she had something to say, not about the theft but about something else, but she didn't really want to. Why? Because it would be an acknowledgment that he was already in the thick of things? He had to get past her distrust of him, her gut-negative reaction at a foreigner horning in on her investigation. He needed her on his side, at least for the time being.

"Am I to assume you've made a connection between Elaine and the missing diamond that I don't know about?"

Mike spoke carefully. She didn't want to alienate the man, at least not yet. "Is she capable of such a thing? To betray everyone like this?"

He turned to face her, his arm stretched out along the back of his seat. "I'm not saying this because she was my friend, my colleague. But for her to steal the diamond— like I told Uncle Bo and Savich and Sherlock, it would be entirely out of character. I can't envision her breaking the law for personal gain, and what other reason would someone want the diamond, if not to benefit from it financially? She fought on the right side. Crime sickened her, if you can understand the sentiment."

Mike nodded. "I do. Everyone in the FBI feels the same way, which is why we're the best in the world at what we do—no offense to New Scotland Yard, of course."

"Of course not. Why would you ever want to offend Scotland Yard?" That shut her up. Oh, he wouldn't mind going head-to-head with the FBI. Give them a run for their money. But he had no problem with trying to stay on their good side, so he said, "We're all on the same side," and shut up.

There was more coming; he could feel the pressure building in the car. Three, two, one, and yes, there she went, her head turning slightly toward him in that way he'd already started to recognize.

She said, "You've got to know that everything is pointing toward one logical conclusion." She paused for a moment. "I have to tell you, if Inspector York *is* involved, this situation is bigger than our personal feelings toward our teammates. All right?"

There it was. She was worried his personal feelings would affect his judgment. He'd be suspicious of an outsider coming into his team as well, especially under these circumstances.

"Fair enough."

"Good."

Nicholas said, "Now that we're best friends, tell me how in the world a priceless diamond goes missing from an exhibit pretty much everyone is aware of and that is surrounded by the best security the art world has to offer?"

Mike shot him a look and accepted the sarcasm, since it was merited. "I think all of us agree it had to be an inside job. Had to be. The person who did it was the same person who caused the power outage, someone really close, someone who'd gotten ahold of one of Peter Grisley's fakes and switched them out in that five-minute window of opportunity."

15

Nicholas said, "Tell me what your forensics are showing. How exactly was the diamond taken and replaced?"

Mike started to answer, and yawned instead.

"Been at it for a while, have you?"

"Sorry. I was up all night. I managed four hours of sleep, but I've got to admit, I'm dragging. My bloodstream needs coffee; that will perk me right up.

"Okay, once Mr. Horsley—Bo—briefs us, and everyone's in agreement with the plan, my best forensic people are standing by to process the room. We'll fingerprint everything carefully, including the fake Koh-i-Noor, of course, and see exactly how the case was opened."

Nicholas said, "Uncle Bo told me the biometrics reports show only he and Elaine accessed the room during the past three days—that doesn't count the five-minute power outage, of course. I don't think Elaine did this. And assuming that's the truth, the thief is most likely already on a plane out of the country. I agree with Uncle Bo, I think we've got a real pro involved here, and a pro isn't going to stick around and glory in his kill.

"Uncle Bo is the first to say that none of the staff close to the Koh-i-Noor have the background to suggest a pro of this magnitude. I'm thinking the background checks on all those people who got within twenty feet of the exhibit room need to go much deeper. We're talking what—maybe a dozen people, on the outside?"

"Sounds about right."

"There must be a great deal of money involved, and we need to be looking at who may be behind a theft of this nature, as well as who the thief might be. I've made a list of world-class thieves who have the resources and cunning to pull off such a theft."

She grinned. "Remember I mentioned the dead Russian in Inspector York's apartment was a foot soldier for the Anatoly crime family? Well, guess what? Andrei Anatoly also deals in stolen jewels, not to mention other criminal enterprises, and we have our local office who deals with them looking deep into their past few weeks as we speak. Another thing: Andrei Anatoly is also an art lover and is on the guest list for tonight's event. I thought we might have a chat with him."

Nicholas said, "I assume you've already heard Savich and Sherlock are here to speak to him as well?"

Mike nodded. "Hearing Dillon's grandmother is Sarah Elliott—that blew my mind. They believe Anatoly is the one behind the theft and switch of one of his grandmother's paintings in the Prado Museum. The crimes echo one another, and I don't believe in coincidence."

"I don't, either. I'll cross-check my list of thieves with Anatoly and his people, see if there's any indication of a match. Maybe Anatoly wants to score one of the most famous diamonds in the world."

"I wouldn't doubt it," Mike said. "We also need to find out if Bo is one hundred percent certain the stone was real when it arrived. It could have been a fake the whole time and no one knew, right?"

"I already asked him. The Koh-i-Noor and all the other jewels were tested before they left England and again when they arrived on American soil. And yet again at the museum, following the indemnity requirements for the gigantic insurance policy covering the exhibit.

"The crown jewels are encased in specially made vitrine display cases with two-inch-thick bulletproof glass, which is impossible to break into. Having the power off is the only untraceable way to get into the case."

"Yep, it was definitely an insider," she said, and unspoken was *Elaine York*.

Mike whipped the Crown Vic across four lanes of traffic and merged onto the Robert F. Kennedy Bridge, which would take them to the East Side. "We're ten minutes out now, if the angels are on our side and traffic doesn't get worse."

He rubbed his neck. "It's been a long day."

"I imagine so. Unfortunately, it's going to get longer. The media is having a field day with Elaine York's murder.

I've already seen it reported on every major station. The talking heads are going nuts, wondering what it could all mean, some of them even questioning the safety of the crown jewels here in the U.S. As for the BBC, they're about ready to pick up pitchforks and light torches and come rescue their jewels. And they even know about Kochen's connection to Anatoly, and you can only imagine what they're saying."

He'd seen CNN as they'd walked through the terminal, but hadn't said anything to her about it. "Well, at least they don't know anything about the missing Koh-i-Noor yet."

"*Yet* being the operative word here. If we don't get the diamond back before the news breaks—" She shuddered. "It doesn't bear thinking about."

No, he thought, *it doesn't.* They were both silent. Finally, Mike said, "Hear me out, okay? Let's say Elaine York was in on the theft from the beginning. Why? Money, I guess, lots and lots of money. She was matched up with the Russian thug, stole the diamond for his people, and both of them were killed, probably by the people she was going to pass the diamond off to. That could mean Anatoly's already got the Koh-i-Noor, and York and Kochen's murderer was another one of his soldiers."

He couldn't very well shoot her, since she was driving. He said only, his voice mild, "That's one possibility. Next?"

"Or Inspector York found out about a plan to steal the jewel, tried to put a stop to it, and got herself killed."

"As my uncle Bo rightly pointed out, she'd have come

to him immediately if she suspected something. That won't wash."

She swerved around a manic bicycle messenger. "Whoa. Idiot. All right. Putting Inspector York aside, is there a market for the Koh-i-Noor out there?"

"There are private collectors who would literally pay anything to get their hands on something this unique. Not to mention the leaders of the countries who think the Koh-i-Noor belongs to them. India asks for it back annually. Pakistan lays claim to it, as does Iran. All three had the Koh-i-Noor in their possession at one time or another, though India held it the longest. Queen Victoria was simply the last to get her hands on it."

"Iran and Pakistan? Could we be dealing with a nationalist with a major grudge?"

"I don't think it's about a pissed-off nationalist, not with Anatoly involved. I suppose it could be about cutting the diamond into pieces for quick sale, but that doesn't play for me. The Koh-i-Noor is far more valuable left intact."

"Then we're talking about a private collector. Like Anatoly."

Nicholas said, "If he has unlimited funds, then yes. If not Anatoly, there are at least a dozen more I can think of to fit the bill."

16

The Metropolitan Museum of Art sat squarely on Fifth Avenue at Eighty-second Street, with Central Park its lovely backdrop. Three huge banners advertising the *Jewel of the Lion* exhibit hung from the parapets between the columns—purple, red, and gold—each with story-high silk-screened portraits of the crown that housed the Koh-i-Noor diamond.

Mike turned off the flasher and siren a few blocks away so they wouldn't announce themselves and make people wonder. She edged the car into a small space a block east of the Met. In front of the museum, people scurried about, and the American flag snapped in the chilly breeze as they walked past.

Nicholas looked up and couldn't help himself: he saw the perfect angles for an attack sniper, counted five possible eagle's nests for shooters, watched the traffic barreling by and the dozens of people walking the streets.

Nothing would happen, but the thought of it made the hair rise on the back of his neck. He pictured Elaine, carefree and alive, walking up the steps, on this same path daily for the past four months. All her energy, all her time, focused on this one place.

Nicholas knew to his gut that Mike and his uncle were right. Someone intimate with the exhibit was the thief, someone who'd covered his tracks perfectly. And it wasn't Elaine. He knew exactly who and what she was. So he had to solve the theft, and he'd solve Elaine's murder. And absolve her.

When they reached the Met's steps, Nicholas said, "I see the museum staff is setting up for the *Jewel of the Lion* gala. It's going to be quite a spectacle."

Mike nodded and pointed. "Those blue crowd barriers are meant to funnel the attendees into the appropriate doors. Nineteenth Precinct will help man the streets tonight. Even with six hundred people on staff, the Met security won't be enough. Look at that huge red carpet they're spreading on the steps. This is a show unto itself. There'll be more paparazzi here, more reps from all the media swarming all over everyone who looks remotely important, than there are political fund-raisers in an election year."

Nicholas looked to the top of the stairs, where a woman with brown hair in a sleek ponytail was watching for them, tap-tap-tapping her boot. When he met her eye and nodded, her smile was clearly relieved. She gave him a tiny wave and a beckoning finger.

He said, "There's our curator, Dr. Victoria Browning. I looked her up online after Uncle Bo told me about her. He said she'd be waiting for us."

Nicholas made seven guards, plainclothes and uniformed, as they followed her into the cavernous entrance gallery. He assumed there were more guards he didn't see; the space was nearly bursting with people. The grand stairs were already covered in flashy red carpet, a vermillion trail upward to the exhibit, and the beehive of activity simply enfolded them as they walked.

Dr. Browning stopped next to the stairs and waited for them to catch up. Despite being smartly dressed in a gray wool sheath with a wide black belt, black tights, and high-heeled black leather boots, she looked exhausted, dark shadows beneath her eyes.

Nicholas shook her hand. "Nicholas Drummond, Metropolitan Police. This is Special Agent Mike Caine, FBI. You're Dr. Victoria Browning."

"Yes, I'm Dr. Browning. Mr. Horsley is waiting for you upstairs. Shall we?"

Browning had a Scottish accent, and Nicholas recalled reading that she was born and raised in Roslin, though he hardly wanted her to know he'd been checking up on her. As they started toward the north elevators he said, "It's very nice to hear a familiar voice. Edinburgh, is it?"

Browning smiled, showing nice straight white teeth and dimples, which made her look very young. "Well done, Detective Chief Inspector. And I grew up near Roslin."

He said easily, "A charming village. Overrun with tourists headed to the chapel, I suppose?"

"After *The Da Vinci Code* made us famous, yes, but you know, I wanted out badly, before the movie, and so I read archaeology at the University of Edinburgh, then did my postdoc research fellowship in art crimes and cultural heritages. Before curating the *Jewel of the Lion* exhibit, my responsibilities here at the Met included verifying the provenance of everything that comes in from the Middle East and India, my specific areas of expertise. You would be amazed at how many fakes and stolen goods we find."

Mike said, "How horribly ironic."

Dr. Browning gave an exhausted laugh. "Agent Caine, you have no idea. Now, before I start screaming at these hordes of people, let's take this conversation elsewhere."

She led them to the oversized service elevator. She used a key and swiped a white plastic pass through the black card reader before she hit the button. As the door slid shut, she collapsed back against the wall, letting it hold her weight, and crossed her arms over her chest. "Forgive me. I'm devastated, haven't slept much worrying about all this. First Elaine, now the Koh-i-Noor. It has not been a good week. And now we're going to have the fake Koh-i-Noor in place tonight for the gala."

Nicholas said, "No one will realize it's a fake, Dr. Browning, you know that."

She gave him a tired smile. "But that's not the point, is it?"

Mike asked her, "So you deal with all kinds of stolen art? I heard the Prado in Madrid found a good quarter of their paintings were forgeries, including a recent Sarah Elliott painting."

"Yes, *The Night Tower*, I heard. It's still hard to believe, isn't it? On the positive side, I also work with both the Museum Security Network and the Association for Research into Crimes Against Art to identify illegal pieces that make their way to our doors, make sure they're returned to their rightful owners."

Nicholas said, "It's been my experience there's a huge market not only for stolen art but for all sorts of artifacts as well. Correct?"

Dr. Browning nodded. "Yes. That's why I work directly with the FBI Art Crimes team as well. I'm not accustomed to seeing our pieces leave the premises without permission."

Mike said, "I'm new to all this. Please tell us more about your security measures."

Browning waved her hand at the card reader mounted by the floor numbers. "This is part of the standard security protocol we have in place. Doors won't close without the pass. This elevator goes only to the secure floors; you have to have both a key and a pass, as you saw, to access them. It's also on camera twenty-four/seven, and so far there is nothing to indicate they were tampered with." She sighed. "Except, of course, for that five-minute power outage."

17

Browning pulled a folder out of the slim black briefcase she'd set on the floor beside her. "Here's the duty roster for the past three days, including tonight's staffing for the ball. We have a huge security team in place." She shook her head and Nicholas noticed the small gold hoops in her ears. "This theft doesn't make any sense at all. I know everyone who works here. They work here because they love art and love our museum. They'd never do anything to hurt us."

Mike said, "No one's been acting strangely over the past few days?"

Dr. Browning shook her head again, making the earrings dance. "Nothing has happened to point suspicion. We were refused all vacation requests for the first three weeks of the exhibit, so it's all hands on deck." She frowned slightly. "Except Elaine. She'd never taken a sick day before, and, of course, the day of the power outage, poof, off she goes. Anyway, there's a new shift coming in at four o'clock this afternoon to staff the ball; we'll have to make sure everyone's accounted for."

Nicholas said, "The diamond isn't exactly a large item to steal. It could have been slipped into someone's pocket, and walked right out the door."

"Yes, that's true. At one hundred five carats, it's a massive diamond, but small enough to fit in your hand. We have the files for everyone who's been in the museum since the exhibit arrived, and we're going through the video feeds to see who was where and when. Assuming the diamond was switched during the five minutes of missing video feed, we're checking the cameras to see if anyone was out of place, leading up to that time, and afterward."

Mike said, "If the diamond is still on-site, it could be anywhere."

"Yes. All the staffers who started their shifts this morning have been asked to stay on until dismissed by Mr. Horsley. They've complied, but everyone knows something's up. Something major. We won't be able to keep this quiet much longer. Our rumor mill is as big as our staff."

The elevator stopped on the fifth floor. Dr. Browning led them down a corridor, their heels echoing in the cavernous silence, through a few turns, then to a gray steel door guarded by two men wearing the black fatigues of Bo's security firm. She said, "VIP tour, guys. We'll be about ten minutes or so." They stood aside without a word, and Nicholas noticed they both carried Glock .40s. Bo wasn't kidding—the security staff was loaded for bear.

Dr. Browning put her palm in the reader and waited for the beep. She said to Mike, "Another layer of security, the biometric reader." She swiped her pass in the reader and entered a code. The door hissed when it broke free of its seal. She said, "This is a low-oxygen environment; it helps keep things nice and fresh. Here we are."

The room was dark, but at its center were three long vitrine cases softly lit from within and full of incredible artifacts—gold and jewel-handled daggers and swords, brilliant earrings and glittering tiaras, and scores of intricately carved gold boxes, all from the Tower of London.

In the elevated middle vitrine, clearly the star of the show, sat the queen mother's beautiful crown on its bed of purple velvet. Nicholas had seen it several times, and it always took his breath away. The history of the jewels aside, they were bloody gorgeous.

And the Koh-i-Noor. Enhanced by the special display lighting, the brilliant diamond shined bright as the stars from its home in the stunning crown. It was insanely large, oval, and the size of an egg. And it was a fake. No one would be able to tell the difference tonight at the gala, no one.

There was a note of awe in Mike's voice. "This is quite impressive, Dr. Browning, but—"

She interrupted smoothly, with a smile. "Do call me Victoria, please. I know. This stone doesn't look fake at all, does it? It's really rather magnificent. That is because it's a perfect replica of the original Koh-i-Noor, which, trust me, is even more spectacular, at least to a trained eye. This replica fits the setting like it was made for it, which technically it was."

Nicholas leaned in for a closer look. "I would never know the difference. Tell us again why you tested it?"

Victoria said, "I received a call from Peter Grisley, who was hired several years ago to digitally map the Koh-i-Noor. There are some great stories about it online, published in a number of places. I'll get one of my guys to pull it all together for you. Someone broke into his workshop and stole his replicas, but he doesn't know when it happened, because he's a snowbird and has been in Arizona since November. He came home for a weekend before flying here to see the exhibit and realized that his replicas were missing, so he called us immediately, knowing something must be up." She paused, staring at the display, and said, "Boy, was he ever right."

18

The air lock hissed, and Bo Horsley came into the exhibit room with a big smile and his arms out.

"Nicholas Drummond. I'm so glad you're here."

Uncle Bo looked so much like Nicholas's mother it was unnerving at times. They hugged, slapping each other on the back. Nicholas said, "It's good to see you, Uncle Bo."

"I'm sorry it had to be this way, Nick, but I'm very glad you came. Mike, thanks for picking Nick up at JFK. You don't look bad for a woman who was up all night."

She shook Bo's hand. "I only need an hour or two of sleep to stay upright with all this adrenaline pumping through my veins. I knew retirement wouldn't suit you. You've been gone only six weeks, yet here you are, back on the treadmill."

"And what a treadmill—listen, Mike, I don't know anyone from Federal Plaza other than you that I'd rather have hunting for the blasted diamond, and finding out why Inspector York was killed. Thanks for being so discreet." He paused, blasted a big smile at Nicholas. "And now you've got my boy here to help you. First off, let me assure you the director of the Met is on board with our plan—no choice, really, since he wants to save his job, his reputation, not to mention all the money the Met would have to pony up. Nick, did you get Mike up to date on what we think happened?"

Nicholas nodded.

"Good. I have something for you."

Bo dropped a small white box into Mike's hand. She looked at it closely, turned it over a few times.

"Is that what I think it is?" Nicholas asked.

Mike smiled. "If you're thinking it's a relay capacitor for an EMP, yes." She turned to Bo. "Where did you get this?"

"Turned up in a sweep of the basement. This is how the thief turned off the power yesterday."

Mike cocked her head to one side, looked back at the fake Koh-i-Noor, tossed the relay into the air and caught it, then murmured, "Five floors away." She looked up. "I realize the most likely scenario is that the thief stole the Koh-i-Noor during the five-minute power outage, which means he or she had an inside helper, someone who could have attached this very effective device to the museum's electrical grid to shut everything down while the thief was switching out the diamonds. I'm thinking we have to look at everyone again, not only the people with direct contact with the diamond."

Bo grinned like a bandit at her. "Smart as a whip," he

said to Nicholas. "You're exactly right, Mike. We're not talking about a dozen or so staff, we're talking the whole ocean of Met employees. We've pulled the files for every employee within spitting distance of the exhibit, but it isn't a small group, believe me, and then there are the delivery people and students and the public who are in day and night. Cross-referencing our security video from the museum with the FBI's new NGI program—next-generation identification facial-recognition technology—will at least get us in the ballpark if there's anyone with a record who's been in and out of the museum around the time of the power outage.

"And another little spanner in the works: we realized the five-minute power outage also wiped the tapes of at least a minute before everything went black, so checking the basement stairs probably won't show us our inside guy. But we'll see. Can you handle integrating the NGI system with our video feeds, Nick?"

"Not a problem."

"Good. Victoria, your job is to make sure no one suspects there's a problem. This is business as usual, a last-minute test of all our security systems before the gala tonight. Would you please get the video feed from the day of the power outage for Nicholas and Mike so they can get started matching it to the NGI database? See if we've hosted any criminals over the past few days."

Victoria said, "I'll let you know when it's ready."

Nicholas wasn't blind. He quirked a brow at Mike. "Any trouble with me finding criminals with you?"

She narrowed her eyes but said, "Of course not. But

remember, the system is pretty new, and we're talking a lot of people, which means we'll probably have a lot of false leads."

"I know a few tricks that might save us some time."

Nicholas ignored her raised eyebrows and reminded himself where he was. Best not to share with her his less-than-legal skills.

Bo said, "Good, good. Mike, did you enjoy meeting Sherlock last night?"

"I've gotta say, sir, Sherlock is pretty impressive, what with her ability to reconstruct a crime scene. We've got what happened at Inspector York's apartment pretty nailed down."

"Don't call me sir. I'm Bo to you now. Maybe something neither of you know. Savich designed the base programs we used for VICAP and CODIS, in addition to adapting the facial-recognition program developed at New Scotland Yard for the FBI." Bo rubbed his hands together. "He and Sherlock are solidly in the loop. They'll be a great resource for us."

Nicholas said slowly, "I didn't realize he was responsible for developing the base programs. Not bad, not bad at all." He grinned. "Don't worry, I'll continue to go easy on him, Uncle Bo."

Mike said, "Bo, are you ready to open the scene and allow my people to come in and process the room? In addition to examining all of the technical security measures, they're going to want to examine the replica for fingerprints. I can have them here in fifteen minutes and they'll be done before the guests are allowed up here."

Bo nodded. "Make the call. We'll have to sneak them in; I still don't want my security staff knowing the diamond is missing. Dress them as caterers; there are hundreds of them roaming around tonight."

"Done."

They heard the air lock hiss, and the door opened. Victoria Browning said, "Sir, we're ready in the communication center whenever you are." She cleared her throat. "I'd like it on the record I think this is a terrible idea. It's my opinion as curator of the exhibit, we should follow protocol and shut down the museum."

Nicholas got the sense this wasn't the first time today Browning had said those words.

"Noted," Bo said, "and I'll make sure you're the first in line to share your thoughts with the director, should our plan fail. At the very least, it might save your job, as well as the director's. Can you manage getting our forensic techs into the exhibit without drawing any attention to them?"

"We'll have to turn off the cameras for the exhibit room so the people in the comm center don't realize we're sneaking caterers in. And I know you don't need reminding, but the jewels are priceless, and incredibly old. We must take special precautions during the evidence collection. As curator, it's my head to roll if anything were to happen to the crown jewels during the course of the investigation."

Mike said, "Anything more, you mean."

Victoria shot her a look, but her voice was calm enough.

"I'm fully aware that my head will roll if the Koh-i-Noor isn't found and returned quickly."

Mike said, "Sorry, Victoria. I didn't mean to intimate you were at fault here. My people are the best, so you can relax. They won't mess anything up."

Victoria looked like she wanted to snipe back, but she took a breath and smiled. "We're all under stress, Agent Caine. Let's go get the video feeds uploaded to the NGI database."

19

A bank of screens took up one entire wall in the massive communication center. Nicholas counted ten rows of five, with separate workstations monitoring access to every nook and cranny of the museum. It was impressive, and he said so.

Bo sighed. "Didn't help us much when it turned out to be so easy to shut down the electricity."

Nicholas said, "Maybe that means we should add a first-rate security expert to master thief. Narrow our focus even more."

Mike said, "Or not. If you could get your hands on the device used to shut everything down, all you'd have to know is how to turn it on and where to fasten it."

Of course she was right. He nodded.

The four of them went up a small set of stairs into Bo's glass-walled office, elevated so he could see everything happening in the room. Bo's phone rang, and he motioned for them to keep talking while he answered it.

Victoria said, "There's a whole new round of staff about to come on the clock, and people are already starting to trickle in for the event." She pointed at a monitor that clearly showed well-dressed people meandering up the entrance steps. The paparazzi hadn't begun their frantic picture-taking yet; they were assembling on either side of the red carpet, waiting for the important and notorious to make an appearance. News vans were lined up on both sides of Fifth Avenue and as close as they could get on all the side streets.

"These early arrivals are probably planning to have a drink or a bite to eat before the gala begins, but the bulk of the people will start showing in less than two hours."

Nicholas said, "We need to move fast, then. Mike, what's your forensic team's ETA?"

"They're ten minutes out."

Bo dropped the phone in the cradle. "You're well in hand with Victoria, so I'm going to go get Savich and Sherlock over here. I'll meet up with you in an hour or so."

"Uncle Bo, call my mobile if you need anything."

Mike sat at a terminal and started typing, pulling the two sets of data together. When the program began to run, a series of mug shots began streaming across the monitor, faster than the eye could keep up with. Nicholas noted that the facial-recognition technology used bone structure as points of reference. It would be accurate to the letter, should a match occur.

Mike said to Victoria, "While this gets started, tell me

more about how Peter Grisley got permission to make the replicas. Could he have something to do with this?"

"I seriously doubt it. He was allowed to utilize the molds from the Queen Victoria cut done in Antwerp in 1852 to digitally map the Koh-i-Noor. He petitioned the palace to be allowed to make the replicas for a research project he was working on. Since they were fakes, no one was worried about them. We were wrong."

Mike looked up from the keyboard. "What do you mean, the Queen Victoria cut?"

Victoria's eyes lit up. "Oh, you don't know the history of the stone? The Koh-i-Noor's story is quite incredible. When it came into Queen Victoria's possession in 1850, it was one hundred eighty-six carats, huge, but alas, hardly beautiful. It was dull and badly cut. Diamonds are meant to sparkle, and this one didn't. At an exposition held to showcase it, it looked even less impressive because it was poorly displayed in a gilded cage on dark velvet. The public complained so much Prince Albert, the Queen's consort, hired a lapidary named Coster from Antwerp to recut the stone from a rose cut to a brilliant, which would make it shine and glow and impress the British people with its beauty.

"When Coster was finished cutting and polishing the stone, it was down to a mere hundred and five carats; on the other hand, it was much prettier. Albert then had it made into a brooch for Queen Victoria. Over the years, it's been the focal point of three crowns, Queen Alexandra's, Queen Mary's, and Queen Elizabeth's."

A mere hundred and five carats. Mike thought of her

mother's precious diamond solitaire, only a carat. Talk about a new perspective.

"Coster came under fire, actually, because the stone was so much smaller, though all the experts rushed to his defense, claimed he did the best with what he had. Nowadays, they might have been able to save more of the original stone, with the laser cuts and all, but back then, it was line things up as best you can, take a crack at it with a hammer, and pray."

Nicholas pictured a man in a leather apron sitting before the stone with a hammer and chisel in his hands, saying, *"Please, God, please, God, please, God."* And whack. He knew it was slightly more complicated than that, but for the most part, luck, or the lack thereof, had played a large role.

Mike leaned back in the office chair, making it squeak. "I thought the name of the diamond was the Koh-i-Noor. Why is the exhibit called the *Jewel of the Lion?*"

Victoria was now lit up like a Christmas tree. "Koh-i-Noor translates to 'Mountain of Light,' but I didn't think that flashy enough to draw the American crowds, but I did want to capture the history of the stone a bit, so I looked to the source—India. When England annexed Punjab in 1849, the youngest son of the Lion of Punjab himself, fourteen-year-old Maharaja Duleep Singh, was forced to hand over his family's most priceless possession, the Koh-i-Noor diamond. Hence, Jewel of the Lion. Do you like it?"

Mike said, "Very much. It's very dramatic. And no wonder the Indian people feel it was stolen from them. It was."

Victoria said, "Incidentally, England annexed Singh, too—he was exiled to Britain for the rest of his life. The poor man wasn't allowed to practice his religion or leave England for decades."

Nicholas was tapping away at his laptop, pulled up a photo of the young Maharaja. "Well, maybe he wasn't so pitiable. He cut quite a dashing figure in 1850s Victorian society, evidently charming everyone he met. He became a favorite of the queen—she was godmother to several of his children—and he was a well-known figure in Scotland, where they dubbed him the Black Prince of Perthshire, because he had darker skin than anyone was used to. He had two wives and eight children, but the line died with them. He was, quite literally, the end of an era."

Mike stared at the photo of a young man, slender and beautifully dressed all in gray. He had expressive dark eyes, and he stood alone and proud for the camera. There was no insolence to mar that unsmiling mouth, but still, Maharaja Duleep Singh managed to radiate an air of defiance. She wondered if he'd come to accept, even love, his new country, given all the honors and attention heaped on him by the queen herself and Victorian society. She asked, "Did Queen Elizabeth like the exhibit name?"

Victoria grinned again. "I don't know if she liked it, but she approved it."

Nicholas said, "Do you know the Koh-i-Noor has only ever belonged to the women of the Royal Family because of the curse?"

20

Mike said, "There's a curse? What curse? Come on, Nicholas, you're joking."

"I don't joke about curses. It says only women are allowed to have the diamond because it brings bad luck to any man who tries to wear it. Trace its history. India, Pakistan, Iran—all historically led by men, and they all lost the diamond in huge, bloody battles. Terrible losses, families killed and torn apart. This went on for generations."

Victoria said, "He's right. The original curse was first seen in 1306 in a Hindu text. *He who owns this diamond will own the world, but will also know all its misfortunes. Only God, or a woman, can wear it with impunity.*"

Mike said, "But why can only women wear it?"

Victoria said, "I've done quite a bit of research on this question. Back in that era, women were greatly valued, as

sages, gurus, even magicians. There were several god-
desses in the holy texts, and the various sects worshipped
the feminine, or *Shakti*. Women were considered pure,
unlike men, who would do anything to get what they
wanted.

"Indian legend says the Koh-i-Noor is the very first
diamond in existence, and belonged to the sun god Surya,
who bestowed it to Krishna. It was stolen from him by a
servant, and because of this treachery, the treachery of a
single man, the curse was born."

Mike asked, "Are there any more replicas out there?"

Victoria said, "Only the two. One is here in the crown,
and the other is still missing. Hence their creator's panicked call to me. Grisley is in some serious trouble. He
should have had them properly secured, but I think this
situation is going to make his problem seem minor. There
is something else—" Victoria's tone changed.

Nicholas's alarm bells went off. His voice was sharp.
"What?"

"Elaine York oversaw the testing of the diamond when
it arrived here at the Met. She used a standard diamond
tester to check all of the jewels. You are welcome to watch
the video feed; you see her testing the Koh-i-Noor, smiling and saying, 'Brilliant. All's well, then,' and they close
up the vitrine case."

She shrugged. "I don't know why we're dancing
around this. It seems clear what happened. It was said all
roads lead to Rome or, in this case, Elaine York. And she
is, most conveniently, dead. And the diamond is gone."

Nicholas said flatly, "You are being disrespectful to a

New Scotland Yard inspector who's been murdered and is unable to defend herself. We will not indict her without a shred of evidence. Do you read me?"

Victoria didn't back down. "I'm sorry the idea upsets you, Nicholas, but facts are facts."

Mike said, "Tell me, Victoria, what did you think of Elaine York? You worked with her for months, both long distance and in person. What leads you to think Elaine had something to do with this?"

"Fact is, I wasn't suspicious until the diamond disappeared. I thought she was a very nice woman, competent and focused. We even had drinks and dinner together on occasion." Victoria looked over at Nicholas. "Elaine even spoke to me about you."

"Did she, now?"

She nodded. "Don't worry, she said only that the two of you had been close, once upon a time. She said you had a fascinating family and a very old home with a ghost. She also said you lied very well, but only when you had to, and she knew she could always trust you. But no matter now. The diamond is gone, and she's gone as well. As I see it, either Inspector York was deeply involved, or something much worse is at play here."

What could be worse? Nicholas wondered.

A red light began flashing on the screen in front of Mike. She stared at the screen. "Well, I'll be. There's a match. We've got ourselves a criminal in the house."

Nicholas bent over the screen. A man's dark face stared back at him, large and rectangular and hard, with dark hair and eyes, a flat nose, and a thin, sneering mouth.

Mike said, "I didn't expect this, I really didn't."

Nicholas said, "What's wrong? We wanted a crook, and we have one."

"Unfortunately, this guy is dead as a doornail at the morgue. Meet Vladimir Kochen, the dead man we found in Elaine's apartment."

21

Nicholas said, "I want to go to Brighton Beach and see Anatoly right now. He's in this. This Vladimir Kochen character coming to the Met proves it."

Mike said, "I know, but it's a forty-minute drive at the best of times. Right now the traffic will be obscene, even with the lights and sirens. We'd never make it there and back in time for the start of the gala. We've got to stay here and keep looking." She paused for a moment, made a decision. "Let me make a quick call." She called out, "Victoria, will you excuse us for a moment?"

Victoria looked annoyed by the dismissal, but after her little speech about Elaine, Nicholas couldn't care less if she was pissed.

He stared after her. "You know, I really don't like that woman." He turned back to Mike, watched her speed-dial a number.

"Ben? Please send three or four agents, a good show of force, to pick up Andrei Anatoly and bring him in for questioning—have them tell him it's about the murder of Elaine York. FYI, we just got an NGI hit on one of his men, Vladimir Kochen. Name sound familiar? The bastard was here, at the museum, so you know Anatoly is somewhere in the mix. Right. Thanks, Ben."

She drummed her fingers on the counter. "Ben Houston is from Art Crimes. He knew Inspector York. About the match—the moment Dillon Savich identified Kochen as one of Anatoly's soldiers, I knew he had to be involved in the theft. We need to move quickly. Truth is, Anatoly wouldn't cop to anything, even to save his own son. And guess what else? We don't have a shred of proof tying him to this, only coincidence."

"Tell me about him."

Her voice went cold. "Anatoly is not a good man. He has lawyers so slimy you'd think they came right out of the primordial ooze. We can rattle his cage, let him know we know he's involved. But we can't hold him, not without something solid."

Nicholas wasn't used to waiting for his prey to come to him, but he didn't see that he had much of a choice. He nodded curtly.

Mike's phone buzzed with a text message. She glanced at the screen. "It's the crew. They're at the loading dock. Let's go down and get them."

Victoria knocked on the door, opened it. "Mike, forgive me for intruding, but your team is here."

"Yep, they texted me. Let's go get them."

"No, I'll go," Victoria said. "I need to get them through security. You two keep doing what you're doing. About the match on your system, Mike, I know the man. I saw him having lunch with Elaine last week."

She started to leave, and Nicholas grabbed her arm.

"Talk."

She stilled and looked down at his hand, at his fingers encircling her arm.

He released her immediately, inclined his head. "Apologies, Dr. Browning. Please, tell us what you know."

She looked at her arm, her jaw tightened. "I don't know anything more. I simply saw Elaine having lunch with him here in the museum café. They seemed chummy. I didn't get the sense she felt she was in danger, but I hardly paid attention. I'll be back shortly. If I'm allowed to proceed."

Mike nodded. "Of course. Thanks for the information."

When she left, Mike said, "I can't allow you to punch her out, no matter what she says, all right?"

Nicholas paced Bo's office. "She has all the answers, doesn't she?" He ran his fingers through his hair, making it stand on end. "It's been a long day."

"Yes, it has. Look, neither one of us has had much sleep, and you've lost a friend."

He was silent, continued to pace. He looked down at the communication center every time he walked past her, as if the answer might magically appear on the bank of screens on the wall in front of them.

"Tell me about the Anatoly crime family."

Mike glanced at the still-running facial-recognition database and wondered if Kochen had been Elaine's accomplice, if he'd been the one to plant the device that knocked out all the power. "They're a pretty typical Russian Mob, loosely organized, not structured like the Italians, and half the time they spend fighting with other parts of the *Bratva*—the Brotherhood. We've gotten them under control in New York, more than three hundred indictments in the past few years, but they're like rats: they breed in the dark corners. Smuggling, arms dealing, credit card fraud, cyber-crime. They're opportunistic and lethal—they never hesitate to kill if they're crossed.

"Anatoly, the big boss—I'll admit it—he's scary, smart, and brutal to those who cross him. He has seven sons from two wives who run the various syndicates, all physically bigger than he is, and twice as vicious. Anatoly, at least, has some semblance of culture, a sheen of respectability; on occasions like tonight, he likes to present himself as a wealthy philanthropic businessman. He's big into the art scene in New York. Likes to get all shined up and come out in public, throw money at things. He's slick, too. We haven't gotten anything to stick to him; he lets the others do his dirty work for him."

"And Kochen?"

"Like I told you, Kochen is one of the foot soldiers, has a rap sheet a mile long. He's been approached to be an informant a few times, and he's been cooperative on the surface but hasn't ever given anything of use. He likes money, and bars and floozies."

"You said Savich wants to talk to Anatoly about the theft of *The Night Tower* from the Prado. He's known for art crimes, yet he supports the Met?"

Mike said, "Yeah, isn't that a kick? Fact is, though, Anatoly is better known for diamond smuggling. It's the best way to move large amounts of money around. Diamonds are valuable and portable. Like I said, we haven't been able to break him. He's been under almost constant investigation since I joined the New York Field Office."

"Sounds like Anatoly indeed has the money to finance stealing the Koh-i-Noor. Do you have a dress, by the way?"

"What?"

"A gown. For the gala. It's black tie. You're going to stand out in that outfit."

She glanced down at her jeans and boots. "Oh. Well, yes, I have one at home."

"You'd best send one of your people for it, then."

He was right about that; time was growing short. She sent a text message, then looked up at him. "Tell me you don't have a tux hidden beneath your clothes, like Superman."

He laughed. "Not this trip. No, my tux is in my bag. I never leave home without it."

"Just like James Bond, are you?"

"I don't think Bond ever has to press his tux."

"Probably not. Look, there's Victoria, back with my crime scene techs Paulie and Louisa. They look good as caterers, don't you think? Let's get this party started, then we can remotely access the interview with Anatoly."

22

Nicholas was impressed with Paulie Jernigan and Louisa Barry. Both were clearly competent, both listened carefully to Dr. Browning's detailed instructions on how the jewels, the room, and the cases should be processed without ruining them. Or upsetting the curator.

When Victoria finished, Paulie said, "Ma'am, no disrespect, but we've already got it figured out. We're gonna use Lightning Spray Redwop on the cases. It leaves almost zero residue, and we can clean it off easy with Rain-X glass cleaner."

Louisa said, "It will work perfectly on the jewels. There's a cone we spray into that eliminates excess so nothing else will be touched."

Victoria had one hand on her hip. "Show me how it works."

They gave her a quick demonstration. "All right, fine

by me. We'll need to work fast, though; the gala will be starting soon. Perhaps we should start with the cases to the side of the Koh-i-Noor and work our way in."

She turned to Nicholas. "The thief probably leaned here"—she made a motion toward the vitrine to the right of the center case—"and opened the case from behind, like so."

She unlocked the case, and he could see exactly what she meant.

Victoria continued. "If there are prints to be found, my bet would be on the inside of the vitrine, and on the pavilion—that's the angled area of the diamond right before the bottom point."

Paulie said, "Dr. Browning, we'll need prints from everyone who had access to this room, too. I have my portable fingerprint scanner with me. We need to exclude the people who've been in the room today. Mike, did either you or Detective Chief Inspector Drummond touch any of the cases?"

"Probably, without thinking about it," Nicholas said.

"Mine are on file, as you know," Mike said. She cocked a finger at him. "Fingerprint him, Paulie."

Nicholas held out his hands, palms up. "This is easier than waking up a print tech in London to have my card sent over."

Paulie was quick and thorough, and within five minutes, they were done and back in Bo's office, Nicholas rubbing the ink off his fingers with an alcohol hand wipe.

"Ah, here's a text message from Ben. They've arrived at Federal Plaza. Evidently Anatoly came quietly enough, outward goodwill, all cooperative. He already had his lawyer with him, since they were headed to the gala together. Ben will set us up to watch and communicate with him remotely."

Nicholas would rather talk to the man in person, but there was too much happening here at the Met, a tense undercurrent he recognized from his many field assignments. His gut told him something was wrong, but for the life of him, he couldn't figure out what.

Mike dialed Ben's number, and when he answered, Nicholas heard him say, "I'll be sending you a remote link in a couple of minutes. Oh, yeah, Anatoly's lawyer's making noises about filing a writ of habeas corpus."

"Let him. Take Anatoly apart, Ben," Mike said, and punched off. She said to Nicholas, "Five more minutes and we'll be all set up."

Nicholas said, "I'm going to do some snooping." He reached into his leather bag and pulled out his laptop.

"Into?"

He eyed her. "The truth? I know you'd rather wait for your people, but time's running out. I'm going into Elaine's journal. Like I said, she used an online diary, has for many years. With any luck, she'll have recorded what she was doing in the days leading up to her death."

"You don't need her computer?"

"Nope."

"You can really break into her journal using this program?"

"Yes. Elaine's data will be under a basic encryption. Won't take me but a minute."

Nicholas didn't bother mentioning he'd been a competent hacker since he was nine, and this would hardly pose a problem.

Mike inclined her head. Sometimes the camel's nose under the tent was useful. "Then have at it. We need all the information we can get."

He hesitated for a moment over the keyboard. *Elaine.* He'd been forcing her from his mind all day, but now she came back, smiling, teasing, arguing in that clipped Oxford accent. His friend. His colleague. Now he would invade her private thoughts. He didn't like it, but Elaine was dead. She had no more privacy, and he couldn't afford to give her any, especially if it meant finding her killer and exonerating her.

With three keystrokes, he launched his program and remotely hacked into her system.

Elaine was fastidiously organized, so he had no trouble finding her journal. It was her habit to write in the morning, stream of consciousness, whatever came to mind.

He browsed straight to the end, saw the entries ended nearly a week before her murder, which was strange, considering how religious she was about recording her thoughts.

He started tracking backward in time.

"You're frowning. What's wrong?"

He glanced up. "Some of her posts seem to have words and sentences blacked out, or missing entirely. Sentences drop off mid-thought." And that made no sense. Why would Elaine black anything out? Or delete sentences?

He flipped through entries going back a couple of months and saw the same strange blackouts. She wouldn't have done this. No, someone else had already hacked in, someone who knew exactly what to erase from Elaine's journal, and how to cover his tracks.

Someone very, very good, and that someone had also probably killed her and taken her laptop.

But Nicholas was better. He might be able to reconstruct the pages. And the entire journal would be cached on Elaine's laptop, if they ever found it.

He felt his adrenaline spike. He hit three keys together and took a screen shot of the journal displayed and copied it to his laptop, then did it twice more, collecting all the information he could for the month leading up to her death.

He flipped back to the screen with her journal to capture another week. It was gone.

"Oh, bugger."

"What's wrong? What did you find, Nicholas?"

He couldn't believe his eyes. The entries were disappearing, one by one. He tried everything, but his actions only made the words delete faster.

"I didn't realize there was a self-destruct built into the system. I thought there were blackouts, but it was the virus deleting the entries. They're all gone."

Mike said, "Why would Elaine have a self-destruct program on her journal?"

"I don't know."

But they both knew that was a lie. Obviously there was

something important in Elaine's journals she didn't want strangers to see. He couldn't stand it.

"I captured a bit of it before it deleted itself. Let me see what's here."

His fingers flew over the keyboard. "Here's a fragment from a week ago. *Brought VK on board.* And the day before that, *Vlad,* then two blank words, *1:00 p.m.*"

"A meeting? And there was nothing more?"

"Victoria said she saw Vladimir Kochen with Elaine at the museum café at lunchtime. It must have been a scheduled meeting."

Mike leaned over his shoulder, reading his screen. "*Brought VK on board.* After a meeting with him the day before? Does it sound to you like she hired him?"

He hated it, hated it. There it was, in black and white. Proof, in her own words, that Elaine was directly involved with Anatoly's soldier.

Mike's phone buzzed. "It's Ben. He's run into a couple of snags, but it won't be long now before he'll have the remote feed up and running." She found herself patting his shoulder, probably the last thing Mr. Super-Spy wanted or needed. "Look, we'll see what Ben gets out of Anatoly. Soon I'll have Elaine's bank records, so we'll know if there are any money transfers to Kochen."

Nicholas scanned the rest of the screen shots he'd captured. Words stood out here and there, fragments, but they made no sense.

He tried a program he'd written to reconstruct coded messages received from assets in the field during his time with the Foreign Office. He fed the copied screenshots into it and watched the words reassemble themselves on the screen in the correct order. He slammed back in the chair, his eyes never leaving the screen.

"Bloody hell. Look at this, Mike."

23

Mike looked at the screen, but it made no sense, and she said so.

Nicholas pointed at the screen. "It's garbled, but there are several key phrases, fragments of thoughts. *Scared something is going to happen. I need to keep myself safe.* She clearly knew something was up."

Mike said, "And you're thinking she hired Kochen to keep her safe?"

"It looks like it. See here, *Vlad escorting me to work. Feel safer already.*"

"But that doesn't make sense, Nicholas. I mean, if she felt like she was in danger, why wouldn't she tell Bo? She was a cop, tough and smart—no, I don't understand this at all. And why, of all things, hire one of Anatoly's men?"

Nicholas was very afraid he did understand. The murdered Russian hadn't only been her bodyguard, he'd also been her accomplice. He said, "She would have told Bo unless she was involved and Kochen was part of it." Saying the words aloud somehow made them more than simply possible, it made them true. But why were they murdered? He knew to his gut there was something else going on here, just as he knew time was running out.

Mike said, "Here's a text from Ben. It's starting. We can talk about it after the interview."

Nicholas had to admit Andrei Anatoly wasn't at all what he'd expected. With his mane of silver hair and black-framed glasses, he looked more like a diplomat or a university president than a crime boss. He was a big man, all buffed and polished, wearing an Armani tux if he didn't miss his guess, being escorted into a small, white-walled, purely impersonal room to a table with four chairs, two on either side.

"He looks a treat, doesn't he?" Mike said. "Talk about false advertising."

Then came a tall, elegant man, slender, fit, tanned, not wearing Armani, but still a well-fitted tux. Both had clearly been intercepted on their way to the gala. Nicholas bet that had made Anatoly mad. *Good.*

The men took seats across from Special Agent Ben Houston. Three FBI agents stood leaning against the opposite wall, their arms crossed over their chests, their Glocks clearly in view of Anatoly, and they looked on with slitted eyes.

Anatoly leaned back in his hard metal seat like he didn't have a care in the world and smiled pleasantly at Ben.

Mike said, "Poor Ben. He's had no rest, and he looks

whipped. He better perk up; Anatoly's lawyer might look like a senator in that beautiful suit, but he's got the personality and instincts of a great white. I've gone up against him before, and I didn't like it a bit."

Ben introduced himself, thanked the men for coming, then said, "Let's get started. As you know—"

The lawyer interrupted him. "Agent Houston, my name is Lawrence Campbell, and I represent Mr. Anatoly. I want it on the record that Mr. Anatoly is here voluntarily, as a courtesy to the FBI. However, he is a very busy man and tonight is the gala at the Met. As you know, Mr. Anatoly is not only a lover of the arts, he is also one of the museum's benefactors. He is naturally very involved in tonight's gala unveiling England's crown jewels. We hope you will not keep him or me long."

Ben said smoothly, "We certainly appreciate Mr. Anatoly's cooperation. Let me hurry right along, then. Mr. Anatoly, would you please tell the whereabouts of one of your men, Vladimir Kochen?"

Campbell said agreeably, "This sort of question is a waste of Mr. Anatoly's time, Agent Houston. We know as well as you do that Mr. Kochen was found murdered yesterday, in, I believe, an English police officer's apartment."

Anatoly nodded. "I was very saddened to hear of Vlad's unfortunate death. He was a valued employee until a year ago, when he left my employ. I have not seen him since."

"May I ask why, then, sir, Mr. Kochen's cell phone records show"—Ben glanced down at several sheets of paper at his elbow—"ah, yes, here it is, at least a half-dozen calls to both your home phone and your cell in the past week?"

Anatoly put a hand on Campbell's arm to quiet him and said easily, "I said I had not seen him for a year, Agent Houston, not that I hadn't spoken to him. Vlad wished to return to my employ. We were conducting negotiations, I suppose you could say."

Nicholas said, "Anatoly's accent is vaguely European, certainly not Russian. I suppose he's been able to smooth it out living in the States—how long?"

Mike cocked her head, "He came with his parents, at the tender age of twenty-two. It's important to him to fit in, and that means getting rid of his Russian accent. He wants to be viewed as a pillar of the community."

On the screen, Anatoly leaned forward, put his hands on the table. "I assure you, Agent Houston, I had nothing whatsoever to do with poor Vlad's death. I am as mystified as you seem to be."

"Tell me, why did Mr. Kochen quit, Mr. Anatoly? Or was he fired?"

"An unfortunate incident. He was not respectful to one of my sons. Yuri told me of it, and I had no choice but to fire him. Our negotiations involved Vlad apologizing to my son and asking his forgiveness. This would have happened if not—" He stopped, gave a creditable Gallic shrug.

Nicholas said to Mike, "This is going nowhere, and Anatoly knows it. He's hardly going to walk in and admit to murdering Kochen and Elaine."

As if Anatoly could hear through the video feed, he said,

"If we are finished here, the gala will be starting soon, and I don't wish to be late. Like every other guest tonight, I wish to see the crown jewels, especially the Koh-i-Noor." And both Anatoly and his lawyer started to rise. Ben shook his head. "A few more questions, Mr. Anatoly."

Mr. Campbell grunted in impatience. "What other questions would you possibly have to ask my client?"

"Be seated," Ben said, steel in his voice. They looked a bit surprised but complied, the lawyer tapping his pen on the tabletop and Anatoly examining his nails in apparent boredom.

Ben placed a picture of Inspector York on the table.

"Do you know this woman?"

Anatoly merely glanced at the photo, and he sounded a little more Russian when he said, "I have never seen this woman in my life. I will say a prayer for her soul."

Ben laid three more pictures beside it, and Nicholas realized they were from Elaine's crime scene. He hadn't seen any of the photos, and the images hit him like a fist to the gut. It was hard, but he tried to focus on Anatoly's reaction, not his own.

Nicholas felt Mike's hand lightly touch his arm. He said, "See how he stiffened a bit as he looked at the photos? He's a good actor, but he knows her."

"I agree. If it were someone else, we could chalk it up to a natural reaction to seeing a dead body, but given who he is, it's hardly likely crime scene photos would faze him."

Campbell said, "We're very sorry we couldn't be of more help. And if there's nothing else, Agent Houston, we really must be going."

Anatoly rose, and his lawyer quickly followed suit.

Nicholas said, "Mike, quickly, tell Ben to ask Anatoly if he arranged for the theft of the Koh-i-Noor diamond."

Mike stared at him. "You're crazy, it'll give everything away."

"Doesn't matter now. Trust me. Do it."

She texted Ben, and Nicholas could see Ben's surprise when he read the text, but then he smoothed himself out and lounged back in his chair. "Mr. Anatoly, one last question. Did you pay someone to steal the Koh-i-Noor?"

Mr. Campbell shouted, "Enough! This is utterly ridiculous. We've had enough of your accusations. We're leaving."

He began to push Anatoly from the room, but Anatoly appeared frozen to the spot.

He looked more than frozen, Nicholas thought, he looked stunned—horrified, actually. It wasn't an act. He gathered himself together, but when he spoke, his voice wasn't all that steady. "Agent Houston, do you mean to tell me the Koh-i-Noor diamond has been stolen from the exhibit?"

"No, sir. I'm asking if you arranged for the diamond to be stolen?"

Anatoly went a deep, unhealthy red, and shouted, "You drag me in here, insult me, and now you accuse me of planning to steal the precious Koh-i-Noor? Understand me clearly, Agent Houston. I have worked tirelessly for the past three years to bring the diamond, indeed, all the crown jewels, to America. I have helped fund this exhibit.

This is absurd, you are absurd! *Poshel na khui, suka, blyad!*"

He continued to rant in Russian, and a wide grin spread across Nicholas's face. "I'd say we rocked his boat."

Mike said, "Do you know what he is saying?"

Nicholas said, "The gist of it, yes. Trust me when I say it's not appropriate for polite company."

Ben said, "Mr. Anatoly, I'll get an agent to escort you and Mr. Campbell out. We'll talk again soon."

He looked directly into the camera, an eyebrow arched.

The feed went dark.

Nicholas said, "Anatoly lied through his teeth about knowing Elaine, and not seeing Kochen recently, but his shock and surprise at being accused of trying to steal the Koh-i-Noor seemed quite genuine. He wasn't aware the diamond's missing."

"But maybe he set the whole thing up. Maybe he was somehow using Inspector York and Kochen, but things fell apart and he had them both murdered. Don't forget the seven sons." She added after a brief pause, "But here's the problem: shooting Kochen full of cyanide? That doesn't sound at all like Anatoly."

24

The Metropolitan Museum of Art
Jewel of the Lion gala
Thursday evening

The streets around the Met glittered under the lightly falling snow and the abundance of jewels and fabulous dresses lighting up the place. Limousines and taxis crowded Fifth Avenue. Some brave souls had defied the elements and were walking in. The paparazzi's flashbulbs were going a mile a minute, making it look like a disco ball spinning outside the doors.

Mike watched the guests drift in, a steady line of Manhattan's elite, plus celebrities and their acolytes, and several flamboyant arty-looking types—models, most likely—showing highlights from the latest fashion lines.

Nicholas said behind her left shoulder, "Your dress is quite lovely."

She turned, nearly cocked a hip, and almost said, "This old thing?" but stopped, since it was too close to the truth.

"Satin keeps well in closets, thankfully. You're quite

dapper in your tux as well." Understatement of the century. His tux fit him perfectly. Fact was, he looked hot and dangerous and very 007. She wanted him to shoot his cuffs and order a dry martini. She said, "At least we don't look like Feds on the hunt."

"Speak for yourself, Agent Caine."

"And there's really nothing for us to hunt, just keep our eyes open. Not that I'm whining—we don't get to attend hoity-toity events like this very often. Nicholas, there's my boss, Milo Zachery, over by the stairs. In the red bow tie, with sandy hair? You need to meet him." She clicked her comms unit in her ear and said, "Sir, I'm sending Nicholas Drummond to you right now."

Mike watched him thread his way through the crowds, all smooth grace and focus, and saw women double-take as they saw him, and she couldn't say she blamed them.

Nicholas came to a halt beside Zachery and his red bow tie. "I'm Drummond, sir. It's good to meet you."

"Ah, Drummond, excellent," Zachery said, and shook hands. "I'm so sorry about Inspector York." He bent his head closer and said quietly, "I heard Andrei Anatoly had an absolute fit when you asked him about having planned to steal the diamond. Ben told me he thought the old buzzard was clear of this crime. You agree?"

Nicholas nodded. "As Mike said, it doesn't mean he didn't want to run the race, he simply didn't make it out of the starting gate in time."

"Your uncle's in the comm center. Ah, there's Agent Sherlock by the bar. I bet Agent Savich isn't far away. Bo tells me you've already met them online."

Sherlock's gorgeous red hair was done up on top of her head with curls hanging down over her ears. Along with dangling black earrings and a nicely fitting black dress, she presented a picture that made her stand out in the crowd. Nicholas thought she looked more dramatic in person, more vibrant.

As for Savich, Nicholas thought he was simply *more* in person, a big, tough man who looked hard as nails, a man he'd want at his back in a dark alley. He looked like he could brawl with the best of them.

Sherlock caught them watching and waved. He nodded in return. Zachery said, "Go fill them in."

Nicholas nodded. "I wanted to thank you, sir, for letting me help."

"If I'd said no, Bo would have grilled me like a steak," Zachery said, "and I'm scared of your uncle."

Nicholas said, "I am, too." He went back to Mike and held out an arm. "Come on, let's go talk to the computer king of the universe."

"I want to worship at Sherlock's feet. I still can't get over how she nailed the crime scene."

Savich saw them coming and held up his hand to the bartender for two more Pellegrino with lime.

Sherlock greeted Mike with a hug. "Mike Caine, lovely to see you again, after what—sixteen hours. The red gown suits you." She held her back. "I got a solid eight hours sleep, but you didn't, I know. How are you feeling?"

"Jazzed, really. So much is happening and so quickly. What will the next minute bring?" Her eyes went to Savich. "I gotta say, Dillon in a tux is something else."

She heard Nicholas say to Savich, "Whenever Uncle Bo talks about your laptop MAX, he lowers his voice to a reverent whisper. I swear he thinks there's magic involved."

Savich said, "Truth is, your uncle's right. MAX gets a daily dose of fairy dust."

Nicholas laughed. "If you swear by it, send me some."

Mike said to Sherlock, "I've never heard of two married agents working together. However does that work?"

Savich settled an arm around Sherlock's waist. "So long as she calls me sir every once in a while, we get away with it."

"He likes to spread this fiction," Sherlock said, and poked him in the ribs.

Nicholas said, "Uncle Bo tells me you have a little boy."

Mike said, "Not just any little boy, Nicholas. Sean is currently the most famous kid in the world—his marriage proposal to Emma Hunt in San Francisco is all over YouTube. When this is all over and done with, I'll show you."

Sherlock said, "He's given us a new challenge. Sean is madly in love with three girls, and a fourth is hovering. I fear he wants to marry all of them, not the thing for a mother's peace of mind."

Nicholas raised a black eyebrow. "Don't tell me all of them are at your breakfast table? Shall I speak to him?"

Sherlock laughed. "Dillon might call you for reinforcements. I hear your uncle Bo and his dad were longtime friends and partners."

Savich nodded. "Bo and my dad used to whoop it up. They'd throw barbecues and invite all the agents over to their houses. I remember all of us kids having a ball. I understand your dad works for the Home Office, which is like our FBI, but you bucked the familial trend and went to work for the spooks in the Foreign Office instead. What made you leave spook world to join New Scotland Yard?"

Nicholas's expression didn't change, but Mike felt it—he'd stepped back, withdrawn. He didn't want to talk about it. What had happened? But he said easily, "For a while all the traveling was fun—shutting down bad spooks, brokering compromises—but to be honest, the constant upheaval, trying to thwart terrorist attacks, got to be brutal. In the end, I wanted to come home, be closer to my family, get my hands dirty on the streets. And London, well, it's quite a challenging environment."

That wasn't the whole truth, Mike could tell. *Interesting*. She looked down at her watch. "Nicholas and I need to get up to the exhibit room before the crowds are allowed up. Two of our top techs are there with Dr. Browning, collecting evidence. I'm hoping our forensic team has turned up something concrete."

Savich said, "Why don't we join you? I want to visit the heart of the museum, see if Bo and his people have spotted any more bad guys."

The four of them headed toward the elevator, weaving through the crowd, the buzz of their voices droning like bees in a hive. Hundreds of beautiful people were tipping back flutes of champagne, accepting hors d'oeuvres from the dozens of caterers who glided smoothly through them, silver platters held high. The cocktail party was well under way, everyone seemed happy and excited, looking for British royalty, not Prince William and Kate, who'd canceled because of a family obligation that hadn't been explained, but perhaps a stray duke or foreign minister accompanying the British ambassador, Sir Peter Westmacott. Wisely, no media or paparazzi with their cameras had been allowed in.

Mike glanced back over her shoulder to see a tall, elegantly thin woman in a form-fitting black gown making a beeline toward Nicholas. What was this about?

25

Nicholas hadn't seen the woman yet. Mike watched him stand to one side to allow Sherlock and Savich access to the elevator first. As he stepped into the elevator, the woman called his name in a cultured British accent, not unlike Nicholas's own.

"Nicky? Nicky Drummond? Is that you?"

Nicholas had only a moment to think *You must be joking* before she was on him. She threw her arms around him, then stood back, both hands on his arms.

"Nicky, it *is* you. I had no idea you were in New York." She looked him up and down. "You look edible, darling. I always liked you in that tux."

He said, voice expressionless, "Pamela. It's been a while. These are my friends." But he realized she wasn't looking at him now, she was staring dead on at Savich. "I am Lady Pamela Caruthers, the founder of *Beauty in Nature*, a very upscale online magazine. I'm doing a spread on the *Jewel of the Lion* exhibit; I'm simply mad for the Koh-i-Noor, aren't you? And you are?"

Savich smiled at the beautiful hard-edged woman standing in front of him. He introduced himself and Sherlock and shook her lovely white hand, her index finger sporting a ruby the size of his knuckle.

Nicholas said, "And Pamela, this is Special Agent Mike Caine."

Pamela gave Mike a cursory look, then moved on. "This is fascinating. All of you are FBI. Why are all of you here, in a law enforcement herd? What's going on?"

"It's a perk," Mike said easily. "Nothing more than a very nice perk. Who are you exactly?"

Pamela laughed and tossed her head back so the rubies around her white throat glimmered. Mike caught the sparkle of diamonds in her hair. "A perk? Come now, dear, that lie will make your nose grow. You ask who I am? Darling, I'm Nicholas's wife, more's the pity."

Nicholas's wife? Mike heard the snark clearly. What was this about?

Nicholas said, "*Ex*-wife, actually. As I recall, Pamela, there was never any pity involved."

Sherlock saw the glitter of anger in Lady Pamela's eyes and threw herself into the breach. "I've read several of your articles, Pamela. The holistic approach to beauty and fashion is a big hit right now."

Pamela stared a moment at Sherlock's hair. "An FBI

agent who is into the holistic approach? Isn't that a lovely surprise. One simply never knows who one's audience includes, does one?"

"No, I suppose one doesn't," Savich said.

"Did you know about my magazine, Nicky? Perhaps you've checked it out after pounding the pavement all day? Maybe talking about me to your mates over a Guinness at the pub?"

Nicholas said, "I really don't do much pounding, Pamela. And my mates aren't the holistic type."

"Such a humiliation for your family, Nicholas, you now a common copper. Now, the Foreign Office—" She gave a sparkling look to Sherlock and Mike. "You should have seen him in Istanbul, right outside the Blue Mosque. Imagine, a spy for a husband, it was all so exciting at first—" She gave an elegant shrug.

"But you were so busy, Nicky. Then after Afghanistan, well, your moods, darling, they became such a trial." She shrugged, her smile brilliant now. "Do you know my magazine has tripled its subscribers since we launched two years ago? The *Jewel of the Lion* special edition goes online tomorrow, and I expect it to be our biggest hit yet."

No one had anything to say about that.

She turned back to Nicholas. "I hope your family does well."

"They do very well, thank you."

She patted his cheek. "Life moves on, Nicky. One of these days you must learn to move along with it. I read about Inspector York's murder. It's all over the news, on the Internet. Everybody wonders what's going on. You're here to find out what happened, aren't you?"

Nicholas said nothing.

Pamela said, "Oh, yes, my father told me he saw your father at the club last week and—he's the Earl of Clarens, you know, and—"

Zachery's voice came through loud and clear on Mike's comms unit. "Bo wants Nicholas, Savich, and Sherlock upstairs. Mike, you stay put, keep an eye on things."

Did her boss think one of the guests would pull the Koh-i-Noor out of his pocket and wave it like a red flag?

Nicholas looked relieved for the excuse to leave. He nodded to his ex-wife and stepped into the elevator with Savich and Sherlock, pressed the button to five. Mike's last view of him was his stoic face as the doors closed.

"He could always run fast, when he wanted to," Pamela said. She gave Mike an indifferent nod and sashayed off, her five-inch Louboutin stilettos clicking on the marble floors. Even when she moved into a crowd, Mike could still see her, she was so very tall and thin and exquisite.

Was he Sir Nicholas? No, he couldn't be, Sir Nicholas was the nearly headless ghost in Harry Potter. Lady Pamela—his ex-wife. Life was like an onion, her mother had always said, you never know what you'd have when another layer peeled away.

What had happened in Afghanistan?

The lights flickered, once, twice. The crowd didn't seem to notice.

"You've got to be kidding me," Mike said aloud. "Now is not the time for the lights to go out."

Zachery's voice came over loud and clear on her comms unit. "Probably the snow, but our people up here are checking into it. What more could it be than a simple power surge?"

"I hope you're right. Can you imagine, eight hundred people wandering around and the lights go out? Pandemonium."

Her cell rang; she saw Nicholas's name on the caller ID. "Hang on, sir, it's Nicholas." She clicked off her comms unit and answered her cell.

"Mike, did you see the lights flicker? Zachery thinks everything is okay, but I know it's not. Something's not right. Get up here now."

26

When the elevator doors finally opened, Mike looked out on chaos. People were stumbling around like the walking dead, coughing, eyes tearing, crying out. The hall was getting increasingly foggy and her own eyes began to burn.

Gas.

Nicholas ran out of the communication center with Sherlock tossed over his shoulder. She wasn't moving. Mike rushed to her side, felt her pulse. It was, fortunately, strong and steady. Whatever was in the gas wasn't deadly.

Nicholas coughed deeply, then turned back to the comm center. Mike shouted after him, "What's happening?"

Nicholas called, "I don't know yet. Tell Zachery everyone in the comm center is down."

She fought panic, hit her comms unit. "Sir, we have

an active attack on the communication center. Everyone's down. Repeat, officers down. It feels like tear gas."

An instant of silence, then, "Copy that, Mike."

She took off after Nicholas, who was dragging more people from the room.

A deafening wail began. The fire alarm.

Nicholas swung the communication center doors wide, sending in fresh air to dissipate the gas. Soon people began staggering out under their own power.

Savich came out with Bo leaning on his shoulder, both of them gagging and choking, their eyes red, tears streaming down their faces.

Mike wiped her eyes and went back to Sherlock, who groaned and tried to sit up.

"Hey, sit still. You'll be okay. What happened?"

Sherlock's eyes were watering heavily. "Some sort of percussion grenade, with gas. Nick was out checking the power grid when it hit, so he escaped. Knocked us all out."

Nicholas cupped her face in his hand. "Did you see who did this?"

"No, I didn't. Where's Dillon? Oh, there you are. You're all right? Did you see anything before the gas blinded you? I had my back to the door, looking at the security feed from the exhibit room."

"I didn't see anything." Savich slumped down against the wall next to her and touched his head to hers. "Are you all right? You're all blurry."

"I'll be fine—my eyes are burning, that's all. I was close to the door. All I remember was someone said Dr. something, and then the fun began."

The elevator doors opened, and Zachery rushed out, barking orders to the five agents on his heels.

Nicholas said, "Your techs, Mike. We've got to get into the exhibit room."

But she was already on her feet, running down the hall, the train of her dress flaring out behind her like a bull-fighter's red cape. Nicholas shouted to Zachery, "The exhibit room—we're going to check." And he ran down the hall after her.

27

Mike was banging on the thick metal door. "It's locked and no one's answering. How do we get in?"

"Bo," Nicholas said, then ran back to the communication center, found his uncle in the hallway beside Savich and Sherlock, wiping his eyes and trying to draw in clean air.

"Bo, how can we get into the exhibit space?"

"I'll let you in, but you'll have to guide me," Bo said. "I can't see a damn thing."

Nicholas walked him down the hall. He realized the fire alarm had been turned off. He hadn't even noticed until now.

Bo said, "The pass is in my pocket. Put my hand in the reader, then swipe the pass."

Mike followed his directions, and the door beeped. "Good job, okay, the code is 35767336." She keyed in the code and the air lock clicked open.

"Stay here, Bo."

"Ready," Mike said, her Glock raised. She held up her fingers, one, two, three, and in they went.

No smoke or gas in here, just two FBI agents sprawled on the floor, unmoving.

"Paulie, Louisa?" Mike dropped to her knees by her people, felt for pulses. There was blood coming from the back of Paulie's head. Both Paulie and Louisa had taken blows hard enough to knock them out.

She knelt up. "They're not dead, thank the good Lord above, but knocked out cold."

There was something wrong, Nicholas knew it. He heard something—

Tick. Tick. Tick.

"We have to get them out of here, now!"

She didn't waste her breath. They dragged Paulie and Louisa out into the hall where Bo was waiting, still blinded by the gas, Sherlock and Savich beside him.

Nicholas said, "There's a bomb in the exhibit space, Uncle Bo. Savich, no, you and Sherlock stay put, you're still half blind. Mike, get Zachery to evacuate everyone and call the bomb squad. I'll see what we have so I can brief the bomb squad when they get here."

Bo lurched toward him. "No, Nicholas, wait—"

But Nicholas cut him off, "I know what I'm doing, Uncle Bo. Mike, get everyone to safety."

When he ran back into the exhibit room, he stopped cold and listened. He'd swear the ticking was louder in the now empty space.

He heard Bo shout, "You have two minutes!"

Nicholas ran to the vitrine cases that held the crown jewels. All looked fine. No, wait, the center vitrine case, the one that held the queen mother's crown with the fake Koh-i-Noor gracing its center—the case was cocked open. The closer he went, the louder the ticking became.

The crown was tilted at an angle away from him. He expected to see the case wired, but what he saw instead was a gaping hole in the crown. The fake Koh-i-Noor was gone—*no*, it hit him. *Not the fake,* he thought. *Bloody hell.*

Tick. Tick. Tick.

No time to waste. He knelt and pushed under the case, saw the bomb attached to the glass.

Tick. Tick. Tick.

There was little light in the room, but still he could see there was no clock on the faceplate, so no way to know how much time was left before he and the room exploded into bits. He looked closer, saw the bomb had multiple wires attached to a cell phone. The sucker could go off at any second; all that was needed was a call to the number.

"Bloody, bloody hell." He needed more light. He pushed himself out from under the case and ran back out into the hall to see Mike standing by the open elevator.

She grabbed his arm. "Everyone's out. We're last. Let's go; the bomb squad's close."

"No time—the bomb's set to a cell phone trigger. I've got to defuse it myself. You get out of here."

He pulled away, ran into the comm center, grabbed a Maglite, and took off back down the hall.

28

Mike didn't think, she simply ran after him. When she got to the exhibit room door, she saw him on his back under the center case.

"Nicholas, are you insane? Get out of there!"

"I should have known you wouldn't do what you're told."

She shimmied under the center case to lie on her back beside him. "I'm here, I'm staying. Tell me what you've got."

"It's a standard cell phone–activated explosive, like they use for IEDs in Afghanistan and Iraq, and suicide bomb vests. Vibration sets it off; the ringer will be set to vibrate, and if the number is called, the movement will cause the trigger to go. I'll use a jamming frequency, remove the phone's faceplate, cut the wire to the ringer."

"I sure hope you know what you're doing. Give me the Maglite, you need both hands for this."

"If I screw up, we'll find out soon enough. Aim the light here. Good."

He heard Tommy Magallan, the head of London's bomb disposal unit, saying over and over, his voice soft and firm, *No hesitation; hesitation means you die.*

He worked with his mobile for a moment, activated the jamming signal, waited ten seconds for it to take effect, and pried off the faceplate with the screwdriver on his Swiss Army knife.

He set the faceplate aside, looked closely at the guts of the detonator. It was attached to a seven-by-twelve-inch gray paper-wrapped brick, most likely C-4, a couple of pounds of it, enough to take down a large section of the museum, not to mention destroy the priceless crown jewels.

He counted *three, two, one,* and snipped the small piece of wire running to the ringer. He used the flat of the blade to edge the battery away from the phone, and time started again.

Safe.

The ticking continued, unnerving and insistent. But that was all right. He knew it wasn't coming from the bomb.

He and Mike pushed out from under the vitrine case and stood. He saw her face was pale, but she hadn't panicked. He righted the queen mother's crown, lifted it to see a small metronome in the shape of a skeleton.

Tick. Tick. Tick.

He used his finger to stop its motion.

Silence.

Where had he seen this skeleton before? He'd had very little sleep for more than a day, his adrenaline was still doing the rumba, and he wasn't firing on all cylinders. But what? Then it came to him.

He said in the silent room, "The Fox."

She was staring at the skeleton. "What fox?"

He handed her the small plastic skeleton.

"What is this?"

"A metronome—a toy, really—meant to scare the crap out of us. It worked, too. When I saw the detonator was a cell phone trigger, well, fact is, they don't tick. I knew there was something else in the room making that noise. She's a devious bitch. She set it up right under the crown."

He shook his head and laughed. "Oh, you clever, clever girl."

Mike said, "Who set it up? I'm clever? All I did was hold the Maglite."

"An excellent job you did, too. Do you remember seeing Dr. Browning when you came upstairs?"

Her brain clicked into place. She said slowly, "No, I didn't see her."

Nicholas said, "Because she wasn't in the comm center. Our *curator* stole the real Koh-i-Noor diamond ten minutes ago, right out from under our noses."

"Browning? But that doesn't make sense, I mean— what's the fox?"

"It's not a what, it's a who. I had no idea the Fox was a woman."

"Nicholas, has the gas gotten to you? You're not making sense."

He said, "The Fox is one of the most notorious jewel thieves in the world. Remember I told you I put together a short list of thieves who had the skill to pull off a job this big, and we wanted to see if they had any ties to the Anatoly crime family? Only a handful of thieves operate at this level, and the Fox is one of them. No one has any idea who he—excuse me, *she*—is. But now we know."

"You're saying the Fox is Victoria Browning? I've got to alert everyone, she might still be in the museum, we have to catch her." She got Zachery on her comms unit, could practically see his brain compute what had happened, then heard him go into action. She switched off. "She can't be far. It's only been ten minutes."

Nicholas said, "She's long gone, and you know it. I'll wager the video will show Paulie or Louisa freeing the diamond to fingerprint it, she whacked them on the head, rolled the canisters of gas into the comm center, and waltzed right out the Met's front door, everything timed to the second."

Mike said, "Maybe the gas is getting to *me*, because if I hear you right, you're saying the real Koh-i-Noor was in the crown, snug in its case, this whole time? It hadn't been replaced with one of the replicas?"

"Exactly what I'm saying. The stone wasn't a fake. The only fake here is Browning. She fashioned herself an incredible identity and background, hired on at the museum and worked her way up until she was curating the exhibit itself. I'm amazed at her patience, and her brain."

"Nicholas, why wait until tonight? She's had four days to steal the diamond, after hours, or the first night the stone was in the building. Why this huge charade? Why wait for half of the New York Field Office and a thousand people to be in the museum to witness the crime?"

"She couldn't do it, not without alerting security. This was her plan all along. She must have engineered the power surge on Wednesday—everyone would focus on those five precious minutes as the time when the Koh-i-Noor was stolen, only, of course, it wasn't stolen. The whole purpose of the outage was to show herself on several cameras far away from the exhibit room, the perfect alibi. She's quite brilliant. Your people did the hard part for her. All she had to do was pocket the diamond, blind everyone, and leave." He took the skeleton from her, flipped it in the air, and caught it.

"And all of us went haring off, looking at anyone but her—looking at Elaine, who couldn't defend herself—" He broke off, then continued, his voice angry now. "We trusted everything Browning dished out. And now she has the Koh-i-Noor. Brilliant," he said again.

"We'll need that for evidence."

"I know."

Mike said, "Do you think she killed Elaine?"

"I don't know. Everything we've been told for the past two days was a web of lies designed to get your techs into the museum and remove the Koh-i-Noor from the crown to fingerprint it. It was the one thing she couldn't do for herself. We have to go back to the beginning, look at everything with a fresh eye."

She saw it now, the elegance of Browning's plan. "That bitch tricked us all."

Nicholas raised the skeleton metronome. "The Fox leaves behind a token at her crime scenes. Something to mock the investigators. I'd say it's working."

Mike touched the head of the skeleton, sent it to ticking again.

Nicholas's cell phone rang, and they both jumped. Nicholas moved in front of Mike instinctively to shelter her from the blast, spreading his arms wide, in case he'd missed something, but nothing happened. He dropped his arms and answered with a curt "Yes?"

Nothing. Empty air. Then a click.

29

She didn't have much time. They knew who to look for now, but she'd still made the call to Nicholas's cell phone—she pictured their surprise, their gut-wrenching fear—she had to admit, it was fun. She knew exactly what Mike Caine and Nicholas Drummond would do next— put a trace on the phone, try to pinpoint the last known location of the call. They'd find it eventually, but in the Hudson River. Smack themselves on the forehead a few times before they figured out exactly how Dr. Victoria Browning, the dedicated, knowledgeable museum curator, had pulled off the theft of the century.

She laughed aloud. Too bad she couldn't stick around and watch the FBI go in circles, the way she intended, but she had a plane to catch.

Her Ducati Streetfighter maneuvered smoothly through the evening traffic as she drove across the bridge. She chucked the phone over the railing and glanced at her watch. She was five minutes out from Teterboro Airport. One advantage to working for Saleem Lanighan was she could afford everything a woman might need to succeed, including a Gulfstream, fueled up and waiting for her.

She gunned the bike, enjoying the kick of power, the engine growling between her legs. It was too early to celebrate, but she would, and soon. Things had gone like clockwork so far.

She frowned. There was one fly in the ointment. She hadn't planned on Drummond. Not only was he cunning and smart, she knew he wouldn't follow FBI procedures unless they suited him. No, Drummond would go on the hunt. He'd been a spy with the Foreign Office, did whatever it took, broke whatever rules he needed to break in order to get the job done. He was coming after her, she could feel it.

She could see him now, organizing, planning, systematically searching. Very intense. Very attractive. Very much like Grant. No, she wouldn't think about him now.

At last she was here. With a wave at the guards at the airport entrance, she pulled through the gates and around to the back of the departure building. Money had changed hands, enough money that no one even noticed her, because, as arranged, the airport cameras had been shut down for a ten-minute interval. She'd found a thick stack of hundreds to be the ultimate motivator.

She'd had the tail number of the Gulfstream altered so it would be very hard to trace ownership. The captain was the only one aboard, and he'd filed a flight plan for

Vancouver, though he was fueled for a journey across the Atlantic instead. He was awaiting her instruction as to where to go when she got on board. Both precautions would assure anonymity, lay a false trail for the FBI to follow.

She knew, of course, the FBI would eventually figure out the subterfuge, but by the time they found out where she was headed, she hoped it would be too late.

She left the bike on the tarmac but kept her helmet on. No sense taking chances, not yet. Her backpack was a welcome weight on her shoulders. She grabbed another, smaller bag from the bike's storage box. She climbed the stairs, and once inside, the captain raised them and secured the door. Only then did she remove her helmet, pull the ponytail holder from her hair, stretch her shoulders, her back. She needed rest. She'd been too keyed up to sleep last night. A long flight was the perfect remedy.

The captain was young, fit, eye candy with big brown eyes. He greeted her with a blinding grin. She supposed it must be fun for him, jetting around the world, never knowing where he would be from one day to the next. She hoped he was competent.

"Bonsoir, mademoiselle." He had a slight Parisian accent. He motioned for her to have a seat in one of the luxurious tan leather chairs.

"I'm ready. Let's get going."

"Where to?"

"Vancouver, remember? I'll give you exact coordinates when we're in the air."

"You're the boss."

Yes, she was. When she heard the engines roar, felt the plane rolling, she knew she'd made it. Five minutes later, the lights of New York winked up at her.

Wishing her well. Bidding her adieu. She waved, laughing.

The phone rang at her elbow.

"We've cleared the New York airspace. Where to?"

"Paris. Alert me when we've crossed into European airspace; I'll give you coordinates then."

"Roger that. There is champagne in the refrigerator, as you requested."

"Thank you, Captain."

A '54 Dom Pérignon, very nice. She poured herself a glass, then snuggled deep in the seat, inserted a small earpiece and took out her iPad. A few taps, and the screen turned an eerie green. She saw shadowy mannequins in shades of grays moving about. She'd used a small cellular repeater that wirelessly boosted the microphones' range, and she could easily hear all the voices from the microphones she'd hidden along the Met's fifth-floor hallway and in the communication center itself.

She turned up the volume in time to hear Mike Caine say, "I'm going to personally punch that bitch when we catch her."

Kitsune raised her glass and toasted the small screen. *"Bonne chance."*

Next she called her employer.

30

A soft voice in his ear interrupted a most delicious dream.

"Monsieur Lanighan? Monsieur Lanighan, sir?"

He came awake immediately, jerked upright, nearly hitting Colette, his secretary. She was naked at his side.

"Monsieur Lanighan, the private line. You have a call." She handed him an encrypted mobile phone, one he'd never used before, because only she had that number.

At last, at long last.

"*Merci*, Colette. You may return to your quarters for the rest of the night. That is all."

She slid from his bed and disappeared without a word, closing the bedroom door behind her. He took a deep breath and answered.

"*Oui?*"

"*Bonjour*, Saleem. I trust the impending dawn finds

the Lion snug in his den? Perhaps with a mate for warmth? I hear Paris is cold tonight."

His heart leapt to his throat. "Kitsune. Do you have my diamond?"

"Where are your manners, Saleem? We've not spoken in nearly two years, and you have no proper greeting for me?"

He touched the scar on his throat. "I will greet you properly if you tell me you have my diamond."

Her voice was light, indifferent. "I am offended, Lion. Your father was much more polite. Yes, I have your precious diamond. Meet me at noon, l'Arc de Triomphe. Repeat, l'Arc de Triomphe. As soon as I confirm the money has been wired into my account, I will give you your prize."

The coded delivery point meant she had encountered problems, making her delivery dangerous. "What has happened?"

"Nothing at all. Everything went smoothly. Any time now the world media will report the theft of the Koh-i-Noor diamond, right from under the FBI's nose. Still, I don't wish to take any chances. There is a wild card in the deck now, and he is good, very good."

"Who is this wild card?"

"His name is Nicholas Drummond, a detective chief inspector with New Scotland Yard."

"So what? He's only a policeman."

"More than that, Lion. He used to be in the Foreign Office. He was, I have heard, a very successful operative."

Saleem calculated how long it would take him to arrive.

He had plenty of time. The Koh-i-Noor was nearly his, nearly in his hands.

"I will be there. I'm paying you fifty million dollars to be smarter than any ex-spy. Do not let me down."

"I will not," she said, and ended the call.

Saleem sat for a moment in the cooling covers, then walked naked to the huge bay window in his bedroom and looked out over his city. The Paris dawn greeted him. He placed a hand on the chilly glass and imagined what would happen once the diamond came home, to him, its true heir. He would succeed where his father and the long line of Lanighan men before him had failed. He would be the one to merge the pieces together. The power of the stone would yield to him, and him alone, and then his world would be changed forever. He smiled, his teeth flashing in the darkness.

31

The media was swarming the Met, going ballistic in their coverage of the incredible events unfolding, so Bo had set up a temporary task force in the basement of the museum, away from the prying eyes of both the media and the Met's board of directors, who were upstairs with the insurance adjusters, steaming mad and tap-dancing hard.

Nicholas listened to Mike speak to Agent Gray Wharton, one of the FBI's top computer experts.

"Gray, assemble a team. Here's what we need: a trace on Nicholas's phone, ASAP, the last incoming call, not older than ten minutes. Get out a BOLO for Dr. Victoria Browning, Scottish national, Ph.D. from the University of Edinburgh. We'll need to get her work visa on file with INS, also her passport, and a photo out to every airport, train station, bus station, car rental. Send a team to her apartment.

"Gray, as you know, this woman stole the Koh-i-Noor, and we're going to have an international disaster on our hands. Her alias is the Fox. Mark her armed and very dangerous, and send me everything as you get it."

She turned to Nicholas as Gray Wharton rushed from the comm center. "Let's go. Bo will be waiting."

They took the service elevator to the basement. Bo was talking to Sherlock, and Savich was hunched over a keyboard, his fingers flying.

They stopped to clap.

Zachery said, "Here's the man of the hour. Good work on the device, Nicholas."

Bo said, "It looks like you didn't waste your time with the bomb disposal unit in London. All of us are grateful for that."

Mike punched him on the shoulder. "You could have told me. I was going to call you Captain America."

Zachery said, "I sent two of the bomb boys with my men to look through the rest of the museum to see if Browning left any more surprises for us, but we seem clear. Here's the deal: Browning hacked into the fifth floor video feeds and erased everything from the start of the gala on. Savich is trying to override and restore the feed."

"Any report on Louisa and Paulie?" Mike asked.

Sherlock said, "They were transferred up the street to Lenox Hill Hospital. They took pretty hard shots to the head, plus it looks like she sprayed them with the same agent from the tear-gas canister. Takes an element of surprise to take down two FBI agents; she planned this to the letter. But they'll be okay, Mike. Everyone's okay."

Mike said, "It could have been so much worse. I'll head up there as soon as we've finished our briefing."

Nicholas said, "Bo, I need everything you know about Victoria Browning."

Bo handed him a manila folder. "Here's her file. She hired on at the Met last spring when they had an open call for security-guards-cum-docents. They handle the tours, plus keep an eye on the artwork. It's a growing trend to hire overqualified people for these positions— kills two birds with one stone. You need a master's or a Ph.D. in art to even be considered. So in addition to being a docent, she was well versed with everything security-related in this museum. She moved up the ladder quickly, was made a curator right before the holidays. When the original curator for the crown jewels exhibit fell ill, Browning was the number-one choice to replace him. She took over every aspect of the exhibit, worked with Inspector Elaine York directly."

Mike said, "Wait, she wasn't the original curator?"

"No."

"I assumed she was the curator from the start. Remember, Nicholas, she told us she named the exhibit? *Jewel of the Lion*. She thought it was catchy."

"How convenient for her, moving up the ladder so quickly," Sherlock said. "What sort of illness did the original curator contract?"

Bo said, "Vertigo. I remember hearing it was a terrible case, too. He ended up taking an early retirement package."

Mike said, "I bet she Hitchcocked him with the

vertigo. Were there any rumblings when Browning got the position? Scuttlebutt? Surely there were more experienced curators who would have been more likely replacements than a newbie."

Bo shook his head. "Before my time. I've only been here six weeks, remember, and Victoria was already the lead dog when my company came on board. I'll have to discuss it with the director and the personnel director. My staff liked her, though. She was easy to work with, tough but nice. She worked hard, like everyone else, but I don't know anything more personal about her than her choice of drink—Diet Coke. We'll have to talk to her coworkers for more."

Nicholas said, "I spent the plane ride over brushing up on the details of the exhibit. My briefing said Browning was chosen because of her extensive knowledge of the crown jewels."

Bo nodded and shook the file. "I have it here, too. A 'preeminent authority,' it states."

Mike said, "An authority? She must have faked her bio."

Nicholas raised his eyebrows. "Faked? Yes, I suppose she could have faked any and all of it, though it would take a bit of doing. The palace vetted her, so she must check out, even with a pretty deep check." He turned to Bo. "I'm sure the Met did as well, correct?"

"We do a thorough background check on every employee, from janitors to the board members." Bo read from Browning's file. "Her employment record and her transcripts checked out, nothing to set off any alarm bells."

"Then we need to go deeper. Ten pounds says her name isn't Victoria Browning."

Savich called out, "Got it. The video feed from the attack is up and running. You're going to want to see this."

32

They watched the grainy video.

Bo said, "Oh, she's very, very good. She programmed the computer in the comm center to create a timed power surge which forced the fifth-floor generators to kick in. Only the fifth floor, mind you. So when she threw the gas canisters and the alarms picked it up, only the fifth-floor alarm went off, not the rest of the building. It gave her exactly the cushion of time she needed to grab the diamond and get away."

Nicholas said, "Savich, rewind it again, to the moment before it all goes black. See, right here. The second Paulie releases the diamond from the setting, Browning takes out what looks like a perfume bottle, squirts it at him, and then Louisa. They're effectively blinded, start rubbing their eyes, and she hits each of them with a police baton, then pockets the diamond. Look at how fast she moves. If I wasn't looking for it, I wouldn't see it."

Savich froze the frame, then advanced it at quarter-speed.

"See, right there." Nicholas pointed at the screen. "Spray, and now the ASP baton is out and she's spinning. She's had martial-arts training, without a doubt." He whistled in what could almost be called admiration. He had to hand it to her, Browning was quick.

Sherlock said, "Those expandable batons hurt, and a blow with one to the head will do some damage. Paulie and Louisa are lucky they weren't hurt worse."

Savich nodded. "So they're down, she scoops up the diamond. She runs to the comm center, throws in the canister. It doesn't take more than ten seconds before everyone is down. She slams the doors closed to contain the gas and heads back to the stairwell. I pick her up again two minutes later, when the fire alarm goes off. Bo, I'm sure you'll find the museum alarms were triggered when she pulled the alarm as she exited the stairwell on the main floor."

Nicholas said, "Then she waltzes right out the front door."

Mike said, "We have to get in contact with the NYPD, get their camera feeds to track her."

Bo shook his head. "We need a warrant for that, and it'll eat up valuable time."

Savich started typing. A few minutes later, the screen split into five squares, each showing intersections and stoplights. He toggled the switch in front of him, and the cameras attached to the feeds turned in unison.

Bo said, "You're slipping. Thought it would only take you a second." He snapped his fingers.

Savich grinned at him. "Let's see where she went."

Mike said, "You hacked into the secure New York City CCTV network?"

"No, that would be illegal," Savich said. "This is the live, public, and very unsecured tourist cam system. It shows every intersection in the area. Perhaps even a better view than our official cameras, since they're bogged down with the new license-plate technology. Let's see where the Fox went."

He backed up the feed and started searching. Mike followed each frame closely. "Wait, Dillon. Right there." She pointed at the top-right quadrant. With a click, it filled the computer screen. He backed it up and hit play, and Victoria Browning's pretty boots walked into the frame and hopped in a cab.

Mike said, "She changed out of her ball gown and back into her work clothes so she'd be less conspicuous on the street. Got her at the corner of Fifth and East Eighty-fifth at 9:39 p.m. She's headed across town."

Savich freeze-framed the camera and zoomed in, then started typing again. "The cabbie's hack license is NY670097. Running it now."

Zachery came into the room. "Bomb squad team leader called. They've finished dismantling the rest of the device Browning planted. They said to tell you well done,

Nicholas. Took some quick thinking to throw on your jammer."

Savich said, "Here we are. The cab is registered to a Daneesh Himsah. I've got his cell, calling it now."

"Told you Savich was good," Bo whispered to Nicholas.

"Yes, and he's on a roll. Let's see how far he can get."

A man's voice came out of the laptop's speakers.

"Hello?"

"Mr. Himsah, my name is Special Agent Savich, with the FBI. You had a fare an hour ago, a woman you picked up at the corner of Fifth and East Eighty-fifth. Where did you take her?"

Click.

"Can you believe that—he ended the call." Savich sounded so surprised everyone laughed.

Nicholas said, "Let's get the NYPD to pick him up. Maybe a face-to-face will—"

A ring interrupted them. Savich clicked the laptop screen. Words scrolled down. "The taxi driver is texting us."

Fare in cab. Thru the CT border booth. Drop off at Tweed.

Zachery said, "That's the airport in New Haven, Connecticut. Tell him to keep it up. We can intercept. Thank you, Savich."

Mike read over his shoulder as he typed in a message to the cabbie.

Proceed as planned. Police will intercept at airport.
Thank you for your cooperation.

She said, "Nicholas, you and I will go. I want to see Victoria Browning's face when we arrest her. First, though, I need to change my red gown for jeans."

33

An MD-530 Little Bird was ready when they arrived at the FBI helipad. Zachery had pulled a tactical unit for them, six men bristling with weapons, silent as the grave, awaiting their orders.

Overkill, Nicholas thought, and said, "Mike, surely they won't be needed."

Her face was set, her tone cold. "She already tried to blow us all up. I'm not taking any more chances."

"Actually, all she had to do was call the number before I disarmed it and we'd all be playing harps. She didn't. She waited until she had to know we'd have disarmed the bomb."

She frowned at him. "Not the point."

They strapped themselves in and put on headsets so they could hear the pilot and speak to one another. The bird lifted off, twisted slightly, then banked right and headed north.

Nicholas looked over to see a grin on Mike's face a mile wide. Her voice crackled in his ear, distorted by the headset. "I love this chopper. I don't get to do intercepts like this very often."

"It's certainly faster than driving."

"Fifteen minutes, tops. We should reach Tweed before Victoria's cab arrives."

"Yeah, we will."

Mike said, "You think there's something else going on, don't you?"

"I'm wondering how we got this lucky."

The pilot spoke in their ears: "We're five minutes out."

Mike said, "Thanks, Charlie," and looked back to Nicholas. "Sometimes gift horses really neigh, don't they? With any luck, we're about to wrap this whole thing up. We'll bring Victoria back to New York and restore the diamond to the crown. And there will be rejoicing in the kingdom again."

Charlie said in their headsets, "I already heard about the theft on the radio. Talk about a brouhaha—I sure hope this comes off easy."

"It will." She turned to Nicholas. "When this is wrapped up, I'm hoping we can get Victoria to talk, tell us how this whole thing went down and who financed it."

He said, "If we do catch her, don't count on her opening her mouth. No thief of her reputation would ever nail the boss. Ever."

"It's against a thief's moral code?"

"In her case, I'm sure it would be."

The lights of the Tweed Airport runway glittered in

the distance, and the pilot broke into their conversation. "Tweed tower has cleared the airspace surrounding the airport and we're on a path to intercept. Are we a go?"

Mike said, "We are a go, Charlie. This isn't exactly a high-traffic airport, but there are still several cabs. Have you identified our target?"

"Yep, we've got a lock on the cab. We have clearance to stop it before it reaches the airport. We'll drop down right in front of it as soon as it takes the exit. Do you know if the suspect is armed?"

"I can't confirm either way. Better be ready for anything, Charlie."

He relayed the message to the tac team. Six heads nodded in unison.

The helicopter banked to the left, circling out over the water before diving back toward the highway. Mike saw police lights turn on, five squads merging into traffic, two ahead of the cab, three behind. It was a beautifully timed intercept. The cab slowed, then pulled to the side of the road.

Charlie hovered the chopper for a moment, and the tac team sprang into action, slithering down cords to the ground. They surrounded the cab, weapons pointed. The troopers stepped in.

It was over in a heartbeat, the cabbie out and on the ground with his hands on his head, Victoria Browning pulled from the backseat. Mike pulled off her headset and could hear her screams over the helicopter's rotors, hear her crying out, "What are you doing? Why are you arresting me?"

The instant Charlie set the chopper down on the road, Nicholas ripped off his headset and jumped out the door, Mike on his heels, her Glock at the ready.

Nicholas yelled before he reached her. "Where is the Koh-i-Noor, Dr. Browning?"

"I don't know what you're talking about." Her black hair blew back from her face, and Nicholas knew this gift horse wouldn't neigh.

"Bloody hell. Who is this?"

Mike lowered her weapon. "I don't know. But she's definitely not Victoria Browning."

34

Mike called over the roar of the helicopter rotors, "It's the wrong cab. We've got the wrong cab." She started toward the head of the tactical unit, but Nicholas grabbed her arm.

"No, it's the same license plate. She duped us. Again. Well, bollocks."

Mike whirled around and made a cutting motion across her neck. Charlie shut down the rotors, and they could hear each other again. The troopers shoved the woman into the backseat of a vehicle, the cabbie in a separate car.

Mike wanted to kick the helicopter skids. "How did she pull this off? Did she get out along the way? Trade places with this woman? Did she set it all up beforehand?"

Nicholas said, "Watch this." He'd uploaded the video

feed Savich sent to his laptop before they left the museum. He queued it up and hit play, froze the video on the figure getting into the cab. He pointed at the screen.

"Those are the clothes she was wearing when we arrived at the museum, without a doubt. The hair matches, and the height. But we never see her face, only a profile." He gestured at the sobbing woman who was now sitting in the back of a state trooper's vehicle.

"This is the same woman who got into the cab. But it's not the Fox."

Mike stared at the screen. "As you say, bollocks."

Nicholas closed the laptop, smacked it with his fist. "Of course it wasn't her. This is the Fox we're talking about, one of the finest thieves in the world. She spent at least a year planning, probably more, with over nine months working at the museum. She had a proper escape plan, too. She'd never be this sloppy, and we should have known it. Let's talk to the woman."

Mike followed him to the trooper's car. She flashed her creds. "Good job on the intercept. We're ready to speak with her now." The trooper nodded and stepped to the side. Mike leaned into the car.

"Step out here a moment, ma'am."

The woman got out of the backseat awkwardly, her hands cuffed behind her back. She had long, dark hair, and looked a bit like Victoria, especially dressed in the same clothes. Enough to fool them all.

She was shaking, crying, and hiccupping, all at the same time. One look at Mike and her sobs gained new volume, and words spilled out, but all Nicholas could make out was *paid me*.

Mike spoke calmly and slowly. "You're not under arrest, you'll be okay. Stop crying, we need your help. I'm Special Agent Caine, FBI. Tell me your name?"

The woman hiccupped again and took several deep breaths. "I'm Tanya. Tanya Hill."

Mike motioned for an officer to remove the cuffs. They watched Tanya Hill shake her hands, rub her wrists, hiccup a couple more times, then say, "I didn't do anything."

"What are you doing in this cab, coming to Tweed tonight?"

"I'm flying to Dallas. There was this call for actresses, and I answered. The lady hired me to put on these clothes, walk out of the Met. She told me to get a cab, ask to go to Tweed, and get on a plane to Dallas. She paid me fifteen hundred dollars, gave me an ID, an invitation to the gala, these really nice boots, everything."

"Is the ID in your purse?"

"Yes, ma'am, Agent ma'am."

A tactical team member handed Mike the purse. "It's clear."

Mike pulled out a black wallet from the green faux-crocodile clutch. Inside was an ID with the woman's face on it, with the name and home address of Victoria Browning. Mike handed it to Nicholas.

Tanya Hill stared between the two of them, and another sob escaped. "I didn't do anything wrong, I didn't, and fifteen hundred dollars is a lot of money—I mean, I paid my rent from this one job. I won't be able to keep the money, will I? Oh, man, I already gave it to my landlord. He'll kick me out if I try to get it back."

Nicholas said, "The money's yours if you tell us all about the woman who hired you."

Realizing the gulag wasn't in her future, the tears dried up and Tanya became positively chatty.

"Like I said, there was a casting call for a reality TV show on Backonstage.com. It looked totally legit, I swear. I answered it last week, sent my book over, and she called me in and hired me on the spot. Said I was perfect. There's no reality show, is there? She lied?"

"Yes, Miss Hill, she lied to you. Did she tell you why she wanted you to fly to Dallas?"

"No."

"What were you supposed to do when you got there?"

"Stay overnight at a hotel near the airport, then fly home whenever I felt like it tomorrow. It was a no-brainer job."

Mike looked at Nicholas, jerked her head toward the helicopter. They stepped away and she said in a low voice, "I'm thinking even if we take her back to the city, put her through another more thorough interrogation, she's not going to have anything that will help us."

"Agreed."

Her cell phone rang, and she sighed. "It's Zachery. I better tell him the bad news." As she spoke to Zachery, Nicholas watched her face change from defeated to triumphant.

She hung up the phone and high-fived him. "They have an active trace on the call Victoria made to you after you defused the bomb. It pinged off a cell tower in Manhattan. Now they know the signal, and they'll be able to trace it. And even better news. Louisa was treated and released, and Paulie's awake."

35

Mike whirled a finger above her head in a circle and called to the tac team, "Back in the chopper, back in the chopper. Charlie, fire her up. We need to get back into the city pronto."

She turned to the troopers. "Give Miss Hill a ride home, get her phone number and tell her we may want to speak to her again." Mike said, "I'm being a dreamer here, but tell her if she thinks of anything else about the woman who hired her to give me a call. Oh, yes, the cabbie helped us, so cut him loose and thank him." Mike pulled a fifty out of her wallet and gave it to the trooper. "He's a good guy. I hope it's enough."

When she took her seat next to Nicholas in the chopper, she said, "Zachery wants us to stop off and talk to Paulie, see if he can tell us anything about what happened before she knocked him out. Charlie, can you get us to Lenox Hill Hospital, ASAP?"

"Will do, Mike."

The chopper whirled into the air and, nose down, flew south toward the city.

"Zachery and Bo talked to Louisa, but she didn't have anything for them. They held a press conference—Bo said it's insanity, what with the evacuation, the bomb threat, and the Koh-i-Noor missing. That tidbit was announced by the director of the Met himself. It's now all over TV and the Internet, going viral as we speak. I hate this level of visibility. Right now the only thing we have to go on is the call she made to your cell phone."

Nicholas was tapping his fingers on his leg. "The last thing I'm going to do now is get excited about tracing the call she made to me in the exhibit room."

"She probably knows how long it takes to get a trace on a wireless signal, so why would she care? Little does she know I have super-agent Gray Wharton on our side, and he has a still-friends ex-girlfriend who's an NSA analyst. She'll rush it right through, and we'll be able to track the phone."

"Maybe it will work, maybe it won't, but she knows we'll trace the call. She wouldn't keep the bloody phone." His voice fell off, and he looked out the chopper window at the lights of New York coming into view.

"We'll see."

Ten minutes later, Charlie set down on the rooftop helipad of Lenox Hill Hospital. They were met by a nurse in blue scrubs who took them directly to the third floor.

They entered the single room to see Paulie flat on his back, arguing with a pixie-haired nurse.

When he saw them, he looked ready to sing hallelujah. "Mike, you're here at last! Rescue me. Tell her I'm fine. I've been hit on the head before; my brother used to thump me all the time when we were kids. I need to get out of here; we've got work to do. Zachery told me about Victoria. I want to help. There will be tons of evidence to gather."

The nurse didn't spare them a glance. "I've told you three times, Agent Jernigan, we have to wait for the doctor. And no matter what you say, he's already told me you can't be released until the morning. Trust me, you won't get out of here sooner. You have a pretty bad concussion from that whack on your head, and we're waiting for blood work to determine what chemical you were exposed to."

Paulie frowned at her. "Bunch of vampires. You must have taken ten quarts from me."

Mike stifled a laugh behind a cough.

The nurse patted Paulie's shoulder. "That's right, dear. We are vampires and we live to draw blood. So lie back and relax. I've given you a little something to help with the headache, and you're going to feel so good in a minute you'll think I'm a fairy princess, not a vampire."

She patted Paulie's shoulder again and said to Mike, "I have to go do rounds. Would you sit on him if he tries to get out of bed?"

"Absolutely. Difficult patients are my specialty."

Mike turned to Paulie, whose face was pale despite his bravado. "Hear her? I'll sit on you if you don't throttle down. You should see yourself with that big bandage on your head. You can't go out looking like that, children will run screaming. So stop squirming and get comfy."

"Eight stitches, Mike, that's all. Only a scratch. Wow, what did she put in my IV? I feel like I'm floating. Is everyone all right? I remember Louisa telling me it was a good thing she was a woman, her head is harder than mine."

Mike sat next to his bed. "Everyone's okay. We haven't much time, Paulie, before you go squirrelly, so tell us what happened."

"Victoria was talking about the curse, told me to be very careful because only women are supposed to handle the diamond. I'd finally released it from the setting and was turning to hand it to Louisa, and Victoria said, 'Sorry about this,' and sprayed something in my eyes. Before I could even start yelling for anyone, wham, I was down. I don't remember much after I hit the ground, outside of hearing the alarms. I'm sorry, Mike." His voice was getting thready, and she could tell he was trying hard to hang on. His head swung back against the pillow. "Ouch."

"Careful. Do you remember anything else?"

He shook his head.

"I'm mad, Paulie, really mad. If we don't find her and get back the Koh-i-Noor, the Brits will declare war and take the White House again. Don't fade out on me, think. Anything else?"

The drugs were working their magic. Paulie's lids were heavy. He blinked a few times and his eyes closed.

Mike caught Nicholas's eye and nodded toward the door.

Paulie's eyes flew open and he sat straight up. "I remember now. She was talking to herself."

He fell back, a hand to his head. "Ugh, that hurts. I was going in and out, but I know she said something like 'Noon at the ark.'"

Mike said, "The ark? Like, Noah's ark?"

"That's what it sounded like. It's all I remember, Mike. I'm sorry."

"Don't be sorry, it's wonderful information. We'll track it down. Agent Savich is recovering all the video she erased, so maybe we can get more context. You rest now, okay? I'll be back to get you in the morning."

Nicholas's dark eyes met hers as they rode the elevator down. "Noon. As in noon tomorrow? That would give us less than twelve hours to catch up to her. It's going to take longer than that to get to Mount Ararat."

She smiled. "I have faith in Savich. He's a magician, he'll figure it out." She got on her cell as they left the hospital and called Zachery. "Sir, we really need Savich to lift the audio from the feed during Browning's attack. Paulie heard Browning say something about *noon at the ark* after she hit him."

36

Mike and Nicholas went with lights and sirens across town to the home address on file for Victoria Browning. The light snow had stopped, and the city looked frosted, park benches and wrought-iron railings silvered in the moonlight.

The streets were slick and nearly empty, and Mike was doing her best not to crash the car as she hurried around the south end of Central Park, then shot down Broadway toward the theater district. Usually jammed with people at all hours, tonight most everyone in Midtown was tucked up in bed, and the trip was going quickly.

Nicholas said, "You're frowning. What's wrong?"

She shot him a look. "I was thinking about what my father would do in this situation. He's the chief of police of Omaha, Nebraska, that's a state in the Midwest—"

"Thank you, they did teach American geography at Eton. And what would your dad have to say?"

"He always told me to check out the stripes first, even if I was sure it was a zebra." She swung around a lone cab with one guy in the back who looked passed out.

"And what have you decided? Is the Fox really a zebra?"

"Not so far. She's anything but, given all the twists and turns she's tossed in our path. I'm hoping her apartment will tell us a lot about her." She stopped at a red light, watched a bundled-up bag lady push her grocery cart piled high with stuff across the street. "I hope she's got a warm place. The temperature's plummeting."

Unlike Nicholas, who felt like he was in a canyon, black monoliths on either side of them, the old woman looked like she knew exactly where she was going. He said, "It's eerie, seeing the city sleep like this, all hunkered down, looming. London rarely gets quiet, but then again, London isn't this overwhelming, so in-your-face."

She said, "It's after midnight and it's snowing. If you're sane, you're inside. I've always thought that in the deep of night, the city knows something we don't know, and always, bad things happen."

Her cell rang. "It's Ben." She put him on speaker so Nicholas could hear.

Ben said, as if in mid-thought, "We're FBI, the most suspicious people in the world, and the most cynical, so tell me, why did we take her at face value? Browning raised the alarm, claimed the stone was fake, and we all believed her. We didn't even check to make sure she was telling the truth. Makes us look like idiots."

Mike knew exactly how he felt. "Well, Bo did check. Victoria used a fake diamond tester, so even he was tricked. So why wouldn't we believe her? She reported a major robbery. She had the credentials, the trust of the museum staff. She engineered the whole thing to get Paulie and Louisa into the room to fingerprint the 'fake' diamond. It was a pretty ballsy plan, and it worked. Yeah, we're idiots."

"Sorry, I had to vent. What are you up to at this late hour?"

"Nicholas and I are on our way to tear apart Browning's apartment."

"Be careful, Mike. This woman is no dummy, she's got more end-arounds than Harbaugh's playbook. She's not predictable, so watch your back."

She hung up and looked over at Nicholas.

He said, "I wonder which Harbaugh he meant."

"You know American football?"

"I am half your species," he said. "Ah, this is the right address."

Victoria lived steps from Times Square, in a building Mike had to admit was gorgeous, inside and out. They'd called the leasing agent, a round and Rubenesque woman in her late forties who smelled strongly of red wine, and she met them in the lobby.

"I'm Special Agent Mike Caine, and this is Detective Chief Inspector Nicholas Drummond. Thanks for meeting us so late." She showed the woman her creds.

"I'm Gillian Docherty. What is all this about?"

Nicholas said, "We need access to an apartment, number 2324, and all the files you have attached to it. The occupant is Victoria Browning."

Docherty narrowed her eyes. "Um, I don't think I'm allowed to give out that information unless you have a warrant."

"We're very concerned about Ms. Browning's well-being. We wouldn't ask if it weren't a matter of life and death."

"You mean *Dr.* Browning. She insisted I remember to call her Doctor. I was the one who leased her the apartment. What's wrong? Is she ill? Is she in trouble?"

Nicholas leaned close to the leasing agent, pitched his voice low. "That's what we're trying to find out. This is a very sticky situation. Be a love and let us in her flat, would you?"

Docherty dimpled, and Mike would swear she batted her eyelashes. "Oh, I see, yes, of course," and Docherty went for the master keys.

Bond strikes again. She whispered, "I may need a tape recording of your voice to use when I run into stubborn witnesses. Well, female witnesses."

He ignored that.

"You lied to her."

"Yeah, but don't worry I'll run off the rails. I have all sorts of highly ethical boundaries. If she'd said no, I would have clubbed her on the head and stolen the keys."

Mike said, "Now, that would be a show worth watching."

"You lied to her, too."

"It was trained into me."

"You obviously were at the head of your class."

Three minutes later they were on the elevator to the

twenty-third floor. Browning's apartment was halfway down the hall.

When they were at the door, Nicholas whispered, "Careful. Like Ben reminded us, she isn't all that predictable, plus she's already set one bomb today."

37

Mike nodded, listened at the door, heard nothing. She drew her Glock, and Docherty gasped.

Nicholas said smoothly, "Perhaps you should wait downstairs, Ms. Docherty, for your safety. We may have some more agents arriving, and we'll need you to greet them and escort them upstairs. Would you mind handling it for us?"

"But shouldn't I, well, my goodness, what has she done? I mean, she's a doctor, right?"

"It's very important you bring them to us immediately." Nicholas took her firmly by the elbow and walked her back to the glass-paneled elevator, and took the leasing file from her as he hit the down button.

Mike had to admire Mr. Aren't I Great. He was beginning to live up to his reputation.

She inserted the door key to Browning's apartment and

slowly turned the knob. When Nicholas was back by her side, she gave a quiet three count and opened the door.

Empty. Strangely empty. There was furniture, but nothing personal. No books on the bookshelves, no afghans or magazines, nothing homey at all. Nothing of Victoria Browning.

He said, "No bomb, so that's something."

Mike waved her hand around. "It's like everything was staged for a showing. Like she'd already moved out."

"Or she never moved in." Nicholas walked to the big windows, undid the blinds. The view wasn't spectacular, there was a building blocking much of it, but a sliver looked north to Central Park. He could see the dusting of snow, the blinking of lights from the occasional car driving toward them down Broadway.

Mike was thumbing through the file. "According to the rental agency, she leased the flat in June of last year, moved in July first. She was paying five thousand two hundred dollars a month."

"What's that—three thousand three hundred pounds, give or take." He took another look around. "Seems underpriced."

"You're used to London prices. This is New York. For the size and location, it's about right." Mike shivered. The heat wasn't on in the apartment, and it didn't have double-paned windows. Cold night air seeped through, finding her neck under the collar of her leather jacket.

Nicholas said, "Isn't five thousand two hundred dollars a month a lot of money in rent on a museum docent's salary?"

"According to her personnel file, even once she was

bumped up to curator, her annual take-home was sixty-two thousand dollars. So her salary didn't even cover her rent, much less anything else."

"It's very possible the person who hired her is paying her way." He leaned against the window. "And paying her a bucketload, you can be sure of that."

"At least we know Anatoly isn't the buyer."

Mike joined him at the window, took a last glance at the city, cold and silent beneath her. She handed him a pair of nitrile gloves. "All right. Let's take it apart."

Mike started in the bedroom. She pulled out empty drawers and checked underneath. Nothing. No clothes in either the dresser or the closet. The bathroom cabinets and shower were empty, too. She tossed the rooms carefully and found exactly zip.

"Nicholas, are you finding anything?"

"No," he called from the second bedroom. "This place is clean as a whistle."

They met in the kitchen. Nicholas opened the refrigerator door. Cold inside, still running at maximum capacity, but empty, wiped clean.

"She knew she was taking off. Cleared everything out. The drawers are empty, bathroom's spotless. Heat's off. She thought of everything."

Nicholas stood quietly, thinking. *What would I do if I were Victoria Browning? If I needed to be completely undercover, off the grid?* "She never lived here."

"But this was the address on her application; the leasing agent remembered getting her the place. And it matches the fake driver's license she gave Tanya Hill."

"She rented it, sure. But she never moved in. No one can keep a place this clean, not if they're living here. It's more proof the Fox is no zebra. She arranged a very precise identity, a full complete background—the works. We can run DNA in here, but we won't find anything, at least that belongs to her. We know Victoria Browning is a false name. Why shouldn't everything attached to her identity be false as well?"

Mike thought about it. "Do you think there's a real Victoria Browning out there who's an archaeologist? Who has no idea someone stole her name?"

"I'll start running the name through all the databases while your team does a forensic sweep."

"Knock, knock! Yoo-hoo!" Gillian Docherty was back, with three FBI crime scene techs. "I found them for you, Inspector Drummond."

"Ah, Ms. Docherty. Brilliant. Thank you."

Mike took her techs aside. "Find me something. This woman has already put two of our people in the hospital. If there's DNA, fingerprints, anything, you pull it and call for me immediately."

"Roger that, Mike. If there's anything here, we'll get it."

"Thank you."

She stepped back and watched them get to work. Nicholas was asking more questions of Gillian Docherty, but it was like trying to get blood from a stone. She didn't know anything, was only playing along so she could flirt with the hot Brit.

Mike tuned everyone out, stood in the living room, looking out over the city, and ran through it again.

No zebra, Dad. What's more, I'm missing something, something really big. If I were a master thief, how would I pull all this off?

A small tingle started in her back, at the base of her spine.

A big job like this, I'd plan it down to the very last detail, then I'd befriend someone who would help me. Someone on the inside I could use, then discard when the time was right.

Someone like Inspector Elaine York.

Surely sometimes zebras could be as devious as lions, too.

38

The Metropolitan Museum of Art
Friday, 1:00 a.m.

Savich had called for some late-night pizzas to be brought in, a veggie delight for him and any other vegetarians, and plenty of pepperonis and sausages for the carnivores. Sherlock was chowing on a piece of pepperoni, happy as a clam. He joined her at a small computer desk.

"Careful. You don't want to spill any of that on your gorgeous dress."

"My gorgeous dress already smells like tear gas, and I doubt that'll come out. And, to be honest here, I'm too hungry to care."

Springsteen's "Born in the USA" wailed from his pocket. "Good timing. There's Nicholas now." He answered the call, put it on speaker. "Before you say anything, Nicholas, a sweep of the Met security offices upstairs showed several cleverly placed bugs. Browning was able to monitor everything we did tonight. We've dismantled them all, but you might think to tell the techs to check her place for bugs as well. She is a very thorough woman."

Mike said, "So she could be listening now? Well, if you are, Victoria, we're coming for you. Savich, give us a minute, we'll step outside the apartment."

There was a brief delay, then Mike came back on the line. "We're clear."

"Did you find anything at her apartment?"

Nicholas said, "The apartment Browning leased was never lived in. Security cameras from the building don't show her entering or leaving anytime in the past month, and it's all they have; their cameras recycle the tapes on the thirtieth of each month. Right now, this woman is a ghost."

"That explains why we're hitting dead ends ourselves," Savich said. "There's nothing on the transportation grid—she didn't get on a plane or train or bus, or we would have found her by now. She may be on the road, driving north to the border, but the facial-recognition system needs more time to process all the faces at the northbound tollbooths. We've alerted Canadian customs to the BOLO, sent it to the highway patrols as well. We're going to need a wider net."

Nicholas said, "She may be hunkered down somewhere in the city, letting her buyer come to her. We do believe she's stolen the diamond for someone, not for herself. If we're right, she stands to gain a great deal of money."

Savich said, "It's nearly two in the morning. I think it would be best to shut down for the night, let everyone get some rest, and start fresh in the morning. We're having a meeting at 26 Federal Plaza at eight a.m."

Mike said, "Yeah, you're right, but I hate letting her get more hours ahead on us."

Zachery leaned over from the workstation. "Time for a break, Mike. Sleep, get some food in you, and I'll see you in a few hours. We need to give the databases time to catch up to her. We'll find her, I know we will. Okay?"

"Yes, sir."

They clicked off, and Savich stowed his phone, yawned. Sometimes the only answer was getting a fresh start.

39

Over the Atlantic Ocean

Kitsune listened to Mike and Nicholas discuss her whereabouts with Agent Savich. She was sorry not to have met him; he sounded interesting.

Her staged apartment was bugged, he'd been right about that, with mikes in all the rooms, like she'd done at the Met. But he didn't realize how thorough she was—she'd also bugged the hallway outside her apartment, all the way down to the elevator. It was a pity she couldn't have miked 26 Federal Plaza, then she could have heard everything the Feds were planning.

She laughed. Mike Caine thought she had only a few hours' head start? She had two years on them. The flat was a total dead end, $5,200 a month well spent. No DNA, folks, except for that fat leasing agent's, so you might as well hang it up and go get some sleep.

If they found her real place, she'd know immediately;

the door was rigged to blow, and an alarm would be sent to her phone.

But she doubted they would. It was many blocks away, in Hell's Kitchen. She'd worn wigs and the clothes of a student down on her luck, plus a baseball cap, every time she went in or out. The rent was paid for another year, and she could disarm the bomb remotely if needed. Kitsune knew exactly how to cover her tracks. She'd been doing it for so many years it was second nature.

When their call ended, she sat back in the buttery leather and ran through the options. They didn't have anything yet, not that she'd expected them to. She knew it was only a matter of time before they figured out the Teterboro Airport connection, but if her luck continued to hold, she'd be on the ground before they did.

But what about Drummond? She wished he'd stayed in London, where he belonged.

No, he wouldn't catch her. All would be well. She would meet with Lanighan, take care of business, and then she'd be gone. Done. Retired. On a small Pacific island, where she'd fit in seamlessly, and no one would think to look for her. Or maybe she could go back to London, speak to Grant—no, he was gone, she had to let him go.

The captain's voice came over the speaker. "Madam, we're in French airspace. Where to now?"

She pressed the button, gave him coordinates. The airstrip was exceedingly private, one she'd used before. There would be no record of the plane even touching down.

She finished the last sip of her Dom Pérignon. An hour to landing. One hour on the road to the meeting site. Three hours to reconnoiter the place, and make sure Lanighan was following protocol, as she always did.

Another twenty-five million in her bank account, which she'd immediately break into packets and transfer into multiple accounts all over the world. Untraceable, even to Lanighan's people, should they try to come back and steal what was rightfully hers.

Lanighan's father had tried to cheat her once, on a stellar Manet she'd lifted from Amsterdam. The payment had been recalled, but Kitsune was faster than the Lion. She'd managed to have the money transferred before he followed through. She'd called him, told him he was a fool. And he'd apologized. He'd come to respect her cunning, all the measures she took to protect herself, and never tried to double-cross her again. Their relationship was fruitful—after the Manet debacle, he'd become her most faithful client, and a lot more. Over the years, a full fifty percent of his collection was gathered by her hands.

She looked at the ground lights below the jet, skimming past too quickly to register. No landmarks. No real certainty that the pilot was listening to her instructions. So this was paranoia. Well, nothing wrong with that. It kept her knife-sharp, always on edge.

She'd earned her nickname the Fox. She was clever and fast, prepared for anything.

Anything.

She glanced at her watch and picked up the phone.

Mulvaney. She smiled as she punched in his number.

For more than twenty years, they'd been together. He was her teacher, her confidant, her father, if it came right down to it, always there for her in good times and not-so-good times, her rock, and she trusted him implicitly. He advised her on which jobs to take, discussed strategy with her. He'd even set up the way she disbursed her money, and he was always willing to jump in and help if needed, and he had a good half-dozen times over the years. She would give her life for him, it was that simple. She'd sometimes thought he tethered her to this earth until she'd met Grant—*Really, Kitsune, you must stop thinking of him.*

The phone continued to ring. At this hour of the morning, Mulvaney should be lounging on the fourth deck of his villa, a warm breeze rustling through the lemon grove below the house, his nose in a book, the first of dozens of espressos at his elbow.

Why didn't he answer? He always took her calls, always.

She punched off her cell. She would try again later, but something nagged at her. She didn't like this, not one bit. Paranoia again. But maybe he was simply busy with something.

She realized she was exhausted. She had an hour until landing and the next part of her plan went into action.

Kitsune closed her eyes and slept.

40

New York, New York
Victoria Browning's apartment
Friday, 2:00 a.m.

Nicholas had to agree with Zachery and Savich: they were spinning their wheels. Even though he was itching to get his fingers on a keyboard and start his own search for Browning, he'd been up for thirty-six hours and needed sleep.

"Mike, let's close it down for the night."

She chewed her lip. "Anything?" she asked the tech she called Mouse.

He shook his head. "A half-dozen bugs, which we dismantled. Other than that, nothing. I'm betting the only thing we're going to find here is yours and Nicholas's DNA."

The woman didn't miss a trick. Mike sighed. "Okay, go on home."

When they were in the elevator on their way down,

Nicholas said, "You think she's got cameras on this building?"

"I wouldn't put it past her."

Both Mike and Nicholas were freezing when they got into her car. She turned the heat on high, rubbed her hands in front of the vent for a minute, then turned to Nicholas. "Where are you staying?"

"On Vanderbilt, between Forty-fourth and Forty-fifth."

"The Yale Club? Swanky."

"You know it?"

Mike laughed. "Only from the outside. Part of being a New York field agent is knowing every nook and cranny of this city. I'll go up against an old-time New York cabbie any day of the week. The Yale Club is a few blocks southeast." She looked right and left and pulled out onto Seventh. "I'm starting to think of my bed with lust in my heart. Past time to catch a few hours."

"Elaine had more trouble when she first moved here, distinguishing the long blocks from the short. She took to running an extra hour each night to learn her way around. She once called and said, 'Nicholas, you wouldn't believe how lost I was tonight.'"

He got quiet.

Her stomach growled, and Nicholas looked over at her. "Hungry, are we?"

"Starved. I can't remember when I ate last; we've been going hard since I woke up. I'm exhausted, but I need something." She smiled at him. "I reheat a mean slice of pizza."

"Pizza sounds good."

She heard something in his voice, something that spoke to her. She understood pain. She understood grief. She understood not wanting to be alone. Too well. And she remembered Jon, and let the pain settle in for a moment. Had he really been gone five years?

"We're only ten minutes from my place. Tell you what, come home with me, it'll be easiest. I live down in the Village, and I've got a lovely long sectional sofa." She continued without pause. "What'd you do in Afghanistan?"

"Is the sofa long enough for me? It's classified."

It could be, but she doubted it; at least what had happened to him wasn't classified. Whatever it was, she figured it must be bad.

She said, "It's over seven feet long, and I have lots of comfy blankets. You left the Foreign Office after Afghanistan, left the spy world altogether, and moved to Scotland Yard. Come on, Nicholas, what happened?"

"I doubt your pajamas will fit me. Let me just say I wanted to be out on the street again, back home, in London, get my hands dirty. Work homicide. Help the helpless."

"You're James Bond. You don't wear pajamas." She drove through a yellow light as it turned red. "At this hour a person's biorhythms are supposed to be low, and they'll spill pretty much everything about themselves."

"I was trained not to," he said. "I won't go to bed commando, as you Americans say, to save you any embarrassment. Let's check out your biorhythms. What's the name of your last boyfriend?"

She spurted out a laugh. "Classified. Tell me about your ex-wife. She's the daughter of an earl?"

Safe subject, she thought, because he straightened and turned toward her. "An earl who's also a very rich man and gives Pamela anything she wants, like backing her online magazine and footing all the bills here in Manhattan."

"How did you two meet?"

"I met her in London, at some party, I forget. Anyway, two years later, I was finishing an assignment in Zurich. She was skiing at Engelberg. We ran into each other at a bar, and it was good to see someone I knew. She shed her friends. It all happened fast, too fast." He slouched down in the seat and closed his eyes.

"Sorry, none of my business."

He didn't open his eyes. "Not a state secret. Pamela loved the thought of my being a spy. It was all fictionalized cloak-and-dagger to her, dangerous and exciting, and sexy, but the reality stopped being fun after about six months. I was gone a great deal of the time, places she couldn't travel with me, and when I was in London, I was usually too wiped to go to parties and bars and wild weekend bashes. And then there was Afghanistan." He didn't shrug, but he could have. "I guess I changed. Settling in London as a copper's wife was the last thing on her mind. She was all sharp edges and snark toward me tonight. She didn't used to act that way."

"She's certainly something."

"She's also the past. Right now, all I want is some pizza, and sleep, and a new perspective."

Mike said, "We made great progress today, you know."

He gave a humorless laugh. "If you think being played for fools is progress, then certainly. Between Anatoly and Browning, our strings have been pulled quite nicely."

41

Hudson Street and West Eleventh Street
Mike Caine's apartment
Friday, 2:30 a.m.

Mike's building was a five-story red brick circa 1970 smack dab in the middle of the West Village. Unlike the rest of Manhattan, there were always lights and action in the Village. Nicholas liked the look of the place. "Nice. Very New York."

Mike waited for a taxi to pass, then turned onto the garage ramp. "They remodeled and converted to condos in the nineties. When I was looking for a place, this one had two major plusses—its own three-level parking beneath the building, and a doorman. Well, three if you count the local restaurants. See the White Horse Tavern across the street? Excellent food, and talk about history."

She pulled her card out of her wallet, slid it into the garage reader, and the iron gates opened inward. She drove down one level and pulled into her assigned spot. "Here we are."

Nicholas stepped out of the car, yawned, then stopped cold. The hair went up on the back of his neck. The garage was very dark, and very quiet, a graveyard of cars, all hunkered down, silent, so much silence. It was the middle of the night, so of course it was filled with shadows—no, something was wrong. He'd learned the hard way never to ignore the occasional punches of intuition, the premonitions that something bad was out there, ready to come at him. He remained perfectly still and listened. He heard Mike talking, but he didn't pay any attention; he was concentrating on any sound that wasn't right.

Nothing.

Mike climbed out of the driver's side, spotted him standing still as a stone beside his door. "What's wrong?" Her hand was already on her Glock.

But he didn't move. There, he heard something. Breathing, carefully modulated breaths.

He motioned her to the front of the car, then stopped again, listened. There, he heard it again, this time not only breathing, harsh and low, but the sound of footsteps sliding over concrete.

A man launched himself from the darkness, swinging a tire iron toward Nicholas's head. He jumped back, but not fast enough. The tire iron caught him on the shoulder, and the force of the blow sent him stumbling to the concrete. Better his shoulder than his head, was all he could think. His shoulder was on fire, but it didn't matter. He lurched to his feet to see another shadow, also male, tall, fit, lean back on the heel of his left foot and kick out with his right, smooth and high and beautifully timed.

Before he could warn her, the man's foot hit Mike square in the head. She went down with a small cry and didn't move.

Adrenaline pulsed through him as the first man came at him again, swinging the tire iron. Nicholas ducked, blocked the tire iron with his forearm, and sent his fist with all his strength into the man's throat.

He dropped the tire iron, grabbed his neck, and went down to his knees, wheezing, trying to breathe. Nicholas had only an instant before the second man, the one he'd mentally dubbed "the kicker," was on him, whipping around to take him down with a kick to the head, as he had Mike.

Nicholas didn't hesitate. He rammed his head into the man's face, sending him back, his arms windmilling to keep his balance.

A gun fired, barely missing his head. Great, this was all they needed. No more silent attack, now it was all-out war.

Nicholas pulled Mike behind her Crown Vic, leaned over her, and said in her face, "Wake up, come on, wake up!" He shook her shoulder as three more shots rang out.

"Stop it, I'm together." Mike pulled herself onto her hands and knees as more shots rang out. She pulled out her phone, called for backup. Her Glock was in her right hand, and her left reached for the gun at her ankle. She slapped her backup Glock 27 subcompact into Nicholas's hand.

They fired, crouched side by side, the Crown Vic their only shield.

Their attackers shot off thirty-two rounds, fast and hard. An MP5, Mike knew. Bullets spiderwebbed the

Crown Vic's windshield, smashed the windows, struck the columns, sending jagged concrete shards in all directions. Nicholas saw a streak of blood snaking down Mike's neck.

A moment of stark silence, then the slap of another clip jacking into place. The first man, the idiot, started firing again, but many of his shots went wild, ricocheting off other cars, smashing glass, wreaking havoc. In the confined space, the noise was deafening.

A bullet narrowly missed Nicholas's head, shattered into the concrete pillar behind him.

Too close. Who the hell were these guys? "Where are the cops?"

"Any second now, they're out of the Seventh and usually really fast." Nicholas remembered Esposito and his Nikes. He fell forward onto his belly and shot under a parked car halfway down a row at the idiot's legs. He yelped, jumped up, and cursed. Then he moved fast, crouching behind the rear tire of an SUV.

He didn't know where the kicker was, but he was clearly the one in charge of this attack. Had he left the idiot behind? Or was he circling around?

More bullets struck the Crown Vic, this time shattering the windshield. Then, suddenly, the firing stopped.

Nicholas touched his hand to Mike's arm. She stopped shooting.

Dead silence. He'd hit the idiot in the foot, so he couldn't be lying dead behind that SUV.

Mike shouted, "We're federal agents. Hear those sirens? You're surrounded. Put down your weapons now!"

Silence. Was that talking he heard? Low, agitated? It was hard to hear anything over their own heavy breathing. He knew to his gut both men were still hiding in the dark, probably trying to decide what to do.

A half-dozen bullets pinged off Mike's car from the left, opposite from where Nicholas believed the kicker was crouching.

Too close to Mike's head, too close.

Bullets began raining on their position again from two directions. The kicker had joined the fray with another MP5.

Nicholas pressed his mouth against Mike's cheek, tasted her blood, and whispered, "The idiot is on the up ramp. I think the guy who kicked you is in charge here. He's behind the dark SUV at one o'clock. I'm going for the idiot, since he's in the open. Cover me," and he took off toward the ramp. Mike laid down fire to cover him, going back and forth between the ramp and the kicker.

Nicholas made it to the opposite side of the garage seconds before the darkness lit up with the flash of bullets. He pressed hard against a column, took two deep breaths, saw the idiot, and squeezed the trigger twice, his last two bullets. He missed, and the idiot ducked away into the darkness.

A heartbeat later, Nicholas was hit hard from behind, and went down face-first, the wind knocked out of him. He managed to fling himself over onto his back, struggling to catch his breath, when the idiot leapt on top of him, straddled him, and punched Nicholas in the mouth. He felt his teeth tear into his lip and tasted blood.

Nicholas jerked up and headbutted him, a sickening sound of flesh against flesh, then hit him hard in the jaw with the small Glock. A shot rang out. The idiot fell sideways, his head hitting the concrete floor with a thick, meaty sound. The man's legs twitched, and Nicholas shoved them off and he rolled spread-eagled onto his back, the scent of his blood hot and thick in the air.

Mike had shot the idiot.

Nicholas came up on his knees, dragged the idiot behind the cover of a concrete pillar, and tore off the black mask. He was young, thirties, dark hair. Indistinguishable, eyes blank, blood spreading out from his back to halo around his body. He was very dead.

Mike shouted, "Nicholas, the kicker, he's running up the ramp."

More sirens now, drawing closer.

Nicholas took off, Mike right behind him. He slowed when he reached the final curve that turned into the street, gestured for her to hold up. He took three more steps, saw the garage barrier. It was closed tight, but the door to the street beside it was wide open.

He heard footsteps and people shouting. He charged through the open door to see light bars flashing, an echo of the cacophony of noises in his ears. An NYPD cruiser skidded to a stop at the curb, two officers bolted from the car, guns drawn. "Stop! NYPD!"

Mike screamed, "Federal agent! Federal agent, don't shoot!" She held her Glock in one hand and her creds high in the other.

Nicholas saw a flash of black to his right. He ignored

the shouts from the cops and edged carefully toward the alley. Mike ran into the alley behind him, shouting over her shoulder, "We need backup!"

The kicker was trapped at the back of the alley, a high fence behind him. He glanced over his shoulder and Nicholas saw a rim of jaw-length white hair under his mask. Of all things, the kicker smiled, then leapt onto the chain link and began climbing, fast and fluid as a monkey. Nicholas's Glock was empty. He knew he couldn't climb the fence, his shoulder was hurting so badly he could barely raise his arm. He could only watch the man pull himself up and over the fence, down the other side, and listen to his light footfalls disappear into the black night.

Mike fired until her gun was dry, but the kicker was gone.

She looked at him, then down at herself. She began to laugh. She choked out, "I don't believe this, I really don't."

"Is your head all right? Believe what?"

"Open your coat and look at yourself. You're still wearing your tux, what there is left of it."

He said, "I doubt the dry cleaner is going to be able to fix this."

42

Three more NYPD cruisers crowded the street, pulling over curbs, into driveways, one even mowing down two garbage cans.

It was mayhem until everyone was clear they were dealing with federal agents. A sergeant arrived and finally sent out men to find the kicker.

Mike sighed. "He's long gone. They'll never find him now, not in a million years. He's fast, Nicholas, and that kick to my head, I'm still woozy. What's this?" She slumped against the wall of the building, and eyed the blood she'd wiped off her face.

Nicholas took a Kleenex from one of the officers and wiped off the blood. "A flying bit of concrete." He felt her head. "And a good-sized lump. You've got a hard head, thank the good Lord."

"Give me the Kleenex, you've got a cut lip."

She dabbed at his mouth. "What's with your shoulder?"

"Tire iron," Nicholas said shortly, and moved it a bit. Better. They watched the NYPD officers hurrying off in all directions.

"How did you know?"

He didn't pretend to misunderstand. She saw he was uncomfortable and said only, "Your gut, right?"

"Maybe. Something felt off when I got out of the car."

She placed her hand flat against his belly. "I'm not feeling you up. I'm thanking your gut."

He laughed, couldn't help it. A Latina officer, her hair in a long braid, gave Mike the idiot's wallet. His driver's license was from Sacramento, California; his name listed as Dennis Palmer.

"It's a fake," Mike said. "See, it's missing the three-color holograph. More false identities, Nicholas. He must be connected to Browning. She must have sent the men after us."

He took the license and turned it over in his hands. "Or Anatoly did. The kicker had white hair hanging down from beneath his mask. I couldn't believe it. He moved like a much younger man. He was fast and well trained, but they came prepared with their MP5s.

"I'm sure the kicker was the one in charge, not the dead guy. If the idiot had been as talented as he is, I'm afraid guns wouldn't have been necessary." He looked toward the dead man now surrounded by techs, a detective from the 7th Precinct, and saw the ME striding up, obviously pulled from sleep, his gray hair a rooster tail on top of his head.

Mike said, "A shootout in the garage in the middle of the West Village. The neighbors must be loving this." She walked away to examine the open door beside the garage barrier. She called out, "Well, how they got in is easily answered. They jimmied the lock. Maybe we can see them on the security video tape."

It was 3:30 a.m. before they were cleared for the night. Nicholas fetched his leather carry-on from the backseat of the wrecked Crown Vic. Mike said at his elbow, "I really liked this car. I put in a call to maintenance, got the night guy. He swore when I come down tomorrow morning, there'll be a new ride here in my spot. Well, not new, you know what I mean."

"So long as it runs and has glass in all the windows, that's fine."

As they took the elevator to the lobby, Nicholas said, "Even though your doorman didn't see anyone out of place, the crime scene techs checked through your flat; they say nothing was disturbed. You need to check, too."

Mike nodded to the doorman, who looked as though he was bursting with excitement and questions, but they didn't slow.

The third-floor halls were as quiet as the garage had been, everyone back in bed after the excitement. Consummate New Yorkers in her building, even the yelling, the bullets flying, the sirens out in front of the building, didn't bother them for long.

Mike's neighbor Frank Pressfield opened his door. "Are you okay? Snot-nosed kid controlling the crime scene wouldn't let me talk to you."

"We're fine. No respect these days, Frank, and here you were, ready and able to tell them what to do. Two guys ambushed us in the garage. One's dead, the other got away." She gestured to Nicholas. "Nicholas Drummond, New Scotland Yard, meet Frank Pressfield, formerly of the Sixty-eighth."

The two men shook hands, and Frank said, "You've had quite the reception, haven't you?"

"Yes, I have." And he thought of Elaine.

Anger, grief, questions, all three welled up in him, and a bone-deep tiredness he knew hours of sleep wouldn't fix. Elaine was gone. She'd died a stranger in a strange land, and it made him sick to think of it. And now whoever had killed her was clearly after him and Mike. But why? They were only two individuals; there were hundreds more FBI agents to take their places.

Rage began to build, at Victoria Browning and Andrei Anatoly, at the man with his white hair, but he tamped it down into his belly, knowing he'd need it later.

"We're going to crash," he heard Mike saying to Frank. "We've been at it all day. Thanks for checking on me."

Nicholas nodded to him and followed Mike into her flat across the hall. She switched on the lights and shrugged out of her coat, and he saw how beat up she was. Her leather jacket was ripped, her jeans covered with grease stains. As for him, the bespoke tux was ready for the trash bin.

In the long scheme of things, who cared?

Nicholas looked around him, from the small entryway

into the living room to his right. It wasn't a large room, but it held charm and warmth. It was cozy. He really liked the stuffed floor-to-ceiling bookshelves, the large sectional sofa that would be his bed, and the single big window that looked out over the street. There were several nicely framed Impressionist prints on the one open wall, and colorful rugs strewn over the oak floor. He walked after her to check out the kitchen, hidden to the left of the entrance, then the bedroom and bath, both down a short hall to the right. Nothing seemed out of place—by either Mike's hand or one of their assailants'.

She said, "All's as it should be. The two guys didn't make it up here. I doubt they even wanted to."

"Probably not. I like your apartment."

Mike smiled. "It's home."

"But remember, the Fox is the master of the bug. We should sweep. Too bad we don't—" He shrugged.

"Hold that thought," she said, and went into the kitchen. He heard her open a drawer. A moment later, she handed him three items: a wand, a control box, and a set of headphones. "Go for it."

"What are you doing with a SuperScout NLJD?"

"Believe it or not, your uncle gave me this fancy non-linear junction detector for Christmas last year."

She watched him go from phone to lamps to vents. Just in case, Mike flipped on her stereo as she walked past, low, and Diana Krall's mellow voice filled the room.

Nicholas appeared in the kitchen doorway. "We're clear. No bugs." He handed her back the equipment. "I wish my uncle had given me something like that for Christmas, but my aunt Emily knitted me a sweater instead. It was purple."

She leaned back against the counter. "I'm glad you came home with me. I'm glad you realized someone was waiting for us in the garage. I'd be dead if not for your gut, so thanks again, Nicholas." She pulled two boxes from the fridge and faced Nicholas. "To be honest, at this moment in time I really don't care about anything other than food—here's pepperoni with mushroom, or plain cheese."

He pointed toward the pepperoni. "May I help?"

"Yes, talk to me. Keep me awake." She slid the pizza into a convection oven, set the timer.

He was rubbing his shoulder. At her raised eyebrow, he said, "For a while there I thought something was broken."

She took a tube of muscle relaxant out of her junk drawer. "Sit down. This and some ice, it should help."

Without a word, he pulled off his torn, bloodstained tux coat and shirt, stripping to the waist.

He was ripped, of course. She admired the work of art, then started rubbing in the muscle cream, slowly, in circles, then pressing deeper. He groaned.

She realized even though she was exhausted—half dead, really—she still needed to distract herself. "Do you know when your uncle Bo told me about his sister, your mom, the actress? I called my dad and I thought he'd explode on the phone. He was in love with your mother when she starred in that TV comedy *A Fish out of Water*.

He watches the reruns whenever he can find them. I'll
have to call him, tell him his goddess's son is in our midst."

"Mom will get a kick out of that. But as she's always
saying, she's more than a pretty face." He groaned again,
rested his head on his hands on the kitchen table while
she smoothed and rubbed and dug in.

"Well, sure, but what do you mean?"

He said, voice muffled, "I get my detective genes from
her. She's solved I don't know how many mysteries in our
village, a regular Jane Marple. When I was a kid, she'd
take me with her, explain all the facts to me, and tell me
it was up to the two of us to deduce what happened."

"Like what? Who stole laundry drying on a clothes-
line?"

"Yeah, and who took three guineas out of the collection plate and who got Millie Hightower pregnant. There
was even a murder that confounded the constabulary. She
solved it." He straightened, moved his shoulders around.
"That's much better. Thank you." He sounded surprised.
"Mind if I use your loo?"

"Of course not."

He picked up his ruined clothes, his bottomless leather
bag, and left her. When he returned, he was wearing a
black T-shirt over his black trousers, back to business as
usual.

He said, "If Anatoly didn't hire the Fox to steal the
Koh-i-Noor, and I don't think he did, that leaves about
half a dozen very wealthy gem collectors in Europe.
Which means—"

Mike's cell phone buzzed. She frowned, looked down,

then sighed deeply. "Sorry, Nicholas. I have to take this. Hello, Timmy. It's very late, what's wrong?"

He watched her face, the flickers of annoyance and bemusement. *Timmy?*

She nodded to him and left him in the kitchen. She was back in under three minutes to see him standing there, arms crossed over his chest, cuts and bruises on his face, a drop of blood dried on his mouth, but he was looking easier, more relaxed. "Who's Timmy?"

She gave him a long look. "Ah, the pizza's done."

"Want to tell me about Timmy?"

She gave him another long look. "Timmy's sort of like my Afghanistan. Come on, Nicholas, time to chow down. We're only going to get maybe three hours of sleep, max, and I want every minute."

43

Naples, Italy
Twenty-two years ago

The day was fine, blue skies and bright yellow sun, the weather tourists to the Amalfi Coast prayed for. She'd hopped the cruise ship in Valencia, Spain, posing as a Taiwanese banker's daughter, taken up quarters in a small empty cabin, and sailed across the Mediterranean without a care in the world. Cruise ships were full of wealthy women and their jewels, and she was getting good practice befriending them, then lifting their valuables. Coming into dock in Naples, the crew knew there was a thief on board, but no one looked twice at the beautiful teenager.

And then she made a mistake and nearly landed herself in a Naples jail cell, known locally as the ninth circle of hell.

But she was young then, and foolhardy. She thought herself infallible, as did all kids her age.

If not for Mulvaney, she might have gone straight to the ninth circle and died there.

She'd roamed the piazzas with the others, dodging in and out of unventilated tourist traps, keeping an eye out for possibilities. The stores in this part of Naples were full of kitschy treasures, designed to suck in tourists and over-charge them for souvenirs made in China.

She spied one decent piece, a square sapphire ring surrounded by brilliants, and she made up her mind on the spot it would be hers. Once everyone had left for lunch and the proprietor had gone to his daily siesta, she went back, easily picked the lock, and waltzed inside.

Unfortunately, the store owner came back to fetch a hat, for the day was warm, and caught her in the act. Despite the fact his stock was mostly fakes and junk, he wasn't going to be ripped off, especially by a teenager who didn't even have the common sense to break in after dark. After screaming at her in unintelligible Neapolitan Italian, the local security showed up, an ape of a man, possibly the man's brother or cousin, but instead of taking her to jail, he dragged her around the back of the jewelry store, the owner following closely, cursing at her.

She saw the building's sidewalk abruptly stopped and the chalky cliffs plunged down into the Bay of Naples. Two more men were waiting there, unsavory men. She began to doubt the ape was a police officer. He held her arm in an iron grip while they all argued among them-selves. She finally caught a few words. They were arguing about whether to toss her over the cliff or have some fun first. The owner wanted to strip her down, see if she had any cash hidden in her underwear.

She was debating the wisdom of trying to kick one where it counted and dive off the cliff herself when she heard a man's voice.

"Kitsune? Kitsune? Where are you? The boat is leaving. Come, my dear, where are you? We really must go."

She saw a tall, beautifully dressed stranger wearing a panama hat come around the building and stare at the four men surrounding her. He paused, then said, "What's this, then, lads?" His Italian was impeccable, and he spoke in the Neapolitan dialect. But he wasn't Italian, she thought, he was too fair, too tall, despite his jacket draped casually over his shoulder, hooked on a finger, like all the European men's. Maybe he was American. Or British. His pale skin was slightly sunburned, and despite the shock of too-long white hair covered by a straw fedora, she made him in his early forties. Old enough to be a father, but this man didn't look like anyone's beloved daddy.

The four men stood stock-still, wondering what to do.

The man turned to her with an avuncular smile and said in charming English, "Kitsune, what have you done, my dear? Didn't I tell you to join us for lunch at Palazzo Petrucci? You shouldn't be out wandering the piazzas by yourself."

She shook her head, unsure of his game, cursing herself for her stupidity. To get caught over an insignificant trifle, she was disgusted with herself. She'd been thinking about running, she was fast, really fast, but the apes had formed a half circle in front of her. Her back was to the sea, so if she jumped, she'd be swimming, not running, if she survived at all.

The stranger began speaking again, directly to the foursome. Bless the gods, within moments, they were all laughing like old friends. She saw money pass among the men, a larger amount to the owner.

The stranger turned to her. "Come with me, you naughty girl." He took her arm and led her away. What should she do? Fight? Run? Come along quietly?

No, better to wait. One man, this was much better odds. When they were a block away, she began to struggle, and he stopped abruptly. He turned to her, his smile gone. "Listen to me, you silly girl. You owe me your life. You must trust me."

"I owe you nothing. I would have jumped and swum back to the ship. No problem."

He'd stared at her, his thumb cutting into the soft flesh under her biceps. And he laughed. "Sorry, my dear, but you would have landed in a heap of rocks." He snapped his fingers. "Then there'd be no more Kitsune."

"Maybe so, but I won't go with you. You'll rape me like those men wanted to."

He looked sad for a moment, then shrugged and knocked her on the head with his fist. She was out cold, then she was floating, rocking. She slowly awoke. She was on a small sailboat, baking in the afternoon sun.

Now she knew what he was. He was a slaver, and he was going to sell her to some sheik. She rolled to her feet and dove off the side of the boat into the Bay of Naples.

The man was above-decks, drinking an espresso and reading. He heard her go in, dashed to the side of the boat, and called after her, "It's more than a mile back to shore. I'm not going to hurt you. Swim back. I have a business proposition for you. See the white villa up there? It's my home. We'll go up and eat. If you don't like my idea, you may leave. I want nothing from you but an hour of your time. You have my word."

There was humor in his voice, and the fact was, she wasn't the best swimmer. She looked up at the house he'd pointed to—a huge sprawling monolith, all white stucco, four stories, set into the cliff. She assumed this was Capri, seventeen nautical miles west of Naples.

She swam back and climbed the ladder. She sat her dripping self on the deck and stared at him.

He threw her a towel.

She said, "No sex."

He touched his chest as if wounded. "Certainly not. I am an honorable man. I could be your father."

Father? Yeah, right. "Then what do you want?"

He smiled. "Lunch. Are you hungry?"

She nodded. She was still young enough to be bribed with the offer of food, particularly after her very busy morning.

"Good. My name is Mulvaney."

He closed the book, and she saw the title. She didn't realize the significance until much, much later. He was reading *Invisible Man*.

44

It was an unlikely friendship, but every mentor needed a protégée, every master needed an apprentice, every Svengali needed an acolyte, so Mulvaney told her.

She stayed the hour on his veranda, listening to him talk while they ate olives and bread and cheese and drank wine. He gave her a glass of limoncello when they were finished, and by then she was hooked, and maybe a little drunk.

Mulvaney was rich, and bored. He was also best known for his alliance with some French nationals involved in a failed attempt to assassinate François Mitterrand, and so was in a kind of pseudo-retirement on Capri until the hubbub died down. Being known, being recognized, was anathema to his purposes. This was his home base, the place he brought no one. No one but Kitsune.

He told her he needed a partner, and a female of her tender years, with a lovely face and figure, would be perfect for what he had in mind—namely, to distract the guards of a Russian industrialist while he went into the man's crude computer and moved his files onto a computer disk, then made his escape.

Was she interested? He'd asked her in fluent Russian. She said yes, in fluent Russian. When his eyes flew open in shock, she casually told him languages came easily to her. He clapped his hands together and laughed.

"I had a feeling about you. Standing there, spitting like an angry cat, caught in the act, the ring in your hand—you did manage to keep it, didn't you?"

She fished the ring from her pocket and set it on the table.

He nodded, and she caught the tone of respect when he said, "Very good, Kitsune. You kept your priorities straight." The smile on his face made her feel warm and happy. It had been a very long time since anyone approved of anything about her. Her parents had been shocked when she'd stolen a watch at the tender age of nine. Ah, well, they were gone, had been for three years now. And she'd been off on her adventures, she liked to call them.

At the end of the meal and drink, they made a bargain. She'd help him with the Russian job, and if they were successful, she would stay on, learn what he could teach, and he would send her out as his replacement until it was safe for him to return to France.

Her role was to steal what she was hired to steal, do it

cleanly, present the prize to the client, and return to him. And if she must, to kill. Whatever she had to do to complete the job.

In return, he would keep her safe and pay her handsomely.

She asked him why he called her Kitsune. He'd said simply, "Because you are as quick as a little fox, filled with cunning and guile, and you have the look of your ancestors, though few would be able to identify your family as being of Japanese descent. You have Indian in you, too. No matter, it is a good name for you. Together we will make it a legend."

He took Kitsune's natural talents and honed her into a weapon more lethal than a bullet, or a knife. She had the touch. A gift. She had the best hands in the business, and no bourgeois morals to ever sway her opinions or her actions. She could disappear at will, switch languages from one word to the next, change looks to add or subtract a decade. She could blend in anywhere. She had no conscience, no qualms. A job was a job, and she was the very best. She took great pride in her skills. She always basked in his approval when she returned, flushed with triumph and money ready for distribution to private accounts.

She remembered in particular the time she'd flown to Berlin to steal a Rembrandt from the foreign minister of Germany, Herr Joschka Fischer. Mulvaney had gotten her enrolled in an exclusive private school as Bettina Genscher from Vienna, and she soon became best friends with the minister's very smart daughter, Liese. Kitsune was twenty-one at the time, yet no one knew she wasn't the same age as Liese, an innocent and sweet sixteen. Soon, Bettina and Liese were best friends, and she was a frequent visitor at the Fischer house. The foreign minister in particular found her charming and well spoken for such a young girl, her German elegant.

After the Rembrandt went missing, she finished the last two weeks in the private school, their top student in a decade, and bid Liese and her family a tearful good-bye.

She would do anything necessary for money, but stealing art, that was her forte.

Mulvaney taught her not only his trade but practical things as well: how to shelter her money, how to use weapons, how to utilize technology and explosives. She became proficient in martial arts. She learned how to cross borders without raising suspicion, learned how to pick the clients who would pay, and be discreet. And most important, he taught her how to stay apart, unemotional. She was never to feel pity for a mark. She was never to lose her heart, never leave herself vulnerable, because that way meant failure.

He put her through university, giving her the vocabulary she needed to mingle among the world's wealthiest men and women. If she were to move in the right circles, she must possess the proper pedigree. They decided archaeology was the perfect cover. After five years putting in the labor in dusty fields and catacombs, an inspired dissertation on ancient Etruscan art, at twenty-five she received her doctorate, a moment of great pride for them both.

As Kitsune's talent grew, so did her reputation. Mulvaney's choice of the name the Fox was inspired. It was gender-neutral, and many of the clients she worked for had no idea she was a woman. She kept to the shadows, made deliveries without being seen.

Mulvaney let her choose her own calling card, assuring her that someday a victim would see her token and know it was the Fox who'd taken his treasure, since she would become that famous. She chose a small plastic skeleton, which made Mulvaney laugh.

At one point, Mulvaney set himself up as her chief competitor, allowing her to ace him out, and letting it become known in the right circles, to help her reputation spread. They shared the profits, and both got richer.

She was soon sought after the world over. Art crime was her true love, though she'd take other jobs, if they paid well enough, and her small token, the plastic skeleton, became her trademark. No one guessed she was a woman.

She had only one rule.

No guns. Ever. She refused to tell Mulvaney why, simply said guns were too unpredictable in the wrong hands, and much too noisy.

Ten years before, Mulvaney had retired from the game. She hadn't understood why he chose to quit; he was vigorous, strong, agile. He had a fast and devious brain she admired. He was getting older, he told her; it was time for him to sit back in the sun and enjoy himself. No, he would never leave her. He would always be there to watch over her, to have her back. She'd come to love him with everything in her, a deep abiding love, a bond stronger than a daughter's for her father. She couldn't imagine him not being a part of her life, a part of her, and she told him so. He'd hugged her, patted her cheek, then kissed her forehead. She felt safe and secure with him. Only him.

He gave her all his best clients; Saleem Lanighan's father, Robert Lanighan, was one of them. Which led her to Saleem, and his fanatical desire to own the unownable. To steal the Koh-i-Noor diamond, possibly the most protected, revered stone in history, part of the very fabric making up the history of England. It would be the biggest, most elaborate job she'd ever attempted.

And then she, too, could retire, perhaps to Capri, perhaps somewhere equally lovely and anonymous, and find a protégée of her own to train.

45

After Lanighan was in contact the first time, she debated long and hard about taking the job at all. Whether it could even be done. She weighed all the options, talked to Mulvaney at length. It took three months of convincing before she even agreed to discuss it with Lanighan, and opened the line of communication in a coded email.

Lanighan's desires were simple and clear. Get the Koh-i-Noor, at whatever cost. And he was paying her more money than even Mulvaney had ever earned on a single job. Of course, it was Mulvaney who'd told her to charge him through the teeth, and why not? For whatever reason, Lanighan wanted the diamond more than anything else in the world. Be audacious, he'd advised. And so she had.

And she remembered a long-ago winter sun, beginning to slip into the sea, casting an unearthly glow in the sky.

Mulvaney had roused himself, walked to the balcony, and stared out over the beautiful Mediterranean. He looked toward the harbor, watching the boats, watching the crowds gather in the outdoor restaurants, watching the shadows grow. Finally he'd turned and said in a meditative voice, "There is a rule you must never break, Kitsune. It is a rule you must never forget, and you must never question it. Do you understand?"

"Yes, sir."

She'd never called someone *sir* willingly, and the word sounded strange in her mouth.

"Good. Excellent. Here is your rule: never ask why."

"What do you mean?"

"When a client wants something, your responsibility is to make it happen. You never, ever ask *why* he wants the job done. It is not your business. Do you understand?"

She nodded, though she didn't understand. She couldn't imagine it, actually, not knowing the why behind a theft, or a murder. And then she thought about what he said, and saw the wisdom in his words.

Asking why would bring her own morality, or lack thereof, into the equation, and could alter her course.

Which could jeopardize the job.

She nodded again, and this time he knew she meant it. And in all her years, she'd never asked a client why.

But the Koh-i-Noor was different. Lanighan didn't want it because he was a fanatic collector. No, it was more. It was an obsession and over-the-top. But why? The Koh-i-Noor was an awesome diamond, steeped in bloody history, but still—and when he'd agreed to pay her fifty million dollars, she wanted to know his reasons so badly she had to bite her lip to keep from asking him.

But she put it aside, because she had a job to do.

She'd long known she was both lucky and cursed with her looks. The pretty teenager had grown into a very beautiful woman. Beauty was a tool as valuable as her treasured lock picks, but it was also a hindrance, because she was easily remembered. Her greatest skill wasn't her ability to steal with impunity, but her ability to camouflage her beauty when needed.

And allow it to surface when it was needed, as well.

When she took up residence in London to begin the greatest job of her career, stealing the Koh-i-Noor diamond from the queen mother's crown, she quickly realized it was time to let her beauty shine through.

His name was Thornton. Grant Thornton. He was a former noncommissioned officer in Her Majesty's Royal Air Force, decorated, dedicated, and driven. He was handsome, and strong and kind. His new post would be in the Tower of London, as a junior member of the prestigious, sought-after Yeoman Warders.

A beefeater.

Guarding the crown jewels.

He was fresh off his third tour of Afghanistan when she met him at a bar in London. He was to start his service at the Tower of London the following week. He was proud as a peacock, drunk and happy, out for a last fun night with his mates before his new post began.

She'd sashayed by in a black dress cut to her navel and

nearly to her waist in the back, and since he wasn't dead, he'd noticed.

They drank together all night. And the next they'd talked. And the next. After three months of dating, he asked her to move in.

She rarely enjoyed playing the role of honeypot, but this was different. Grant was an intelligent man, a handsome man, a generous lover. He treated her as an equal, not as a plaything. She liked him.

Not loved. That would be too dangerous. But it wasn't the worst assignment she'd ever had.

Beefeaters lived on-site in the Tower of London, in apartments that dated back to the 1300s. Their families lived with them, wives and children. There was a pub on-site, a doctor, a chaplain, everything the men and their families could possibly need. The women often worked outside the walls, but the men, they had no need to leave.

When Grant proposed, Kitsune accepted both the stunning cushion-cut diamond and the offer to move inside the Tower walls.

Working from the inside out was her favorite way to do business.

She knew there were background checks being done. She had a healthy respect for the British; they took nothing at face value, especially a stranger in their midst. She'd heard only the American FBI was more stringent.

She used an identity as close to her real world as she dared. Julia Hornsby was the expatriated daughter of a Scottish father and a Japanese mother. She'd studied art history at the University of Leeds, hadn't, however, done anything of note with her degree, and was currently underemployed in a truly disturbing modern art gallery in Notting Hill.

Grant, for all his military expertise, was a trusting soul, but the members of Her Majesty's government were not. To enhance her cover, Julia quit the Notting Hill dead-end job, rented gallery space near Peckham, filled it with some cheap art she bought at Tesco, and went to work there dutifully each weekday. Her flat nearby was barely furnished but stacked full of large, sweeping Jackson Pollockesque canvasses in various stages of finality. To anyone checking, she was an unsuccessful, undiscovered, not terribly motivated artist, which explained her woeful lack of income, or tax files.

It was thin, but enough. Mulvaney knew his stuff. The background checked out, and she was approved to move into the Tower with Thornton.

Once she was in, her plan was straightforward. The crown jewels were protected by some of the finest security in the world. It ran by computer, with redundancies to make sure if one system failed, another would replace it seamlessly. All she needed to do was hack into the computers, cause a systemic failure, wait for the secondary security to pop online, disable it as well, then use Grant's physical keys to access the exhibit, and wrench the diamond free of the crown.

Stealing the diamond wasn't her primary issue—it was difficult but not impossible. Getting out of the Tower with the diamond, now that would take some finesse. They would know something was happening when their security systems went down. She needed a distraction.

The grounds were patrolled constantly. After dark, the stoic beefeaters traded their blue-and-red uniforms and bearskin caps for dark fatigues and automatic weapons. They might as well have been on patrol in Afghanistan.

Being a part of the fabric of life within the Tower was the only chance she had to escape. If she was recognized, knew the daily password to leave the gated walls, she had a chance. She would need to sicken herself, something dreadful that would be beyond the abilities of the Tower's doctor, something that necessitated a trip to the hospital. Perhaps even make them think she'd been hurt by the thieves in order to make their escape.

Out from behind the walls, she would give herself the antidote and escape, Lanighan's diamond in her pocket.

It was a dangerous plan, and Mulvaney thought her daft for even trying. He knew about the man she'd made fall in love with her, Grant Thornton, and he'd questioned her closely about him. She hadn't fallen for him, had she? One never fell in love with a pawn or a mark. It could easily lead to failure. No, she'd assured him, she hadn't fallen in love with Grant Thornton. She wasn't that big a fool.

She was three weeks from executing her plan when the queen struck a deal with the Americans to bring the queen mother's crown, along with a few other pieces of the crown jewels, to the Metropolitan Museum of Art in New York City, to celebrate the queen's diamond jubilee.

She rethought her approach. It would take more time, but she figured Lanighan wanted the diamond so much, he'd force himself to be patient, to wait. He was already in for twenty-five million dollars, he really had no choice, not that she'd tell him she'd changed her plans.

46

Every job had its own stroke of luck. Be it small or large, it was an undeniable truth. The trick was to recognize how to use the smallest bit of luck to your advantage.

The day Kitsune heard about the Metropolitan Museum of Art exhibit, she began combing New York museum job listings. And her bit of luck presented itself—the Met was hiring, and she was well qualified for the position. All she needed was to get through the doors; she could finagle the rest once she was in.

Mulvaney pulled together the Victoria Browning identity in record time, which told her it was already in existence. A good thing—she wanted to be as clean as she could be.

When he couriered over the paperwork, she memorized all the details, burned the file, created her online persona, and applied for the docent/security guard position. She felt confident her skills and qualifications would land her the position, and she was right. The Met responded with an interview offer within twenty-four hours.

Grant was the next to go. She broke it off and moved out, leaving him reeling. She reeled as well when she'd had to pull off the gorgeous antique cushion-cut diamond, passed down from his grandmother. It hurt more than she'd expected, hurt to see the shock in his eyes, the knowledge dawning on him that she was serious, she was leaving, and never coming back.

But she closed her heart, surprised by how much it hurt. She assured Mulvaney she didn't care about this man, and he applauded her actions.

The flat was shut down, the lease let go on the gallery, her email closed. Once London was buttoned up tight, she made an appointment to deal with a more immediate problem: Victoria Browning had chocolate-brown eyes.

The exhibit was many months away, far too long to wear colored contacts without attracting notice. They were fine for temporary jobs, but not for anything long term; an observant person would notice them slip here or there, and they were never perfect. She'd done this particular surgery before; it was a hassle, nothing more, and reversible.

Through Mulvaney, she knew an excellent, discreet doctor in Bern, a leading laser ophthalmologist by day, and by night, he attended to people with special needs, like her. The process was identical to cataract surgery, with a clean lens to replace the cloudy one. But the clean lens in her case was tinted brown and laid on top of her own iris. After two days of tears and a feeling of grit in her eyes, they healed up nicely.

Her hair was next. She preferred it short—again, wigs were easier to manage without excess hair to cover—but for this, she wanted excellent extensions. With the help of a talented stylist near Hyde Park, she ended up with Princess Catherine–styled dark hair that tumbled past her shoulders and was a few shades lighter than her own hair.

A wardrobe was purchased, muted grays and browns with some elegant dresses, lots of leather and suede and trendy heels, some old, battered sleep things from a secondhand shop, creased jeans, University of Edinburgh sweatshirts from ten years ago, and the like.

Then she flew to New York, to start a new life.

The Met hired her on—she knew they would. Her qualifications screamed at them. They considered themselves lucky she was even interested. An apartment was next, something she could stage, something not too ostentatious. She searched for a week before she settled on the Archstone, then found the garret hidey-hole in Hell's Kitchen for actual day-to-day living.

And then it was simply a matter of making herself indispensable to the Met staff.

Within a few months, her excellent mind realized and valued, she moved up to the position of assistant curator. But time was running out. The exhibit was due in New York in only a matter of months, and she was not in the proper position to execute her plan.

The curator had to go.

An illness, then, one that incapacitated but wouldn't kill. Something a man of his age would be forced to deal with and, with a sorry shrug, retire.

And then she was in the clear. She applied for the curator's spot, was given the position, and all was right in the world.

47

New York, New York
26 Federal Plaza, FBI Headquarters, twentieth floor
Friday, 8:00 a.m.

The conference room was full of people, drinking coffee, talking, eating the Danish stacked on several plates.

Then Paulie came in looking rather worse for wear, a stunning black eye peeking out from his forehead bandage.

Mike gave him a hug. "Paulie, it's good to see you back among the living. How are you feeling?"

He touched the bandage. "I've got a headache the size of Manhattan, but the vampires were good to me. I'll live. Louisa is in the lab running the evidence from the Met. We didn't get any prints; the whole room had been wiped clean. It wasn't a total waste, though. Louisa had a brainstorm, went back early this morning and took samples from Victoria Browning's office. No prints, but she might have left some DNA."

Better than nothing.

Paulie continued. "Everyone came out unscathed, and it could have been so much worse. She could have blown that bomb, but she didn't. So it seems Browning is only a thief, not a murderer."

Nicholas said, "Or she didn't see the point in destroying countless treasures from all over the world."

Agent Gray Wharton patted Paulie's shoulder, and the two of them argued a moment about a Danish versus a bear claw. Gray did indeed look like a computer geek, Nicholas thought, thin, bespectacled, in his early forties, and clearly not at all concerned that he was rumpled and creased, beard stubble on his chin. He nodded at Nicholas. "Gotta love a meeting this early in the morning."

Nicholas smiled. "You Yanks clearly feel sleep is overrated."

Mike saw Savich and Sherlock huddled with Bo. What was that all about?

Zachery tapped a pen against the rim of his coffee cup. "All right, everyone take your seats, let's get started."

She sat beside Nicholas, feeling like something the cat dragged in, whereas he looked sharp this morning, dressed in a charcoal suit that looked straight from a presser, a blue tie, and a fine blue shirt. Something he'd pulled out of a magic compartment in his little leather bag, she supposed.

What she needed was a gallon of coffee and a big fat dose of adrenaline. She saw him slowly rotate his shoulder. Well, he hadn't gotten off scot-free from their short war. When she'd lain in her bed last night, thinking about the battle before she went to sleep, it hit her that the whole attack had lasted less than five minutes. It had seemed much, much longer.

Zachery got things started, meeting each person's eyes as he told them about the attack in Mike's garage six hours before, ending with, "So that's why Nicholas has some bruising on his face and Mike has a lump on her head the size of our missing diamond. One bad guy is dead and as yet no legitimate ID on him. He's not in AFIS. We're spreading out the net to Interpol."

Mike knew to her boot heels there wouldn't be any ID coming from anywhere. She said, "Nicholas, tell them about the Kicker."

"Where'd that moniker come from?" Ben asked.

Nicholas said, "He's the one who kicked Mike in the head. I was chasing him down an alley. I saw some white hair had slipped down out of his black ski mask. The thing is, though, he didn't move like he was old. He was fast and smooth, and when he kicked Mike in the head, his leg swept up and his follow-through was perfect. He was in charge, no question in my mind. I'm thinking he has to be working for Victoria Browning, aka the Fox."

Zachery said, "We'll find out. Now, because Mike and Nicholas are both skilled and fast—"

"And lucky," Mike said.

"And lucky," Zachery repeated, "both of them are fine. People, we had a hard night. But everyone's alive, and we know who the thief is. We've started bigger cases with a lot less.

"Everyone's been hammered with the media reports on every TV station, and all over the Internet. Not a surprise this theft is the biggest, splashiest news all over the world.

"But we're being crucified, along with anyone even remotely connected to the Met and Dr. Victoria Browning. Needless to say, Director Mueller isn't happy, nor is the president of the United States. Not to mention the insurance people, who are trying to shift blame to get out from under some of the upcoming crushing payout if we don't get the diamond back.

"Unfortunately, there's nothing we can do to stem the tide, no excuses to make. We're in the spotlight until there's a worse catastrophe somewhere in the world. There's only one thing we can do: we have to find the Koh-i-Noor, and fast. Now, Gray, where are we with finding Browning?"

Gray Wharton stood up. "Here's what we know." He dimmed the lights with a remote. A slide came up on the screen, and Dr. Victoria Browning stared out at them, studious, elegant, understated, and wearing a complacent Mona Lisa smile Mike wanted to slap right off her pretty face.

"This is not Victoria Browning. We don't believe there ever was a Victoria Browning. We believe we have fact and fiction expertly mixed to create this identity. It's very possible this woman is indeed a British citizen, thirty-eight years old, who grew up in Scotland and attended school there. According to her passport records, she entered the United States in April of last year on a work visa.

"We believe she created this identity specifically for this job. In other words, she's legit up to a point. The best lies are based in truth, and according to everyone who worked with her at the Met, she *was* an expert on the crown jewels, and had contacts in the archaeology world that couldn't be faked, which means she might have indeed gained her doctorate from the University of Edinburgh. We will verify once we upload the university's records.

"However, to our everlasting despair, they're having a snowstorm over in Scotland, and there's no one at the school to transmit the records. It will be a day at a minimum before we can access that information."

Ben said, "Sometimes I hate that we have to play by the rules and can't hack into the university records."

Nicholas smiled, threaded his pen through his fingers.

Sherlock said, "When did Browning cross paths with Elaine York?"

Ben said, "Last year. Elaine worked with Victoria long distance on the exhibit until she moved to New York four months ago."

"Were they friendly?"

Ben nodded. "They worked closely together and seemed to be friends. I know they occasionally went out after work for drinks and dinner."

Sherlock said, "Is there anything new on Inspector York's murder?"

Mike said, "A tenant thought he heard a struggle

around lunchtime this past Wednesday. We have Vladimir Kochen entering the apartment building at eleven forty-five a.m. with Elaine. She comes stumbling out half an hour later, disoriented and bleeding.

"We have a security video from a bodega across the street. We're comparing all the people entering and exiting her building, and running them against her facial-recognition profile. It's entirely possible Browning was disguised and we missed her."

"Or it's someone we haven't considered yet," Zachery said.

Nicholas said, "What you told Mike and me last night at the hospital, Paulie, about one of the words you heard Victoria say—*ark*—it's bothering me. What if it wasn't *ark* she said, but something rhyming, like *park*, for instance. *Meet me at noon at the park*, which makes more sense than *Meet me at noon at the ark*."

Paulie said, "Could be, Nicholas. I was pretty out of it."

Mike said, "Dillon, you don't think it's possible to reconstruct the audio during Browning's attack on Paulie and Louisa?"

"I just thought of something else to try. I'm going to see if I can work some magic," and Savich rose and left the conference room.

Zachery nodded to Gray, and he flipped to a new slide. "These are the canisters and explosive material retrieved from the Met and analyzed last night. The C-4 chemical signature matches a bombing in Tripoli last May. The canisters are standard-grade tear gas, and there was a smaller canister of a chemical we haven't identified yet; it's what made everyone feel sick. The attack was definitely meant to disable but not kill."

Zachery said, "Any trace on how the C-4 got into the country?"

"No, sir. It's possible it was made here and shipped over there, too."

Zachery rolled his eyes. "Like we need that hitting the news." He asked Ben, "Do any of your Russian Mob friends use explosives?"

Ben shook his head. "Not like this. I suggest we farm the test results out to counterterrorism, let them have a go."

"Done. I don't want to be in wait-and-see mode, people. What can we do right now to move this case forward?"

Mike said, "Andrei Anatoly, sir. Though he says Kochen wasn't a part of his team anymore, it was one of his soldiers murdered in Elaine's apartment. Maybe Anatoly planned to steal the Koh-i-Noor but simply wasn't the first in line. We need to talk to him again."

"Ben, you're on that. Mike, you're to stay focused on Browning."

"But Browning and Anatoly could have ties we haven't found yet," Mike said. "Ties that could involve Inspector York."

"Sure they could," Zachery said, "but let Ben keep on him. You and Drummond figure out what Browning's real name is and where she was living. She'll have a trail. Go find it."

Mike nodded.

"Gray, continue your sweep of private airports. She's somewhere. Let's see if she left the U.S. Okay, people, we have a priceless diamond to track down and the media hard on our heels. We need answers, and quickly."

48

Mike took Nicholas to her office, a small blue-paneled cubicle down the hall and around the corner from the SAC's conference room.

He thought of his own office back at New Scotland Yard, the spacious room, the large window. Mike could reach her arms out and touch either side of hers.

"Cozy."

She nodded. "Yeah, yeah. It's humble, but it's mine. Have a seat. I'll get logged in and create a secure thumb drive for you so you can access our classified network. You'll find everything you'll need there. Our computer systems are divided: green is for general stuff and is unsecured. We can access the Internet, email, Facebook even. Red is classified and secured. Its only access is internal, to our secure FBI Scion network. We won't want anyone watching what you're doing, so I'm going to set you up on the red side. No monkeying around, okay?"

He was amused. "Me? Never."

She narrowed her eyes at him. "Don't kid a kidder," she said, and handed him the thumb drive to work from.

Nicholas was impressed. He had enough computer power before him to find out everything about Victoria Browning, particularly if she did indeed have records from the University of Edinburgh.

He'd logged in to the system when Mike's phone rang. She glanced at it. "It's Zachery's office." She picked up the phone.

It was Zachery himself, not his secretary. "Whatever magic Savich used, it worked. I've got the audio from the actual theft and Browning's attack on Paulie and Louisa. Get in here, you need to hear this."

"On our way." She hung up and stood. "Savich came through. Let's go." They hurried down the hallway and were in Zachery's office a minute later.

Zachery welcomed them with a big smile. "Not only did Savich get the audio in the exhibit room cleaned up enough so you can tell Browning said *ark* all right, but in French, as in *L'Arc de Triomphe—meeting is in Paris tomorrow at noon*. Gray also just found out the Teterboro feed was down for about ten minutes. Their air traffic control tower confirmed a private jet left during that time. Browning paid two guards to shut the cameras down while she entered the grounds and boarded the plane. We've arrested the two men, and one decided to talk. He said her plane filed a flight plan to Vancouver—a lie, of course. A Gulfstream could easily make it to Paris with the same amount of fuel.

"Your plane is wheels up in an hour. I'll square it with the French authorities, and you'll be met at the airport. Get her, guys, and bring the diamond back."

Mike was so jazzed she nearly hugged Nicholas, who was grinning and rubbing his hands together. Once back at Mike's desk, Nicholas said, "Good thing I never checked into the Yale Club; I already have my bag. Do we need to swing by your place?"

She gave him a long-suffering look. "Nope, I have everything right here." She opened a lower drawer and pulled out a nylon bag. She added her laptop and a Glock .40.

"Let's move." She hoisted the bag. He didn't dare offer to carry her bag, but instead gestured for her to lead the way. She wasn't dragging any longer, she was energized, shoulders back, moving out in her long-legged stride, those biker boots of hers covering a lot of ground fast. She looked strong and fit, and she smelled good, too— jasmine, maybe, close to the scent his mother wore. He'd been too knackered yesterday to fully appreciate the complete FBI package.

The elevator shot them down to the garage, where Mike's replacement black Crown Vic was waiting. They tossed their bags in the back and jumped in.

The snow was melted, but the sky was gray and dreary. Mike made a series of turns and took the Lincoln Tunnel to Jersey.

"Where are we flying from?" Nicholas asked, strapping himself in.

"Teterboro as well. I'd like to knock some heads together before we take off."

After navigating tight traffic for a couple of blocks, Mike looked over at Nicholas. "You're quiet."

"Running it all through my head. From my brief research on the Fox, she works alone. She's known for getting herself in place months in advance for big jobs. In this case, the planning had to take a year at least. Amazing that she could hold to her role for so very long.

"She doesn't make mistakes, and so far from what I've read, she doesn't kill people. If she had something to do with Elaine's death, I don't think it was part of any plan. But who knows? I've been wrong before."

Mike was through the tunnel now. "You're stewing. What else?"

"We could be flying right into a trap. The Arc de Triomphe in Paris at noon. It seems too easy."

She gave him a cocky grin. "Don't worry, we're not going to parade in there all alone. You heard Zachery. He's getting us backup as we speak. I'm not worried about Victoria." She waggled her eyebrows. "What I worry about is the terrifying curse."

"Yeah, laugh all you want, but you'd be smart not to diss it."

Mike said, "Come on, Nicholas, isn't archaeology full of curses and warnings to deter tomb raiders and the lot?"

Nicholas ran his hands through his hair and rotated his shoulder. He wished he had more of her muscle-relaxant cream. At least her big sectional sofa had been comfortable. He said, "True, but if you look at the history of the Koh-i-Noor through the ages, you'd be hard-pressed to discount the warning entirely. We Brits aren't a superstitious lot, but no one wants to test it out, for all that. The history of this stone is a bloody one. How much do you know about Colonial Imperialism?"

"I know the British loved their colonies, and some of us weren't so keen on that idea, which caused a big tea shortage for a while." She flashed him a smile that he couldn't help returning. The biker librarian was pretty when she lighted up. She was smart, too, and quick, as witnessed by her skills in the garage last night.

He continued. "All the tribes and countries who possessed the diamond have fallen, and that's why we Brits heed the warnings. We have no intention of following suit."

Mike gave him a curious look. "How do you know all this stuff?"

"My great-grandfather, the sixth Baron de Vesci, was one of the last viceroys to India. The Koh-i-Noor was a favorite topic of his."

She gave him a brooding look. "Am I supposed to be calling you *Sir* Nicholas?"

He laughed. "I have no honorary, Mike. My grandfather is the baron, and my father his heir. I'm simply DCI Nicholas Drummond. I have no real part in the family business."

"But your father works for the Home Office, right? He wasn't part of the family business, either. What is the family business?"

"Have you ever heard of Delphi Cosmetics?"

She glanced over at him. "You're kidding."

"My grandfather is eighty-six, and he still deals with the managing director every single day. He's even let my mother in the door, despite her being a provincial American."

"They make great lip gloss."

He laughed.

"So no cosmetics for you. Did your granddad and your father approve of your becoming a spy?"

He smiled. "I guess Granddad thought it sounded swashbuckling, but my father knew the truth—Foreign Office operatives work in a dirty, nasty business, little trust from anyone, covert jobs that don't always go as planned, that many times end in tragedy and—" He stopped talking. After a moment, he added, "Now I do what you do, which is far more rewarding."

He could see she had more questions, but he didn't want to answer. He was tired, had already talked too much.

49

Once the FBI Gulfstream was hurtling east at four hundred fifty knots, Mike tucked herself into the big leather seat with a couple of pillows and blankets and fell asleep immediately. First some work, Nicholas thought, then he'd join her.

He hacked into the University of Edinburgh system and immediately found Browning's records and another photo. Her limpid brown eyes smiled at him from underneath a brown fringe, all innocence and excitement. It was the face of a student ready to break the shackles of small-town Scotland and experience life in the big city. It was not the face of an international jewel thief. Again, he was struck at how very talented she was at presenting herself as someone she wasn't, someone who didn't exist.

He started digging. Ten minutes later, when he was at

the point of admitting defeat, he saw a red flag. The electronic file had been created two years prior. While it was possible the university was simply bringing old records into the electronic age, Nicholas knew that wasn't the situation here; he'd worked another case with a terror suspect who'd attended the University of Edinburgh, and all their alumni files had been online for at least four years.

Break one for the good guys.

He thought back to the conversation with Browning in the elevator of the Met, about art crimes. She'd claimed to work with the Museum Security Network and the Association for Research into Crimes Against Art.

It turned out that the Museum Security Network had an excellent firewall, but it wasn't enough. A few clicks and he was into their records. Sure enough, Dr. Victoria Browning was on the rolls. He dug deeper, looking for the initial date of the file. There. Also two years prior.

The ARCA website also listed her as a member in good standing. As of two years ago.

He drummed his fingers on the arm of his seat, thinking. Knowing what he'd continue to find. While she had an excellent identity on the surface—passport, license, all the identification would match—this particular Victoria Browning hadn't existed before two years ago. And he was probably one of a small number of people who could discover this information. He was willing to concede that Savich was another. With the skills Browning had displayed, he was beginning to think she was on par with them. Possible, but she was turning into Wonder Woman. It was more likely she had someone else, someone close to her, a master hacker. Something else to explore, but not now.

He looked at the timeline he'd drawn up. The plan to steal the diamond had been in play for at least twenty-four months, if not longer. But according to Elaine, the *Jewel of the Lion* exhibit was only a year in the making.

He called a friend, Miles Herrington, who worked in the office of the queen's private secretary at Buckingham Palace. Miles also had the dubious honor of being Hamish Penderley's stepson. Nicholas trusted him to be discreet, both on the request and about not telling his father Nicholas had been in touch.

Miles answered immediately. "Drummond, you dog. Tell me you've found the Koh-i-Noor."

"Not yet, Miles. I'm working on it."

"Tell me you're going to get it back before the government falls or declares war on America. Better yet, I should find the Lord Chamberlain and put you on with him. He's already been crowing about his plans to boil you in oil when he gets his hands on you."

"Good to speak to you as well, Miles."

"You're embroiled in the scandal of the century, mate, and from what I've heard, it was of your own doing. Don't expect rose blossoms when you get back."

"I'm aware," Nicholas said. So Penderley was talking about his insubordination. Not good.

"Miles, I'm flying to Paris right now to stake out a

meeting the thief arranged. Have you ever heard of the Fox?"

"You mean, Teddy the Fast Fox, the kids' cartoon character on the telly?"

"Wrong fox, but never mind. When did you strike the deal with the Yanks to send the jewels to New York?"

"Let me think, we were deep into the plans for the queen's jubilee, and the Met approached us for a single event in the U.S. I believe it was more than two years ago. I'd have to check the exact date."

"Please do. I need to know everyone who was in on those discussions, and who would have firsthand knowledge the Koh-i-Noor was under consideration to go to America."

"Whatever for?"

"There was a leak, someone who knew the negotiations were under way and talked about it."

Miles sounded horrified. "You don't believe someone on my staff is responsible?"

"It must be someone in those initial talks, yes. Whether it was purposeful or not remains to be seen. In any case, word got round to one of the most successful jewel thieves in the world that we were sending the crown jewels to the States. You can do the math from there."

"Bugger me. All right, I'll start putting together a list."

"Thank you. And Miles? Hurry."

They hung up. Things should come together quickly now. He hoped. He looked over at Mike, dead to the world. Within two minutes he was asleep himself.

———

M ike woke with a start. She'd been dreaming, chasing Timmy, ready to smack him because he'd stolen her tennis racquet and she couldn't catch him. She hoped it wasn't a portent. She sat up and stretched. Nicholas heard her stir, opened his eyes and gave her a big smile. "Have I some interesting news for you."

"Oh, yeah? You had a vision?"

"Not quite," and he told her about Victoria Browning being two years old. He didn't mention hacking into the records of the University of Edinburgh, but of course she knew. He recognized it in her eyes the moment she decided to give him a pass. She got up, got them some bottled water and some sandwiches.

The ham sandwich tasted good—that or he was starving. Same with Mike, since she was on her second sandwich, this one egg salad. He said, "Like I said, Browning's identity was created two years ago, at the very beginning of discussions to bring the Koh-i-Noor to America, long before Elaine was chosen to mind the exhibit. Whoever orchestrated this has a contact high up in Her Majesty's service."

"It's hard to keep secrets, Nicholas. Especially of this magnitude."

"True. The Fox must have been engaged to steal the diamond when it looked like we would cut a deal with the Met. She created the Browning identity, came to America, and was hired on at the Met. It's her specialty, assimilating into the fabric of the piece she's tasked with stealing. She's done it before."

"So who is she? Wonder Woman?"

He had to grin. "Funny, that's what I was thinking as well. I keep circling around both who she is and who hired her. Paris, London, New York. A plot at least two years in the making. Too many threads, too much time has passed. We must figure this out," and he stood and walked the short length of the plane, stretching his legs, his back, rotating his shoulder. Better, definitely better.

He pulled another bottle of water from the small fridge in the galley. "I've been thinking. Elaine's laptop must have had details of the museum's security protocols. The blueprint for the theft, so to speak."

"So? Browning worked at the museum. She already had access. So why would she need Elaine's computer?"

"She wouldn't."

"Yet it was stolen from Elaine's apartment. Someone thought it was important. But who?"

Nicholas said, "I'm thinking Andrei Anatoly. He wanted the diamond, Elaine wouldn't help, so he killed her."

"But Elaine was concerned for her safety. She hired a bodyguard. I suppose it's possible she didn't know he was part of Anatoly's mob, but Elaine wasn't a stupid or careless woman. I think she knew exactly who she was getting when she hired Kochen. Don't forget, Nicholas, she didn't say anything to your uncle Bo about any threat or danger."

Talk about a tautological argument. Mike said, "Which

brings us back to the fact that Elaine was involved in the theft."

He drank the rest of the water and sat back down. "It's time for a little help."

He got out his mobile and rang the only other person who might be able to assist them.

"Savich? It's Drummond. I was hoping you could set MAX on a task for me."

50

Savich said, "I heard you're on your way to Paris. Let me tell you what I'm doing before you tell me what you need.

"I've discovered from Interpol files that the Fox has struck at least ten times over the past ten years, and those are only the jobs they can document. They're sure she goes back further. We need to find out who she really is, and who's been paying her. If I can find the money trail using the stolen items as a baseline—" Savich paused. Nicholas heard him typing in the background.

Nice to be on the same wavelength with someone, Nicholas thought. This was exactly what he'd wanted Savich to do. The typing stopped.

Nicholas said, "There must be some data on who she worked for in the past, simply through the news accounts of the thefts, especially if any items have been recovered. She hasn't exactly been subtle."

Savich said, "I'll correlate the dates of the known thefts and where they happened, and then we should be able to get a partial geographical profile. If we can track her current movements off the profile, we can also follow money transfers from financial institutions in those areas and match them up. If we're successful, we can extrapolate her recent money transfers and track her current employer."

"That's exactly what we need."

Savich said, "Email me everything you find, as you find it, and I'll add it to the profile. The relationships we uncover should be enough to send you in the right direction."

"One more thing. Since you're already into the Interpol files, cross-reference the list with people of Indian, Pakistani, or Iranian descent. Maybe this theft has a bigger canvas. Whoever hired the Fox has major quid, not to mention patience. There's something there, I can feel it."

"Always trust a hunch," Savich said. "I'll be back as soon as MAX spits out some results."

"Thanks, Savich. Give my best to Sherlock."

He hung up and sent the email, then turned to Mike, who was also on her mobile. She held up a finger and kept talking and nodding as she took notes.

A moment later, she hung up. "The fingerprints done during Browning's background check for employment at the Met were faked. They match the prints for the Browning identity."

Nicholas said, "And they discovered the fingerprints were entered in your AFIS database two years ago, right? Why are you grinning?"

"No one can spend day in and day out working in an office without leaving something of themselves behind. Louisa said Browning had wiped her office thoroughly, but she noticed some tooth marks on the pencils. She tested them, and shazam—DNA. Browning chewed on her pencils, and forgot to throw them away. They're putting it into the system now."

"Well done, Louisa. But if there's no DNA on file, there won't be anything to match it to. Unless we catch her."

"*Until* we catch her," Mike said, "and you're right, but don't forget what we can get from DNA. We can determine eye color and racial makeup, and at the very least we'll be able to reverse the mitochondria and search for family members as well. Louisa tells me she'll have the results within twenty-four hours."

"Excellent. Anything else?"

He watched her unbraid her hair, smooth it free with her fingers, and begin to rebraid it, her movements sure and fast, weaving in three separate hanks of hair. "Gray said the additional bodega video feed showed a strange man entering Elaine's building the morning of her murder. They canvassed the entire apartment building, spoke to everyone who lives there, and no one can identify him."

"A him. Not Victoria Browning disguised?"

She shook her head. "It couldn't be Victoria, he was too tall. And too thin. So we could have our killer on video. Remember, Gray has an ex-girlfriend at the NSA? She came through with the trace on the cell phone. Browning threw it in the Hudson River on her way to the airport, but it turns out they found another call, made from a cell phone with a sequential serial number to the one that called your phone during the attack at the Met. Gray figures they were disposable cell phones bought at the same time, a two-for-one package. The call from the second phone was scrambled, but it originated over the Atlantic, heading east."

"Browning?"

"The timing's right. They ran the number she called, but there was no answer. She called it twice in one hour."

He sat back in his chair, rubbing his fingers along his chin, staring straight ahead, toward the cockpit. He was rotating his shoulder, trying to regain full motion. He needed to shave, not that it mattered, Mike thought. It enhanced the *Don't mess with me or I'll twist off your head* look.

Nicholas jumped up from his seat. "Of course. The two calls she made, all that expert computer work—she does have a partner."

She hated to rain on his parade, but they had to consider everything. "She could have been calling the buyer to let him know the diamond was on its way."

"Why wouldn't the buyer answer? Especially if he'd been waiting two years for this call."

"Why wouldn't a partner answer?"

He threw himself down in the seat again. "I don't know. But a job of this magnitude, I know she has someone to work the back end. It's very rare to have a thief, or an assassin, do a job without someone to facilitate—vet the jobs, handle the money, those types of things. It makes sense she would have someone behind the scenes, and of course she would guard their identity with her life."

"But you said nothing in her background speaks of a partner. The Fox is known for going it alone."

"Yeah, but I was wrong."

Mike said, "Then we need to find out who the partner is and where he or she is. We can't afford to be surprised again."

He reached across the aisle and slapped her on the knee. "You know, I may have to steal Agent Wharton from you. He seems to earn his keep."

"I won't give him up without a fight. He's one of the best in the FBI."

Her cell phone rang again.

"It's Zachery." She put the call on the speaker. He sounded excited.

"Mike, divert the plane. The Fox didn't go to Paris. Agent Wharton and the NSA got lucky. Using satellite footage of European airports within the plane's fuel range, they've tracked the false tail number to a private airstrip in Megève, France. The French authorities have her pilot in custody. She's headed for Geneva, Switzerland."

51

Kitsune slept through the plane's approach and landing, which was just as well, because the small landing strip's position gave the illusion the plane might fly directly into the side of the massive mountain Mont Blanc before it banked sharply and landed.

She woke when the wheels touched the ground and the engine fired into reverse. She yawned and stretched, and dug a warm coat out of her bag. It was cold out; she could see the snow on the Alps, cotton white, backed by the azure sky.

The pilot taxied to a stop and came out of the cockpit.

"Will you be needing my services again today?"

She thought about it for a moment. She'd planned to send him away, but to be safe, it wouldn't be a bad idea to have him primed and ready.

"Do you ski?"

"Yes, ma'am, I do."

She gave him a charming smile. "I will be a day. Enjoy the slopes. I will meet you back here on Sunday morning. Six a.m. Don't be late."

She descended the stairs to the waiting car. A black Mercedes sedan, as requested. The driver held the door.

When she was safely inside, he got behind the wheel and said in French, "We will be in Geneva in one hour, mademoiselle."

The divider went up between the front and back seats, and she hit the mute button on the speaker. Once secure, she dialed Mulvaney again.

No answer. She clicked off, set the phone in her lap. The Arve River flowed to her right, following the highway, silted by glacial water to an eerie green. It looked wrong, as wrong as she felt. Mulvaney had now missed three check-ins. She knew what his silence meant. He was either taken or dead.

She pushed away the gut-wrenching fear at losing him; she couldn't afford to think about him now, but the pain was still there, hot and deep. *No.* She had the job to complete. She had to deal with Saleem Lanighan, deliver the diamond, make sure the money was transferred properly. She saw Mulvaney in her mind's eye, warning her that Lanighan wasn't his father, who learned his lesson quickly—no, the son couldn't be trusted; she'd have to be very careful.

She needed to take extra precautions with this exchange. When she was confident he hadn't double-crossed her, only then would she hand over the safe-deposit box key to the diamond. He wouldn't like it, but it was the safest way for her. And where was Drummond? Close, she knew it. He was close.

She made a few adjustments to her hair and clothes, looked out the window to see the geyser peak of water in the distance, the Jet d'Eau, at the center of Lake Geneva, a lovely sight.

She checked her watch; right on time. She had two hours before she was to meet Lanighan. Considering the situation, she was glad of their set of coded meeting points. Even if Drummond had tracked her down, he'd be waiting for her in Paris, not Geneva.

She realized she was more concerned about him than she was about Lanighan. A few more distractions might be necessary to keep her safe. Just in case.

The driver followed her instructions well. The car stopped in front of the Deutsche Bank off Quai des Bergues exactly one hour after he'd picked her up in Megève.

Kitsune dismissed the driver—she could walk everywhere she needed for the rest of the morning—and entered the building. She immediately cut across the lobby into the courtyard and went out the north entrance. It was a five-minute walk to the Basilique Notre-Dame. She wound her way around the streets on foot, looking in the plate-glass windows of the stores along the way, until she was certain no one was following her.

The day was cold and clear, the city bustling around her. Geneva was always one of her favorite cities, even in winter, when the lake sometimes roiled and splashed over its banks, encasing the cars and boats and walkways along its length in ice.

She walked back toward the lake and went into the exquisite lobby of the Bank Horim.

One last errand, then thirty minutes later, she walked a bit up the Quai du Mont-Blanc, stopped for an espresso at the Hôtel de la Paix to shake off the chill.

She was nearly finished. Once the money was transferred and carefully redistributed to safe places, she would go directly to Bern, restore her blue eyes, and fly to Capri, to Mulvaney. She wouldn't accept that something had happened to him, that he'd suffered an accident or a heart attack. No, he would be all right, welcoming her with a smile and a glass of his favorite Capri Falanghina. She would be with him again soon, and they would laugh together about all her adventures in New York.

Grant Thornton's face flashed into her mind. When this was all over, maybe, just maybe, she could get him back. Mulvaney wouldn't like that she'd fallen for a mark—it went against everything he'd taught her—but it was her life, her decision. Was she asking too much from the universe? Probably. But at the thought of him, a smile lingered on her lips.

Five minutes later, the espresso was gone. It was time.

52

Saleem was traveling on a false passport, under the name Rolph Heyer. It was easier to fool the border guards than customs agents in the airports, which was the purpose of driving across the border.

The border crossing was backed up, cars slowing to nearly a standstill. He lowered his window and breathed in the chill air. He felt good. He was close now. So close.

When asked for his papers, he handed them over with a smile. Image was everything. He was relaxed and capable. Nothing to fear. His face was not known to be a part of any criminal enterprise. Rolph Heyer was a businessman, a careful, cunning businessman, and entirely legitimate.

A few moments later, the car thoroughly looked over, his passport swiped through the reader, he was given the go-ahead to move forward.

The rest of the journey was uneventful, and four hours later, as he pulled off the highway into the streets of Geneva, his mobile rang. Colette. At last.

"Tell me you have good news."

"Yes, sir, I do. I have received the call. The package has been secured."

He relaxed. "Excellent, Colette. *Merci*."

"Do not thank me yet. We lost Rathbone."

"Was he taken or killed?"

"He is dead, sir. I was told there was no way to recover the body, but there is also no way to discover his identity, since he was never in the system, either in Europe or in the U.S. He is not a liability."

Lanighan sighed. Rathbone was one of his favorite henchmen, lethal as a rattlesnake and twice as fast, but smart, never even arrested. He'd been with Saleem for many years, always willing to do anything he asked.

"This is a terrible loss. But it is the price we must pay. Many men's lives have been sacrificed in the pursuit of the Koh-i-Noor. He will be remembered as a hero." The eulogy finished, he said sharply, "Now, where is the package secured?"

"In the warehouse, in Gagny."

He hung up the phone, quite satisfied.

There was too much at stake to take the risk of allowing Kitsune to double-cross him. Too much money, too many variables. She'd been sloppy, letting the FBI close in on her as she was leaving America. Showing off, no doubt, proving the Fox was smarter than the world's best law enforcement.

He was a patient man. Yes, he was. The power he would wield was worth waiting for. But he would have to be very careful and not take any chances, because now he had another variable in the mix.

Lanighan had a room booked at the Beau-Rivage, at the edge of Lake Geneva across from the Jet d'Eau fountain, as their plans dictated. He checked in, took his bag to his elegant suite, and went out on the balcony, watching the huge plume of water rising nearly five hundred feet in the air.

His meeting with Kitsune was in two hours. She was sure to be nearing Geneva at this point, and he would soon hold the Jewel of the Lion itself in his hands. He shivered with excitement, with the promise of what was to come.

He closed the doors to the balcony and ordered raclette and champagne to be delivered, then took a scalding hot shower. He dressed carefully, then went out onto the balcony to enjoy a cocktail while he waited.

Mont Blanc glistened in the distance, and Saleem had a rare moment of peace. He was alone, he was about to fulfill his lifelong dream, and he had insurance to assure the smooth transition of the Koh-i-Noor diamond into his possession, for a much smaller price than he'd bargained.

Of course, at his death, his father was comforted by the knowledge his son would carry on the search, as he'd done for his father, and his father before him, and he'd suggested Saleem use the Fox, and yet, he wondered again, as he had many times over the past two years, why hadn't his father told him the Fox was a beautiful, soulless woman?

He was long dead now. It didn't matter.

The promise of the stone's power wasn't a legend to Saleem—it was real. He was the Lion, and soon he would have the famed Koh-i-Noor in his possession, and everything he wanted would finally be his. Nothing could stop him. He could feel it in his bones.

53

Mike said, "Switzerland, sir?"

"Yes. We got lucky. The French had a satellite passing over when she arrived. Facial recognition confirmed it was the Fox, though I didn't recognize the woman in the still photos as Victoria Browning. Her hair is short now, black, and she's smaller, if that's possible. Talk about a master of disguise.

"The car, a Mercedes, took A40 to the A411 northwest toward Geneva. The license plate was obscured, but the satellite picked up the car entering the city limits an hour later.

"The driver dropped her at the Deutsche Bank in the city center and left. The Geneva police are looking for him, but if he's anything like the pilot, he knows nothing of use. She seems to hire new people with every job. She doesn't have a set group of people she uses again and again."

Nicholas said, "It's much safer that way. There's very little chance of being able to turn someone against her. You lost her after the bank?"

"Yes. We're in touch with the police in Geneva to get the camera feeds, but nothing yet. All we know for sure is she's in the city.

"Pierre Menard will be your contact on the ground; he's a FedPol agent stationed in Geneva. He's a bulldog, likes Americans, and you can always count on him. Mike, I've texted you his number. He's expecting your call."

Mike said, "We'll get in touch with him and go straight to the bank when we arrive, see what she left behind. We'll call you when we're on the ground."

She hung up and pressed her call button. The pilot came on the air. "We need to reroute to Geneva, Switzerland. How long will it take to get there?"

"Hold on a moment, Agent Caine, let me get a new flight plan. I'll be back to you in five minutes."

She turned to Nicholas. "Geneva?"

"Best banking in the world."

"What do you think she's up to?"

"Maybe the buyer put her money in a Swiss account and she has to sign for it in person."

Mike's face fell. "She'll probably be gone before we get there."

"Don't be a pessimist. Look, she anticipated we might trace her call and sent us to the wrong place at the wrong time. But she's here. We're going to get her."

"You think she had prearranged codes with the buyer, something like *L'Arc de Triomphe at noon* means Geneva, dinnertime?"

He nodded. "I expect you've hit it head-on."

Mike hated to admit it, but she felt a grudging respect for Browning. "She has thought of everything."

"And we've gotten bloody lucky, tracking her to Geneva. She knew we'd find her trail, but not so quickly. We have the element of surprise. We've underestimated her before. We won't do it again."

The pilot came over the speaker. "We're on course to Geneva, Agent Caine. We'll be landing in less than two hours."

Mike keyed the switch and said, "Roger that," then pulled up the text from Zachery. "Have you dealt with FedPol before?"

"The Federal Police? Yes, many times. I've had mixed success with them. Interpol doesn't have agents in the field the way we do, they're really more data crunchers. FedPol works closely with them. Every major European country has a branch. Honestly, there are so many layers of international law enforcement that bureaucracy gets the better of them, but right now, we need someone who can move freely around the European theater. We'll see if Menard is a help or a hindrance."

Spoken like a true spy.

"Zachery said he's a bulldog, plus, since I'm an American, we know he'll at least like me. Let's just see how much," and she rang Menard's number.

"Menard, here. Is this Agent Caine?"

"Yes, and Nicholas Drummond from New Scotland Yard."

"Drummond, I've heard of you. You used to be Foreign Office, *oui*? You may know a friend of mine, Jacques Bouton."

Nicholas laughed. "I know him well. What's the old bugger up to these days?"

"Retired, but you never can leave, can you? Even though he's up in his chalet in Chamonix, he still manages to butt in to our cases. He spoke for you, said you could be trusted."

"I appreciate the vote of confidence." Bona fides established, he asked, "Do you know where our target is now?"

"We're searching. The Geneva police have been cooperative, but there is nothing yet. When will you arrive?"

"Two hours."

"I will meet you at the airport. Good-bye."

Nicholas said, "He should be a help, which is good news. If he and Bouton are friends, he'll know how to bend the rules. You know, I think he likes me better than you."

She went silent for a moment, then said, "Who's this Bouton character?"

"He's a friend, one of my old contacts. We worked together on a nasty case about five years ago, in Algiers. And if Menard knows him, we're in luck." He paused a moment. "To catch the Fox, we might have to jump over the line."

Mike kicked off her boots and drew her feet up on the

leather seat. "We aren't flying to Europe to bend the rules, Nicholas."

"The only rules that matter right now are the Fox's."

Mike was already shaking her head. "Come on, you know the FBI doesn't play fast and loose with the law."

"I know."

"Yeah, of course you know. But you also think the Fox was involved in Elaine York's murder, and you want revenge. I can see it on your face, Nicholas. But our job is to solve this case without breaking laws and compromising ourselves."

His voice went cold. "If you think I'm going to allow my grief for Elaine to influence me in this investigation, you're dead wrong. Apparently I know a lot more about you than you know about me."

"You absolutely don't know anything about me."

He shifted in his chair, eyebrow raised. "You told me about your dad, the chief of police in Omaha, quite the achievement for the son of a farmer. I also know he did two tours in Vietnam and received a Purple Heart and a Silver Star. Your parents are still married—happily, by the looks of it. You have a younger brother, Timothy. Unfortunately, I didn't have time to check him out. He called you in the middle of the night last night. I guess there's a problem with your brother, since you said he was your Afghanistan, sort of—"

She cut him off. "Stop right now. This is all Google stuff any moron could find out about my family. It has nothing to do with how I choose to do my job. I don't wave my wand and decide what's appropriate for the given situation. My *rules*, as you call them, separate me from the people I hunt. It should be the same for you."

His face remained expressionless, and his voice was light, but she wasn't fooled, not for an instant. "Believe it or not, the Elaine I knew was a lot like you. And you know what? I could always count on her to have my back, no matter what I asked. I do hope I can count on you."

She fingered the Glock on her hip and said, her voice as light as his, "You're a lamebrain, you know that? Don't worry about me. I've never backed down from a fight in my life. But we won't break laws, Nicholas. We won't become criminals to catch criminals."

54

Nicholas didn't reply. He picked up the phone and called Savich again.

"Sorry, I don't have anything for you yet."

"I have one more thing to add into the search. Our suspect walked into a Deutsche Bank in Geneva half an hour ago."

"Ah, that will help. Good work. I'll add it in, see if anything changes." They hung up, and Mike's email dinged.

"Finally," she said. "Video feed from Elaine's building is here. Why would they keep the tapes off-site? Took us forever to get it."

Nicholas sat beside her as she opened the feed on her laptop. It had been taken from the camera in the building's lobby, and the time stamp read 10:14 a.m.

They saw a tall, thin man wearing a black jacket and

slacks with a hank of white hair under a black watch cap. He walked with confidence, looking neither right nor left, but away from the camera, so they couldn't see his face. He had a key to the building's door. He let himself in, and as the heavy glass swung closed and he passed the camera, they saw the small backpack on his left shoulder.

"That's the man who attacked us in the garage, Mike, I'm sure of it."

The video fast-forwarded to 12:10 p.m. They watched the man exit. He was wearing a Yankees baseball cap now, and his jacket was apparently reversible; it was now a light gray. As he walked out the door he again tilted his face down so the camera couldn't catch any details. All they could see was a thin knife-blade nose and a small smile playing on his lips. He turned and they had a full-on shot of the lower portion of his jaw, but only for a fraction of a second, and then he strolled out of the frame. The video stopped.

Mike said, "He looks awfully happy for someone who just committed a double murder."

"He looked happy last night, too, when he was trying to kill us. Play it again."

She rewound the tape. "He's a professional. He's aware of the cameras, knows exactly what to do to avoid them. I don't know if there's enough to run him through the facial-recognition database."

"Zachery's email says they're trying." She played it again. "Who is he working for? He doesn't look Russian, does he?"

"Not really, no. Are the cameras on the street able to

capture where he goes? Does he have a car, or does he walk away?"

She scanned the email. "This is all we have. I'm sure they'll send us more if they find something else."

"Play it once more. Watch the backpack he's carrying."

She looked closely.

Nicholas said, "See, as he exits? Look how much farther down his torso the bottom of the bag is. He's carrying something heavy, something he didn't have when he went in."

"Elaine's laptop?"

"Most likely. Can you ask Gray to see if he can identify what sort of backpack it is? It may give us something."

"Nicholas, you're grasping at straws."

"It's better than nothing."

He was angry now. It was bad enough imagining what happened, but to see Elaine's murderer, a smile on his face, almost as if he were whistling, casually strut out of the building without a care in the world? It burned him. And poor Elaine had followed him out several minutes later, stumbled to the river, and fell to her death.

Mike laid her hand on his arm. "We'll get him. You know we will."

He realized his hands were fisted, and he relaxed them. "I hate being in the dark, and I don't like being played for a fool. We're still ten steps behind these buggers, and it's starting to tick me off."

55

It was nearly noon, gray and overcast, windy, no sun at all. After three hours of sitting here watching Anatoly's fancy Mediterranean-style mansion, Agent Ben Houston still hadn't seen any movement—no one turning on lights against the gloom, no one coming out to get the paper, walk a dog, drive somewhere, nothing, which meant Anatoly still had to be at home.

He looked down at his watch. Savich and Sherlock should be here soon, and together they'd go knock on Anatoly's door, and they would question him about the stolen Sarah Elliott painting from the Prado. Ben still thought it amazing that Savich was Sarah Elliott's grandson.

Ben continued to stare at the silent house, as if willing something to happen, anything. He'd like to go in there before Savich and Sherlock got here and beat the living crap out of Anatoly, force him to tell the truth about Kochen and Elaine.

He banged his fist on the steering wheel. It didn't help thinking about Elaine. Rules were rules; the law was the law.

He wondered what Mike and that dude from Scotland Yard were doing. Ben had thought Nicholas Drummond smart enough, but he took chances, and Ben bet he'd cut corners when one got in his way. At least he'd defused the bomb in the exhibit room—talk about a big chance. He sighed. They did have one thing in common: Elaine York. Ben felt the familiar pain settle in his belly.

He was bored with this view. He started up the Crown Vic and moved a block north, which gave him a clear shot of three sides of the house, and settled back in to watch and wait for Savich and Sherlock. His cell rang. It was Sherlock. They'd been held up another thirty minutes.

Ben tapped his fingers on the steering wheel. He knew two of the seven sons lived with Anatoly. No mother, no wives, no children. Only the three grown-ups, all bad to the bone. He wouldn't want to play poker with them. He couldn't imagine them being good losers. Actually, he wouldn't want to eat breakfast with them, either.

And that made Ben realize he was hungry. The bagel he'd inhaled for breakfast was long gone. He'd seen a pizza place as he'd come in, Papa Leone's. A pepperoni sounded good. After their meeting with Anatoly, maybe he could talk Savich and Sherlock into a slice.

One more drive by, Ben decided, and started up his

Crown Vic. He drove slowly by the Anatoly mansion, and lo and behold—he saw the front door wasn't closed.

Why hadn't he noticed before? Because something had happened, something he hadn't seen. Adrenaline poured through him. He wasn't about to wait now. But no way was he going to approach the house by himself, not after Anatoly had looked at him last night like *Wouldn't you look good without a face?* And Anatoly would be glad to oblige.

No time to wait for Savich and Sherlock, no time to call in other FBI agents. Instead he called the Brighton precinct. Three minutes later, a blue-and-white NYPD cruiser sharked around the corner, two more cruisers in its wake. These boys knew whose house this was.

Ben waved at them as they slowly pulled to the curb. A sergeant approached him, an older guy, going bald and sporting a growing paunch. His nameplate read *F. Horace.*

"What's the problem, sir?"

Ben stuck his creds in his face. "Special Agent Ben Houston, FBI. I had a chat with Mr. Anatoly last night down at Federal Plaza. I'm expecting two other agents, but not for maybe twenty more minutes, and I didn't want to wait." He pointed to Anatoly's front door. "It's open, but I haven't seen anybody go in or out for the past three hours."

"And you're wondering why Mr. Anatoly would leave his front door open. Gotta say, I'm wondering, too. Let's go check this out," and Horace opened the snap over his Glock. He waved to the other officers, telling them to stay outside, wait for the two FBI agents that were expected, and keep their eyes open. Then they set off.

Ben pushed, and the front door swung in easily.

He stopped cold. Not good, not good. "Smell that?"

"Blood," Sergeant Horace said, all humor gone. "I don't like this, I really don't." He laid a beefy hand on Ben's shoulder. "Listen to me now, Agent Houston, in case no one taught you, be sure to walk carefully. We don't want to disturb any evidence, okay?"

Ben didn't know where the manic grin came from. "Thanks for the wise words, Sarge. I'll be extra careful."

Horace's gruff laugh was his only reply.

The two men walked, guns drawn at the ready, through a vast entrance hall decorated to the hilt with what looked to Ben to be Italian antiques. They followed their noses and stopped cold when they reached the huge vaulted kitchen, modern, shiny, pristine except for the three bodies pressed together in the middle of the kitchen floor, hands tied behind their backs. Two had fallen forward, one canted over as if he were sharing a secret with the man next to him. They'd all been shot in the back of the head, execution-style.

Sergeant Horace keyed the mike on his shoulder. "We need the crime scene unit and an ME out to Anatoly's place. Triple homicide." He turned back to Ben. "We gotta clear the house. Step careful."

As Horace cleared the bottom floor, Ben went up the stairs, Glock steady in his hand.

In the second bedroom on the right, he found another body slumped on the floor, a male Caucasian, his back against the door frame, sitting in a pool of dried blood. His eyes were open, slightly gummed over, and he was facing the bed. He was dressed in black from head to toe. His hands were cupped around a wound in his stomach. He'd taken a while to die, Ben thought, looking at all the dried blood on his clothes, black now, stiff.

This man wasn't big like the Anatolys. He had to be one of the shooters, had to be. So there were a minimum of two shooters, but his partner hadn't shown him any love. He'd left him to die, and that was cold, real cold. Ben searched the man's pockets but found no ID, no nothing.

The room itself was a mess, the bed unmade. It smelled of dirty laundry and, oddly, old toast. One of the sons' rooms, then. He pictured the shooter coming into the room, and the son was fast enough to grab up a gun and gut-shoot him.

Had the son gone downstairs then, only to end up dead on the kitchen floor? He'd had a gun, he knew something bad was going on, but it hadn't mattered. Whoever was waiting downstairs had overpowered him.

Ben methodically went through the rest of the rooms upstairs, then called down to Horace, "Upstairs is clear. Got a body, gut shot. Looks like he was part of the crew who broke in."

"A quadruple homicide? Now, ain't that something on a beautiful Friday."

Ben rejoined him in the kitchen. Horace pointed at the bodies. "That's Anatoly in the middle, and the younger ones are two of his sons. Someone was really pissed off. Nice of the killer to off them in the kitchen, no ruined carpet.

"But how the hell did he manage to get the drop on all three of these badasses? I just can't see that." They both stared down at the bodies.

Ben said, "Had to be more than one person responsible for this, had to be. Like you said, they were three very big strong men, even Anatoly."

Horace nodded. "Plus, those Anatoly sons are meaner than hungry crocodiles. Their old man used to be, but he's mellowed out, doesn't kill those who piss him off himself any longer, just gives the orders. You need to see this."

Ben followed Horace into what looked to be Anatoly's office. The room hadn't been ransacked. What looked to be an original Picasso had been gently lifted from its spot behind the huge mahogany desk and carefully placed against the wall. And there was a wall safe, the thick metal door hanging ajar.

Horace said, "There's still packs of cash, legal papers, and lookee here—half a key of coke."

Ben said, "That's weird. If they found what they came for, why leave the cash and the drugs?"

"If I was the badass who broke in here," Horace said, "I sure wouldn't have left the C and C. I wonder what they did take out of that safe?"

Ben holstered his Glock.

"No clue." He looked up to see Savich and Sherlock appear in the living room doorway.

56

Savich and Sherlock looked down at the three dead men on the kitchen floor while Ben filled them in.

"There was another body upstairs, most likely one of the killers. Whoever did this had to be big and strong and fast. These three couldn't have been easy to take down, much less forcing them to kneel and accept being shot. They were really bad news."

Sherlock dropped to her knees, studied the three faces, flesh slack and gray, eyes all open, staring at the floor. "This is really bad," she said. "Really ugly, but no anger, no rage, all business as usual, I've got to say. Very controlled. In, do the job, and out. Didn't take long."

Horace said, "Yeah, that seems right, but how? Just holding a gun on them doesn't seem like enough. And I can't see these three cooperating. No muss, no fuss, just kill us?"

Sherlock lightly touched her palm to the side of Anatoly's face. "He hasn't been dead all that long, maybe two hours, more or less, the ME will tell us." She frowned, then she sniffed. She looked up at Savich. "Dillon, guess what?"

"Busy guy," Savich said.

"What busy guy?" Horace asked. "What did you smell?"

Sherlock said, "Nothing, Sergeant. We had a cyanide case yesterday, but I don't smell it here. Ben, you know Kochen was shot with a tranquilizer gun, disabled, then murdered. He was a big guy; the killer didn't want to take any chances. I think that's what happened here, too."

Ben said, "You think this is the same guy who murdered Kochen and Elaine?"

She nodded. "Like you said, the dead men were all big, strong, and vicious, all in prime physical condition. I'd bet my next paycheck all three were unconscious before he dragged them in here, lined them up next to each other, and shot each in the back of the head." She paused for a moment. "Then he reholstered his gun, job done, and went back to take whatever it was he wanted out of the safe."

Horace said, "The killer wasn't alone. Agent Houston found another bad guy upstairs, dead, obviously shot in the gut by one of the sons."

"Then when the son came down yelling and blasting," Savich said, "the man shot him with the tranquilizer gun, dragged him into the kitchen and killed him, and arranged him with his father and brother. I wager we'll find some casings and maybe some holes in the banister or in the walls, maybe even his gun."

Sherlock said, "He didn't torture them because he knew where to find what he was looking for. He didn't need them. But why kill them? Maybe because he was told to kill them, or maybe it was simply a reward to himself for a job well done."

Ben said, "The dead guy upstairs, he bled out, and I don't think it was fast. His partner left him."

Savich said, "No, he wouldn't care at all, would he?" and he nodded to the three bodies. "Let's look at the safe again, see if we can't find a clue to what the killer wanted. And I'd like to look around to see if I can find *The Night Tower*."

Horace frowned. "What would a night tower be doing here? What is a night tower?"

Savich smiled. "My grandmother is an artist. *The Night Tower* is one of her paintings. It was stolen from the Prado in Spain. We're following a rumor that Mr. Anatoly here had it taken and replaced with a fake, but it was spotted."

Savich was leaning over to check a tattoo on the neck of one of the sons when two young men the size of linebackers ran into the kitchen, looked at the three dead men, and one of them screamed at the top of his lungs. Savich straightened, and both of them yelled curses at him and jumped. One of the men was waving a gun, the other his fists, both radiating out-of-control fury, Savich their target. Two NYPD officers came screaming in after them, guns drawn.

Time seemed to freeze. Ben saw one of the men strike Savich in the shoulder with a huge fist, sending him stumbling back against the big kitchen island. He saw the other man raise his gun, but then, in a move so fast it was a blur, Savich swung his leg up, sharp and hard, clipped the guy's hand, and sent the gun flying across the kitchen. He turned fast, leaned forward, and slammed the outside of his hand against the other man's throat. He stopped then and stared calmly at the young man who was cradling his hand, sobbing, his nose running.

It was over in less than three seconds.

Horace stared at Savich. "As my son would say, dude, that was very fine." Then he picked up the gun, clicked out the magazine, barked at his officers, who were both wild eyed and panting, "We've got it under control. Get back outside, both of you. I'll deal with you later."

He leaned over the young man who was sobbing and cradling his broken wrist. "Yuri, calm yourself down. I'm NYPD. These are FBI agents. None of us killed your father or your brothers. We found them like this. They were executed."

Yuri wiped the back of his hand across his nose, raised tear-filled eyes. His brother was still wheezing, holding his throat, trying to get up. Horace said, "You, too, Toms, get yourself together. At least Agent Savich didn't kill you."

Sherlock slowly rose. She said to the young men, both now staring blankly toward their dead father, their two dead brothers, "We're very sorry about this, Yuri, Toms. But you must steady yourselves." She nodded toward

Dillon. "This man isn't good for your continued health if you don't get a grip on yourselves. All right?"

An hour and a half later, Savich, Sherlock, and Ben stood on the front doorstep of the beautiful Italianate mansion and watched the two coroner's vans drive off down the street, three Anatolys in black body bags inside one and one of the killers in the other. Techs swarmed through the house while officers canvassed the neighborhood. Savich agreed with his wife: the same man had killed five people in a matter of days; possibly it was also the same man who'd attacked Nicholas and Mike the previous night.

"Smart guy, aren't you?" he said quietly. "And you're not new to this. I'll bet you've been at it a lot of years now." He looked up to see the sun burst out from behind the gray clouds. The wind still snapped and cut, but it was becoming a beautiful winter day.

He said to Sherlock, who'd come up to stand next to him, "The killer wasn't interested in the Picasso, merely set it against the wall by the safe. There were also two Manets, one Pissarro, and a gorgeous Berthe Morisot still hanging on the walls, all of them very valuable, and I doubt they were stolen. Nor was he interested in the cash or the cocaine. And we have no clue what he was after. Did you think he found what he wanted?"

"Yes," she said, "I have a strong feeling he did. He didn't take the other goodies because he's the consummate professional, a very well-paid consummate professional."

Savich said as he pulled up his coat collar, "No sign of *The Night Tower*. I wonder if we'll ever find grandmother's painting now?"

Sherlock didn't think so, but she said nothing.

Two hours later, Savich and Sherlock accompanied Louisa and a forensic team to Anatoly's Midtown office because, Savich told her later, he'd simply had this feeling.

He found a small hidden room off Anatoly's office. The room was climate controlled, the lighting perfect. In the center of the room sat a comfortable armchair. Twelve paintings were beautifully hung on the white walls. One of the paintings was his grandmother's *The Night Tower*.

57

True to his word, Agent Pierre Menard met them on the tarmac at Geneva International. He was a short, neat man with graying temples, wearing a beautiful charcoal three-piece suit.

Some bulldog, Nicholas thought. Well, they'd soon see.

He bustled them into a white Toyota Land Cruiser with POLICE stenciled in blue on the side and bright orange stripes around the back, and started into the city.

Nicholas hadn't been to Geneva in several years, but the city hadn't changed. The architecture was eclectic—hypermodern buildings mixed in with classic French and medieval churches, side by side. The city still housed the world's finest watchmakers, with twenty-foot-high signs clinging to the sides of the buildings. Rolex. Patek Philippe. Montblanc. Hermès. Every luxury a discerning shopper could need was headquartered and built here in the city of time.

Mike watched the scenery flow by, entranced by the modern glass buildings and huge parks buttressed by neoclassic lines. It was her first time in Europe, and she felt straight off the boat, stepping onto a strange shore.

Menard wasn't much of a talker, though his English was quite excellent. Nicholas wanted details, but Menard shook his head. "I am sorry, Inspector Drummond. All I know is what we have already spoken of. We are going directly to the bank. When there is news of a sighting on the cameras, they will call. Who is this woman you're chasing?"

"The Fox."

The name perked him up. "The art thief? *Mon dieu.* No wonder you are here. The Fox is a legend. But you say he is a she?"

"Yes. Tell us what you know about her."

He was driving with his right hand, the left hand hovering by the edge of the window, two fingers together as if he normally smoked and flicked the ashes out of the crack. "There are many warrants, of course, across several countries. She steals very valuable paintings both from private collections and museums, does not matter which. But she is also known for stealing very valuable jewels, some priceless, like the Koh-i-Noor. We have never managed to track her down, of course, because she is very good."

Mike said, "You admire her. Why does everyone admire her so much? She's a common thief."

Menard shook his head. "*Non*, she is an uncommon *voleuse de bijoux*. To be a jewel thief of this magnitude, never identified, hunted for so long, but never caught? The Fox is *magnifique*. And to think, she is a woman." He grunted a very French sounding, "Huh."

"I plan to put the handcuffs on her myself," Mike said.

Menard mumbled something she thought was "Good luck," and she shot Nicholas a look. He shrugged and rolled his eyes.

Menard said, "You will see the Koh-i-Noor theft is dominating all the news channels. It is pervasive, even to the villages in the Pyrenees. The FBI is being given big pokes in the eye, yes?"

"Yes," Mike said. Menard didn't sound all that upset about it.

"I have even read blogs about the theft, although the idiots writing the blogs are writing fiction, since they could not possibly know exactly what happened. Your British news stations are foaming at the mouth. Ah, it is a terrible thing, is it not?"

Nicholas only nodded. "Has the Fox ever been accused of killing people for money, or does she only steal?"

Menard again flicked his fingers out of habit. "I remember a rumor of an assassination—maybe ten, fifteen years ago—some Italian gun manufacturer near Milan, but there was nothing proven. It remains an unsolved case, and I have not heard of anything since. And now she has stolen the Koh-i-Noor."

He sounded so intrigued, Mike wanted to punch him.

Menard continued. "The media is also playing up many

nefarious plots regarding your British Inspector York's role in the theft."

Nicholas's voice was cold. "The Fox might be involved in her murder."

"I must say this surprises me. Ah, we arrive."

Mike could see Lake Geneva ahead, and the huge water plume called the Jet d'Eau. The promenade was lined with people, ignoring the chill, enjoying the show. She got out of the car, checked her weapon on her hip. This wasn't exactly how she'd always dreamed of visiting Europe.

Despite the shining sun, a cold breeze whistled through the city. Nicholas turned up the collar of his coat and looked at Mike, shivering in her leather jacket.

Menard said, "The wind is brutal today. You should see when the waves form on the lake and the water splashes over onto the streets. We are lucky, this is a warm winter."

Mike shivered. "You're saying it could be worse?"

Nicholas laughed. "What, and you a New Yorker? I thought your blood was thicker than this." But he moved to shelter her from the worst of the wind. "It's momentary; we're going to have to cross the street to get into the bank. Yell when you're ready."

Menard had already started across. "Nicholas, you speak French, right?" Mike asked.

"Well enough. Geneva is trilingual—French, German, and Italian are all the official language—but everyone speaks English. You won't have any trouble getting around, I promise."

"Good. Because I doubt my high school French will

do more than get us to the bathroom successfully. I'm ready now. Let's go."

They dashed across the Quai des Bergues, the wind cutting at their heels. Once inside the Deutsche Bank, Mike took a second to warm her face with her hands.

They were greeted by the bank manager, a short, rotund man with merry eyes and lovely white teeth.

"*Bonsoir*, mademoiselle, messieurs. You are the FBI the Cantonal Police told me to expect?" His pleasant manner made her think he'd been warned to make nice.

"I'm Detective Chief Inspector Drummond, and this is Special Agent Caine."

"And I am Agent Pierre Menard, with FedPol. We require your assistance."

"I am Tivoli, and I will do all within my power to help. How may I assist you?"

Nicholas handed Tivoli a picture. "Have you seen this woman? She came to the bank earlier today."

He glanced at the photograph and shook his head. "No, monsieur, I have not."

"Are you sure? Look again. She may have asked to access the security boxes. Her hair would be short and black, not long and brown."

Tivoli's eyes lingered on the photograph, but he shook his head. "I am most sure, monsieur. It has been a busy day. One of my men is out sick, thus it is I who have been handling the vault today. I would remember her. We sent our videotape to the police when they called, but I also checked the tapes from the time frame, and saw no one who matched her description. I am sorry."

Nicholas said, "Thank you, Monsieur Tivoli. We appreciate your help."

They stopped in the lobby next to the scrolled front doors.

Mike said, "Now what?"

Nicholas ran his hand over his chin. "The Fox isn't stupid. She would have taken precautions, made sure if she had a tail, she could lose them. Driving up to the Deutsche Bank in broad daylight, plain as you please, was a bold move. It was also a brilliant stroke of camouflage. She came in here"—he pointed toward the other end of the lobby—"and she probably walked right on through. We have the police looking at the wrong tapes."

Menard agreed. "I will ask for more surveillance video to be examined. To come to a bank first—it seems an odd thing to do."

Mike said, "We were thinking she might be here to accept payment for the theft, but you're right, it could all be a smoke screen. We can't even be positive she's still in Geneva."

"I was told the pilot of her plane said she sent him skiing, and would meet him in twenty-four hours. Do you believe she meant to keep this appointment?"

"Yes, why not?"

Menard said, "Then she must still be in the city. We will find her. Come. Let us get a hot drink, and I will call for a deeper search."

58

Menard knew exactly who to call and, better yet, where to go. Within ten minutes they were inside a small café drinking steaming espressos, waiting on news about additional footage from the cameras around the Deutsche Bank. Mike was grateful for the warmth; the wind off the lake had her chilled through. Nicholas, Mr. Aren't I Great, seemed unaffected.

He asked Menard, "Are you an expert on art crimes?"

"I am."

"We are narrowing down a list of people who could afford to bankroll a theft of this magnitude. Let me ask you, in your experience, why would anyone steal the Koh-i-Noor? It's one of the most famous pieces in the world, so they couldn't resell it. It couldn't be displayed without running the risk of someone telling the authorities. The buyer would surely know the British will never stop hunting for it. So why this stone?"

Menard tossed back his espresso in one gulp, and Mike stared. The coffee was steaming hot; his throat must be made of asbestos. He set the tiny cup on the counter so he could use his hands to help him speak. A very expressive man, Menard, and smart, she thought, very smart, and very committed. They'd lucked out. She was wondering when he was going to make it clear he really liked her, the American, best.

"You must think of art theft this way: there are usually three possibilities. In this case, for this particular diamond, and similar pieces which have such a strong historical path, there are four."

He raised his hand and started ticking the list off on his fingers.

"One, to sell it. Then you are dealing with a profiteer, and they have no style, no panache. It is simply a transaction, and it is most likely already gone, out of your reach. Two, if it was taken to return it to its rightful owners. Then you're looking for a zealot, who is very dangerous, for he will try to kill anyone who gets in his way. Three, for the prestige of having such a piece. A collector, then, who will be the hardest of all to trace, because he will quietly hold on to his prize and never share it with the world."

"And the fourth?" Nicholas asked.

Menard's face grew grim. "A man who has stolen the diamond because of the legend attached. This man would be unpredictable, dangerous, a man who would destroy the diamond before he gives it up."

Mike said, "Which do you think we're dealing with?"

Menard splayed his hands. "I do not know, mademoiselle, but we shall hope it is not the fourth, yes?"

Nicholas sipped his espresso, hot as fire, thick as tar, delicious. "Have you heard of the Fox working with someone?"

"No. Never. My understanding is that he—she—always works alone."

Nicholas said, "She made two calls to the same number while she was flying from America to Europe. Neither was answered. Mike's government is running the number, and we should know soon who it belongs to."

"I am sorry. I have never heard of her working with anyone."

"What about against someone? Who is her competition?"

Menard nodded vigorously, signaling to the barman for another shot of espresso. "Ah, this I can answer for you. There are three: a Frenchman from Algiers, dead now. He was shot by a security guard in a botched attempt on the Tate Modern and bled to death on the floor. He was called Goyo. The second is Ruvéne—he successfully lifted three Cézannes for the Russian government and was caught two years ago near Prague. He is in jail for life.

"The third is the Ghost. He has been in business far longer than anyone else I know of. No one knows his nationality, but he takes only the biggest jobs, the most prestigious, the most challenging and dangerous. He has either retired or died, for his name and his signature have not been seen in over ten years."

Mike asked, "What was the Ghost's signature?"

"Explosives. They were used as insurance. He would wire the place and leave a small warning note behind. If he was allowed to steal away, he would not blow up the rest of the museum, or the house, or wherever else he had taken his prize from. After twenty-four hours, the clocks on the bombs ran out, and they were deactivated. Crude but effective. He always got away."

Nicholas felt his adrenaline spike. He looked at Mike. "Sound familiar? Menard, the Fox wired the *Jewel of the Lion* exhibit to blow. I was able to defuse the bomb before she followed through."

Menard pursed his lips. "Very interesting. A nod to the great one, perhaps, or simple coincidence?"

"I don't know. Do Interpol or FedPol have a physical description of the Ghost?"

"The jacket on the Ghost contains an anecdote someone told an interviewer at one time. The man saw a ghost when he was a child, and it turned his hair stark white. This is all we know about him."

Mike and Nicholas both sat up straighter.

"This means something to you?"

"Yes, it does." Mike loaded the video and pushed her laptop across the table. "We received this feed today, from the scene of Inspector Elaine York's murder." She hit play.

Menard watched with interest. "A man with white hair."

"Could it be the Ghost?" Nicholas asked.

He shrugged. "I don't know why not. Send the feed to me, I will load it into the FedPol database. Perhaps there will be something to match it to."

Mike did, and Nicholas said, "One more thing. This man was probably one of two men sent to kill Agent Caine and me last night in her underground garage. We fought them off, and one was killed. This one"—he tapped the screen—"got away. I saw white hair sticking out of his ski mask. He was tough, and fast, a martial-arts master."

Menard was getting excited. "So the Ghost could still be with us? But why was he in New York, and why attack you, and Inspector York? He wasn't involved in the Koh-i-Noor theft, was he?"

"Maybe," Mike said, "the Ghost is her partner and guarded her back."

Nicholas said, "I'll email Zachery and Savich, give them this additional information."

Menard's mobile rang while Nicholas sent the email. He listened, then a smile broke out on his face. He hung up and said, "Let's go."

Nicholas typed in a couple more words, then jumped to his feet. "You found her?"

"We found where she was two hours ago. Bank Horim. It is across the way."

59

ank Horim was a block and a half down the street, along the lake. They hurried, Nicholas restraining himself from breaking out in a sprint. They were closing in, he could feel it. Could feel the Fox nearby like she was giving off a scent.

Sirens began to wail. A cop car drew closer, summoned by Menard.

Menard had short legs and a smoker's lungs; he was puffing to keep up. "Swiss banking is a global business. Horim is very private, very discreet, has branches in Zurich, Geneva, Luxembourg, and Singapore, and offices in Russia, Hong Kong, and Israel." He had to stop to catch his breath. "I hope they are as helpful as Monsieur Tivoli at Deutsche Bank." But he sounded doubtful.

They entered the building and asked for the manager. They were shown into a small glass office, and were quickly joined by a tall older woman wearing a sleek black suit. Her strawberry-blond hair was cut in an elegant bob. She didn't smile, but she did nod to each in turn as they showed her their creds. She said in a lilting accent, "I am Marie-Louise Helmut. What can I help you with?"

Menard said, "Madame Helmut, we are looking for a woman who came into the bank two hours ago. We need to know what business she had here." Nicholas showed her Browning's photo.

She said, in a formal voice, "Assuming I've seen this person, you know I cannot share this information with you. We have the strictest privacy policies to protect our customers. Without the proper papers, I will not be able to speak to you."

Nicholas took a step toward her, aggressive as a wolf. Helmut immediately recoiled, obviously alarmed.

Mike saw the look on his face and the way he readied himself, but when he spoke, his voice was very quiet. "This is a matter of the utmost urgency, madame. Look again."

Despite being wary of him, Helmut stared him down. "We need the appropriate paperwork."

"Hold on." Menard whipped out his mobile and made a call to the local police. "This is Menard. I am at Bank Horim. We need armed men at the entrances. In case our suspect returns."

He hung up and smiled pleasantly at Helmut. He handed her a card. "If you change your mind about cooperating, call. Otherwise, it is going to look like a siege in here until the warrants are executed. And you will not get any banking done because we are going to interview everyone who was in the building, all morning long."

"See here, Monsieur Menard, there is no call to be this way. I am bound by our privacy laws—"

Nicholas shoved the photograph in front of her face. "What did she do while she was here? Tell us now or you're going to be tied up for weeks with regulatory checks on each of your accounts. Your bank participates in the International Anti-Money Laundering and Terrorism Acts. We have the right to discovery on your clients, the money you move, everything. And we'll spend all the time we need being very, very thorough."

She looked like she wanted very much to shoot them but couldn't. So she said, "She did no business with us. She simply asked for directions."

Nicholas said, "Stop wasting our time."

"It is true. She did no banking."

Mike stepped in. "This is a matter of life and death. This woman is a fugitive; she is extremely dangerous. We need to know what she was doing here."

Helmut closed her eyes for a moment. A small frown crossed her face, then her shoulders straightened, her decision made. "The lady in the photograph inquired about the purchase of a safe-deposit box. I informed her there was a waiting list of over two years for the security section." She looked down her nose. "We don't do 'walk-ins,' as you like to say. She was very upset. I sent her to Sages Fidelité, on Place de Chevaleux. They perform a similar service without the wait. Or the security, but this did not seem to matter. She was quite urgent about it."

She gestured toward the door. "This is all I know. Please, I must return to my work."

Nicholas was vibrating with anger. "After all that, you mean to say you've been stalling us over a matter of directions?"

Helmut crossed her arms over her chest. "I am protecting my bank and my clients. I would prefer for you to leave now."

Menard said, "Not yet, Madame Helmut. My officers are on their way. You will understand we cannot take your word for it. We will need your video feeds for the day."

Mike's phone dinged with a new text message. She looked at it and breathed in hard. Nicholas looked over at her.

"What is it?"

"Mr. Menard, Ms. Helmut, please excuse us for a moment."

Menard nodded at them and stayed to face off with Marie-Louise Helmut. Mike walked out onto the street, Nicholas behind her.

"What is so important that you'd pull me away from a suspect in the middle of an interrogation?"

She merely showed him the message from Ben.

Nicholas read it aloud. "Andrei Anatoly and two of his sons are dead. Call me when you can. Savich has news for you, too."

Menard joined them.

"She is lying through her teeth but is handing over the video feeds. What has happened?"

"News on another facet of the case, in New York,"

Mike said, "and it's a doozy. One of our initial suspects has been murdered. A mobster named Andrei Anatoly. Heard of him?"

"I do not know this name. What would you like to do?"

Nicholas said, "Tell us about Sages Fidelité."

"They are much less intransient. They would do business with a rhinoceros, should it have the right amount of money. I must stay here and gather the video. You should take a taxicab, they are a long walk from here."

A cab pulled over at nearly the same time Menard raised his hand. Nicholas said, "We'll be back as soon as we find anything."

The moment she saw the three police officers walk away from the front of the bank, Marie-Louise Helmut calmly picked up the phone.

60

Mike called Ben from the cab as they raced through the streets of Geneva, put him on speaker so Nicholas could hear.

"Hey, Mike. Good timing."

"What in the world is happening there?"

"Other than I'm up to my butt in dead mobsters and wished I had a beer, nothing much."

"Ben, quit being funny and tell me what happened."

He did, then said, "Sherlock thinks it's the same guy who killed Kochen and Elaine. He could also be the guy who attacked you and Nicholas last night in the garage. As for his dead partner, he simply left him to bleed out. Savich thinks he found what he wanted.

"Two more sons, Yuri and Toms, came in, saw their father and two brothers dead, and attacked straight off.

Savich put them both down, neat as you please. So far no one in the neighborhood saw anything.

"Now, back to the Fox. The bomb boys have a signature on the C-4 explosive from the Met exhibit. It's out of Tunisia. They're looking to compare it to the explosive used on Anatoly's safe. No tests yet, but they think it's the same.

"Neither Yuri or Toms Anatoly know what was in the safe. There are three more sons. We've called them to come in and talk to us. Paulie and Louisa are tearing the place apart, but so far, nothing you wouldn't expect in a huge house like this one."

Nicholas said, "Ben, we have a tentative ID on the man with white hair—we think he's another master thief called the Ghost. Could be he's partnered up with Browning. We don't know exactly how he ties in to the theft of the Koh-i-Noor, but he does."

Ben whistled. "Lot of coincidences piling up. And you know how we feel about coincidences."

"There aren't any. You got anything else, Ben?" Mike asked.

"Yeah, one other thing. We got a warrant in, and I tracked Elaine's funds. She paid Kochen three equal installments of five thousand dollars apiece."

Nicholas said, "Any indication why she paid him this money?"

"No. You guys watch your backs, okay? There's some bad people around."

"We will. Call me if you find anything else."

She punched off her cell and turned to Nicholas. "Ben's right. Talk about a case twisting in on itself."

She saw his expression was remote. When he replied, his voice was distant. "So Elaine *was* paying Kochen."

She lightly touched his arm. "I'm sorry."

He shook himself. "Doesn't mean she's guilty of anything yet, Mike."

The cabdriver slowed, slid to the curb, and grunted at them, "Three euros."

Nicholas handed the money through the slot. "Here's our stop. Let's go see what the Fox was up to, and maybe things will begin to make sense."

61

Saleem was eight when his father took him to visit his grandfather one last time before the old man was expected to die. At his request, Saleem was left alone in the study for an audience with the dying Lion.

The fire was the only light in the room. His grandfather's chair sat squarely before the fire, close enough for the old man to warm his bones. There was nothing wrong with his hearing. The moment the servants softly closed the door behind them, he commanded, "Come here to me, boy."

Saleem edged forward. His grandfather had changed so much since their last visit. The man who'd held him on his knee and hugged him close was gone, replaced by this ancient gray thing sitting too close to the fire.

He knew his grandfather was very sick, and suddenly

Saleem was scared of him. He smelled wrong, and his eyebrows were thick, like hairy caterpillars, with stray hairs growing out like feelers.

When he was within a few feet, his grandfather's arm snaked out and grabbed him, pulling him close. The musty smell of death overwhelmed him, and Saleem coughed.

"I need to tell you a story, Saleem. I am dying. It is important for you to know what this means."

"Why are you dying, Grandfather?"

"My heart is broken, young Saleem. It has a hole that cannot be fixed. So it slows and doesn't push the blood through my body. Feel how cold my hands are, how blue my nails."

He touched the boy's forehead, and Saleem jumped. It was like setting a large cube of ice against his skin.

"Shall I add more wood to the fire, then? Will it help warm you?"

The old man shook his shaggy head. "It will not work. Now listen to me, and listen well. You are about to be given a secret so important you can never share it with another soul. Do you understand what I mean when I say a secret?"

"I can't tell anyone, or I'll die."

A spark of humor showed in the old man's eyes, and Saleem briefly saw the man he remembered, peeking out from the gathering black. He smiled, pleased to make his grandfather happy, and said, "Tell me, Grandfather. I will never tell a soul."

"Good, Saleem, good. I must whisper these words to you. Come closer."

Saleem bent his head, and his grandfather spoke, his old-man breath foul and hot on his face. "You are of a long line of men whose one job in this life is to guard a most ancient and valuable secret. See the box on the table there? Fetch it to me."

The rosewood box was small and brown, with an intricate lock. "Where is the key, Grandfather?"

"I will show you. Bring me the box and the small knife lying beside it."

Saleem did as he was asked. His grandfather took the box in one feeble hand, set it on his lap. His fingers were gnarled, but he cut his thumb surely with the ivory-handled knife. The blood welled from the wound, and instead of wiping it away, he laid his thumb against the latch of the box. Saleem heard a deep clicking noise, and the latch sprang free.

His voice shook. "Blood? Blood opens the box?"

His grandfather smiled. "Not any blood, Saleem. Our blood. The blood of the Lion. We are the descendants of the Lion of Punjab, and it is our line which was given this great gift. We, and we alone, are the guardians of the stone."

He lifted the top of the box, and within lay a crystal-clear rock, slightly misshapen, not quite an oval, and the size of his grandfather's fist. It didn't look grand or exciting, and Saleem was disappointed.

"This is your destiny, Saleem. It is one part of the most

ancient diamond in the world. Once, our ancestors possessed a great stone, given to Krishna himself by Surya, the sun god. He who owned the stone had the power of the world in his hands. This power could not be bought, it could only be given, or"—his voice hardened—"taken by force."

He took the stone from the box, held it up. The flames reflected off the diamond, and Saleem looked into its depth. He could swear he saw marauders riding horses, heard their screams as the dust rose beneath their hooves, heard the steel swords clashing and clanging.

Saleem jumped back, but his grandfather's hand was hard on his arm, and he pulled him close again. He smiled. "The stone speaks to you, Saleem, for you are the rightful descendant.

"Look. Now you will see the effect it has on me. Holding the stone makes me young again, heals my broken heart."

Saleem stared. Gone was the old man, and in his place was another, younger man bursting with health.

"Grandfather, what has happened?"

His grandfather didn't answer him. He set the stone back in the box, and the din died down. The latch clicked shut of its own accord.

Then he said, "Without its brothers, it won't heal me for more than a moment." Saleem watched him drain of life again and become once more gray and slack and smell of death.

"This is only one piece of the original stone. The most secret piece, one no one knows of except the carriers of the stone's blood. You are a carrier, Saleem, and with my death, it falls to your father, and to you. You must fulfill your destiny, Saleem. You must unite the three stones."

"If you had the three stones, Grandfather, would you be well and young again? Would you never die?"

"Do not think like that, Saleem. Each man's life must have a beginning and an end."

62

Young Saleem was confused. "I don't understand, Grandfather."

"I mean a man should not extend his life through magic. Let me tell you the story of the three stones." The old man took a sip of his tea. "The original diamond was cleaved in two by our ancestor, Emperor Aurangzeb. He owned the stone, as his father and grandfather had before him. Word spread of the stone's value, and it became known throughout the lands. It was written that the stone's value could sustain the world for two days. The entire world, not only a small part of it, Saleem. You realize what this means? If you held the stone, you would be seen as a god, and so he was.

"Holding the stone also gave Aurangzeb the sight. He knew what was coming, knew his kingdom would be ransacked, his diamond stolen from him, and the lands would fall to strangers and he would not be able to prevent it. He came up with a plan. He engaged the Italian lapidary Borgio to cut the stone, ostensibly so that it would be made more beautiful and be remarked upon by all with more envy and awe.

"Publicly, it was said that Borgio mangled the job, taking the incredible seven-hundred-and-ninety-three-carat diamond down to a mere hundred eighty-six carats. Despite the huge mistake, Aurangzeb displayed this smaller stone for the world's amazement.

"Privately, however, Borgio had been instructed to cleave the stone into two parts. Aurangzeb kept the larger piece for himself. He placed it in a small rosewood box for his descendants and hid it until he was dying and told his son, and so it passed from generation to generation."

He tapped a long finger on the rosewood box on the table.

"Later, when the British stole the smaller stone, now called the Koh-i-Noor, from Duleep Singh, your great-great-great-grandfather, they cut it further still, to make it pretty for the paltry British.

"Hear me well, young Saleem. The stone cannot be destroyed. And the dust from this final cut was gathered into a bag, and overnight, it healed itself, and thus became the third brother."

The old man coughed, and Saleem gave him more tea, wiped his chin. He sank back in his chair, his voice growing softer and farther away.

"Not only will it forever heal itself, it will heal man, as well." He pointed at the box. "This is only one piece of the original stone, the largest, as I've told you. You must find the other two and unite them. If you cannot, it is your sacred duty to pass this piece of the precious diamond and the truth behind it to your son, so he may continue the quest. Why have I told you, instead of waiting for your father to pass the legend along?" His grandfather smiled, a funny smile that made Saleem want to laugh. "I do not believe in chance, Saleem. I believe in redundancy. Now both descendants know. It is safest, I think."

Saleem was very quiet. He was confused and upset. All this talk of stones and death and healing, he did not know what to make of it. His grandfather was a very old man; perhaps he was raving mad. He did not understand this redundancy.

Saleem tried to pull his arm away from his grandfather's clawed grasp, but the old man held tighter.

"The diamond's prophecy, Saleem. You must remember the prophecy. The world only knows part of it, the curse of the Koh-i-Noor:

> *"He who owns this diamond will own the world,*
> *but will also know all its misfortunes.*
> *Only God, or a woman, can wear it with impunity.*

"Only our family knows the second part of the prophecy. This is our secret:

"When Krishna's stone is unbroken again,
the hand which holds it becomes whole.
Wash the Mountain of Light in woman's blood,
so we will know rebirth and rejoice."

Saleem would say anything to get away now. "I will remember."

His grandfather's voice strengthened, echoed throughout the room. "The stone gifted to our people by Surya through Krishna is in three pieces. The largest piece you've now seen for the first time. The second piece resides in the Tower of London, stolen by the British marauders who knew not the true power of the stone. And the third piece, the reassembled parts from the cut Koh-i-Noor, disappeared in 1852, when Queen Victoria had the stone recut to please her people. You and your father must find the two stones and bring them home, and reunite the three stones together again."

He fell back against the velvet chair, exhausted. His eyes closed, and Saleem wanted desperately to run from the room.

Yet he wanted to touch the gleaming stone again, hear the shouts and the screams, feel the power and the excitement.

The stone had spoken to him. He had heard its voice.

Saleem's hand crept toward the box, and his grandfather's eyes shot open. His voice was strong and clear.

"This is your destiny, Saleem. Your life will be consumed by this quest, as it consumed me and now consumes your father. Know this: all before you have failed. But if you do succeed, Saleem, you must see the stone home."

"Home?"

"Back to India, to the Kollur mine. You must unite the stones and throw the diamond back into the earth, in its proper place. If you do so, our land will rise again and prosper, using its strength to make the soil strong. You will be recognized as a hero, as the one who restored us to our appropriate place of strength in the world."

He hugged the boy to his chest.

"May luck be with you always, Saleem."

The following day, Saleem's father took him aside in the gardens.

"You were given your duty?"

"Yes, Papa."

"Do you understand what it means, Saleem?"

He shook his head. "No, Papa."

Robert Lanighan sat on a stone bench, beckoned his only son to sit beside him.

"When I was your age, your grandfather told me the story of the lost stones. I too did not understand the significance of this task. You are very young, Saleem, but it is time for you to be strong, like me."

He'd roared then, like a lion, making young Saleem giggle.

"You try."

Saleem roared and roared, stomping around the

gardens until his father was bent over in laughter. This happiness felt better. Saleem liked to see his father laugh.

He drew him close, into a hug. "Your grandfather died last night, an hour after he passed along the legacy to you. You must always keep him close, Saleem, in your heart. His love, and mine, will keep you pure. You are now a man of the Lanighan family. We will carry on where your grandfather left off. Somehow, we must find the missing stone and take back the Koh-i-Noor from the British. We must unite the three stones.

"One last thing, Saleem. There can be no personal gain from this quest. Always remember your role, your duty. No man himself may hold the power of the united stones. It will cause madness and despair. Only the land is capable of sheltering the diamond. If I do not succeed, and you do, you must swear to me you will see the diamond home."

"I swear it, Father."

And he meant every word, when he was eight years old.

Years later, when his father had fallen ill, he became frantic to obtain the two missing pieces. He commissioned thieves to steal the Koh-i-Noor from the Tower of London, but they failed again and again, until the British began to suspect who was behind it. Nor could he ever find the part of the diamond that reassembled itself after Queen Victoria's final cut. He sent Saleem across the globe following dead leads, but the third stone always remained hidden.

At the end, when it was clear he wasn't going to survive, he bade Saleem come to the hospital. Fragile from his illness, his skin paper white, he took Saleem's hand in his.

"My son. I have failed. My failure means my death. I have no more time. You must dedicate yourself to the search. You know the power of the stones, and you will need it. I tell you now, bring them together and heal yourself."

"I am fine, Father. I haven't been sick since I was a boy."

His father shook his head, pain flooding his eyes.

"You are not sick now, but you will be, for I have seen it. Find the third stone, Saleem, liberate the Koh-i-Noor from the British, and unite them. Only then will you save your own life."

63

Kitsune walked northwest through the city until she spied an anonymous street that backed to an elementary school. She followed the Rue de la Navigation, through the turnstiles that accessed the walkway, stopping cars from interrupting the children at play in their schoolyard, then up a quiet one-way street.

She took a room at the Hotel Kipling, stashed her bag in the room's safe, showered and dressed, then went next door to the Lord Jim Pub on Rue de Lausanne to have some food before the meeting with Lanighan. It was an English-style pub, full of afternoon revelers drinking microbrews and shouting their drunken opinions at a football match playing on all of the bar's big-screen televisions. She ordered bangers and mash and wondered, as she had many times, if this would be her last meal. She saw Grant's face and forced away the sadness and regret.

The food arrived. She forked warm mashed potatoes into her mouth, savoring the salty onion gravy, as authentically British as any she'd had near the River Thames.

She ate slowly, enjoying the meal.

Part of her preparation to steal the Koh-i-Noor diamond was to become an expert, to learn every single aspect of its storied history, even the lore. Especially the lore. She'd found deeper legends, ones she'd only half believed, rarely spoken of, long forgotten in the stone's tragic path through documented history.

During her studies, she'd come across an old parchment that posed the idea of the three stones. When she'd read it, she'd shaken her head and dismissed the idea as absurd, possibly the result of an opium dream. Now she worked to recall the story, picking over the words to find the truth behind them.

According to the parchments, Sultan Aurangzeb was a visionary. He knew others would kill him for the diamond. To be safe, he had Borgio split the stone in two, and while publicly parading the smaller stone known as the Koh-i-Noor, he'd secreted the much larger stone in a place no one knew.

Over the centuries, this secret was passed down from father to son. While the Koh-i-Noor was fought over, bled over, stolen, and retrieved at the cost of hundreds of lives, the larger piece was kept hidden, safe, its whereabouts passed down from generation to generation.

The parchment claimed a long-ago prince's son was born blind, and when the father pressed the stone to the child's forehead, his sight was restored. If the stone could heal—but that was ridiculous.

Could Saleem actually believe this?

Three hundred and fifteen years later, according to the parchment, when Prince Albert had Coster cut the diamond down further, the dust was collected, placed in a velvet bag, and stowed in a safe to be used to edge a skaif to cut more diamonds. This was the normal course of things; any time a diamond was cut, the dust was collected and recycled.

The next day, when the bag was retrieved to be put into service, the young lapidary who picked it up felt something bulky within. The parchment claimed that the diamond dust had reformed into a small stone. Shaken, the fellow shared the story with his wife and fled to Germany to put the stone in his family's safe. He was found dead on the train to Berlin, his body stripped of its treasure.

And so the third and final piece of the diamond was lost to history forever.

Three stones. A legend only the most dedicated fans of the Koh-i-Noor even knew existed. To hold the three stones in your hand was to have the power of ten thousand men. Its measure was greater than gold, and the man who owned such power would control his destiny, and the destinies of many others.

The curse, though—she had to believe it was real. Every man who'd believed himself lord and steward over the Koh-i-Noor met with a bad end. Only God or a woman could wield the power properly, that part of the warning was quite clear.

Legends. Stories meant to entertain men, to educate, to foster a desire to hunt treasures long lost to the mortal world.

One stone, cleaved into three pieces. One piece, now in her possession, sought after by a man who clearly believed in the magic of merging the three stones.

If the fragments of stories Saleem's father had shared with her were true, his family had held the largest piece of the diamond for more than four centuries.

Kitsune knew where the third piece was hidden, because Mulvaney had told her.

Only a true descendant of the original Indian line would have the power to unite the stones.

Kitsune shook her head. She knew what the prophecy foretold, but it all seemed too incredible to believe.

She paid her bill and checked her watch. It was time to meet with Lanighan, then leave her old life behind forever.

64

Geneva, Switzerland
Hotel Beau-Rivage
Friday, early evening

One conversation thirty years ago had set him on an exhausting path. *Unite the stones, and it will heal man.*

To hell with man.

From his sixteenth year, Saleem wanted the god's diamond, not for India but for himself. Saleem's father had been right. Saleem needed the stones united to heal himself.

He often wondered, if they had retrieved the Koh-i-Noor and its mate in time, would his grandfather have truly been healed? He'd seen the man's face clear of its wretched pain and age when he held the one large piece, seen it with his own eyes.

Would his father, saddled with kidney disease, have lived beyond his sixtieth year?

Would Saleem himself have sickened in his teens, his body have been pumped full of the poison that put him in this desperate position now? Cured, alive, but unable to father a child?

And last month, at his annual physical, a ritual he took very seriously, his latest blood work showed an overabundance of white blood cells. The leukemia he'd battled as a teenager was back. He was running out of time.

With the three stones united, he would be healed and forever immortal. Not only would he have the Koh-i-Noor this very day, he also finally had in his possession the lost seventy-seven-carat stone from Antwerp. If his father had any idea his old friend Andrei Anatoly held his diamond all these years, he would have killed the man himself.

No matter. Anatoly was dead, and the smallest piece of the diamond was now safe in a Paris warehouse, awaiting its brothers.

He would return to Paris, open the locked box, marry the three stones, and be healed. Then he would sire a son.

Behind him, he heard a soft knock at his door.

65

Saleem opened the door to his suite. Two years since he'd seen her last, and she still took his breath away. But something was different, wrong. Her beauty was diminished. She was only a woman after all, not the mythical creature he remembered.

And then it hit him.

"Your eyes."

She waved a hand in dismissal. "A necessary evil. May I come in, or are we going to do this transaction in the hallway?"

He stepped back and allowed her entrance. He stuck his head out the door, looking right, then left. The hall behind her was empty; she'd come alone, as instructed.

He shut the door and turned to see her watching him. She set her backpack down on the table and opened it.

"You have the Koh-i-Noor."

"Of course. Let us do our business and go our separate ways. You are prepared to transfer the funds?"

"Let me see it first."

She held out her hand. There was a small envelope, only a few inches big, inside her palm. "Money for the key."

Saleem said, "Key? Key to what? Where is my diamond?"

"Safely stashed away where you will be able to claim it. As soon as I've confirmed the money is in my accounts."

Was she indeed planning to betray him? Well, he'd been warned, and he was ready for her. "Why have you not brought the diamond to me?"

Kitsune pulled back her hand.

"Did you honestly believe I was going to walk in here and hand you the stone? Do you take me for a fool, Lanighan? This is how business is done. You know the proper procedure. I see the weapon you carry under your coat. Did you plan to shoot me dead the moment you have your diamond?"

They were circling each other now, Kitsune watching his hand carefully for any sign he was going for the gun in his pocket. He was not the same man she'd met two years earlier. There was something different about him.

He's desperate, she thought, finally recognizing the problem. *But why?* What had happened over the past two years?

It didn't matter. Mulvaney had warned her she shouldn't trust Lanighan.

"I will ask you once more. Where is my diamond?"

"The Koh-i-Noor is safe. You transfer my money, and I will tell you where to take the key. I keep my bargains. I always have. Do you?"

He was becoming enraged. She recognized the signs and took three steps back, put her weight on her back foot, ready to defend herself.

He whipped the gun from his pocket and jabbed it toward her chest. "I have been warned of your duplicity, your intention to take my money and the Koh-i-Noor. I will not allow you to do this. I want my diamond, and I want it now."

She spun, pivoting on her left foot, and her right leg clipped the gun from his hand, sent it skidding across the floor. She followed with an elbow to his jaw, snapping his head back, knocking him into the table. She darted across the room to the weapon, raised it, aimed as he turned and started toward her.

Her voice was ice. "Stop. Right now. Or I will shoot you, Lanighan, and you will get nothing."

He dropped his hand to his side. His rage was barely controlled. He said between clenched teeth, "It seems the warnings against you were correct."

"Who would say that about me? I always play by the rules. You're the one acting like an amateur. Now, I'm going to watch you transfer the money, then I will give you the key, and we will part ways, each satisfied our end of the bargain has been upheld."

"Very well. Give me the key. An act of good faith."

Without lowering the weapon, she tossed him the small envelope.

"It is a five-minute walk from here. Now transfer my money."

"You will come with me."

She shook her head. "If you try to walk out this door without transferring my money, I will shoot you dead and keep the diamond for myself."

"Where is the diamond now?"

"Bank Horim. You can see it from here, Saleem. Go out on your balcony and look to the right."

He considered her for a moment, then shrugged and went to the balcony. The outside air was biting, and the sun was disappearing rapidly. He turned to the right and saw the pulsing blue and white lights half a mile away.

"Kitsune. Come here."

"So you can throw me off the balcony? No, thank you."

"Come here now!"

She edged carefully toward the open door. She saw the lights immediately, realized there were police cars in front of the Bank Horim.

Her mobile rang, a secure number. It was Marie-Louise Helmut.

The older woman's voice was a whisper. "People are asking about you."

"What people?"

"An American FBI agent and an Englishman from Scotland Yard, plus a French FedPol agent. I am holding them off as long as possible, but they know you were here, and they are bringing warrants. I will not be able to stop them from opening the box."

Drummond had found her. She'd known he would; deep down, she'd known. But how? How had he found her here?

Kitsune couldn't allow them to open the box, not while the stone was inside.

Kitsune said, "You must open the box yourself and remove the contents."

"I cannot, the FedPol agent is still here." Then Helmut said, "I did send the man and woman to Sages, as you instructed. If only the third agent would leave, I could retrieve the contents of the box unnoticed."

Kitsune's heart sped up. A chance, then.

She said, "Do what you have to do. Make it happen."

She turned to Lanighan.

"There is a problem, but I am handling it. Meet me back here in two hours."

She didn't wait for an answer, turned and left so quietly he wouldn't have known she'd even been in his room if he hadn't seen her with his own eyes.

66

Sages Fidelité was not a bank, it was simply a small building with a counter separating the foyer from three walls of floor-to-ceiling safe-deposit boxes. Mike and Nicholas burst in the door at a run, and the attendant behind the counter jumped to his feet and threw his hands in the air. He looked so scared Mike had to bite back a laugh. This was going to go better than it had at Bank Horim.

The boy was the assistant manager, a gawky youth who didn't look old enough to shave. Tomas was his name, and he was happy to share all he knew, though, alas, it wasn't much.

He looked at the picture and nodded enthusiastically. "Yes, she came in this afternoon and rented a box. She paid up front, the nonresident of Switzerland rate, for two years. Then she put something in the box and left."

"Let us into the box."

The wide Adam's apple bobbed. "Without her key, there is no way to open it."

Nicholas banged his fist on the counter. "Find a bloody blowtorch, then. Get the box open, right now. And let us see the paperwork."

The kid knew a serious man when he saw one. "No, no, don't do that. I have a master key. We're not allowed to use it, though; it's only for emergencies."

Mike touched her fingers to her Glock. "This is an emergency. Open the box."

The boy swallowed and handed over the paperwork, then ran into the back for his master key.

Mike said, "This place isn't very secure."

"If it were one of the banks, this would never happen. They'd have to drill the lock out. There's no guarantee of safety in a place like this." He looked down at the paperwork. "Cheeky girl—she rented the box in the name Duleep Singh."

Mike asked, "Duleep Singh? The last rightful owner of the Koh-i-Noor, before it was handed over to the British, right?"

"Yes. She's playing games with us."

The boy came back with the master key, opened the lock of the safe-deposit box, and quickly stepped back. Nicholas pulled the gray plastic box from the wall.

It was light. His heart began to pound. Was this it? Had they found the Koh-i-Noor?

Without waiting to set it on a table, he opened the box. There was only a piece of paper inside.

"I'd hoped it was the diamond. No such luck."

He pulled out the paper. There was a list of numbers. No rhyme or reason to them that he could see.

"What is it?"

Mike took the paper from him and studied it. "Bank accounts. They're consistent, each with thirteen numbers. Numbered accounts. We better let Savich throw this into the mix."

"What's that written on the back?"

She flipped the paper. Written in an elegant cursive were eight words. *This is all you get. Leave me alone.*

Mike said, "Do you think this is directed at us, or to someone else?"

Nicholas looked down at the message. "It has to be someone else, since she shouldn't know we're here. But we're a step closer."

He saw the young man watching them warily.

Nicholas dropped the box and crossed the floor in three steps, grabbed the boy's collar, and jerked him up on his toes, got right in his face. "What else did she do while she was here?"

"N-Nothing, sir."

"You're lying. Did she buy another box?"

The boy was silent. Nicholas shook him. "Which one is it?"

"She didn't, I swear."

He said to Mike, "Call Menard, have him send over his officers to arrest this man."

"Wait. Wait. Okay. She did rent one more box."

Nicholas let him go. "So she paid you to keep quiet about it, did she, Tomas? Too late now. Open it."

This box was heavier than the first. Nicholas carried it to the small Formica-covered table in the center of the room. He began to lift the lid, saw a flash of blue velvet and the clear, clean lines of molten glass.

The Koh-i-Noor.

Then the lid caught. He stopped and, holding his breath, he slowly and carefully allowed it to close.

"Everyone, don't move." Still holding the lid carefully closed, he fished in his pocket for his Swiss Army knife with its small attached flashlight.

He eased down onto his haunches until he was eye level with the edge of the lid, and keeping it less than an inch open, flashed the light inside.

There was the Koh-i-Noor in the box. Surrounded by wires.

Bloody hell.

He thanked the Almighty for the instincts that had just kept them all alive, and gently laid down the lid. Without moving, without raising his voice, he said, "Mike, it's rigged to blow. Get the boy and walk outside. I'm right behind you."

She didn't hesitate, grabbed Tomas's arm. "Come with me, right now."

When he was sure they were safely outside, Nicholas carefully eased his hand from the lid, praying he hadn't jostled the bomb. It was meant to explode the moment the lid was lifted past a quarter of the way open.

He slowly and silently backed away. He was still in one piece, which meant he hadn't tripped the pressure switch. It didn't mean they were safe, there could be a secondary timer, or it could work on a mobile signal, like the bomb in New York. It was surely divine intervention they all hadn't been blown to kingdom come.

No way would he try and disarm this bomb himself. He needed to leave the building as quickly and calmly as possible and bring in the experts, with their robotic counterparts, to deactivate the switch.

He backed toward the door until he felt the handle under his hands, then turned swiftly and stepped outside. The freezing air bit his face, and he breathed a deep lungful. *Too close, Nicholas. Too bloody close.*

The glass door swung shut behind him, and he searched for Mike. She was across the street with Tomas, her face white. She was scared. And she was shouting at him, her hands above her head, arms waving wildly.

His mind registered her screams, and he felt rather than heard the glass shatter behind him with a ferocious burst of heat and an ear-blasting explosion. He dropped to the ground, rolling into a ball, protecting his head, as the explosion roared around him, glass and metal twisting and hurtling outward, shooting out fire that burned his hands.

He couldn't hear anything, see anything. It was all black.

67

Kitsune watched Drummond and Caine talking to the boy, manhandling him, and the idiot caved and opened the box for them. At least he'd followed her instructions—if a couple came in looking for information, he was to give them the box with the paper in it.

If Saleem Lanighan came in, it was a different story.

But Drummond had scared the daylights out of the kid, and he'd brought out the second box. The box meant for Lanighan.

Her left thumb was on the detonator, the right held a monocle trained on the Sages Fidelité lobby. She was safe, across the park, but well within radio range.

She watched them talking about the bank account numbers in the first box. She saw Caine flip the paper over, saw Drummond snatch it from her and read her short message, meant for them.

This is all you get. Leave me alone.

More discussion, then Drummond got physical with Tomas and she knew it was all over.

All it would take was a minute press of her thumb, a hint of pressure, and this would all be over.

No more Drummond. She recognized she was full of righteous anger, a feeling she remembered well from when she was younger and less disciplined. She'd acted on emotion only once. This couldn't be about rage. This was about survival.

She'd wanted it to be Lanighan to open the second box, to blow himself off the face of the earth, because it would mean he'd betrayed her.

She held the detonator in her hand and watched. No, she wouldn't have to blow up the box, Drummond was going to open it and do the job himself.

She heard Mulvaney telling her once, twice, perhaps with the planning of every tough job: *Redundancy is your friend, Kitsune.*

She gritted her teeth at the thought of her mentor, pushed him from her mind. She needed to be clear for this. There would be time enough later to find out what happened to Mulvaney.

She watched Drummond stiffen, and she knew he'd realized the bomb was there. She watched Caine drag Tomas from the building, and run across the street. And she watched Drummond slowly lower the lid, then slowly step away from the box. His life was in her hands.

She hadn't wanted it to end like this. She swallowed, breathed deeply, forced herself to calm.

Do it.

You have to survive. There is too much at stake.

Do it do it do it!

The front door opened and Drummond was outside—

Do it now.

Her thumb twitched, and it was over.

68

The car shook with the force of the explosion, but Kitsune put it in gear and drove away, counting on debris from the explosion and the bursting flames to cover her escape.

Two blocks from the explosion, on a quiet, unmarked street, she found a small gray Fiat, still running, the owner probably running into the house to get something. *Perfect.*

She abandoned the rental in the small driveway of a town house, threw her things into the Fiat, and was gone all in under a minute.

She forced herself to calm, to think, to figure out what she was going to do now. The sky was already darkening. She would be all right. She had two more clean identities in her bag, both prepared for her by Mulvaney, and there was no one better than him. Where was he? No, she couldn't think about him just yet, too much to do.

She started west immediately. The border was only a few kilometers out of town, and she wanted to make it through before they'd been alerted about her.

Since all available personnel would rush to the scene, including the FedPol agent, Helmut would have enough time to secure the box and its contents. She'd better come through, Kitsune thought, since she was paying her a small fortune.

Lanighan had betrayed her, just as Mulvaney had warned he might. She hadn't seen it coming, though. She thought back to the night in Paris with him two years before; she'd weighed, judged, and decided his desire for the Koh-i-Noor would keep him on the straight and narrow. He was a businessman. He knew how things worked. So what had changed? Why did he now consider her the enemy? Why had he believed *she* was betraying *him*?

A thief who would hand over the goods in person was a fool, hardly professional. He knew this. Give him the key, make sure her money was transferred, and everyone was happy. It should have worked seamlessly. Instead it was all unraveling.

Those precautions she'd set into place were going to save her now, not only from Lanighan but from the authorities, too.

She bit her lip hard enough to taste blood. It would have to suffice for the moment, until she could feel Lanighan's blood on her hands.

She changed quickly, pulling on a new wig and pulling out the appropriate ID from the base of her backpack. She called Marie-Louise Helmut at the Bank Horim.

"Did you secure the package in the safe-deposit box?"

"Yes, madam. A fortuitous happenstance, there was an explosion nearby. Even the FedPol agent went to deal with the emergency. You will not be coming back to the bank, I presume?"

"No. Send the contents to the Café Papon, on Rue Henri-Fazy."

"I know it."

"I will be there in ten minutes. Have your person waiting in the women's loo."

"Ten minutes." Helmut rang off, and Kitsune felt her control slide back into place. Ten minutes and she'd have the diamond back in her hands. She pulled the Fiat into the light traffic, checked the mirror to see if anyone was following.

She made it to the Café Papon in five minutes, walked to the counter, bought a croissant and a coffee. The television set above the cash register had an alert on the screen, the local station running news of the bombing, showing the horrendous carnage, the flames bursting into the sky, raining down debris. It was the only local event, she thought, dramatic enough to replace the outrage over the stolen Koh-i-Noor.

She listened to the rapid-pace French. Three injured, none dead. So Drummond hadn't died in the blast. He was in the hospital, then, and that would slow him down, surely long enough for her to get herself, and the diamond, away from Geneva.

A young woman entered the coffee shop, walked directly past Kitsune toward the back. Kitsune followed her to the bathroom.

It was an expert handoff, the diamond was now heavy in her pocket, and Kitsune was gone. As she climbed back into the car, she thought maybe she needed some help with things after all. At the very least, it should surprise the hell out of him.

69

Lanighan raced back to the balcony at the sound of the explosion. It shook the railing and rattled the windows. He saw the ball of fire plume into the air, then smoke, black and thick, well up, blacking out the sky.

Where was Kitsune? Was she responsible for this?

Thirty minutes later his cell rang.

She said only, "I need your help."

A moment of surprise, then he said, "And I need my diamond."

"I have it, but I can't get back across the bridge to your hotel because of the fire. The police from America and Britain are after me—how, I don't know, but they're here."

"I assume you set the bomb. You were so careless they didn't die?"

"I tried, but they managed to escape the blast. One of

them is injured. I don't know how badly, but I don't want to take any chances. I'm sure both of them will be at the hospital, at least tonight. When they leave, don't kill them, just get them off my back for a while."

"And my diamond?"

"You will get your diamond when you meet me in Paris. You know the time and place."

His suspicion and distrust sounded loud in the silence. "Very well, I will handle things. I will see you in Paris."

There was a click, and his cell went dead.

Saleem slipped his cell into his pocket, packed his bag, and left the suite. He took the stairs to the basement, checked his BMW—who knew if this was a trick and she'd planted a bomb on his car? He saw no bomb. He was out of the garage and onto the Quai du Mont-Blanc less than two minutes after she called. Better to cross the border now before the police started cracking down.

He made a call as he weaved his way out of downtown Geneva and pointed the car west. The phone was answered on the third ring. He explained his needs and hung up, fully satisfied his demands would be met. He'd get the agents off her back forever. Then he would get his diamond and deal with her.

He dialed her number, and she answered with a curt "Yes?"

"I have made the arrangements. Tell me how you've bungled this so badly. From the way my father talked, he considered the Fox to be above mistakes. I begin to believe you are not worth the vast amount I agreed to pay you."

She heard it in his voice, beneath the smooth, civilized

words he spoke, and she knew absolutely he would betray her, and so it pleased her to say, "You will listen, Saleem. The wire-transfer numbers from your first payment to me in Paris allowed me to track down other account amounts you've used to pay other thieves over the years. I placed a list of these numbers in a Sages Fidelité safe-deposit box. If my list survived the explosion, it is possible for an accomplished forensic accountant to trace the accounts back to you, don't you think?"

He froze in shock. He knew to his gut she was telling the truth, but wait, no, it didn't matter, since he always closed those bank accounts after each transaction. But given enough time . . . He said very softly, "You bitch."

She laughed. "That's right. Now, shut up and listen to me closely, because I am not lying. I have every intention of honoring our agreement. I know you've been very careful over the years, just as I know it's very unlikely anyone could ever trace the accounts back to you.

"You will consider this a warning. I will lead the police directly to you if you try to betray me. Do you understand? Your empire is in my hands, Saleem. Honor our agreement."

"That is all I ever intended. It is you I do not trust."

"There is no reason for you not to trust me. You know my reputation. We will try again tomorrow. Remember, I have the diamond in my hand. Now, slow those agents down."

His voice was clipped, rage bubbling. "Unlike you, I don't screw up," and he threw the mobile onto the leather seat next to him and gunned the BMW's engine, letting it snarl as he hit the A4 out of Geneva.

A police car flashed past him, heading into the city.

With an eye on his rearview mirror, he took the ramp for the highway, northwest toward Paris, then set the cruise control to one hundred twenty kph, fast enough so he wouldn't seem suspect among the other drivers.

Arrogant, stupid woman. In Paris, she would learn exactly how much power he had over her.

70

Geneva, Switzerland
Friday evening

He heard his name from a distance, and felt hands shaking him. He didn't want to wake, wanted to drift back into the sweet oblivion nestling him deep, but there was pain now, bright and sharp in his back, and so he opened his eyes.

Flashing lights. Voices, screaming, calling. He tried to focus, but his eyes wouldn't work right. A woman's voice in his ear, calm, controlled, a touch of fingers, feather light. "Nicholas? Can you hear me? Answer me."

Her voice was familiar somehow. He searched for the woman's name. Mike. Mike Caine. Her blond hair was swinging in his face. He reached up, whether to push it out of his face or hug her, he didn't know, and she wrapped her arms around him. He felt the warmth of her tears and smiled. Better. Even pain lessened in a woman's arms. She was soft and warm, and her hair smelled like flowers, and wild grass. Jasmine, he thought.

Then she pulled away from him, and pain sliced across his lower back like a hot knife. He gasped and was gone again.

When he awoke the second time, the confusion, the heat, the noise were gone. The air around him was quiet, deathly so. Something cold was across his face; pulses of chilly oxygen pushed into his nose. Low, steady beeps, the thrum of his own heart in his chest, pounding hard. The smells were different, antiseptic and unnatural. Hospital. He was in hospital.

"Nicholas? You're back. No, stay with me. Stay awake now. Listen to me. You're going to be okay."

His vision swam into focus. Mike was sitting on the edge of his bed, his hand held between hers. She had a black smudge on her cheek. He wanted to reach up and wipe it away, but his arm was curiously heavy.

She leaned in and kissed him on the mouth, fast and light. "You listen to me, you lamebrain. Trying to get yourself killed was not part of the deal."

His voice wouldn't come. She gave him a sip of water. It tasted better than his grandfather's favorite single malt, Glenfiddich. His voice came out a croak. "What happened?"

"You blew up the building."

It was coming back now, bits and pieces, the blue-white gleam of the diamond in the box, the red and orange wires, the hot explosion at his back.

"Not me. I closed the lid."

"You should have told the bomb that. The moment you stepped out the door, the whole building blew. You had a shard of glass in your back, plus several cuts from the shrapnel. The doctors removed it all. And your hands were burned a bit. You most likely have a concussion, and your hearing might be messed up for a while. Mine's finally getting back to normal. It was a big blast."

He couldn't feel his back, and panic began to creep in. "My back?"

"You're probably numb from the lidocaine. They had to stitch you up a bit. You're going to be sore, but you're all right."

"Anyone else hurt?"

She shook her head. "Some people were banged up, but everyone's okay."

He looked around the room, small, white, one chair. The blinds were closed. It seemed like night to him, though. "How long have I been out?"

"A few hours. You were bleeding badly, and you were unconscious. I thought—well, you're okay. Tomas was scared for you, too. Yes, he's all right. Last time I saw him he was shaking like a leaf, stuttering as he tried to answer the police officer's questions." She touched a hand to his cheek. "Don't do that again, all right?"

"I'll do my best," and he smiled, though it hurt, and leaned back against the crackly pillow.

"Menard and the Geneva police are all over the bomb. The fire was confined to the one building, which was amazing. C-4, it looks like, on a detonator. Was it similar to the bomb at the Met?"

"No. There was a pressure switch. She wasn't playing around this time."

Mike's lips pressed together in a grim line. "No, she wasn't. And when we catch her, I'm going to beat the crap out of her."

He wanted to laugh, but suddenly it all came back, and he started to sit up. "Did they find the diamond?"

"No, don't try to get up. You're hurt."

She pressed on his shoulders and eased him back down. It took him a moment to control the pain. "The diamond. The Koh-i-Noor. It was in the box. The bomb surrounded it. The box was wired to blow the moment anyone opened it."

"Are you sure, Nicholas?"

"I am. Have them look. Did the boy Tomas know about the bomb?"

"No. As I told you, he was totally freaked out. I heard him tell the police about Browning. He admitted she paid him well to direct us to the first box, the one with the account numbers in it. The one with the bomb was meant for someone else, a lone man, Tomas said, with dark hair and eyes."

"The buyer," Nicholas said.

"Probably," Mike said. "I guess if things went wrong, she needed to take him out and destroy the evidence. But we forced Tomas to give us the second box—and kablooey. I better call Menard, tell him about the diamond."

Mike made the call, and Nicholas allowed himself to float for a minute. She came back and sat down on the chair next to him. She didn't touch him. "They'll look, but it's too hot to go in now." She leaned forward, stared him straight in the eye. "Seriously, Nicholas, you scared me to death."

"When we find her, after you beat the crap out of her, I'm going to strangle that woman. She's tried to blow me up twice now. I'm starting to take this personally."

"Tell me, what tipped you off? You realized there was a bomb and told us to leave."

"I did?"

"You did."

He didn't remember, then, "Wait—the box felt wrong. Too heavy. I could tell something nasty was in there."

Again, she touched her fingers to his face. "Let's hear it for your fine instincts. You've saved my life twice in as many days. I owe you one."

"Actually, you owe me two, but I'm not counting." He tried to smile, but it hurt too much. On the other hand, he was alive, and he would heal. "Browning, the Fox, whoever she is, she's upped the ante. A lot of people could have been hurt or killed today. Mike, we're so close, we can't stop now."

She bent over him again, pushed his hair off his forehead. "We won't stop. But you need to stay here overnight. The doctors think the concussion is mild, but they want to keep an eye on you. Let the drugs work. We've lost the trail, anyway; she's gone for now."

He wasn't going to argue. Moving around was going

to be difficult until his head cleared. He'd been concussed before, knew if he did too much too soon, he'd end up vomiting on the floor and right back in the bed. And since they'd shot something really good into his IV, he really didn't want to move, because he was floating high, up there at the ceiling. Now Mike was lightly rubbing his temples, and it felt very nice. He felt calm, and let go.

He heard her voice from a distance. "That's right. Relax. I'm here. Nothing bad will happen."

Just like his mother, he thought, and slept.

71

Nicholas passed a restless night, full of strange drug-induced dreams, and was vaguely aware of being poked and prodded every hour on the hour by the nurses. Mike slept awkwardly in the chair by his bed.

He awoke at dawn, his head still aching, but he could see much better. He searched the room until he spied a wall clock. Five in the morning. Twelve hours after they'd walked into the Sages Fidelité and all the fires of hell had burst into the world.

The Fox was certainly gone by now, Mike was right about that, as was the Koh-i-Noor.

Mike opened her eyes to see Nicholas sitting up in bed. She saw his eyes were clear, his face only slightly bruised.

"Hey, dude. Go back to sleep."

Nicholas said, "I'm up. I'm feeling better. Did you hear back from Menard? Did he find the diamond?"

Mike gave it up. "No sign of it. Chances are the heat of the explosion reduced it to sand. I don't know if heat will destroy a diamond, but I hardly think anything could survive strapped to a brick of C-4."

"It would depend on the blast radius. It could have survived and they simply haven't found it yet."

"I was thinking about it last night. I don't think it was the Koh-i-Noor at all. It was the other replica, and the bomb was her insurance policy."

Of course it was. He'd clearly damaged his brain.

"Menard and his men found nothing at Bank Horim. According to the bank's logs, there *was* a safe-deposit box leased around the time she was there, but when they drilled it open, it was empty. The manager, Madame Helmut, claimed she didn't know a thing about it."

"Do you think she was lying?"

"Menard thinks so. About the Fox, the police found an abandoned rental car late last night a block away from a report of a stolen Fiat. Menard told me the border police have a photo of the stolen car passing through the Swiss-to-France at ten last night. A single woman, passport registered to a Stephanie Arle, resident of Calais, France. She was blond, but from the snap photo, it's definitely her."

"I wonder where she's headed now."

"There have been no Fox sightings since the border. She clearly has several identities at her disposal. She may be laid up somewhere, or ditched the car and stolen another one." She paused for a moment. "Remember, Paris was the first place she was supposed to go. It's only a four-hour drive from here. She could be driving there to meet the buyer."

It made sense. "Do we have anything yet on the bank account numbers we found in the safe-deposit box at Sages Fidelité?"

"Unfortunately, you must have set the list down when you opened the box with the explosives."

Had he set the paper down? He didn't think he had. "Check the pocket of my pants. No, wait, try my wallet. I think I stashed it in there."

Mike pulled the plastic bag from under the hospital bed that held the smoky remains of Nicholas's clothes.

She pulled out his bloodstained pants and stuck her hand in the back pocket, careful not to cut herself on the small shards of glass embedded in the fine wool. The leather wallet had shaped itself to the curve of his butt, and wasn't that nice?

Sure enough, in between the euros and dollars she found a small slip of paper. She pulled it out and waved it in his face.

"Hallelujah, Nicholas, you saved it."

He started to smile, thought better of it. Now that he was becoming more alert, everything hurt, especially his face. And his eyebrows. And his ears. Even his teeth felt sore.

"Call Savich. He can add the account numbers to the database he's working on."

Mike typed away on her cell phone, copying the numbers, then hit send and looked up to see him watching her. She could tell he was hurting, and she hated to see it. She really was going to smack that bitch when they caught her.

"Good thing you have your magic leather carry-on," she said, holding up his pants. "These clothes are ruined."

"And I so dearly loved those pants."

A bit of a joke, but it was a good start. He was going to be okay, thank the Almighty.

She said, "Louisa sent me a note late last night while you were getting stitched up. The DNA taken from Victoria's chewed pencil was a familial match to an entry in CODIS. Did you know we've been matching our Combined DNA Index to international profiles through Interpol?"

That perked him right up. "And?"

"The Fox has a brother. And aren't we the lucky ones— he's in prison, serving life without parole for murder. We'll go talk to him, see if we can't get some background on this woman. Maybe he even knows where she is."

"Where is he?"

"La Santé. In Paris. I've already set the arrangements. As soon as you're well enough to travel, we'll head to the airport."

"All roads lead to Paris, it seems. Tell me about him."

"Henri Couverel is his name, and he's got a jacket a mile long, from petty street stuff to murder. Drugs, mainly. The murder he's in for is his dealer. The man was stabbed a dozen times, and Couverel was found high as a kite, sitting in the man's blood. He does not at all fit the profile for an explosives expert jewel thief."

"So you don't think she's ever worked with him?"

"No," Mike said, "and from his history, he's much too

scattered to have ever been any use to her. She's a precision instrument, honed by years of practice. He's a sledge-hammer in comparison. Selling drugs is the least of it. According to the file, he's a heroin addict. You know heroin addicts aren't known for their cleverness."

He sat up again, ignoring the pain in his back and the urge to vomit. "I'm well enough now. Let's go."

"Big bad tough guy, aren't you, James Bond?"

"Yes. Yes, I am."

"Lie back, Nicholas. The plane doesn't leave until eight a.m. whether you're ready or not."

A nurse came in, checked him out, drew his blood, and offered him a sedative, which made him snort. He swung his legs off the edge of the bed to go shower. His head swam for a moment, then righted itself. The pain in his back where they'd stitched him up was a dull throb.

He was fine. Sore, but fine.

The nurse said from the doorway, "If your lab work is normal, you are being discharged in an hour. Maybe sooner, given what a macho guy you are. Oh, yes—try not to faint in the shower."

72

He might want to crawl, but he didn't. Nicholas managed to follow Mike from the hospital lobby, ignoring the pulling sensation in his back every time he took a step.

He saw that yesterday's sun was gone, replaced by gray skies and a bitter cold wind that whipped through the buildings. Snow was coming.

He was going slow, but it felt good to be up and moving, and the brisk air helped clear away the cobwebs from the concussion. There was a black Mercedes sedan waiting for them at the curb.

Mike said, "Menard was kind enough to send a car for us. We're not that far from the airport. You'll like this even more. The driver is the man who drove the Fox yesterday. We can have a chat with him on our way, see if he remembers anything."

Nicholas held the door for Mike when something buzzed his ear. He reached up to swat it away just as five holes appeared in the side of the car.

He whipped sideways, dropped to the cement curb, yelled to Mike, "Get down, get down," but she was already shouting at him to do the same. Her Glock was out, and she tossed him her backup Glock 27 off her ankle.

As more bullets hit the car, he began returning fire, covering Mike as she pushed the driver out of the car and yelled at him, "Go, go, go." She began shooting toward the gunfire as the driver darted inside the hospital doors.

Nicholas shouted after him, "Call the man who arranged for you to pick us up, tell him what's happened."

Mike was crouched behind the open driver's-side door. Nicholas pulled open the passenger-side door. "Where are the shots coming from?"

Mike said, "Up the street, to the right. I make two shooters. They've got us pinned down."

Nicholas sighted down the barrel of the gun, saw the men she was talking about, a block away, in a Land Rover similar to the one Menard had picked them up in, minus the orange police stripes.

He squeezed off two shots, hitting their windshield and cracking the glass into a spiderweb.

All went silent, then they heard the throaty growl of a Land Rover revving its engines. It started toward them with a squeal of tires, bullets flying.

Nicholas turned and yelled, "They're going to try and ram us. Let's get out of here. Where are the bloody keys?"

Mike yelled back, "The driver took them with him into the hospital."

Nicholas dove across the front seat and smacked the butt of the Glock once, twice, and the plastic panel cover under the steering column split off. He ripped out the wiring harness, heard Mike yelling, "Hurry, hurry," as two shots smashed into the windshield at eye level.

He sparked the two wires together, and the Mercedes engine roared to life.

"Got it. Get in, get in!"

Mike slammed the passenger-side door closed. Nicholas jammed his foot on the gas, and the Mercedes shot from the curb. The Land Rover was coming head-on. He sliced the car to the left, catching the Land Rover's bumper on the grille with a rending screech.

The force spun them around and he worked the wheel smoothly, allowing the car to turn one hundred eighty degrees, and now they were behind the truck.

Nicholas said, "Take them out," and floored it, bringing the car closer. The shooter on the passenger side stuck his head out the window and sprayed them with bullets.

The driver gunned through an intersection, leaving skidding cars in his wake, and Nicholas shot through behind him, the wheel alive in his hands.

"Take the shot, Mike, go for the tires."

"I'm trying," Mike said. "Hold the damn car steady."

"Where the devil are they headed?"

"Toward the Jet d'Eau, I think."

Northwest, then. He saw the Credit Suisse building to their right, then the Land Rover whipped across the bridge on Rue des Moulins, then turned right onto the Quai du Mont-Blanc.

He said, "The road will open up in a minute. Try not to kill any tourists."

She pointed at a police car swinging out in front of them, flashers going wild. Nicholas swerved around the car and caught sight of the Land Rover again.

He urged the Mercedes closer, gunning the engine to the red line, thanking all that was holy the car was an automatic.

He got his left hand out the window and squeezed off a few shots, which hit the tail of the truck and did no damage to the tires. He cursed and tried again, ducking back into the car when he saw a black semiauto come out the driver's-side window.

"AR-15 fire incoming. Can you take out the driver?"

He swung the car wide to the left so Mike could angle for a shot, ducked as the machine gun sprayed bullets across the front of the Mercedes, pockmarking the windshield and hood.

Nicholas began to laugh. "It's bulletproof glass. What luck. Mike, stay behind the glass and take them out."

As they flew through the city, they were gathering cop cars like a magnet to filings, a stream of wailing building behind them. The shocked faces and angry horns of oncoming drivers flashed by, but Nicholas ignored everything except the bumper of the truck in front of them, getting closer and closer.

The driver of the Land Rover was good, swerving all over the road to keep them from hitting anything vital, but Nicholas was better. He maneuvered the Mercedes right behind them, then shouted, "Hold on," and gunned it, slamming into the tail of the truck. The Land Rover veered off to the left but held it together, shooting back at them.

The road opened up, and they accelerated so fast Mike was forced to brace one hand on the dashboard to keep herself upright. Nicholas backed off a bit, evened the car's direction, and then yelled, "Do it!"

Mike took careful aim and pulled the trigger, and the Land Rover's back left tire blew with a squeal and a puff of white smoke.

Nicholas shouted, "Now! Get the right one."

"I'm trying," she yelled back. She shot a good dozen times but missed.

The lake was on their right; the blue-gray winter water looked cold and forbidding. Boats bobbed off their docks, and Mike realized they'd left downtown Geneva.

"There's a sign up ahead; it says sixty kilometers to Lausanne."

Nicholas was surging up toward the Land Rover again. "The road's going to get tight up ahead as we go into Bellevue. When I pull next to them, Mike, I need you to hold the wheel."

"No heroics, Nicholas."

"Never. I'm going to take out the driver and we'll be able to force them off the road."

Cars came toward them as they rushed up the road,

weaving and honking. Nicholas ignored them, carefully pushing the Land Rover into the less occupied streets north of the city. They were lucky it was a weekend, the traffic would have been terrible during the weekday rush hour and more people would be at risk.

There was an opening ahead, the lake showing through the heavy trees next to the road.

The man in the passenger side of the truck pulled his entire upper body out of the window and sighted on them.

"Now, Mike. Hold the wheel and put your foot on the gas."

She moved to take his place, and he slid his upper body out of the window and took careful aim, ducking as the AK spat bullets back at them.

"Here you go, you bugger." He caught the driver's eye in the rearview, rolling and mad, and took careful aim despite the wind whipping him backward. He emptied his magazine into the driver's-side window, saw the fine spray of blood across the glass, and pulled back into the car.

The results were immediate. The Land Rover squirreled hard to the left, hit the concrete barrier and ricocheted off to the right, through the metal guardrail, which launched it into the air. It twisted as it toppled over the edge and caromed down to the water head over tail, before crashing through an old wooden dock and landing upside down in Lake Geneva.

Nicholas pulled the beaten-up valiant Mercedes to the side of the road. Mike was out the door immediately, Nicholas right behind her, their weapons drawn, but there was no need—the Land Rover and its occupants were sinking down into the freezing water.

It was over.

To Mike's astonishment, Nicholas started laughing. "You want to know something? My back doesn't hurt at all. I feel bloody great."

The sirens were on them. The Geneva police screeched to a stop, blocking the A1 in both directions. Officers scrambled down the bank to the submerged truck, and two took defensive positions in front of Mike and Nicholas, shouting in French, "Drop your weapons!"

Mike held up her FBI credentials. "I'm Special Agent Michaela Caine, FBI, and this is Detective Chief Inspector Nicholas Drummond, New Scotland Yard! Call FedPol Agent Pierre Menard; we're working with him."

She looked at Nicholas and shook her head, her ponytail swinging in her face, trying to catch her breath. "You call that no heroics?"

73

Menard caught up to them as the divers arrived. Nicholas and Mike were drinking hot coffee out of foam cups and being questioned by a pissed-off young Cantonal Police captain. After shooting up the main thoroughfare through Geneva, causing countless wrecks during the course of a high-speed chase, ending with a car in Lake Geneva and two missing bodies, the captain wasn't inclined to allow them to leave the city, but Menard flashed his FedPol badge, spoke a few curt words in French, and he backed off, even more pissed off than he'd been when he arrived.

Nicholas said, "No one was hurt, I hope?"

"Only the two you chased into the lake," Menard said. "What can you tell me about them?"

Nicholas said, "Both dark haired and medium height, late twenties to early thirties. One was Caucasian and the other was Egyptian, maybe. I thought I heard a few choice phrases I've overheard in Cairo before. As to who set them on us, that's the more troubling question. Either the Fox called in some hired muscle, or these guys belong to the buyer. To go to this extreme, it's got to mean they're panicking, which means we're getting close."

A diver in a wet suit broke the surface with the truck's license plate in his hand.

Menard said, "I am thankful you and Agent Caine escaped more injury. It is probable the Land Rover was stolen, but we will trace this plate and find out to whom the truck belonged, and with luck, it will lead us to your buyer. And when we have a positive identification on the two assailants, I will let you know. I will meet you in France tonight.

"Now, the young captain will not detain you. We have secured your flight to France. It would be best for you to leave sooner, rather than waiting too long. I will manage this. But you must go now, or the captain might shoot all of us."

Mike touched Menard's arm. "Thank you, monsieur, you've been a great help."

He took her hand and kissed it. "My pleasure, of course." He handed Nicholas a Glock .40.

"My own. You may need this. Be careful."

74

The flight from Geneva to Paris took only forty-five minutes, and the drive from Charles de Gaulle to La Santé Prison another twenty-five. Nicholas wasn't feeling so great now. He was covered in a fine sheen of sweat when they arrived. Mike was worried about him, but he was a stubborn man, determined not to look like he was hurting, so she kept her mouth shut.

They were met by the warden of La Santé. Her name was Lucienne Badour, a striking brunette in her late forties, heavyset but with long, shapely legs more suited to dancing the cancan than walking the filthy prison halls. She spoke very nice English with a strong Parisian accent.

She met them at the gate, got them signed in, and brought them to the entrance of the infamous prison. She stopped before they entered the first door.

"May I ask why you desire a meeting with Henri Couverel?"

Nicholas shook his head. "It's a matter of national security. We must speak with him in private, with no one listening. If he knows he's on camera or tape, he may not be frank with us, and we don't have time to sort out lies."

"Is it pertaining to the Koh-i-Noor diamond? I understand it was stolen from the Metropolitan Museum of Art Thursday evening. It's all over the news." She turned to Mike. "Forgive my curiosity. Your boss, Milo Zachery, arranged this meeting. He told me a bit about what was happening."

Mike said, "I'm sure he did, Madame Badour, but we are not at liberty to discuss the matter. May we see Monsieur Couverel now?"

Badour gave them a beautiful Gallic shrug. "You can see him, but whether he will speak to you is another matter. He is not a cooperative inmate."

Mike had been in her share of prisons. La Santé had a reputation as one of the worst in the world. The suicide rates were enormous, inmates battled infestations, overcrowding, lice and rats, and one another. She had to admit, the long, gray corridors weren't cheerful. They would go for twenty to thirty feet and meet another gate, which was opened only after the gate behind them was shut, locked, and cleared. It took a solid twenty minutes to weave their way inside the dank concrete walls.

Nicholas said, "Madame Badour, has Couverel made any requests which you've denied?"

"Hundreds. He knows most of the drug pushers in Paris. Many officials want information from him, but it always comes at a price. Cigarettes, privileges, television. His most fervent demand, however, is beyond my control."

"What does he want?"

"A transfer to Clairvaux Prison. Out of Paris, out of this—" She broke off, swinging her hand around, and finished with a short "muck."

"And if I could make this happen? Would he be more cooperative?"

She studied him for a moment. "You must have sway with the French authorities."

Nicholas said, "Enough."

Mike remembered his Foreign Office ties, and realized that yes, he did have the pull for such a move.

Madame Badour realized he was serious as well. "Then I will not stop you from making the offer as leverage. We will wait here for Couverel. It won't be long. He isn't dangerous; we keep him in the mixed cells. Four men to a cell, they are confined twenty hours out of the day. He's been in isolation a few times, but he's been well behaved for the past two years, so he's been given work privileges. He folds pamphlets for a company we do business with. Oh, here is Couverel now."

Even as bad as the prison was, Mike was still shocked at the man's appearance. His dark hair was lank and greasy, and heavily streaked with white. His clothes were torn and dirty. He hadn't seen a razor in at least a week, nor water for bathing, it seemed. French prisoners didn't wear uniforms as they did in American prisons. They depended on the kindness of family and friends to provide fresh clothes. Couverel was obviously on his own.

She didn't think Couverel looked well enough to stand the interview, much less many more years.

He sat down hard at the chipped Formica table and stared at them. Mike and Nicholas sat themselves opposite him.

Nicholas turned to Madame Badour. "You'll excuse us?" It wasn't a request.

She pursed her lips and walked out. The steel door shut behind her with a loud clang, and they were alone with the prisoner.

Nicholas asked, *"Parlez-vous anglais?"*

Couverel shrugged. *"Non."*

Nicholas continued to speak in fluid French, and Mike struggled to keep up with his fast, idiomatic speech. Couverel was paying attention, and when Nicholas switched to English mid-sentence, he followed along.

Liar. He did speak English.

"The lady does not have enough French to follow. We will continue in English."

He shrugged again, a spark of humor in his eyes. *"Oui, cochon."*

Nicholas ignored the insult. "You look a bit like your sister."

Couverel's eyes narrowed. "I have no sister."

"Of course you do. We have DNA matching her to you. Where is she?"

Couverel stared at the table, flicked a nail against the edge.

Nicholas leaned into Couverel's face. "Listen to me very carefully. You have something I want. In return, I will give you what you want—a transfer to Clairvaux Prison. If you're truthful, I will make it happen. Lie to me"—Nicholas shrugged, placed his large hands on the table—"you will remain here to sleep with the rats."

75

Couverel settled deeper into the hard metal chair, chewed on a ragged, cracked lip for a moment, then said quietly, "If you can get me to Clairvaux, I will give you what you want."

Nicholas said, "Consider it done. You have my word. Now, your sister?"

Mike said, "We need a name, Henri. What was she called?"

"We called her Victoire. We were separated at a young age. She went to live with a family in England; I was left behind. I was old enough to be on my own, she was only a child."

Victoire. Victoria in English. As Gray Wharton had said, the best lies were always based in truth.

"Our parents left us when she was five. I did not know if they died or were killed or simply did not care anymore.

I found out later they were murdered. We were put into the Clesde Champs orphanage and stayed off and on for five years. Victoire had a family who liked her; they took her away, and I have not seen her since."

"What were your parents' names?"

"Isobel, she was my mother. My father was Henri as well."

"Couverel?"

"Oui."

"And the family who took her?"

"No idea. The woman, she had light hair and eyes. I remember thinking it would be clear Victoire was adopted; she looked nothing like the woman."

"Victoire Couverel. How old is she?"

"Four years younger than me. I am forty-two."

Mike was surprised. He looked to be in his late fifties if he was a day.

She said, "And you haven't seen her since you were fourteen and she was ten?"

"That's correct."

"No contact at all?"

"No." But he looked away, down and to the left as he said it, and they both knew he was lying.

Nicholas crossed his arms. "Clairvaux Prison awaits if you tell us the truth, Henri."

Couverel sat back in the chair, scratched his neck. Something came off in his fingers; he examined it for a second, then casually flicked it away.

Mike shuddered. Couverel caught the movement and

smiled at her. His teeth were crooked but in surprisingly decent shape, considering. His voice was dreamy.

"Do you know they keep Carlos the Jackal at Clairvaux? I should like to meet him. He was here for a time, inside La Santé. But kept isolated. A celebrity. I suppose they didn't want him to give us ideas."

Nicholas was getting impatient. "Henri, I'll make sure you get a personal audience with him, but only if you tell me the truth. When did you see Victoire last? I know you've seen her recently, so don't lie."

He sniffed and lit a cigarette he'd probably stolen. "I speak the truth. It has been twenty years since I last saw her. She does not care about me, I do not care about her. I have no idea where she is or what she's done to bring you to me. I don't care, either. If you see her, remind her she has a dying brother." He took a long drag on the cigarette and shrugged. "Who knows? Maybe she will send me some money. Or her friend will."

Nicholas flattened his palms on the table and leaned close. "What do you know of your sister's friends, Henri?"

His eyes flickered. So this was the lie. He said slowly, unwillingly, "Perhaps I have heard of a man she knows."

"Go on."

"He is, how do you say it in English, *un fantôme, oui*?" A ghost. Nicholas felt his heart speed up.

"A ghost?" Mike asked. "You mean the man is dead?"

Henri lit a new cigarette from the smoking ember of the old one. He nodded. "Yes, a ghost. But he is not dead."

"You have to give us a bit more to go on, mate."

"I cannot give what I do not have."

"What's his name?"

Silence.

Yes, Couverel was afraid of this so-called ghost. Who was he?

"Where did she meet him?'

Silence.

Mike said, "Come on, Henri. Help us out."

"*Un fantôme*. You look, and you will see."

"Tell us more about the people who adopted Victoire."

Couveral didn't move, didn't speak, didn't meet their eyes.

76

Couverel looked caught between the Devil and a hard place.

Nicholas waited, then stood up. "Say good-bye to Clairvaux, Henri." He turned to Mike. "Let's go."

"The family who took Victoire, the man was some kind of missionary. He traveled, to foreign countries. I remember because they asked what sort of shots Victoire had." He snapped his fingers in disgust. "As if she were a dog they had rescued from the gutter."

Nicholas had seen Victoria snap her fingers in that same dismissive way in New York, at the Met, while they were still on the same team. Was it simple genetics, or had Henri seen Victoria more recently than he claimed?

Nicholas doubted it, because Couverel wanted Clairvaux more than he was afraid of the ghost. Nicholas rubbed his hand across his chin. He hadn't had a chance to shave, and the stubble was thick. "Shots. A missionary. Were they taking her back to England, or somewhere else?"

"I do not know. And I swear to you, I know nothing more. Clairvaux—will I go there?"

Nicholas said, "Yes, you will go to Clairvaux."

Nicholas went to the door and pressed the buzzer. Moments later, Madame Badour appeared, and they stepped from the room. She shuttled them through the first two gates before saying, "It sounds as if you had success."

Nicholas nodded. "Expect the request to come for his transfer to Clairvaux, but don't release him to their custody until I give you the go-ahead. I need to make sure the information he gave us was the truth."

The woman spoke without irony. "You may count on me to do my duty, Monsieur Drummond."

They wound out of the prison's heart, through the clanging gates, and she bid them adieu at the cement bench she'd collected them from two hours earlier.

Mike couldn't get out of the prison fast enough, and she could tell Nicholas was anxious to be gone and follow the lead, too. It wouldn't take long to verify the information regarding Victoria's adoption; it would be in the state records. The ghost. *Fantôme*.

She said, "Couverel said the ghost was Victoire's friend. I assume you made the connection, too, between Henri's *fantôme* and our master thief, the Ghost."

"Yes, I did. He's a busy man, this *fantôme*."

Mike nodded." This is the last bit of evidence we

need—they have to be partners. And maybe the number she was calling on the plane belongs to him. We can track him through the number."

"It fits, Mike. Menard told us the Ghost was a retired assassin. No wonder Couverel was so terrified to tell us about him. The *fantôme* has already murdered five people we know of in the past couple of days. At least he told us enough about her adoptive parents to track them down."

He didn't argue when Mike took the keys from his hand and got behind the wheel. He climbed in beside her, and she turned the engine over. Heat began shooting from the vents of their rented Peugeot, and she rubbed her hands in front of the stream of air. She was cold through, and it wasn't only because of the winter chill.

"You're quiet. Still hurting?"

He was hurting, the adrenaline of the chase wearing off. He could make it awhile longer, though.

"I'll do. I'm going to look up the parents' murder as we go. Do you need directions?"

"No, I have the GPS. But I do need to know where we're going."

"A destination would help, wouldn't it?"

"Yes, and having a plan might be good, too."

"I think our first priority should be finding some food. I'm famished."

"Do you know, I don't think I've eaten a proper meal since this case began. You, either."

"Drive west, toward the Eiffel Tower. We'll find something suitable along the way."

She put the Peugeot into gear and pulled out. Forty

minutes later, they were seated at Café L'Ardoise, steaming cups of café au lait at their elbows and croissants on the plates in front of them. Nicholas's computer was open, and he was reading out loud between bites.

"Isobel and Henri Couverel. This is interesting: they were murdered. During a robbery gone wrong, it seems. Henri Couverel was a shopkeeper; his wife was an artist. Oils, watercolors, the like. They were mugged, and fought back. Both were shot and left on the street. Their assailant was never caught."

"So they left two kids, five and nine. No family to take them in. Does the orphanage have good enough records?"

"There should be records of an adoption. And if her name really is Victoire, we can search from that angle, too."

He typed in the name of the orphanage. "Oh, bugger. The orphanage burned down in the nineties, and there are no online records. We'll have to go at this the old-fashioned way, through the state system, and it's going to cost us time."

He took a big bite of bread, washed it down with his coffee.

Mike played with her spoon, dipping it in and out of the coffee absently as she thought aloud. "The murders will be easier to track. Even though it's a cold case, the French police will have the records. As for the adoptive parents, let's assume parts of her story for the Victoria Browning identity were real. She did have a Scottish accent. It could have been faked, but that's hard to do for months at a time. So let's look for missionaries near

Roslin, Scotland. Her brother said England, but it was a long time ago. Perhaps they brought her home before they set out on their voyages, or came back to Scotland after their mission was accomplished."

"Good thinking. I'll tackle the adopted parents. Would you like to use your considerable American charm to get the murder information from the French?"

"If it's a cold case, I doubt it will help, but I'll call Zachery. He's got a friend over here. This same friend is also the reason we were able to get into the prison so easily. In the meantime, you may want to think about where we're sleeping tonight. Not to mention, I'd like a shower." She yawned, not bothering to try and hide it. "And a nap. And I'd like to take a look at your back. After our car chase in Geneva, I want to be sure your stitches aren't ripped."

He arched a black eyebrow at her. "I have the accommodations covered. We're going to the Ritz, on the Place Vendôme. We'll regroup, as you Yanks like to say, and you can strip me down."

77

When they arrived at the Ritz, the valet took the car, and Mike stared at the white awnings of the swanky hotel, wondering how, exactly, she would write this off. She couldn't afford to stay here, but she wasn't about to say so to Nicholas, who was holding out his arm and smiling like they were on a date. She laughed to herself. A very demented date.

She tucked her arm in his and he whispered, "Follow my lead."

They entered the hotel and walked to the desk. A young blonde with her hair drawn back in a messy, casual bun looked up from her computer to greet them, and her face broke into a wide smile. She spoke in rapid French to the woman next to her, who scurried away, then acknowledged them with a nod.

"Monsieur DuLac, welcome back to the Ritz."

"*Merci*, Clothilde. *Comment ça va?*"

She dimpled at him. "I am well, Monsieur DuLac. It is good to see you again. Will you be staying long?"

"At least one night, perhaps two."

She glanced at Mike, who suddenly felt very American, very tall, and very underdressed in her motorcycle boots and jeans.

"One room or two?"

"A suite would do nicely, Clothilde. Two bedrooms."

"Excellent." She handed him a key. "Shall I send up your usual?"

"That would be lovely. For two, if you will. *Merci*, Clothilde."

Mike followed him across the elegant lobby, past the Bar Vendôme. Nicholas paused for a moment to watch the small flat-screen TV. A panel of jewel experts on a local news station were yelling over one another to see who could condemn the Americans more for the Koh-i-Noor theft. He shook his head. It wouldn't stop until the diamond was back. Once on the elevator, Nicholas smiled at her. "All right?"

She grinned back. "What was all that? Who is Monsieur DuLac? And do I want to know what your *usual* is?"

"DuLac is one of my better covers. I used to come to Paris often when I worked for the Foreign Office, and DuLac served me well. I didn't see any reason to walk in and announce who I really was. Besides, we'll be well taken care of now. You can freshen up and we'll have some dinner. Without food and sleep, we're going to be worthless to this investigation. I need to spend some time on the computer, tracking some of these identities. We're getting enough information on this woman to pull together a real profile. I think the Fox's days as an anonymous master thief are coming to an abrupt end.

"Even though we have no idea where the Fox might be, she seems to have a sixth sense about us following her. She may have assumed, or hoped, I was dead after the explosion, but she will find out quickly enough there were no fatalities. I certainly don't need her calling around to hotels to see if anyone by the name of Drummond or Caine has checked in."

Smart man. "You look like you could use a pain pill. You haven't had one since we left the hospital this morning, and we've had quite a day."

Actually, he could use a whole handful of pain pills. He said gruffly, "Mike, if I need mothering, I'll call home."

They rode to the sixth floor, and Nicholas led her down the blue-and-gold hallway to their suite.

"Did you know the Ritz was supposedly the first hotel in Paris to have en suite bathrooms?"

Mike said, "Good to know. At this point, so long as it has hot water, I don't care where the bathroom is."

He opened the door and let her go in first, then pointed to the left. Without examining the room, which looked like the inside of a castle, or the view, which looked expansive—she caught a snatch of the Eiffel Tower; you really could see it from everywhere—she excused herself and went inside.

The bathroom did indeed have hot water, and a

gorgeous marble shower with buttery soft peach towels. She stayed under the steaming waterfall for a good fifteen minutes, washing away the travel dust, explosion residue, worry, fear and two days of exhaustive searching for what amounted to a very well-equipped and pissed-off ghost.

She did her best thinking in the shower. She was certain the Fox was in Paris; where else would she be? She thought about the adoptive parents—missionaries—and about the new life the Fox had led with them. Was it good, bad, or maybe it didn't matter? The Fox had become a criminal regardless.

She was interrupted by a knock on the door.

"Go away. I'm never coming out. This is the most glorious shower I've ever taken."

Nicholas laughed. "You may think differently when I give you this news. Savich called. He has a money trail. And the food's arrived."

She couldn't get dry fast enough. She spared a quick glance at her clothes—no sense getting back into them right away, and she'd rushed in here so fast she'd left her bag in the other room. She pulled on the thick robe instead and joined Nicholas in the living room.

He'd had a shower, too. His hair was still damp, and he smelled good. Unlike her, in her anonymous bathrobe, he looked as sleek as a panther in a black zipper-neck sweater and gray wool trousers. Where did he stash all these wonderful clothes? He had to be coming to the bottom of his magic carry-on.

A tray was on the table with a variety of cheeses, bread,

and fruit. A bottle of wine was open, but she ignored his offer of a glass and instead poured herself some water.

"So what did Savich have to say?"

"I told him I was going to get you out of the shower so he could tell us both. He should be calling back any minute."

"I better grab some clothes."

"Don't dress on my account."

She arched an eyebrow at him. "In your dreams."

Nicholas grinned. "And was I dreaming, or did you kiss me last night?"

"You were definitely dreaming."

"And was I dreaming when you called me a lame-brain?"

"That you didn't dream," she said, and grabbed her bag and carried it into her room.

When she returned a few minutes later, he said, "Eat something. The coffee and pastry weren't enough."

She helped herself to a plate and sat with her legs drawn up, eating Brie and grapes. She looked tired, and he couldn't blame her. He'd been drugged up, but still he'd gotten a good ten hours. He couldn't imagine she'd enjoyed much rest in that chair.

"After we talk to Savich, we'll work the computers, find the trail. And stick around here tonight. You need some rest."

She swept her arm around. "This is nice."

It *was* nice, which was the reason he'd wanted to bring her here. Half showing off, half wanting to give her some kindness, after the kindness she'd shown him last night.

He said, "You're a good partner, Mike."

He caught her by surprise. She paused for a moment, then said, "You know what? You are, too."

He laughed. "When do you want to examine my stitches?"

78

Paris
Saturday afternoon

Kitsune stopped for an espresso and a bathroom break at a roadside travel station. She was dragging. Paris was an hour away; she needed to hold it together a bit longer, then the job would be finished and she could rest. This was why she trained so hard, and saved her energy between contracts; once she started a job, proper sleep and food weren't priorities.

She set the empty cup down on the bar. The place was filled with tourists: teens in tight jeans and mismatched colors, flirting; harried parents with small children; the odd lingering glances of single men. Normal. It was all so very normal. She didn't remember ever having normal.

She turned to leave and heard her mobile ringing from her jacket pocket. She drew the phone out and looked at the screen. It was Mulvaney.

She shouted with relief. She ran out of the building, jumped in her stolen Fiat, and answered the phone.

"Mulvaney! Thank God, I've been so worried!" She got hold of herself. "Well, it's about time. I thought you were dead."

"Hello, Kitsune." Her heart stopped. *No. Please, no.*

"Lanighan?"

"You'll get your man Mulvaney back when you hand over the diamond."

Her heart pounded at her temples, fear clogged her throat. "What have you done to him? Where is he?"

She knew who held the power now. Lanighan's voice held both contempt and pleasure. "You will do exactly what I say. No more mistakes, no more trying to screw me out of my diamond. You give me the Koh-i-Noor, in person, and I will let him go."

How had he found Mulvaney? They were always so careful. And how had he managed to take him? No one took Mulvaney, he was too smart, too fast—

Control, she must gain control. She must be calm. She said, "I do not understand why you have done this. I have given you my word, and two years of my life in the pursuit of your dream. I want you to have your diamond."

He was breathing fast, so mad now he was nearly shouting. "I'm to blame here? You're the one who put my bank accounts in the hands of the FBI. You're the one who gave me a key to open that rigged safe-deposit box. You would have blown me up!"

His voice dropped; he was struggling for control.

"Damn you, you bitch, you sliced my throat in Paris. Consider this payback. You're going to do exactly what I tell you. Bring me the diamond, and you get your precious mentor back."

She was shaking, she was so furious. She yelled, "You idiot! That was not a fake key! You let Mulvaney go right now, or I will disappear with the Koh-i-Noor forever. You won't be able to unite the three stones."

She heard the sharp intake of his breath. She knew he was planning something crazy with the diamond, she *knew* it. She'd shaken him; now it was time to press her advantage, to be calm and take control again.

"Yes, Saleem. I know what you think you can do. Why else would you want the Koh-i-Noor? All the men in your family have tried and failed. What makes you think you are any different?"

Saleem ignored her words, and went for the jugular. "You're killing him, Kitsune. Every word, every minute that ticks by, Mulvaney dies a little more. A finger, an ear, so much I can do. I am serious. You bring me the diamond at nine p.m., to my home, or I will cut him into little pieces."

He hung up.

Kitsune buried her face in her hands. She felt hollowed out with failure.

She'd bested the father. Somehow she would best the son. She had to regain the upper hand. Lanighan was mad if he thought she would now hand the diamond over in person—he'd kill her without hesitation, and Mulvaney as well. She patted her backpack. The diamond was safe.

Now she had to find out where he was holding Mulvaney, and end this.

She put the Fiat in gear and got back on the road, thinking furiously.

This was not the first attempted double-cross she'd faced. But it was the first time a job had ruptured into her real life. Again, she couldn't believe Lanighan had managed to find and take Mulvaney. He was the most careful man she'd ever known.

They'd worked together for more than half her life, more than twenty years now, and never been linked. Anyone who knew their names saw them only as rivals, and she and Mulvaney had laughed, toasting each other with the Krug he so loved to drink. Tears stung her eyes. She was afraid, not for herself but for him. Had she done something to allow this to happen? Or maybe she'd been naive, trusting their measures were infallible? It didn't matter now. She had to stop Lanighan, had to, no choice.

She wanted to kill him, she wanted to feel the point of her blade sink into the thin flesh of his throat. She wanted to watch him realize he was dead.

A righteous killing, but first she had to figure her way through this.

Think, Kitsune.

Lanighan had driven from Paris to Geneva so there would be no record of his face at the airports or train stations while this hubbub about the diamond raged on in the news. His car would have been searched at the border, which meant Lanighan hadn't held Mulvaney in Geneva.

Where, then?

In Paris. Lanighan's empire was run out of the City of Light. His first and only meeting with her had been at the Paris Ritz. Before their first meeting, she'd done a property records search. Lanighan had four private holdings where a covert operation could take place. Mulvaney was surely being held at one of them. She needed more information.

Saleem Lanighan was not the man his father was. He was arrogant and sloppy and cared only what happened to himself. He thought money solved everything. Nor was he comfortable operating far away from his base, which meant he kept precious possessions close. And at this point, Mulvaney was precious.

79

Nicholas's computer chimed. He opened the secure tele-
conference, and Savich's face popped up on the screen.
Mike recognized the furniture from the FBI's conference
room, which meant they were on the CIVITS secure
videoconference network. They could say anything
without worry of eavesdropping. Even the screens were
pulled on the picture windows—they could see out, but
no prying eyes could see in.

Nicholas said, "Hello, Savich. Good timing."

"You have Mike now?"

Nicholas shifted so Mike's face appeared over his
shoulder. "She's right here."

"Hi, Dillon."

"Hey, Mike. I've been at it all morning with MAX,
and here's what I've found. The numbers you sent were

wire transfers for a variety of banks. I've emailed the file
to you, Nicholas; you should have it now."

"I have it open."

"All right. I didn't find all the money yet, but I narrowed down three possible buyers for the stone. As you
guys know, the banks are hard to crack; numbered
accounts are the best way to stay under the radar when
you're moving large amounts of money. It's not like
anyone will funnel millions of dollars through Western
Union."

Nicholas laughed. "Life would be so much easier."

"It would. Based on everything we've compiled so far,
I'd pay special attention to the first person on your list.
I'm going to keep at it, see if anything else matches. We're
putting all three men under surveillance immediately. I'll
call you back if I find anything more."

Nicholas closed the chat and looked at the email from
Savich. The top entry was a man named Saleem Lanighan.
Mike scrolled through the attached photos. He was a
handsome man, dark hair and direct brown eyes, a square
jaw, but he wasn't smiling, and Mike thought he looked
cruel.

Mike said, "Dark hair, dark eyes. Remember what the
kid from Sages Fidelité said? None of the other three
match the physical description. Lanighan could be the
one."

Nicholas read Savich's dossier aloud.

"Lanighan is thirty-eight, educated at Oxford, a resident of Paris. He has a second home in the Loire Valley.
He took over his father, Robert Lanighan's, art and

antiquities business, plus the man's huge art collection, when he died five years ago. Lanighan was in *ArtReview*'s top one hundred three years running, is known for his philanthropic work on behalf of new artists and new galleries.

"He sits on the board of three separate companies, employs almost a thousand people in Lanighan Enterprises—they do international import-export—and regularly travels to China, Singapore, Hong Kong, and Tokyo in search of treasures. If this is our guy, there's a good chance the Fox is here, too."

Mike said, "He's entirely too respectable, don't you think? But rich as Croesus."

"Well, without the money, none of this would work. Lanighan sounds like the winner to me. On the surface, he's exceptional, but the man's father was suspected of orchestrating several art thefts. Where does Savich find this information?"

"Didn't Dillon tell you he used magic dust?"

"Yeah, I should have believed him. Would you look at this. Lanighan's mother was Amelia Thomas-Collins." He sat back, lost in thought. "Now I know why the name Lanighan sounds so familiar."

Mike raised her eyebrows. "Why?"

"Last summer, there was a rumor about the lineage of the Lanighan family; the rags ran stories for three weeks. The gist of it was the Lanighan line was illegitimate, the issue of—" He stopped speaking, his eyes suddenly very far away.

Mike said, "Issue of who? Nicholas, what is it?"

He said, slowly, "Lanighan must believe he's the last descendant of Duleep Singh. The last Lion of Punjab."

"The safe-deposit box in Geneva was rented in the name Duleep Singh."

"Just so. Remember when Singh was brought to England to give Queen Victoria the Koh-i-Noor, he became the toast of Britain and Scotland? He was on the social circuit, and society loved him. Queen Victoria even stood as godmother to several of his kids.

"He had eight children with two wives, but none of them had children of their own, so the line died out. Some said in the day that this is the true curse of the Koh-i-Noor."

"The end of the line. I see."

"The big scandal from last year came about when a historian realized one of Singh's sons supposedly fathered a child with Lady Grace Lanighan, Countess Wiltshire. A bastard child, who in turn sired his own line. He wasn't given a title; he was a second son, and clearly illegitimate. Though supposedly he looked exactly like his father, much to the earl's dismay."

He stood up and started to pace the room. "It wasn't spoken of publicly then, mind you, not at the turn of the last century. I believe the child was born in 1898 or '99, and no one wanted to accuse the countess of getting a leg over with someone other than her husband, the earl.

"Historically speaking, the child was of no consequence. His older brother married and produced a son, a proper heir, and no more was spoken of it. However, the family line died out after all the sons were killed in the war, and the title became extinct."

"Gotta love primogeniture."

He glanced at her coldly, and she shrugged. "What? I watch *Downton Abbey.*"

"To continue. Now, if Saleem Lanighan is the child of the illegitimate Wiltshire line, he could be an actual blood relative of the Lion of Punjab, the last true owner of the Koh-i-Noor diamond before it was taken."

"That would be incredible. What if he is a blood heir? Who would care?"

Nicholas sat back on his chair, crossed his arms over his chest. "We're dealing in conjecture, and legends. *If* Saleem Lanighan is the son of the line, then he is the rightful heir to the Koh-i-Noor. Not that it matters, because the British will never give it up. I know there's more to this. But what?"

"I don't know, but we better order some coffee. It's going to be a long night."

80

Kitsune walked into the black skyscraper known as Tour Areva like she owned the place. The lobby was quiet, only a single security guard sat behind a half-moon desk. He was leaning back in his chair with his feet up, watching a video on his monitor, some high Hollywood production in the middle of a battle, from the screams and explosions and screeches coming from the computer. He snapped to when he saw her approach but didn't turn off the movie.

"May I help you, ma'am?"

"Bonsoir." She didn't stop walking, merely flashed a pass at him, too quickly for him to read. "My boyfriend left his phone in his office. I'm going to run up and grab it for him."

"I'll need you to sign in."

She abruptly turned, grabbed the pen from his hand,

and scribbled on the white sheet of paper, then kept moving.

"I can't read this. Where are you going?"

"Twenty-third floor. I'll only be a moment."

He nodded—how much of a threat could this small woman be, after all—and went back to his movie.

She smiled as she reached the elevator. She'd talked her way past hundreds of security guards in her day.

She took the elevator to the twenty-third floor, then ran up the stairwell to twenty-five.

Lanighan's offices were down the hallway, and his state-of-the-art security system didn't hold out long against Kitsune's deft tools. She put the rake in the lock and pulled the trigger, listening to the tumblers whine, then clunk open.

When the latch on the door opened, the security system began giving off a quiet beep every second. She slapped a counter up on the wall, attached two metal butterfly clips to the alarm, and within moments, the counter had identified the numbers of the system's passcode, inputted them, and bypassed the system. The alarm turned off with a small squawk, and all was silent.

She would have approximately three minutes before the alarm company registered the system at Lanighan Enterprises had been turned off and notified Lanighan of the breach. With luck, the guard downstairs wouldn't be notified for five minutes, but just in case, she needed to work quickly.

Lanighan was first and foremost an art lover, like his

father. On his computer was a comprehensive list of all the holdings of Lanighan Enterprises, and where each piece of art was kept.

Since he was holding Mulvaney hostage, she'd take his art away. Most of his net worth was tied to the collection. Wipe it out, and she'd take his fortune with her.

He'd left his desktop computer in sleep mode to save energy, and, luck of all luck, it didn't have a password on it.

"Stupid man."

Whereas Kitsune's talents lay in physical extractions—it was said she had the softest hands in the business—Mulvaney was getting older, and his natural aptitudes had become slightly more cerebral. Corporate espionage paid very well, and Mulvaney designed many of the tools he used to gain information himself. Kitsune made heavy use of them in her jobs as well.

She inserted a thumb drive into the terminal and copied over Lanighan's hard drive. The thumb drive contained a nifty little virus Mulvaney had cooked up that deleted the master files and all the backups from the host computer as it transferred. Not only would she have the information on the art collection, her thumb drive would be the only link to his company's files. Payroll, insurance, assets, everything. It would take great effort to re-create—effort, time, and money.

She counted down as the files deleted themselves from his system, whispered to herself, "Come on, hurry, hurry."

Two minutes to go.

She took a lap around his spacious office, bigger than her flat in London, with a spectacular view over the city.

She stopped to admire the paintings on the walls. He had a small Cézanne she was tempted to cut from its frame, just to be spiteful. It would serve him right.

The thumb drive beeped, and she pulled herself away. Maybe another time.

Back out the door, silent and careful. She reset the alarm, relocked the glass doors, ran down the two flights of stairs, and grabbed the elevator down.

Less than three minutes, all told. Not bad.

She walked out the front door, waggling her own mobile phone over her head as she walked past the guard. He ignored her, and she was gone into the night.

81

Nicholas was deep into rereading Lanighan's file when there was a knock at the door to the suite.

Mike was combing the files from the French authorities on the elder Couverel's mugging and murder. She set her laptop aside and said, "There's the coffee. I'll get it. I'm telling you, Nicholas, I'm pretty sure there's nothing useful in these files. The case went cold thirty years ago, and no one has done any work on it since."

She crossed the room and opened the door. Nicholas heard a strangled cry and bolted from the couch to see Mike hurled backward into the living room and slammed against a chair. A dark-skinned man burst in after her, a suppressed Beretta 92S in his hand.

The man ran into the suite, his eyes on Mike, his Beretta aimed at her head. Nicholas came in hard from the side, buying him a moment of precious surprise. He kicked out at the man's knee, but the man whirled about and leapt back, only taking a glancing blow to his thigh. He grunted in pain, but it barely slowed him. He brought his gun to Nicholas's chest, Mike forgotten.

Nicholas whipped his leg up to kick the gun out of his hand, but the man pulled his arm back in time. Nicholas jumped into him, slammed his fist into the man's neck. The man's head flew back, and as Nicholas spun around, he grabbed the man's arm and sent his elbow into his gut, once, twice. He grabbed the man's wrist and clamped his fingers hard into the soft flesh. The man screamed and the gun went off, an obscene sound, then fell and skidded across the floor. The man's fist hit Nicholas's forehead, and he staggered back, seeing lights.

Nicholas heard Mike shout, "Get away from him, Nicholas!" He knew she wanted to shoot the man. And the man did, too, because he grabbed on to Nicholas, trying to use him as a shield, dragging him toward the door of the suite. But he couldn't hold him.

Mike watched the fight turn into a vicious brawl. She had her Glock out, but the men were moving too fast to get a clear shot—blocking and countering each other's strikes as they destroyed the furniture in the suite, and themselves.

Nicholas took a hard blow to the shoulder. He pivoted and grabbed the man's neck with one arm as he punched him in the kidneys, vicious blows that would fell a giant, but the man managed to squirm away—how, Mike didn't know, he was that good. He stared at Nicholas for a split second, then took off at a dead run out of the suite. Mike fired once, twice, but missed him.

Nicholas yelled to Mike, "Call it in, I'm going after him," and ran out the door.

The man was at the end of the hall, going through the emergency door to the stairwell. Nicholas sprinted after him, made it through the door in time to see a black-sneakered foot running up toward the roof. He squeezed off three shots, but the man didn't stop.

Up three more flights, and the man threw open the door to the roof and slammed it shut behind him, slowing Nicholas for a moment.

When he eased open the roof door, Nicholas was met with a deep silence. It was dark, but there was enough ambient light from the streets below and the rising full moon to make out shadows and shapes.

There were plenty of places to hide up here. The housings for the air-conditioning units acted as dividers down the length of the roof; the man could be behind any of them.

Nicholas held himself perfectly still, listening. There, labored breathing coming from about twenty feet away. He edged forward, his steps light on the gravel. Ten feet, five, then the door to the roof opened, light flooding the dark, and the man jumped up like a quail flushed from the brush. He ran hard down the roof.

Mike joined him, whispered fiercely, "Let's get the bastard." They could see the man bobbing and weaving, and fired.

There was a muffled grunt and the man stumbled. *Good,* Nicholas thought, one of them had hit him.

Mike peeled off to the other side to flank him. Three more steps and Nicholas tackled the man. They rolled to the ground, twisting, punching, kicking, trying to gain an advantage. Nicholas saw blood and realized a bullet had nicked the man's rib cage. Why didn't it slow him down? Nicholas flipped him onto his back, jammed his elbow in the wound, and wedged his forearm under the man's chin.

"Who sent you?"

The man gurgled, and Nicholas eased off, only to get a vicious hit in the back, knocking him sideways. The man was up on his feet, his fists lashing out. Nicholas rolled over and up and went at him. He struck him in the face with his fist and saw blood spurt out. He'd broken the man's nose.

Mike kicked out the man's right knee from behind, and he collapsed forward. Nicholas clamped down tight on the man's windpipe.

"Who sent you?"

The man shoved backward with all his strength, knocking Nicholas into the air conditioner's housing, slamming his head into the metal unit, but Nicholas hung on. Still the man came at him, trying to slam his fist into his throat, a crushing blow meant to kill him, but Nicholas got his hands up in time.

The man kicked out again with his leg, blood dripping down his chin onto his chest. Nicholas was in a berserk fury now, punching and jabbing and kicking. Mike screamed, "Don't kill him, Nicholas, we need him!" but the only noise he heard was his blood thundering in his ears.

Nicholas shoved the man backward, and as he lost his balance Mike shot him in the leg. He howled in pain, and his leg buckled. He was too close to the edge of the roof. Nicholas saw him stumble and fall, and grabbed for his wrist, but his palms were slick with blood and he couldn't hold on.

With a scream, the man disappeared over the edge. His body struck the dormer window frame, then toppled down to the sidewalk onto the Place Vendôme below.

82

Nicholas and Mike looked over the edge. The man had landed facedown, arms spread-eagled out on the concrete, his neck clearly broken. She didn't want to see his face.

Nicholas slid down the wall, breathing hard. Mike eased down beside him, reached over and swiped the blood off his nose and mouth. She picked up his hand, saw the torn knuckles. "Not too bad." There was blood all over his chest. "You're bleeding!"

"No, no, it's his blood. Sorry I couldn't keep him alive, Mike."

"I wish I'd shot him in both knees."

Nicholas laughed, couldn't help it. He got up and pulled her with him. "Damnation, woman, you're the one covered in blood. Where did he hit you?"

She blinked at him, mute, then stared down at herself and passed out without a sound.

He eased her down onto the roof. Her nose was bleeding, and she had a cut lip. He ripped her shirt open and pulled it down. The man had shot her in the arm. A bullet to the biceps, through and through, into the meat of the muscle, not the bone, thank the good Lord above.

He ripped the sleeve off and used it as a tourniquet, then ran his hands over the rest of her body. No more injuries. She'd be okay. He pulled her against him for a moment, thankful and quiet, then stood up and hoisted her over his shoulder. He heard a whisper of a laugh.

"That tickles."

"Stay still. I need to get you down the stairs." She relaxed against his back, and he carried her down the stairs to their room.

Their suite looked like a war zone. At least the sofa was still in one piece. He laid her down, and she looked up at him and smiled.

"Aren't we a pair? Do I look as bad as you do?"

He smiled back. "I don't want to look. Stay still, Mike. I hear the sirens. We're going to be crawling with cops any second now. Did you call it in?"

"Yes. Before I went up after you to the roof. Let me sit up." She realized then she had a split lip from the man's fist in her face when she first opened the door.

"Now who's being the tough one?" he asked, but helped her up, loosened the tourniquet, happy to see that the wound was bleeding only slightly.

He said, "We're going to have matching stitches."

She wanted to tell him she would have more fun checking his stitches than he would hers, but she didn't. She said, "Who was that man?"

"I don't know. He's dead. Look, it couldn't be helped. I still can't believe he wouldn't give up."

She couldn't believe it, either.

"I've never seen anyone fight like you do. It's brutal."

Nicholas said, "It's Filipino Kali with a bit of karate thrown in. I'll teach you, if you'd like."

She cocked an eyebrow at him. "Maybe you'd better wait to see some of my moves first."

83

Hotel security wasn't happy to have a shootout on their roof and a dead man on the street at the front doors. The local flic from the commissariat de police, who introduced himself as Monsieur L'Agent Foulard, insisted on interrogating them for twenty minutes, despite their badges. It was only Menard's arrival that put a halt to it.

After Foulard was gone, Menard said, "I was told your former suite needed a lot more than a simple dusting and clean towels. Do tell me how you managed to end up on the roof with an assassin."

Nicholas said, "Fewer people on the roof than in the lobby."

Menard grinned, showing a gold back tooth. He turned to Mike. "Agent Caine, I hear you're being difficult. You should be treated at the hospital."

Mike said, "I think we're better off sticking together

and staying here. Whoever's after us isn't going to give up simply because we've killed three of his men."

Menard said, "We have an ID on the two men who ended up in Lake Geneva—César Arnault and Claude Soutane, local freelance bad guys."

Nicholas said, "We think we know who hired them. A man named Saleem Lanighan, a British national who makes his home in France."

"I know this man. He is big in the art world. What makes you think he is behind this?"

"Everything is pointing his way. If you could trace the men in Geneva to him, that would pretty much nail it. The man who went off the roof wasn't local muscle, he was a pro. Tough, vicious, and committed to seeing us dead."

"I heard the flics mention the name O'Brien. If this is the same man I know, you're lucky to be alive. Talk about a pro—he's never failed before tonight."

Menard rose. "I need not remind the two of you to take care. Agent Caine, do as the doctor tells you. Keep your arm in a sling, and no more fights—at least for a couple of days."

Mike said, "It's only a flesh wound."

Menard gave each of them a long look. "I will try to trace the men in Geneva to Saleem Lanighan." And he took himself off to deal with the mess downstairs.

Nicholas's computer chimed.

It was Savich. Nicholas opened the chat.

"Good to see you're both still upright."

"We're fine," Nicholas said. "The man who attacked

us is dead, and Menard is going to try to connect him and the two men in Geneva with Saleem Lanighan."

Nicholas and Mike filled Savich in on everything they'd learned, from Couverel to the Ghost, who was undoubtedly the man who'd murdered the Anatolys and Elaine York and Kochen. Mike told him how they believed the Ghost was connected to the Fox. "But we still don't know who he is or where to find him," Mike said, "only that he exists. He could still be in New York."

Nicholas told him about Saleem Lanighan's direct line back to Duleep Singh, the brother of the Lion of Punjab, and the newly discovered scandal about his affair with the Countess Wiltshire.

Savich said, "I'm going to have to tell Sherlock she was right. She said she knew down to her size sevens we'd find the answer to the theft of the Koh-i-Noor in its English roots."

"Kiss the woman's size sevens, Dillon," Mike said.

Savich laughed. "Now, for my contribution, I've found the money trail for one of the Fox's accounts. Over the past three years, there have been four money transfers from the Bank Horim to a Smith Barney account, which then pinged out to a bank in Curaçao. The money left Curaçao and went to Israel, where it was disbursed back into five numbered accounts at a Horim branch in Tel Aviv. Clean as a whistle."

"For how much?"

"Each transfer was for five million dollars."

Nicholas was impressed. "Twenty-five million bucks.

That isn't a half-bad payday for a single job, and I imagine there's another equal share owed her on delivery of the Koh-i-Noor. Does it say who the accounts belong to?"

"As you know, the bank doesn't have names attached to the accounts online, only numbers. You'll have to get a warrant for the names tied to the numbered accounts. Though I wouldn't count on it being anything other than multiple false identities, and therefore meaningless. The Fox seems to have plenty of identities."

Mike said, "You're right, Dillon, she does. Assuming this is the Fox's money, why would she circle back to the same bank? Is this the safest way to move the money around?"

"With as many accounts as it pinged through, yes, it's a very safe way to launder money. I wouldn't have found it if I wasn't specifically looking for these types of transfers from this specific bank and cross-referencing by the account numbers you found. All the Swiss banks are good, but she must trust this bank implicitly. I'd be willing to bet she has someone on the inside at the bank running these accounts for her."

Nicholas arched a black brow. "Marie-Louise Helmut, perchance?"

"Probably," Mike said, then turned back to the screen. "Dillon, did you see any direct ties to Saleem Lanighan?"

"No, not yet, but I bet the originating account will trace to him. Since it's been closed, there's no foolproof way to tell. Maybe you'll have more luck on your end. One more thing. Nick, I'm sorry to have to tell you this.

But last week there was a money transfer from this Smith Barney account to Elaine York's bank account as well. One payment of two hundred thousand dollars."

Nicholas felt the news like a punch to his gut. It was over, no more trying to pretend Elaine was innocent.

He said only, "Thanks, Savich. We'll take it from here."

"Be careful, guys."

They closed his computer, Nicholas looked at his watch. Nearly eight. Mike was watching him. "Are you okay?"

"Yes, of course. The question is, are you?"

"Like I said, 'tis only a flesh wound."

"You're lying. I admire that. Okay now, we know Lanighan is based in Paris. Find out where he lives. Later tonight you and I are going to go watch his house and see if he has plans."

"What about the Fox?"

"If she's making a delivery to Lanighan, he's the one we need to track. Like you said, she seems to have a sixth sense about us on this case. Who knows? Maybe she'll come to us."

84

Ben Houston was deep into Anatoly's files when Zachery called him into his office.

Ben gathered his things and walked the hundred feet to the executive suites on the twentieth floor. Normally at 2:00 p.m. the leadership would be in their daily big-dog meeting, but since it was a weekend, only a few stragglers were around. Even Maryann, the secretary to all the Criminal Division SACs since the late eighties, had gone home. But her boss hadn't. When Zachery closed and locked the door behind him, Ben went on red alert.

Something big was going down.

Zachery gestured to the black leather couch instead of his round conference table. "You've been at it for hours. Take a load off."

Like everyone else working this case, Ben had managed only a few hours' sleep for the past few days. Safer to take the chair. "If I get on that couch, you'll never get me off it. What's happening, sir?"

Zachery stood at his window, staring out across the East River into Brooklyn, his arms behind him. "Nicholas and Mike found the buyer for the diamond; Savich has verified it."

"Who is it?"

"A wealthy businessman, Saleem Lanighan, supposedly a direct descendant of the Lion of Punjab, who was the one who surrendered the Koh-i-Noor to Queen Victoria."

"So Sherlock was right," Ben said.

"Yes, she was. However, we have lots more work to do, Ben. The NSA has sent over the trace of the phone number the Fox called from her plane. They confirmed the signal, and we've been able to track it. The owner of the phone has been in New York for the past week. He left the country last night, bound for Paris. We ran his face through the NGI facial-recognition database, and it matched the photo of a British national who tried to assassinate François Mitterrand two decades ago. Interpol believes this man is the Ghost. They're sending us everything they've got, which isn't much.

"It seems likely the Ghost killed not only Elaine York but Anatoly and his two sons, and attacked Mike and Nicholas in the garage. We've also identified the man killed at Anatoly's. His name is Jason Rathbone, and he works for Saleem Lanighan. There were no prints in the system, but there was a DNA match on CODIS."

Zachery said, "Savich told me Elaine's bank account

shows a two-hundred-thousand-dollar deposit last week. So she was being paid, but for what? By whom?"

Ben couldn't bear it. He'd hoped everything would be explained, that Elaine would be exonerated. But no. Ben said only, "I don't know, sir."

Zachery came over and sat in the chair opposite Ben. "I don't know, either. We need to find the tie between the Ghost and Elaine and Anatoly. They're all mixed together in this, but we don't know exactly how.

"Track this Ghost character, Ben, and find out what he took from Anatoly's safe. Can you do that for me?"

"Of course, sir. I'm on it."

Ben left Zachery staring out the windows, and went back to his desk. He called Mike first thing, to warn her so she'd know about the Ghost, but she didn't answer her phone, so he left her a message to call him as soon as she could.

And then he settled himself at his desk to mourn Elaine York and find a killer.

85

Kitsune checked into a small, quiet hotel on the West Bank, took a room sight unseen, and was barely inside the door before she plugged the thumb drive into her laptop and watched the files upload. Hundreds upon hundreds of files, every one a valuable link to Lanighan's enterprise. It gave her great satisfaction to hold the heart of his world in her hands.

If Mulvaney was close by, she would find him in these files.

She set the laptop down on the small desk and opened her bag. She wanted to hold on a bit longer, but there was no help for it, she needed fuel and rest. The hotel provided fruit at the front desk. She'd taken three apples and a banana, had jerky and granola bars in her bag from her stop at the travel center. She ate while the files began to load, then took a shower. She set her alarm for two hours of sleep and drifted off immediately.

She woke refreshed, though still tired. She took a handful of vitamins loaded with ginseng to help her stay awake and focused. She drank water, stretched, and made a cup of herbal tea.

While she was sipping her tea, the files finished uploading. She scrolled through them, down to the *S* files—the security folder—hoping there were protocols of the security systems from Lanighan's warehouses. She was in luck; there was a folder inside labeled *DropCams*.

There were at least fifty camera feeds to go through. With a sigh, she settled deeper in her chair and began opening them one by one.

She hit pay dirt on the eighth folder. The screen was separated into five squares, two large squares showing the first-floor interior of a warehouse, and row upon row of what she knew must be artwork, and three smaller squares on the bottom showing individual rooms on the top floor, one a very large office. And in the office, she saw Mulvaney, tied to a chair, his arms stretched tight behind his back, a gag in his mouth. He was slumped over, asleep or dead, she couldn't tell. The video was too grainy to see if his chest rose and fell. She saw flashes of light, shadows moving outside the range of the cameras. She realized whoever was in the room with him was taking photographs.

She took a deep breath to calm her rage, looked at the file, saw the address—it was a warehouse in Gagny Neuftrois. Forty minutes away.

She hadn't wanted to believe Lanighan, but now she had no choice—she'd seen Mulvaney with her own eyes. She felt tears burn her eyes, shook it off. She'd save him, she had to.

She scanned the remaining files, saw a few more attached to the Gagny warehouse. She opened them and read through the information, found the corresponding video feeds for the cameras on the grounds.

She wasn't surprised the outside cameras showed armed guards patrolling the perimeter. She counted fourteen men in fatigues, cradling AR-15s to their chests, all in a state of readiness she'd seen from professional soldiers. They fairly screamed mercenary.

It made sense to have security, of course, with the treasures he had inside the warehouse. But this—fourteen heavily armed men sweeping around the building in a clearly coordinated pattern, this was overkill, and done for a reason: Lanighan knew she was coming.

If it was a war he wanted, she was happy to bring it to his door. One against fourteen wasn't the best odds, but she'd dealt with worse.

She spent the next fifteen minutes drawing up plans, making lists. She had a storage unit near Paris that held everything she'd need, units similar to ones she had all over the world. Tools were needed for her work, and it paid to be prepared.

She looked at her watch; she was supposed to meet Lanighan at 9:00 p.m. back at his apartment on Avenue Foch, but she had no intention of doing that. She put away her computer and called him.

86

Paris
Avenue Foch
Saturday evening

Lanighan answered on the first ring.

Kitsune said, "Change of plans. I want to meet at the warehouse in Gagny where you're holding Mulvaney. Meet me there at midnight. I will bring you the stone, and I will take him out with me."

He showed no surprise, not that she'd expected him to, because he knew by now she'd been the one to break into his office and found where he'd hidden Mulvaney. A showdown, then, not an exchange. She knew he would try to kill both her and Mulvaney and take the diamond. No doubt in her mind.

He said, "Aren't you the clever one? No more tricks, Kitsune, or he dies slowly, one piece of him at a time."

"I want Mulvaney released first, then I will give you the diamond. You must show me proof, Lanighan, that he is alive. Then I want the remainder of my money."

"Is that all?"

"No. I want to be there when you unite the three stones. I want to see the legend come alive before my eyes."

She heard his breath catch, but when he spoke, his tone was cool. "I don't know what you mean."

"Saleem Singh Lanighan, son of Robert Lanighan, grandson of Alastair Lanighan. Four generations back, your great-great-grandmother lay with the son of the last Lion of Punjab and got pregnant. She passed the child off as the son of her husband, but her maid knew the truth, and she talked."

"You simply recount the scandal the British rags have sensationalized."

She continued, her voice calm and slow. "Blood runs true, Saleem. Unless I am totally mistaken, you already have one-third of the great stone, the largest piece, kept hidden by the males in your family for hundreds of years. I have another third, the Koh-i-Noor. May I assume you hired another thief to steal the last third of the diamond from that piece of rotted horsemeat known as Andrei Anatoly?"

He didn't answer.

"I thought so. You should have hired me to steal both parts of the diamond, but you didn't. You hired Mulvaney. And then what did you do? You repaid him with treachery. Of course you always planned to betray me as well. You've already proved that.

"You are beneath contempt, Saleem. Your father would be disgusted at what he spawned."

He held silent.

"As I said, I want to see you unite the three stones."

Saleem said, "I do not know what you're talking about."

She said,

> *"He who owns this diamond will own the world,*
> *but will also know all its misfortunes.*
> *Only God, or a woman, can wear it with impunity.*

"That is the curse passed down, the curse all know, but it isn't the end to it, is it, Saleem?" And she softly spoke the two sentences he thought he was the only living person to know.

> *"When Krishna's stone is unbroken again,*
> *the hand which holds it becomes whole.*
> *Wash the Mountain of Light in blood,*
> *so we will know rebirth and rejoice."*

"How do you know my family's legend, Kitsune?"

She laughed softly. "I told you when we first met I knew *everything* about you, Saleem. I meant it. You are not the first Lanighan I've done business with who sought the diamonds. You know I worked for your father. I know he must have told you of me—the Fox. He needed the stones as well, and like you, he was running out of time."

She heard his breathing become hard and fast as he realized the truth.

"He hired me to find the third stone, but he died before I could locate it. He also told me why having the three stones was so important to him."

Saleem couldn't take it in. Why hadn't his father told him what he'd done? He'd told Saleem about the Fox, but not that she was a woman, that she was Kitsune. He tasted his father's deceit, his betrayal, and it was hot and rancid. His own father, sharing their precious family secret with a common thief. He could do nothing to his father, but he would kill her with his bare hands.

Kitsune said, "You should know by now I am a woman of my word. It is a simple bargain. You will share the moment with me, and I will walk away, with my money, and my friend, and I will be satisfied."

He realized then that his father had not told her about needing a *woman's* blood. Why hadn't he? He smiled into the phone. Her request was too good to be true. He no longer had need of Colette.

He said, "Meet me at Gagny at midnight, and we will both gain what we want."

87

Mike was typing one-handed on her computer, the light from the screen making her skin glow. She was tough, and he admired that. He knew how much a bullet hurt, but she had barely missed a step.

Nicholas said, "Any luck?"

Mike nodded. "Lanighan has offices in La Défense, and he lives on Avenue Foch."

"Not a surprise," Nicholas said, "Avenue Foch is one of the posher areas of Paris. Residential neighborhood, very expensive, perfect for our Mr. Lanighan."

Mike said, "He has several warehouses where he stores all his art. The biggest is in Gagny, east of downtown Paris. He has over twenty-five hundred paintings and sculptures, both religious and secular, in his possession at any given time."

She turned the laptop around so he could see the

warehouse at Gagny. "For a crook, he's incredibly legitimate. He's on the cultural advisory board at CERN, bankrolled an exhibit at the Louvre, is a majority shareholder in a startup fashion business which has gotten serious legs, even made a failed bid to buy Christie's auction house. He owns several smaller entities, including—drumroll, please—Sages Fidelité. They have over one hundred branches across Europe and Asia. Lanighan has serious money. He could afford to buy pretty much anything; last year he beat out Qatar's ruling family on a lost Pissarro painting. Forty-eight million dollars."

Mike sat back and shifted her arm to a more comfortable position. "There's one other thing I came across you might find interesting. Lanighan's been married three times, had a slew of affairs. He's been connected to any number of rich and elegant women. Yet he has no children. He was sick as a kid, leukemia, and had chemotherapy treatments. It worked; he was cured, and obviously survived. But if you're right about him being the last in a long line of descendants, and he has no siblings, and no children—wait, maybe his wanting the Koh-i-Noor isn't about the obsession to own a unique artifact, maybe instead it's about something else entirely, something very personal, something he believes connects only to his family, to his line."

Nicholas said, "Okay. But what exactly does he want the Koh-i-Noor for?"

"I don't have the foggiest idea. Sorry, something flashed in my mind, but—I really don't know. Maybe he really is an obsessed collector or maybe he really does feel deeply that the Koh-i-Noor should come home to him and to India because it's part of his heritage."

"Keep your brain flashes going." Nicholas checked his watch, stood up, and pulled on his jacket. "It's time for us to go see what Mr. Lanighan is up to."

88

Nicholas had his hand on the door to leave the suite when his mobile began blaring "London Calling."

Mike's eyebrow rose. "The Clash?"

He shrugged. "This will be Nigel."

"Who is Nigel?"

"My butler." Ignoring her incredulous look, he answered the call. "What's up?"

"Sir, you received a package today, from America."

"Yes? Who's it from?"

"Inspector York, sir."

Adrenaline shot through him. "Open it, Nigel."

He heard a ripping in the background, then, "There's only a thumb drive. Shall I pull it up on your computer?"

"Yes, hurry, Nigel. Open it and email me the contents immediately."

"Yes, sir. Please let me know if there is anything else I may do for you."

Nicholas ended the call, reloaded his email over and over until the new mail registered. It was a .wmv video file. He hit play, and Elaine's face appeared on the screen. He stared at a woman he'd respected, admired, and trusted for three years—and more, he thought, so much more.

"It's Elaine York," Mike said from behind him, and couldn't help but compare the woman on the screen to the body she'd stood over three days before. The gray bloated face—no, she wouldn't remember her like that. She'd remember her like this—studious face, beautiful dark hair, serious eyes.

"Yes, let's see what this is about," Nicholas said, and hit play.

Nicholas, let me answer your first question. Why am I sending you this video instead of an email or calling? The answer is, I can't take the chance of your email or mine being seen, or hacked, or your call overheard. The truth is, I need your advice. I'm afraid I've gotten in over my head.

Let me start at the beginning. There's a woman who works here at the Met, Victoria Browning, and we've become really good friends. One night, two weeks ago, we were at a club, drinking entirely too many Manhattans, and she told me about the legacy surrounding the Koh-i-Noor diamond. Not the curse everyone's heard of, no, the explanation for the curse. Get this—she told me there are three diamonds that are supposed to be married together, and when this happens, if the person holding the united stone is sick—not just of a cancer or a bad heart—he'll be healed forever. Yes, forever.

At first I thought Victoria had downed too many drinks, but then I thought of my mother, her brain destroyed by Alzheimer's, and I'll admit it, I started to pay attention. A huge diamond that could make you immortal? I thought of the romance of it, the mystery, and, well, the possibility there really could be magic at work here, a sort of magic I've dreamed of all my life. Just imagine—three pieces of one huge stone, Nicholas, put together, and they'd heal.

Victoria then told me the Koh-i-Noor is one of the three pieces, someone in Europe has the second, and she believed a man here in New York has the third. She didn't tell me his name.

The next day, I realized I was still hooked. I had no real hope of getting the stones together, but verifying that a man right here in New York City had one of the three—I realized I had to know. And I said why don't we go see this man and verify if he does indeed have the second stone. Hey, maybe we could work a deal. Then maybe we get our hands on the stone in Europe, and maybe we could borrow the Koh-i-Noor.

Victoria said we might be able to get two of the stones, but the Koh-i-Noor, no way the Royal

Family would ever loan it out for a mad experiment like this. But I was enthralled; I wanted to try, to be the one to bring the magic to my mother. You doubtless think I've lost my mind. You're probably right. Still, Victoria stared at me like she was looking deep into my soul. She was clearly intrigued by the idea, and I knew I had to convince her to go see this man. She finally agreed. And I laughed and said it's our own quest, Victoria, ours alone.

She didn't tell me the man's name until we reached the thirty-fourth floor of a huge Midtown building—Andrei Anatoly. I had no idea then that he was a Russian mobster, probably evil to the core. He let us in, and Victoria came right out with it and asked him if he had a special diamond in his possession.

Anatoly stared at her, then at me, like he was memorizing our faces, which, as it turns out, he was, and then he threw back his head and laughed and laughed. He told us he didn't know what we were talking about, and ordered us to leave.

The next day, I was notified that two hundred thousand dollars had been wired into my account with a note that said, "Leave it alone." I asked Victoria if she'd put the money in my account, but she said she didn't know anything about it. She said it could be Anatoly wanting us to back off. Why would a mobster do that? I asked her, but she only shook her head. I offered to split the money with her, but she insisted I look at it like a windfall, and use it for my mother. I could tell she didn't want to pursue this any further, either.

I think now it was Victoria who gave me the money. Why? Because she felt guilty about telling me about the diamond, and she was worried about what Anatoly might do.

I kept the money, Nicholas. Another stupidity. But when I thought of my mom and how she needed it so desperately—I needed to keep it to help her.

Even though I backed off, the next day I saw two thugs following me. I knew then Anatoly hadn't sent the money, and I knew I was in trouble.

I met a Russian man, Vlad Kochen, in the cafeteria in the Met. He told me he saw men following me, and that he could take care of it. I felt ridiculous going to Bo with this, especially because of the money, and besides, what on earth could I say to him? So I paid Kochen to watch my back. He said to trust him, he would take care of it. Sure enough, the next day the young thugs were gone, but there was another man watching me. He was older, thin, white haired. And there was something about him that scared me more than the young thugs. I asked Vlad about the man, but he didn't know who he was.

To be safe, I asked Vlad to get me a pistol.

That's all, Nicholas. What will happen now? I don't know, but I'm going to send the money to my mother. I don't care who sent it to me, Mom needs it.

As for Victoria, she is avoiding me. I think she's very sorry she ever said anything to me about the three diamonds. Maybe she's afraid, too.

I have to say life is never what you expect. All my life I wanted some magic, something that was of the unknown, the inexplicable. I laugh thinking about being careful about what you wish for—I miss you, Nicholas. I hope you are well and happy and that you haven't strangled Penderley, or the other way around.

And the screen went blank.

89

Nicholas had to stop himself from throwing the laptop across the room. Why hadn't she come to him sooner, called him, anything? She might not be dead.

He said, "I wondered why Lanighan wanted the Koh-i-Noor specifically. I mean, what would he do with it? Now we know. You were pretty close to the mark, Mike. He's sick, and he wants the stones because he thinks he can put them together and heal himself. We need to call Ben and Zachery. I think it's pretty clear now what was stolen from Anatoly's safe yesterday.

"The white-haired man—the Ghost—he stole the third diamond out of the safe after he murdered Anatoly and his sons."

Mike said, "Sounds right. Ben called while the video was playing. Let's call him back." She dialed Ben, who answered immediately.

"Finally, I've been waiting for you to get back to me. The NGI facial-recognition database found a match with Interpol crime scene footage from two decades ago, an attempt on François Mitterrand's life. We've identified a man named William Mulvaney, aka the Ghost, early sixties, six foot one, thin frame, white hair. We were right about all of it. He not only killed Elaine and Kochen and attacked you guys, he also killed Anatoly and his sons, but we still don't know what he stole from the safe."

Mike said, "I know what was in the safe." And then she told him about Elaine's tape, what she'd done, finishing with, "Supposedly, the three stones together can heal sickness. We think Saleem Lanighan believes it, and he's the money behind the theft and the attacks." She paused, then said, "Ben, Elaine had nothing to do with the Koh-i-Noor theft, nothing at all. She was innocent in all of this."

Ben was silent for a moment, then said simply, "Good. That's good. But if Elaine wasn't involved, why did Mulvaney feel he had to kill her?"

Nicholas said, "Because she found out about the third stone, and he couldn't take the chance of her telling someone. Or, very possibly, because Anatoly told him to."

Ben sighed. "So needless, all of it. You also need to know, we've verified that Mulvaney flew into Paris last night."

Nicholas said slowly, "It's all coming together. Thanks, Ben."

A brief pause. "You guys be careful. Savich has hooked up the surveillance on Lanighan whenever you're ready to start watching him."

Nicholas said, "We're going over there at nine." Mike hung up, and Nicholas said, "All right. Let me make one more call."

He dialed Miles Herrington's number but got no answer. No help for it. He called his boss, Hamish Penderley, at home, braced for the deluge. After two days of ignoring the man's emails and calls, he had a bit of explaining to do.

Penderley surprised him, though. He answered the phone with a gruff "About time you surfaced." But the berating he expected didn't come.

"Sorry, sir. I've been rather busy."

"Yes, I suppose you have. We heard about the explosion in Geneva. Cut it a bit fine there, didn't you?"

Nicholas was relieved; apparently, word of the other two attempts on their lives hadn't gotten back to him. He said, "Yes, sir. Even have a few stitches in my back as a result. Have you heard anything from Miles? He was supposed to be following the leak from the palace on the plans for the Koh-i-Noor exhibit."

"My son doesn't check in as regularly as he should."

"Ah, well, then. If you should speak to him, tell him I'm waiting."

"Is this what you called me about, Drummond? First you defy my orders and run off to America, now you want me to be the messenger boy from my son to you? You have some gall."

"No gall, sir. I'm working closely with the FBI; they've been most cooperative. We've identified Elaine's killer, an assassin named Mulvaney, also known as the Ghost, and we believe we understand his motive for killing her. She was innocent in all this; it was a terrible mistake."

Penderley said, "I knew Elaine couldn't be involved. The Ghost, you say? I've heard of him. He's a legend. He was just a kid we were told. It was rumored he was behind a series of bombings in Northern Ireland while I was in the academy. We had to work the scenes; they pulled the trainees onto the ground to support the regular coppers. I'll never forget it. From what I know, he disappeared from the stage several years ago. It was widely assumed he was dead."

"Apparently, he's not dead. What else can you tell me about him?"

"There's a dossier of information in our database, but it's sketchy at best. He's a dangerous man, Drummond, maybe more dangerous than you. Keep me informed. And Drummond, watch your back."

"Will do, sir."

He hung up. It looked like he'd have a job to return to when all was said and done, though Penderley would find a way to punish him—probably with training exercises at Hendon for six weeks—but he wouldn't be cast out.

Mike was watching him. He gave her a mad grin.

"It's nearly nine p.m. Let's go see what Lanighan is up to."

90

At five minutes after nine, they heard a car start up and drive around from the garage. The door to the building opened and Lanighan came out. He looked angry. They watched him get into the waiting car and slam the door. The wheels on the Mercedes squealed as the car whipped away from the curve. What had him so pissed off?

Nicholas gave them a moment to put some distance between them, then pulled out after him.

"Keep an eye on them, Mike, they're going fast."

They were circling around the Arc de Triomphe now.

She said, "There they are, turning to the right. Let me count, fifth turn off the roundabout, onto the Champs-Élysées."

Nicholas downshifted instead of braking as the car flew out onto the street behind the Mercedes. He could see it up ahead, nearly a quarter of a mile down the street. He floored the gas pedal, and the Peugeot leapt forward.

Mike said, "He's headed east. Gagny is his biggest holding, and the only one east of the city. That must be where he's going."

"I'll lay back a bit. Is he using his mobile?"

She checked the computer in her lap. "I've tapped into the wire Savich has on his phone. No outgoing calls."

"I'm sure that will change."

Ten minutes into the drive, the tracker on Lanighan's mobile lit up.

"Got one. Outgoing, from Lanighan." Mike turned up the volume on her laptop. Lanighan's voice was scratchy.

Is everything prepared?

It is.

Is the bitch there yet with the stone?

Not yet. She'll come. She wants her money too much to betray you. It's all she ever cared about. Relax. How long until you arrive?

Thirty minutes, no longer.

I'll be waiting.

The mobile went dead.

Mike's cell phone rang almost immediately.

"Hey, Dillon. You guys get that?"

"We did. The call was made to the same phone signal we have on record here. Lanighan was talking to the Ghost, William Mulvaney."

Mike said, "So who's he working with? Lanighan or the Fox?"

Nicholas said, "Well, we're going to find out soon enough. Savich, is Menard set up to meet us at Gagny warehouse?"

"Yes. He has a team with him."

Nicholas said, "Be sure to tell them to stay well back until we signal for them. We're going to go in first and see what's happening. We don't need this blowing up in our faces and turning into a bloodbath."

"Be careful," Savich said, and hung up.

"He's not going to be alone, Nicholas. We need Menard and his men."

He didn't argue with her. "I have no issue with having Menard's men backing us up. But the last thing I want is a massive show of force before we know what's happening inside that warehouse."

Nicholas lagged back, and Mike couldn't see the Mercedes anymore. He shut off the lights, let the moon guide him. "When Mulvaney talked about the Fox, he sounded bitter, maybe angry. I wonder what that's all about."

Five minutes later, they could see the road dead-end at a large gate, topped with a camera.

Mike said, "Stop here. We don't want to announce ourselves yet." She pointed to the camera. Nicholas pulled the car to the side of the road. It was quiet, and very dark. The warehouses were deep into the grounds behind the gate. There was no movement here.

"No help for it," Nicholas said, "we'll have to go over the fence. Can your arm stand it? Or should I cut through?"

Mike shook her head. "Nicholas, we need to wait for Menard's men."

Nicholas shot her a grin. "No, we don't. Are you with me or not?"

She thought about the three assassins Lanighan sent to kill them, thought about taking a nice swing at the Fox, bloodying her lip—it took exactly two seconds before she said, "Let's go."

"Let's start out with a bit of reconnaissance."

He reached up and turned off the interior light and opened his door carefully. He loaded his bag on his shoulder. She could see his face; he was having fun, the idiot.

She felt strong; she felt right. She checked her Glock and followed him out of the car. It was a war she wanted to fight, a war she intended to win.

91

Gagny Neuf-trois, Paris
Lanighan's warehouse
Saturday night

Kitsune went over the fence at the back of the warehouse and climbed to the roof of the next building in the compound.

She could see the gate to the grounds, the parking lot, and half of the building proper.

She knew Mulvaney was inside, knew Lanighan had hurt him. He was probably in pain, wondering where she was, if she had a plan to save him. All she knew for sure was that she was going to destroy Saleem Lanighan tonight.

Lanighan's Mercedes came into the warehouse parking lot at ten minutes to ten. She trained her monocle on the car, watched Lanighan get out and hurry inside the warehouse. He shouted something to his driver, but she couldn't make out his words. She could tell, however, he was mad. At her? Good. Mad meant off balance, and that would make her job easier.

The warehouse had windows high up on the second floor, and she could get only an idea of where people were from the shadowy movements behind the lights.

She counted off until she saw him again on the second floor. Thirty seconds. There was probably a single stairwell and hallway. She'd loaded the blueprints for the space, and knew the building was divided into two areas—an open bottom floor, where large paintings and sculptures were kept, the space large enough for a decent-size truck to drive in and out. She knew the setup was sophisticated and fully automated, knew hundreds of paintings were kept on racks electronically programmed to slide out from the wall for easy access and storage.

The second floor had a very large office, where the manager of the warehouse worked and where occasional buyers came to see art Lanighan was selling. She was convinced this was where they were holding Mulvaney.

She saw the guards patrolling the grounds were only casually alert. They weren't expecting the show—namely, her—until later, which was the reason she was hitting them now.

With her left hand, she screwed the suppressor into the threaded barrel of the H&K MP23. She hated guns, always had, after the long ago *incident*, as she often thought of it, with her parents, but she wasn't about to go in without one. The H&K fit her hand nicely, the suppressor giving it only a few ounces of additional weight. She tucked it into the custom-made leather holster, felt for the two tear-gas canisters she had placed in the pockets of her black cargo pants. Four knives were in place, two strapped to her outer thighs, two to her stomach in a cross-handed pull.

She did square breathing, in for four counts, hold for four, out for four, hold for four; when she felt the familiar clean emptiness, she started down off the rooftop.

She went silent as a cat through the night, her eyes adjusted to the darkness, the moon guiding her steps, sure and quick. Five hundred feet to the warehouse. Three hundred. Two. She swallowed and slowed, listening for the guards in case they circled around the back of the warehouse.

Nothing. She was clear.

She drew her gun, walked forward, watching for the metal staircase she needed to climb to the second-floor window.

A voice spoke from the darkness: "Stop, right there."

She whipped around, crouched, gun pointed, finger already putting pressure on the trigger, but she realized she couldn't risk firing yet, not outside. Even suppressed, it might bring the guards.

Decision made in a split second, her movements quick and sure, she holstered the gun and whipped a Ka-Bar knife out of its sheath on her thigh. The weapon made a vicious whisper as it left the webbing, and she readied it, sharp edge out.

A man took a step from the darkness and said, "I wouldn't do that if I were you."

Drummond!

She lashed out at him, and he danced back, away from

her lunge, back arched and stomach drawn in. Close, but she didn't get him.

She pulled out the second Ka-Bar and sliced back the other way, forcing her way forward, balancing her weight on the balls of her feet. He stepped back just as a cloud floated in front of the moon, effectively blacking out the scene.

Knives poised and blind, she went for him again, a shadow in the dark. His fist shot out and hit her face. Pain radiated out from her cheek, and she gasped, ducked, and swung out her leg to trip him, but he was gone, fast as lightning. He was behind her, his hand in her hair, jerking her head back, exposing her throat. She jabbed one knife backward, but he twisted in time and she missed again.

He wrapped his hand hard around her right wrist and pulled her toward him. A mistake, that. She could throw him now. Leg forward, balanced on her toes and ready to spin, knowing the move would drive him over her shoulder, but she froze at the touch of hard metal against her temple.

"Drop the knives now, or I'll take great pleasure in dropping you where you stand."

It was Mike Caine.

Time stopped for a moment. She heard her own heavy breathing, felt the blood dripping from her nose, and wondered if Drummond had broken her wrist.

Kitsune said, "If I drop the knives, they're going to make quite a bit of noise, then the guards will come. You'll never make it out alive."

Mike grabbed a Ka-Bar from her hand and tossed it behind her with a clatter. Nicholas removed the gun from her hip holster, and took the other knife away.

He wrenched her arms behind her back, and Mike tossed him her handcuffs. He latched them on, then turned her around and grinned, his teeth flashing white in the light of the moon.

"Hello, Victoria."

92

Nicholas retraced their path to the fence. There was a perfect body-size hole where he'd cut through the metal. Mike went first, watching for guards, cleared the road, then signaled the go-ahead. He pushed Victoria through and followed after her.

He wanted to tell Mike she'd put a stop to the fight at just the right moment because he didn't know how much longer he'd have been able to dodge those knives. He felt a small wetness at the base of his spine; most likely he'd torn open his stitches. He certainly didn't need any more.

When they reached the car, Mike got into the back with Victoria, her Glock pressed hard against her ribs. Nicholas got behind the wheel, and quietly pulled the car away.

"Where are you taking me?" Her voice shook a bit, not

from fear, Mike thought, but from the pounding adrenaline.

Nicholas said, "Away from here. We want the Koh-i-Noor and we want it now. Where do you have it hidden?"

Kitsune laughed. "You seriously think I'm going to hand it over to you?"

"Yes." He might as well have said, *Don't, and I'll kill you myself.*

"Where are you taking me?" she asked again.

Mike wondered the same thing but contented herself with keeping the barrel of her Glock against Victoria's ribs.

Nicholas took turns too fast, going deeper into the Parisian suburbs. After fifteen minutes, he pulled into a small alleyway behind a row of town houses. "Mike, back in three, don't let her move an inch," and he got out of the car.

Kitsune said, "You take orders rather well, don't you, Mike? Lying down for the man, huh? Why? You don't work for him. Surely you're too smart to be sleeping with him. Why don't you think about this: you help me and I can give you more money than you've ever dreamed of."

Mike really would have liked to beat the crap out of this woman. Such a pity, but she couldn't, not with her in handcuffs. She gave her a big smile. "Screw you, Victoria."

Kitsune didn't move, didn't say another word.

Nicholas appeared on Kitsune's side of the car and opened the door. "Come. And be quiet about it."

Kitsune saw her chance, opened her mouth to scream.

Nicholas yanked her out of the car and smashed his hand over her mouth. He whispered, "I said, be quiet."

She tried to bite him, so he clouted her hard over the ear, enough to stun her, and dragged her into the rear entrance of the town house.

Mike followed, silently applauding.

Nicholas tied Victoria to a chair in the kitchen, arms and legs, and gagged her with a dishrag he found in a drawer.

Mike felt Victoria's pulse, strong and steady. *Good*. She wasn't hurt badly. She turned to Nicholas, who was sitting on the table, leaning forward, his elbows on his knees, watching.

Mike said, "Now we're breaking and entering?"

He grinned at her. "Safe house."

From his time as super-spy, of course.

"Now what?"

He gestured toward Victoria, who was coming around enough to open her eyes. She was making mewing noises behind the gag.

"Now she gives us the whereabouts of the Koh-i-Noor." He hopped off the table and pulled the gag from her mouth. Mike gave her a drink of water.

Nicholas said, "Don't bother screaming; this place is soundproof."

Kitsune cocked her head to the side, eyed him. "And to think I waited for you to leave before I blew the bomb in Geneva. What a mistake that was."

"Yes, it was. Where is the Koh-i-Noor?"

"It's still in Geneva."

"Okay, Victoire Couverel. Yes, we've met your brother, we know about your parents, about their murder. We know about your adoptive parents, the missionaries. And look at you. You grew up to be the notorious thief known as the Fox. Fact is, I know enough about you to know you'd keep the Koh-i-Noor close. Now, where is it?"

She was stunned. But she'd never let him see it.

She gave him a sneer. "I see you've done your homework."

Nicholas said, "Listen, all we want is the diamond. You give it to us, and you'll live the night."

"I did not lie. It's in Geneva. In a safe place."

Nicholas was advancing on her when his mobile rang. After a moment, he pulled it out and glanced at the screen. Penderley.

He said, "Mike, convince our guest of the smart course of action." He threw her the Ka-Bar knife he'd lifted during the fight. Mike caught it, expertly twisted it in her hand so the blade was pointed out, directly at Victoria's lily-white throat.

It was a nice move. He went into the living room and answered the phone with a brusque "Yes?"

"I've spoken to Miles," Penderley said. "The leak on the jewels traced directly to the Tower of London."

Nicholas asked, "Are the Yeoman Warders the only ones outside of the queen's people who knew this was even being discussed? Has anyone left their ranks suddenly of late?"

"No, but last year there was an engagement that broke

up. The man's name is Grant Thornton, and his fiancée walked out on him. No one's ever heard from her again."

"Photo, please?"

"It's in your email."

"Hold on." He switched apps to his email, pulled up the photo. He looked at a tall, dark-haired, well-built man looking down at a smiling woman who was staring directly into the camera without knowing the shot was being taken. It was Victoria Browning, of a sort. Her hair was darker, and her eyes were a different color, a sparkling light blue, and her smile was genuine. The combination made her exotic instead of merely pretty.

"That's our girl. Do you have the man in custody?"

"No. No one thinks he knows a thing about any of this, so we're simply keeping an eye on him."

"Okay. If we need leverage, you can haul him in. If he and the Fox were engaged, perhaps she had real feelings for him. I'll be back in touch soon."

93

Nicholas hung up and went back to the kitchen. Mike looked one second away from belting Victoria. She'd obviously said something to tick Mike off.

He turned one of the kitchen chairs around and straddled it, laying his arms along the top. Relaxed, not a care in the world. Mike stepped away a few feet, crossed her arms over her chest.

Nicholas smiled. "Victoria. Victoire. What shall I call you?"

"Kitsune. You may call me Kitsune."

"Kitsune, Japanese for fox. So are you Japanese? Your heritage seems a bit muddled to me. Like a dog from the pound."

"Woof."

He stood up and leaned over her. "Let me tell you how

this is going to work. You are going to give me the Koh-i-Noor, and in return, I'll put in a good word for your friend Grant Thornton. You remember him, don't you? He's the one who gave you the information about the Koh-i-Noor stone moving to New York months before it was publicly announced? As we speak, he's being transferred to the tombs in London. Into a mixed cell. You know how they love the pretty boys. Word gets out he's former SAS and they'll want to make an example of him."

She paled, couldn't help it, and Nicholas thought, *Got you*.

Kitsune raised her chin. "He has nothing to do with this. Nothing, and you know it."

"I beg to differ. As does Her Majesty's government. Thornton will be stripped of his rank, his work, his pension. He will be an outcast from his world, a pariah. On top of his humiliation, he'll go to jail for the rest of his life. If he survives the night, naturally."

He walked around her, circling his prey. "A man like him, who's dedicated his life to queen and country? You've destroyed him, Kitsune. It's all on your head. He lost everything because he had the misfortune to fall in love with you—a fraud, a chimera, only the illusion of a woman who didn't really exist."

Kitsune closed her eyes and saw Grant. Beautiful, innocent Grant. He would be the one to suffer, and she'd done it to him. The Brit was right about that.

"I'll save him if you give me the Koh-i-Noor."

She gave him a long look, weighed his word, he knew, weighted him. She said finally, "I have conditions."

Nicholas stopped his pacing, went back to his chair and sat, eyebrows politely raised.

"You're hardly in a bargaining position, but let's hear it."

"Grant walks, no stain on his character, and he returns to his job. Has he been told about me?"

"No."

It was an unutterable relief. She nodded. "He will not be told about any of it. Not about me, not about Lanighan. Nothing."

"All right. And?"

"Lanighan is holding a man in the warehouse. He is important to me. See that he's freed and I'll tell you where the diamond is."

"Ah, now, Kitsune, you're going to have to do better. If you want our help, you tell us up front where the Koh-i-Noor is, and then we'll talk about meeting your conditions."

She shook her head. "My friend first. And your word, as a gentleman, that he will not be harmed."

Mike stepped in. "Are you talking about William Mulvaney?"

Kitsune couldn't believe this. Did everyone on the planet know about Mulvaney?

"Yes. His name is Mulvaney."

"What's he to you?"

"A friend."

At Nicholas's raised eyebrow, she added, "More than a friend. He is my mentor, my partner. He is a man I have known more than half my life."

"You sound like you would give your life for him," Mike said.

Kitsune said simply, "Yes."

"*Is* he your friend? A man you would trust with your life? A man you would sacrifice yourself for? Is he really?" and Nicholas queued up the phone conversation they'd overheard on their way to the warehouse.

"Is the bitch there yet with the stone?"

"Not yet. She'll come. She wants her money too much to betray you. It's all she ever cared about. Relax."

Mike said, "Is this the voice of your *friend* Mulvaney?"

Kitsune rolled her eyes. "Please, I know how you work. You can manipulate anything, make Drummond here sound like the president of the United States."

Mike said, "Yep, that's certainly possible, but take a look at this. We couldn't have screwed around with this. We took this from your car at the warehouse."

She put Kitsune's laptop on the table and opened the lid. The video camera feed from the warehouse was still running.

Mike backed the feed up, set the small computer in Kitsune's lap.

"This was shot less than an hour ago."

Kitsune looked down, saw the time stamp, and saw Mulvaney walk out of the warehouse, upright, unfettered, tossing off some remark at the man who stood nearest the door. He was by no means tied up, nor did he seem to be under duress. On the contrary, they were laughing.

What is going on here?

Nicholas said, "We have it all, Kitsune. Lanighan kept detailed records."

"You're lying." She smiled. "I destroyed everything."

Nicholas smiled back. "No, you didn't. We got there before you. Remember Savich? He's been on Lanighan for a day now, and guess what? Lanighan saved all your emails. All your planning, every detail. And we found emails between your friend Mulvaney and Lanighan. Let me read one to you. This is dated a year ago.

"You can't trust Kitsune. Did I mention her name is Victoire? Her full name is Victoire Couverel. She was a careless little gutter snip, no more than sixteen, when I saved her from jail in Naples. I saw the potential in her and trained her myself. She has betrayed me, and she will betray you as well if she has a chance. Use this information wisely. Watch your back around her. I will bring you Anatoly's diamond. I will send the account number when I have secured the stone from America. Once she's made delivery of the Koh-i-Noor, kill her. You need the blood of a woman to fulfill the promise of the stone. If you can't do it yourself, I will do it for you."

"*Stop!* Stop, now."

"Betrayal tastes pretty rank, doesn't it, Victoire?"

"Bloody bastard." Her voice was flat, unemotional. Shock, Mike thought, the woman was in shock.

Kitsune's head dropped. She was tired, so tired. She didn't understand any of it. She hadn't betrayed

Mulvaney. She would cut off her own arm before she'd even consider betraying him. Why had he said that she had? What did he mean about needing *her* blood to fulfill the promise of the stone?

She wanted to weep. Why did the man she'd loved more than her own father hate her now? What was she going to do?

94

Her world was crashing down around her ears, and yet here she was clearly plotting and assessing. Nicholas could practically hear her thinking.

He said to Mike, "Call Menard. Tell him to take the warehouse. We'll transport Kitsune to the Préfecture de Police, let them start the paperwork to extradite her to America."

Her voice rang out in the small kitchen. "No."

He glanced back at her, but kept talking to Mike. "We'll want a full assault, he has plenty of help. If we overwhelm them—"

"No!"

He stopped and gave her his full attention.

"What?"

She spoke through clenched teeth. "I will help you. I

will give you everything you want, and more. But we must do it my way."

She was taking a huge risk. But this was Mulvaney, and she had no choice. He had given her back her life—no, he'd done much more. He'd given her a life. Even if he hated her enough to betray her, she still owed him.

"You can't take the warehouse by force. There are safeguards."

"Explosives, you mean?"

"If Mulvaney is involved, yes. Many. He'll have the entire place wired to blow."

Mike paused before she hit send on her cell. "What exactly are you proposing?"

"You allow me to go as I'm supposed to. I'll get the detonator from Mulvaney. When I signal, it will be safe for you to enter."

"You're joking, right?"

She said quietly, "I will give you information. Everything I know. About his crimes, and those of mine it is safe to reveal. You will get the biggest assassin in the world, close hundreds of open cases, both thefts and murders and espionage. Then I will give you back the Koh-i-Noor."

Nicholas said, "What do you want in return?"

"I go free. No one looks for me. I'll take my money from my accounts and the money Lanighan paid me, and I will disappear. This was my last job. I'm retiring. No one will ever hear from me again."

Nicholas said, "What's to make us believe you'll honor your end of the bargain?"

Mike said, "Yes, I'd like to hear this."

Kitsune said, "The truth? The one man I've ever trusted has betrayed me. I want to know why. He killed Elaine." She met Nicholas's eyes, and he saw the pain not hidden deep enough in hers. "The minute I heard about the cyanide, I knew he'd done it. He's used it before; it's a trademark. It was unnecessary, a waste. Elaine had done nothing. Nothing at all, but it didn't matter. And the tranquilizer gun. He always said using it kept him from bruising his knuckles, and he'd laugh because he's one of the best fighters I've ever seen. He taught me everything.

"And Grant—" She broke off, and was silent.

"What do you care for Elaine?"

"She was my friend, too. And she's dead because of me, because of what I told her. I didn't realize at first that she really wanted to believe the prophecy, but she did, she was so excited about the possibilities, the magical possibilities—Mulvaney didn't need to kill her, she was harmless."

Nicholas said, without expression, "Yet you were perfectly happy to let her take the fall for stealing the diamond. You were the one who told us she met with Kochen."

She shrugged. "I was alive; she wasn't. I had to save myself."

Nicholas said, "Elaine told me about the prophecy. Three stones would heal the sick."

Kitsune said, "It's even more than that. Lanighan believes uniting the three stones will bestow immortality. His father believed it, too."

Nicholas was fascinated. "You tried to steal the Koh-i-Noor for his father as well?"

"No. His father told me the prophecy and hired me to find the lost stone, the one Anatoly ended up with. But I didn't find it in time for him."

Nicholas said, "I want a listing of everything you've ever stolen so we can put it to rights."

"You must know I can't do that, Drummond. You'll get me killed. It's one thing to fail, but I've been in business for a very long time, and there's no way I'm going to drop the dime on my other clients. I will tell you what I stole for Lanighan's father, and everything Mulvaney did. He and I never shared clients. If my clients are dead, and there is no threat to me, I will share the information. Will that do?"

Nicholas saw Mike wasn't happy. He said, "Come with me."

Kitsune heard them talking in the background, then Mike making a series of calls. She could hear anger in her voice. Kitsune didn't like her, but she respected her. Perhaps, in another life, young Victoire Couverel would have grown up to be more like Michaela Caine. But the thought of being a cop nearly made her laugh aloud.

After fifteen minutes, Nicholas came back and said, "Yes. We are in agreement."

Kitsune was careful to show no expression. She only nodded. "Good. I will have the information for you, and you will have a signed, notarized paper for me declaring my immunity from prosecutions by the U.S. and Great Britain for my role in the theft of the Koh-i-Noor, and blanket immunity from any other crimes you may see fit to try and hang on me."

"But first the Koh-i-Noor. Hand it over."

"What time is it? I can't read my watch."

"It's nearly midnight. Eleven-forty, to be exact."

"Then you need to get me to the warehouse right away."

Mike snorted. "We aren't letting you anywhere near that place alone."

Kitsune said, "You have no choice. I stashed the stone there, and you'll need me to get to it."

95

While Nicholas pulled on a Kevlar vest, Mike circled him like a wolf about to attack.

"Nicholas, you can't let her go in alone."

He gestured for her to put on her vest as he used the other hand to pull the Velcro together tightly across his ribs, ignoring the pain in his back as he did.

"Of course not. I'm going in with her."

"You lamebrain, that's crazy. You know she'll turn on you."

"Actually, no, I don't think she will." He looked over at Kitsune, sitting quietly in the back of the Peugeot, armed men standing close. "Our Fox is in love. If she hates Mulvaney right now, and hates us for capturing her and putting her feet to the fire, she loves Grant Thornton enough to sacrifice herself to keep him from losing everything."

Mike planted herself in front of him, hands on her hips. "How do you know she isn't faking cooperation?"

Nicholas grinned as he pulled the last Velcro strap into place. "I'm thinking that's why Mulvaney betrayed her. For him, it's not about the money, or the prestige of the job. It's about his heart. You remember the bitterness and anger we heard in his voice when we overheard him speaking to Lanighan? You saw the letter, and the way she reacted. This man was a father, a cherished mentor, a man she trusted beyond reason. He saved her, kept her safe. Trained her, but she did the one thing neither of them anticipated. She fell in love with a mark.

"And that's the kind of betrayal a man like Mulvaney can't handle, especially if he loves a woman who doesn't love him back, at least not in the way he wants. I suspect he loved her as much as he hates her now."

"But he's old enough to be her father."

He arched a brow. "Feelings don't have years attached. You're right, though—for her, Mulvaney was indeed a trusted, beloved father."

She gave him a long look as she tugged on the vest. "Don't give me any crap, I'm going in with you."

She expected him to argue, but he didn't. In fact, he actually looked relieved. He put his hand on her shoulder. "I can't think of anyone I'd rather have with me."

"If you get us both killed, I'm going to be very angry with you."

He shot her a grin, then called to the men: "Gather round. Here's the plan." He laid out the blueprints of the warehouse, gave assignments, showing the snipers their positions. "You'll form your perimeter here, and when Mike gives the go-ahead, you'll converge and take out the guards." He finished with a smile. "As for us, Kitsune, Mike, and I go through the fence and split at the warehouse. Kitsune will go in the front, and take the guards with her. They won't be expecting anyone else, so I'll be able to sneak in behind them. Mike will go up the fire escape and cover the room from outside. Once we're all in place, we go in, get the diamond, and get the hell out. Any questions?"

One of Menard's men asked, "Shoot to kill?"

Nicholas nodded. "Try not to take out Lanighan or Mulvaney. We need them."

Nicholas said to Menard, "In case it all goes awry, I trust you'll be there to mop things up?"

"Give me the signal, my friend, and we'll take them all out. Try not to get yourself blown up in the meantime."

"I won't. Mike, are you ready?"

"Ready. Are we giving Kitsune Kevlar?"

Kitsune had been taken out of the car and was standing a few feet away. She said, "No. They'll know something's up if I go in bulked up. I'm supposed to be handing over the stone, and I'm supposed to think Mulvaney is a hostage. They'll keep up the charade long enough to get the stone in their hands."

Nicholas said, "Okay, time's up. Where's the diamond?"

She took a deep breath and grinned at him. "It's in Lanighan's briefcase. He carried it into the building when we were here before."

Mike rounded on her. "Why should we believe this?"

"Because it's the truth. I went to Lanighan's house earlier this evening, looking for Mulvaney. Everything on this job has gone wrong, so I protected the diamond the best I knew how, which was fulfilling my end of the bargain in the hopes Lanighan would do the same. I put the Koh-i-Noor in the lining of his bag. He has no idea it's there. I knew you were on my back, too. It was the only way I could think to keep the stone safe until the delivery."

Her hand went down her shirt, and she withdrew a blue velvet bag. "It's a good thing you're a gentleman, Drummond. A more thorough search would have turned this up." She dumped the stone into his hand. "They're amazingly well done, for fakes. Peter Grisley should be proud of his work."

Nicholas ran his fingers along the stone. "Good job stealing the replicas."

She smiled. "I really only needed one, but I thought, who knows? The second one might come in handy. And it did, in Geneva."

She took the stone back from him, replaced it in the bag, and thought, *Thank goodness they aren't experts and don't have a diamond tester. They'll never know they just handled the real Koh-i-Noor.*

She said, "I do have one question."

"Yes?"

"What are you planning to do with the other two parts of the diamond?"

Nicholas said, "I assume there will be a number of

people higher up the food chain who will make that decision. We can't worry about it."

"Should something happen to me, Nicholas, you must destroy them, along with Lanighan. He's the last in his line. It will stop with him."

They began to walk to the fence.

Nicholas said, "One last thing. If the prophecy is true, the stones can't merge without a woman's blood. He's going to try and kill you, Kitsune, to make it happen."

Kitsune was quiet for a moment. "Let him try."

96

Saleem Lanighan paced the second-floor office, full of anticipation and excitement for what was to come. She should be here soon. Fifteen more minutes, and he would unite the stones and be cured of the leukemia. Cured of every illness forever.

He was nervous, too, since he had no idea what to expect. His life's work, the work of every male in his family for generations, was culminating right now. Since no one had gone before, he was breaking new ground.

But he knew exactly what he'd do tomorrow.

Healed, he would set out to find the perfect woman to sire his child.

One of his guards came to his side. "Sir. She's here."

Mulvaney turned from the window. "She's walking up to the gate. She's carrying a small backpack."

"Good. Have the men bring her in."

Lanighan realized his hands were shaking and he wanted a drink, several. Would it hurt—uniting the three stones? Would the cancer be killed immediately? A flash of his grandfather's face, pink and smooth, unlined as he held the stone, came to him, and he decided no, it wouldn't hurt. It would be wonderful.

Mulvaney said, "Steady, man. Steady."

Lanighan opened eyes he didn't realize were closed and smiled. "I am ready." He turned to the guard. "Bring her to me."

He looked to Mulvaney. "Are you going to let her think she's rescuing you?"

Mulvaney said, "Of course. And then I'm going to give you her blood to do your magic."

"And then you'll kill her?"

"Once we have the blood, we won't need her anymore."

The door opened, and the guard brought Kitsune in. She looked scared. *Good,* Lanighan thought. *She should be scared*.

The guard said, "She was carrying these."

He laid out a semiautomatic pistol, two knives, and two tear-gas canisters.

When Lanighan was sure the guard was out of earshot, he rounded on Kitsune.

"Where is the Koh-i-Noor?"

"Where is Mulvaney?"

"Don't you want your money first?"

"I want to see Mulvaney."

Mulvaney stepped from behind the door, and Kitsune's face went blank with shock.

"Your loyalty becomes you, my dear."

She looked from him to Lanighan, swallowed, and said, "William? I don't understand. What is this? I believed you were his prisoner."

He picked up her knives. "Oh, no. Come here to me, little fox."

She took a few hesitant steps. Lanighan grabbed her arm and yelled, "No. First the Koh-i-Noor."

Mulvaney smiled at her, a bitter smile, one filled with shadows and hate. "Yes, where is the diamond?"

All pretense gone, Kitsune's eyes turned hot and dark, and despite himself, Mulvaney took a step back. "You betrayed me! You're working with him. Why, William? What could I have possibly done to make you hate me so much?"

It was as if the dam had burst. Mulvaney yelled at her, "I gave you everything, you faithless bitch! I saved you from the gutter, trained you, taught you endlessly. Damn you, I loved you! I made you the center of my life. We were together. We were meant to be together always.

"And how did you repay me? I've seen your computer history, Kitsune. I know you've been checking up on that man Thornton. Hoping against hope once you showed up with fifty million dollars he'd take you back. You were going to leave me for another man, walk away from your life, our life. I spent years making things perfect for you, making you perfect for me. We were supposed to be together. You are the one who betrayed me!"

Somewhere deep she'd known but simply hadn't wanted to face it, to accept that such a thing could be possible. She said calmly, "I never betrayed you, William. You were like a father to me, and I loved you like a father. I gave you everything I could give you."

"No, you did not give me what I deserved, what I wanted. You gave what should have been mine to Thornton—he was nothing more than a tool, someone to throw away when you had no more use for him. What did he do for you besides screw you? Damn you, Kitsune, he was nothing, and yet you chose him over me."

"No, I did throw him away because I had to, because of the job. And you've been spying on me this whole time? You're pathetic! A pathetic old man."

There was nothing more to say. Kitsune reached into her shirt and withdrew a blue velvet bag, tossed it to Lanighan.

"Here's your bloody stone. I'm leaving."

Lanighan looked from Mulvaney to Kitsune. "Is your drama played out? Good. Now, Kitsune, you and I are not done. You will give me something else, something I must have. It will be your final gift. Hurry, Mulvaney, do it now!"

Mulvaney lunged at her, grabbed her arm, twisted it behind her back, and began pummeling her kidneys with hard punches. He outweighed her by a good forty pounds, and he knew all her moves. He'd taught them to her, after all. But she was much younger and very fast and strong, and she fought him with everything in her, twisting and punching and kicking.

Lanighan ignored the battle and opened the bag, dumped the Koh-i-Noor into his palm. It was luminescent, sparkling, lit from within, recognizing its true master. The great stone was his at last.

He went to the small table in the corner, where he'd set his grandfather's ancient rosewood box.

Using the bone-handled knife he'd brought from his family's estate, he cut his finger, laid the wound against the golden lock. The hasps began to turn with a creaking noise he remembered as if it were yesterday, and the lock sprang free.

He opened the box and looked down at his grandfather's huge stone, and the smaller one retrieved from Anatoly's safe. Both were dull in comparison to the Koh-i-Noor, their internal fire hidden. He pulled them from the box and laid them next to one another. He heard a noise begin. It was as if they were greeting one another, a small hum growing louder and more insistent. He pushed them closer together and the hum became screams. He put a finger on each of the stones, caressing them, giving them thanks.

The screams built, louder and louder still, beating at his mind, but he didn't look away from the incredible stones before him. They were so beautiful, yes, and now they were pulling together, as if drawn by an unseen force, though the lines between them were still clear. Not fully united, not fully one again. Not yet.

He stared into the heart of chaos, became one with it, then he rose above it, looked down, and marveled. He picked up the stones, cupped them tenderly in his hands.

Their heart was calling to him, and he knew it was time. When he spoke, his voice was stronger and louder than the screaming. It was the voice of a god.

"Bring me the woman's blood."

Mulvaney was tiring, but he didn't slow. His knife slashed a path in front of him, sending Kitsune back, closer and closer to Lanighan. Kitsune was focused on him, her own knives jabbing, tearing, and she rent the sleeve of one arm. She saw blood well up, but it didn't slow him. He continued advancing, forcing her back, ever back, toward Lanighan.

Lanighan screamed, "Now!"

Mulvaney grabbed her hand, jerked her arm straight out, and sliced her from wrist to elbow. She screamed in pain and the shock of the wound, numbly watched the blood pour from her arm.

Lanighan held the stones beneath the flowing blood. When they were red with her blood, he threw back his head and yelled to the heavens, "It is done!"

The screaming stopped.

Lanighan looked at the stones in his bloody hands and saw a light—blue, transparent, blinding in intensity, and it seemed to outline the edge of each stone. It whirled around the stones, merging them, and soon the edges were no longer to be seen. As the stones became one, they vibrated in his hands, and a whine began, growing louder and higher, like an electrical wire pulled taut and plucked. The light grew brighter and brighter, spearing out, encompassing the stone, his hands, the room.

He felt the light move into him, felt the small poisonous

cells in his body pop as they were destroyed. He was on fire, and he hurt, hurt so badly, pain rising from every part of him. The stone—it was killing the cancer, and it was killing him. His heart pounded hard and fast, and his breath grew short. He tried to let the stone drop, but he couldn't. The light moved through him and around him, and suddenly it coalesced into one narrow beam and split through the top of the warehouse, arcing up into the night sky, piercing the heavens.

And the killing pain left him and poured itself into the light, becoming one with it. He couldn't look away, it was pure and powerful, and it was born of him. Night became day, and he stared into the face of his own sun, followed its pulsing rays upward through the night sky and beyond, to the soul of the universe. Now he understood the very nature of its being, of man's being. He was its king, its master.

He was perfection.

He was a god.

The ground began to move under his feet.

97

Voices, loud, angry voices, then there was nothing, no sound at all. It had been only moments, but it seemed much longer since he didn't know what was happening. Then Nicholas heard Kitsune screaming. He tapped the comms unit in his ear. "Mike! Now!"

He heard her yell to Menard's men, "Go, go, go!"

Nicholas had wanted to stay close to Kitsune, but six guards had followed her up to the big office on the second floor and he'd been forced to hide in the shadows. When the guards heard Kitsune scream, they didn't rush into the office. Obviously they'd been ordered not to come in, and they wanted to do something, but there was no one to tell them what to do.

When the building began to shake, the decision was made for them. All but one of the guards took off down the stairs to get out of the warehouse, and Nicholas heard the staccato gunfire from Menard's men taking them out. The last guard started for the doorway, weapon up. Nicholas came up behind him, hooked his arm around his throat, and twisted, then threw him to the floor.

Nicholas ran into the room. He saw Mulvaney throw Kitsune against a wall. Mulvaney turned and saw him, and incredibly, he smiled, the same smile he'd given Nicholas as he'd escaped over the wire fence in the alley behind Mike's garage. "I wished I'd killed you. But now's a good time, isn't it? You've made your last mistake, boyo."

Nicholas saw the detonator in Mulvaney's hand. He fired, shattered his hand, but the bullet was too late. Mulvaney had already pushed the button, and the floor was buckling under their feet.

The noise of metal wrenching apart was brutal, and then came the wall of flames behind him. No escape back through the door. He saw Mulvaney fall to the floor, heard him cursing, cradling his wrist.

He saw Lanighan standing in the corner, his eyes— exalted, that was it, his head thrown back to the heavens. A long, thin scream tore from his throat. Nicholas saw he had something in his hands. It was the three stones, but now they looked like one, and they were covered with blood, Kitsune's blood.

Nicholas shouted, "Mike, Lanighan, stop him!"

She jumped in the window and crossed to Lanighan in three strides, turned him around, then put her fist to the soft spot under his jaw. His eyes rolled back in his head and he went down.

Mulvaney was on one knee but coming back up when Kitsune appeared from behind him and kicked him, hard, in the back. He sprawled onto the floor face-first, and she darted over to Lanighan.

The fire was whipping madly toward them, the walls starting to go up in flames around them.

Mike was pulling at his arm. "Nick, we've got to get out. Come on. Come on!"

He saw Kitsune through a thickening veil of smoke on her knees by Lanighan, the blood from her arm streaming over his face. She was hurt badly; he needed to help her. He took a step toward her, but she rose and rushed to him, pressed something hard into his hand.

He looked down and saw it wasn't the three stones united, it was simply the Koh-i-Noor, and it was covered with blood, her blood. What had happened to the other two stones?

Kitsune's face was highlighted by the inferno behind her. He saw her mouth move: "Go."

He made a grab for her, but she raced back toward Mulvaney.

Mike screamed, "Nicholas, come on, come on! I'll get Lanighan." She pulled him up and threw him over her shoulder and carried him to the fire escape. Nicholas climbed out the window, and she shoved Lanighan at him.

Together, they got Lanighan down the rickety metal stairs as Menard's men came running. Nicholas literally threw Lanighan at them. He saw the building was a raging inferno, pulsing with the heat of the flames. He started back to the fire escape.

Mike grabbed his arm. "No, Nicholas, it's too late!"

He turned briefly to look at her and said only, "I have to go back for her," and she watched helplessly as he began to climb the ladder rungs.

The metal was hot under his hands, and the higher he climbed, the hotter it became. He reached the window but could see only billowing endless flames, the black smoke threading in and out in a mad dance. He yelled her name again and again.

Then he saw her. He yelled her name again. She turned and smiled, gave him a small salute, and turned back into the fire. He saw her standing over the body of her mentor, and Nicholas would swear he heard the sound of a bullet over the crackling roar.

She was gone.

He climbed back down the fire escape, and saw Menard's soldiers had gathered up the remainder of Lanighan's guards. One of Menard's men said, "We have four down out front. The firefighters are on their way."

Mike stepped to his side, gripped his shoulder. Her face was black, covered in soot. He slowly reached up a hand and wiped her cheek.

"Are you okay?" she asked, and began running her hands over his chest, his arms. "Nicholas, listen to me. You're bleeding, bad, but I can't find the wound. Where are you hit?"

His ears hurt, his throat was raw with smoke. His hands were blistered from the heat of the metal. He looked down to see his shirtfront was covered in blood from where he'd wiped his hands. "I'm fine. It's not my blood, it's hers. Kitsune's gone. I think she shot Mulvaney."

It had all happened in a split second.

Mike hit him on the shoulder. "You scared me again. Stop doing that."

He reached into his pocket and pulled out the Koh-i-Noor, still smeared with Kitsune's blood.

Mike stared at the bloody stone. "So she gave it to you after all."

He saw Kitsune's face again, saw her smile, saw her walk into the heart of the fire. He cleared his throat. "She'd never hidden the Koh-i-Noor in Lanighan's briefcase. She had it all along; it was in the blue bag. I saw her pry it out of Lanighan's hand, and she gave it to me."

Mike didn't say anything. She'd seen Kitsune lean over him, but she hadn't seen anything else, at least not clearly.

They turned and watched the fire, listened to the smaller explosions rip through the warehouse as the charges that Mulvaney had laid ignited. Nicholas could swear the Koh-i-Noor was warm in his hand, but when he looked down at it, he saw that the skin of his palms was burned and beginning to blister.

Mike asked, "Nicholas, did you see the other diamonds?"

"No." Had he? He simply didn't know.

"All that precious art on the bottom floor, all of it destroyed."

The roof started to collapse, the corrugated metal walls buckling with an unearthly groan. Nicholas put his arm around her shoulders and turned her away.

"Enough. Let's go home."

98

Mike came out of her bedroom the next morning to find Nicholas already showered, dressed, and sitting at the table in their living room, eating a croissant that she wanted to rip out of his hand.

He looked up and smiled at her. "Good morning. Before you ask, yes, my stitches survived." He saw her arm was back in a sling. No wonder, given the way she'd jerked Lanighan over her shoulder last night. "How about yours?"

She waved him off. "All good."

She sat at the table and stared at the beautiful plate of food in front of her—café crème, yogurt, croissants with strawberry preserves, and a big fat brioche.

He said, "Best of all, here's coffee. You'll need your strength. Our debriefing is in half an hour."

She asked, "How are your hands?"

"I'll do." They fell into comfortable silence as they ate their breakfast.

Mike wiped the crumbs off the front of her shirt, glanced at her watch. "Okay, it's time to fill them in on our adventures last night." She opened her laptop and tapped into the CIVITS secure videoconference feed. The twentieth-floor conference room appeared on the screen. Zachery, Ben, Gray, Savich, and Sherlock were sitting around the table.

She waved a croissant at them. *"Bonjour."*

Light laughter, then Zachery said, "It's already all over the news, all over the world, and viral on the Internet. The Koh-i-Noor saved, but no details. Probably one of Menard's men saw you with it but didn't know how you'd gotten it. After we get things clear, we'll hold a press conference here.

"I'm very glad to see both of you alive. Is the warehouse fire out yet?"

Nicholas answered, "At last count, there were two hundred firefighters and forty-five engines on scene, and the thing's still burning. Mulvaney knew his business. All the surrounding warehouses went up in flames, too. The fire spread nearly half a mile through the area. They had to evacuate all the homes."

Mike said, "Not to mention every ounce of evidence was destroyed and all the priceless artwork stored there. It will be a week before the hot spots die down enough for a forensic examination to begin."

"Any bodies recovered?" Ben asked.

"Four guards who were near the doors, firing at Menard's men, and one guard from the second floor."

Zachery asked, "The Ghost? The Fox?"

Nicholas shook his head. "The last time I saw Kitsune—the Fox—she'd knocked Mulvaney out. He was facedown and unconscious near the doorway where the fire was coming in fast." He paused for a moment, and added in an emotionless voice, "She was bleeding heavily. She gave me the Koh-i-Noor, then walked back into the flames." He didn't mention the gunshot because he didn't know if Kitsune had used it to kill Mulvaney or herself. He didn't want to know.

"How's Lanighan?" Savich asked.

Mike said, "He's in a secure unit at Hôpital Saint-Antoine. Menard told us he's retreated into his own mind, chanting sutras. He won't answer to his name, won't recognize anyone around him. The doctors don't know if or when he'll ever recover.

"All of you now know what Lanighan wanted to do—merge the three stones and heal himself. Become immortal." She nodded to Nicholas.

He said, "I can't describe what I saw last night as well as I'd like, but here goes. I saw Lanighan standing in the corner of the big second-floor room, his face lit up, his arms outstretched toward the ceiling, and he was cupping a huge bloody stone in his hands. He looked, well, maybe like he saw something no one else had ever seen before, he looked like he'd been blessed—I know that sounds strange. Really sorry, but nothing more than that." He paused for a moment, then added, "You remember Lanighan had leukemia as a teenager and went into remission. Recently the leukemia returned. And I, well, I asked the emergency-room doctors to test his blood." He paused a moment. "His blood work came back entirely normal."

There was silence, then Savich said, "Are you saying the legend had truth at its core? That reuniting the three parts of the diamond cured him?"

"All I'm saying is he no longer has cancer. Perfect health, at least physically. I can't tell you more because I don't know any more."

Everyone was quiet. Sherlock finally broke the silence. "You said the Fox gave you the Koh-i-Noor. Is it damaged in any way?"

Nicholas said, "Both Mike and I have examined it thoroughly and we can't see anything wrong with it. It's in the safe here in the room. I suppose the insurance indemnity folks would like it returned to the Met so it can be replaced in the crown."

Zachery said, "You bet. Last time I saw the director he was rubbing his hands together, saying he now expects the *Jewel of the Lion* exhibit will draw twice as many people as they'd planned; it'll be the event of the century. Hey, it'll probably be the start of a new legend. Once he hears the details, he'll probably give you guys a lifetime membership to the Met."

Nicholas said, "I'm glad someone will benefit from all this—" He waved his hand. *This what?* he wondered. *Waste? Tragedy?* He supposed some good had come out of this, but frankly all he could think about was the needless loss—Elaine dead, Kitsune killed in the fire.

Savich said, "Not only will the Met burst its seams with visitors to the exhibit, but Bo still has the contract. The Met has asked him to double the security."

Sherlock said, "Yep, Bo's a happy camper."

Zachery asked them to run through the previous night's events, then once more, with a dozen questions thrown in. He finished with, "Job well done, people, and thanks, Drummond, for your minor assistance to the FBI." And he laughed.

Savich said, "Nick, would you mind sticking around for a moment? I'd like to talk to you alone." The conference room emptied around him.

Nicholas said, "Sure, Savich." He glanced at Mike.

She said, "I'm outta here; a nice hot shower calls my name."

When they were alone, Savich said, "I have a proposition for you."

Up went a black brow.

"Nick, you've got talent, and insight, and let's be honest here, you take crazy, stupid chances and you're a bit uncaring about your own hide. I also think you've got the luck of the Devil, and that's never something to discount. However, the important thing is you get results."

The brow was still up. "You're very kind."

Savich grinned. "No, I'm not kind at all. I'm being entirely selfish here. I want you, Nick. Would you consider leaving New Scotland Yard and joining the FBI?"

Nicholas nearly spewed out the coffee he'd just drunk. "What? You want me to join the American FBI?"

"Yes. You'd have to go through the proper channels to apply, but with your spook and cop experience, your facility with languages, and your computer skills, you're a match with what we're looking for. You're thirty-one, only a year over the average age for our entrants.

"You work well with our agents, and you've scored a big win recovering the Koh-i-Noor. I'll even put in a good word for you. You'll have to go through the academy at Quantico like all the other agents. It won't be easy, and I can't guarantee you won't wash out."

Nicholas said, "After all that, it would be a shame to blow the landing, wouldn't it?"

Savich laughed. "I can't promise, but I think I could get you assigned to the New York Field Office. It seems to me you'd be a good fit there, and from all the signs, Zachery thinks you're a pretty handy guy to have around. I'd want you to work with my teams in Washington, D.C., as well, on a case-by-case basis."

It was finally sinking in. The FBI. Nicholas Drummond, a cop with New Scotland Yard—the American FBI. He said slowly, "I hadn't thought about another life-changing move, Savich. I really appreciate what you've said, but I'll have to think about it, long and hard." Only he didn't, he realized, he really didn't.

"All I can ask. Hurry, though. The new academy class starts soon. Now, you and Mike get home safe. And again, congratulations."

Call ended, Nicholas sat back on the sofa, staring out at the Parisian sky. Rain had begun to fall. He hoped it would help put out the warehouse fire.

The American FBI.

Mike came into the living room. "Yeah? So will you be the first Brit in the FBI?"

"Agent Caine, were you eavesdropping?"

"Sure. Did you know he was going to ask you to come aboard?"

He shook his head.

"Will you? Will you come join us?"

He laid his arm along the back of the sofa. "What do you think, Mike? Do you want me to join you?"

She gave him a long look. He looked like he'd been in a major-league brawl and he'd won, just barely. He didn't look at all like Mr. Aren't I Great. What he looked was tough and dangerous and tired, and beneath it all was a deep well of excitement, and perhaps a dollop of uncertainty.

She said slowly, "Well, Dillon is right. All in all, you're not a bad cop. You've got a pretty good brain. Trust the academy to train you up, make you into a real agent. Then yeah, maybe I could deal with having you in New York."

"I'm blushing. You and Savich, both of you heaping all these compliments on my head."

She joined him on the sofa and took one of his battered hands in hers. "I wouldn't be surprised if the queen makes you a knight or something."

He felt the warmth of her flesh as she cradled his hand.

It felt good. He realized she smelled like jasmine and wild grass again. He said, "Well, fact is, even though I hate to admit it, I couldn't have done it without your help."

She cocked her head to the side and regarded him thoughtfully. "We make a pretty good team, don't we? If you come to New York, I wouldn't say no to having you as a partner."

"You're saying if I join the FBI, you'd have my back?"

She patted his bruised cheek. "Stitches and all."

99

Nicholas turned onto the drive leading to his family home, Old Farrow Hall, or OFH, as everyone hereabouts called it. In the spring and summer the branches of the ancient lime trees intertwined above like a secret tunnel. In mid-winter, everything was naked sticks and branches—alien, yet still achingly beautiful, at least to him.

Once through the ancient stone gate, another half mile and the hall itself loomed before him, three stories of four-century-old red brick with stone quoins, gables, and turrets. Home. He pulled into the roundabout, the gravel crunching under his tires.

A small man with a tonsure of gray hair circling his head stood by the open door, dressed in a fine gray morning coat, crisp white shirt and tie.

"Good morning, Master Nicholas. Hurry in, now, the rain is coming down harder."

"Morning, Horne," Nicholas said, and stepped into the central core of the old hall. "You're looking well. Nigel sends his best."

Horne's expression at the mention of his beloved son didn't change, since age-old precepts of decorum prevented it, but he did allow a full-bodied "Ah."

Nicholas pulled the hamper from behind his back. "Can you sneak this in for me, Horne? I don't want Cook Crumbe seeing I've brought pastries from Fortnum and Mason for my mother."

Horne's nose twitched. "Of course. No sense in upsetting her. Your mother and his lordship are waiting for you in the breakfast room."

"Thank you, Horne. I'll head there straightaway."

He passed through the grand entrance hall and made his way toward the back of the house to what had been labeled the breakfast room by some ancestor centuries ago. He smelled cinnamon and apple and cardamom. Cook must have made apple tarts for breakfast, his favorite. All hail the prodigal son. He hoped they wouldn't kick him out.

The long, narrow breakfast room gave onto the sweep of the back lawn. A row of six tall windows overlooked the lower garden and the labyrinth, a fetching scene, even with the rain scoring down the glass. A fire crackled in the grate; the room was a bit too warm, but that was the way his grandfather liked it. Nicholas didn't mind, not today.

His grandfather, Eldridge Augustus Nyles Drummond, eighth Baron de Vesci, was ensconced at the head of the table in the master's hand-carved chair, his buttocks cradled by a decades-old crimson velvet cushion thicker than Nicholas's fist. He was halfway through a bowl of Cook Crumbe's solidly bland Scottish porridge, welcomed his grandson with a swirl of his spoon, his voice gruff. "Nicholas, my boy. About time you joined us. You're late."

"The score of vehicles I nearly ran off the M11 getting here wouldn't agree with you."

The baron wheezed out a laugh.

"Good morning, Mother. I like that jumper you're wearing, matches your eyes."

The old man harrumphed, spooned in more porridge. "The demmed thing doesn't match her eyes at all."

Mitzie Drummond laughed as she lightly laid her hand along his cheek, leaned up, and gave him a kiss. "Good morning, sweetheart."

"Where's Father?"

Mitzie said, "On a call, talking to the Home Office about some nonsense in the Middle East he shouldn't have to worry about." She shook her head, the perfectly maintained blond bob swinging forward. "He had tea, said he needn't have anything more."

Nicholas turned to Horne. "Would you ask him to join us, please? I have some news I'd like to share."

Mitzie narrowed her eyes at him.

"What sort of news?"

"Let's wait for Dad, shall we? What's been happening round here?"

Mitzie took the hint and began filling him in on the

leak in the West Wing roof, and how she was certain Gwynne Willis, the town butcher's wife, was slowly poisoning her abusive husband—served him right—and she was having trouble with her moral compass since she'd just as soon see the husband belowground. Did she have proof of this? She nodded, sadly, but said no more.

A few minutes later, Harry—Harold Mycroft St. John Drummond—joined them. He was taller than his son, fit and lean, a full head of black hair, distinguished gray at the temples. Nicholas stood and shook his father's hand in greeting. He took his seat and poured some tea.

His father's every motion was done with economy and purpose, like his grandfather, Drummond hallmarks. He was a man of infinite calm, which made him an excellent diplomat, and a man of common sense and reason. He was not, like his son, with his impatient, impulsive American blood, a man who ever leapt before looking carefully at the terrain beyond.

Properly fortified, Harry leaned back in his chair. "What's this news then, Nicholas?"

Nicholas also poured himself a cup of hot tea, stirred in milk and a bit of sugar. Liquid courage. He took a sip and said, "I've decided to join the FBI."

Dead silence, all eyes staring at him. Well, he had their attention. There was more dead silence.

"I've been accepted to the FBI Academy in Quantico, Virginia. It's twenty weeks of immersion training. I'll probably be assigned to the New York Field Office with the same people I worked with to find the Koh-i-Noor."

He looked around the table at the shocked faces. "Well, say something."

Harry studied his son's face. "You already changed direction once when you left the Foreign Office for New Scotland Yard. You are certain you wish to make another change?"

"I'm sure."

Harry sat back and looked at his dark-eyed, dashing son. He took after his mother, with his handsome face, his spirit, his bullheadedness, traits that made Harry proud, and profoundly worried on occasion. Nicholas had spent his entire career avoiding any hint of favoritism, of nepotism, striking out on his own from the very beginning. His son had courage, and honor, which made him, his father thought, a fine example of Drummond blood. And sometimes he was a wild hair, doing something so unexpected it left one speechless, something Harry recognized in his own father.

His mother was biting her lip. "You'll move to New York? When will we see you?"

"I'll come home as often as I can, I promise."

She shook her head. "I always knew your uncle Bo would drag you into his den of thieves."

Nicholas said mildly, "It's not the old Wild West, mother. It's your country, too."

She waved an elegant hand. "Of course it is, Nicholas, it's simply too far away for my tastes." She sighed. "I suppose this is a wonderful opportunity for you, but—" She didn't finish; instead, she came to give him a hug, and he relaxed. This, telling his family, was the part he'd dreaded. Penderley hadn't fought him at all, even wrote him a glowing recommendation. Nicholas suspected Penderley was probably happy to get him out of his hair more than anything else.

He stole a look at his grandfather, who appeared to be ignoring all of them, still studiously eating his oatmeal. He was eighty-three, his back ramrod-straight, his eyes still the rich Drummond brown, always sharp and assessing. The only real acknowledgment of his age was his thinned hair, and, well, not to belabor it, but his ears and nose seemed to grow bigger each passing year.

Nicholas was the grandson of a baron; there were no two ways around it. The heir twice removed, as Penderley had sometimes called him if he was feeling jovial. There were responsibilities to come in his future, but not now. His grandfather was hale and hearty, his father as well.

No, not now.

Finally, his grandfather put down his spoon and met his eyes. "Don't forget where you come from, Nicholas. This is your home, and it always will be." He said again, "Don't forget."

Nicholas smiled. "Never."

EPILOGUE

They walked in unison out of the thirteenth-century Norman church, a slow march in step with the beatings of their hearts, one hand clasped on their belt buckles, the other hand steadying the heavy coffin on their shoulders. Nicholas felt the edge of the wood digging into his neck, a last connection to Elaine York, and it was pain. At least the pain reminded him he was alive when so many others weren't.

He'd seen Mike sitting in the middle of the church, her head covered with a ridiculous confection hat she'd told him she'd found near Harrods in London. She'd laughed, adding that the enthusiastic saleswoman had assured her it was just the thing for a stylish funeral. Elaine would have loved it, since she couldn't wear hats and was wildly jealous of women who could. Elaine's mother, who looked rather marvelous in hats, sat with her companion near Mike. She now had a much-needed

$200,000 safe in her bank. Kitsune had seen her friend done rightly by, at least.

Nicholas thought she understood what was happening, though he wasn't really certain. She'd been mentally clear, though, when, taking his big hand in her small ones, she'd said to him, "Please bury my daughter here, Nicholas, in Farrow-on-Grey. She loved it so." And then she'd sort of faded away, back into the soulless prison in her mind.

Nicholas looked over the top of the coffin at Ben Houston, his head bowed, grief pouring off him, and he felt his own throat close.

Elaine was being buried as a decorated officer, with all honors, as she deserved. Her friends and fellow officers from London were here, all still in shock, not really understanding what had happened, since she was in New York to be a minder, not a police officer. And Penderley, silent, bearing the weight of Elaine's coffin on his shoulder.

He heard a throat clearing and looked over at his uncle Bo, walking in front of Ben. Nicholas was grateful for his presence. It would make the next few days easier, having him here.

When it was done, when Nicholas had said a silent prayer over her grave, the sky opened and rain began to fall in heavy sheets, crying for him, crying for them all.

Friends from the Yard were going around to The Drunken Goose, Farrow-on-Grey's fifteenth-century pub, with its small windows of square-cut glass, ancient oak beams, and hot, sweet air, Penderley with them. But Nicholas didn't want to go, he wanted to go home and strip off the damn funeral suit, take a shower, and have a drink. He crossed the church graveyard to Bo, who laid a hand momentarily on his shoulder; then the two of them turned to wait for Mike and Ben. Once they were together, Bo said, "Let's get out of here."

The drive to Old Farrow Hall took only a few minutes. They were all silent.

Cook Crumbe had prepared a spread for them, of course, so when they arrived, all shaking umbrellas and ducking out of the way of Mike's enormous hat, Horne shepherded them into the dining room and saw to it everyone had a drink and some food.

Nicholas nodded to the old man who'd taken such care of him and his family for so many years. He cleared his tight throat. "Thank you, Horne."

Horne only nodded and said in his most formal voice, "Of course, Master Nicholas, of course."

"Inspector York told me she appreciated your kindness to her."

Horne bowed his head, then said, his voice austere, "She was a young woman deserving of kindness. I will miss her."

Mike watched Nicholas speaking to the Drummond butler—butler!—she still couldn't get over having a butler in the modern world. She'd noticed his accent was deeper, his voice more clipped, when he was at home. It had been a hard day on him—a hard week, really, what with telling his parents he was joining the FBI. She would have loved to be a fly on the wall when he'd made that announcement. He'd told her his parents and his grandfather, even

Horne and Cook Crumbe, had taken it well, but she thought he was just trying to make himself feel better about his decision.

And then he'd arranged for Elaine's funeral, seen to Elaine's ill mother. Mike was very pleased that Elaine had had time to send her mother the $200,000 before she'd been killed.

She knew this huge rambling house with its hundreds of years of life and all its endless dramas was a deep part of him, and would always be his touchstone. As for her parents, she'd told her dad how his heroine, beautiful Mitzie Drummond, was a gracious, loving woman who solved mysteries in her spare time.

Mike looked at Mitzie across the room. She'd left it all behind, fame and fortune, to marry Nicholas's dad, a man very unlike his son. Tall, aloof, but when he smiled, it warmed his face and made you smile in return.

Nicholas's wily old grandfather had asked her if she intended to take care of his grandson. And not five minutes later, Nicholas's mother had asked her the same thing. And not five minutes after that, Cook Crumbe had stirred from the kitchen and asked if she would take care of Master Nicholas. She told them all the same thing: yes, she would take care of Nicholas Drummond, they could take that to the bank.

She ate one of Cook Crumbe's delicious shrimp prepared with some sort of curry and watched and listened.

Horne waited until Nicholas had eaten and had a few sips of single malt before handing him a thick package.

"A woman came with this while you were out."

Nicholas only glanced at it. "Can't it wait?"

"She said no, sir. She wanted you to open it the moment you came home."

Something in Horne's tone made Nicholas look up sharply. "Who was she?"

"I couldn't say. She was small, though, with dark hair. Bonny blue eyes, so light—"

Nicholas thrust his drink into Horne's hand and grabbed the package from him, ripped it open. Everyone stopped to watch him. He pulled the thick stack of paper from the envelope; saw the familiar blue backing indicating a legal document.

Mike asked, "Nicholas, what is it?"

He thumbed through the pages, then started to laugh. "It's a deposition. Almighty God in heaven, it's a bloody deposition."

"From who? About what?"

"There are hundreds of pages. I will be damned. This contains information on Mulvaney's thefts, all the murders, everything she promised."

He looked up and said simply, "Kitsune. She's alive, and she kept the bargain."

London
March

The rooftops were slick with frost, the sun just beginning to break through the gloomy sky. Snow again, she could feel it. She adjusted her position slightly, made herself more comfortable. She stashed the ATN night-vision goggles, pleased she'd chosen the PVS7s. Wouldn't do to have anything less than military grade. They'd served her well on her overnight sojourns this week.

She brought her monocle to her eye and checked it once. All was quiet. In their quarters, their tiny apartments, men were waking, beginning their morning routines. Women were showering, preparing breakfast, readying themselves to go out into the world. The men stayed behind; this was their work and their home.

She saw him then. Her pulse quickened, her breath became shallow, and something moved deep inside her.

She set the monocle down and poured the last of the tea from the thermos into her cup. She drank, letting it warm her, then checked the monocle again. The watch was changing, the guards in camouflage bristling with weapons.

The gates would open to the public at 9:00 a.m. The most dynamic and wondrously grim landmark in London would see throngs of people streaming through the gates, despite the weather. Though late March now, the air was still a bone-deep cold and seeped through puffy down jackets.

Today, Kitsune would be among them, bundled in her jacket, as she had every day for the past week.

Today, she would approach him. Ask to speak. Ask for forgiveness.

She was prepared, overprepared, but it was the only

way she had the courage to try. Today everything would change. He'd either turn her away or take her back. There would be no in between. He wasn't the type to stay friends.

Ignoring the lingering pain in her forearm, she packed her things and crawled down the slick roof. The wound was healing, but she'd have the long, thin scar forever.

The window on the tenth floor was still cracked, and she slipped inside, taking a moment to make sure nothing had been disturbed. It wasn't just a stroke of luck construction had started on the building closest to the Tower of London. She'd bought the building and commissioned the renovation. Through a shell company, of course. She wasn't about to let anything else get in her way. And she saw a profit down the road as well. She'd been able to observe unmolested for days.

She said a small prayer as she changed clothes, stashed her black camo that blended so perfectly with the night-time rooftops, and became the young researcher from the University of Edinburgh again, jeans, trainers, jumper, and mac, hair in a ponytail, the false brown irises restored to their natural, startling blue, the odd genetic anomaly that should have led her to a career in modeling instead of the life she'd led. She wouldn't change her old life for the world, but she'd bid it farewell back in Gagny.

She pulled the satellite phone from her bag, scrambled the signal, and placed a call to a mobile number she knew by heart.

His voice was deep, clogged with sleep. She'd woken

him. She couldn't blame him for sleeping late. He deserved rest after all they'd been through. And his life was undergoing a sea change as well.

"Drummond here."

"Thank you," she whispered, then ended the call before he had a chance to react.

Time to go.

With a smile, she gathered her bag, walked to the elevator, and disappeared.

AUTHOR'S NOTE

Koh-i-Noor—say it aloud, pause for a moment. Do you feel the fleeting warmth of light bathing your face? Or perhaps the pull of something you don't understand, but you know it's in the deepest part of you, the part that recognizes magic?

Imagine, this incredible stone was once 793 carats—the size of a man's fist, the prized possession of the god Krishna. Now imagine betrayal and a curse passed down through the ages that promises death, chaos, and destruction to any man who tries to keep the Koh-i-Noor close.

The stuff of legends, you say, but in truth the Koh-i-Noor did indeed pass from bloody hand to bloody hand, and always devastation followed in its wake. A long ago Sultan had the Koh-i-Noor cut from 793 carats to a mere 186. It came to Queen Victoria in 1850 and it was she who wanted to shine it up. The once massive Koh-i-Noor of 793 carats ended up 105, and that is its size today.

The Final Cut is based on fact. What I have created is the personal Lanighan family legend passed down from father to son for generations:

When Krishna's stone is unbroken again,
the hand which holds it becomes whole.
Wash the Mountain of Light in woman's blood,
so we will know rebirth and rejoice.

I hope you enjoyed *The Final Cut*, written with love
and great excitement and a touch of magic.
Say "Koh-i-Noor," and just imagine.

—*Catherine Coulter*
and J. T. Ellison

HISTORY OF THE KOH-I-NOOR DIAMOND

Legends claim the Koh-i-Noor diamond belonged to the great god Krishna until a treacherous servant stole it from him while he slept, and thus the curse was born.

He who owns this diamond will own the world, but will also know all its misfortunes. Only God or a woman can wear it with impunity.

Other stories have the Koh-i-Noor discovered in a riverbed in 3000 B.C. alongside its pink sister, the Darya-i-Noor, residing today in Iran.

The first time the Koh-i-Noor enters into written history is in 1305 as a stone weighing an extraordinary 793 carats. It passed from hand to hand as regimes rose and fell, always coveted but never bought or sold, only gained through conquest.

THE FIRST CUT

In the seventeenth century, Emperor Aurangzeb, the last of the great Moghul leaders, wanted to impress a French gemstone expert who was searching the East for rare and special stones. Aurangzeb gave the Italian lapidary Borgio the task of polishing the diamond for the visit. Borgio bungled the job, taking the 793-carat diamond down to a measly 186 carats.

It mattered not; the value of the stone was still overwhelming. It changed hands many more times, through blood and trickery, even going to Pakistan and Persia before returning to India. Thus, all three countries lay claim to it, and regularly petition the British government for its repatriation.

HOW THE KOH-I-NOOR DIAMOND CAME TO QUEEN VICTORIA

In 1850, Maharaja Duleep Singh, the last Maharaja of Lahore and the youngest son of the famous Lion of Punjab, was dethroned by the British, his country (Punjab) annexed. He was forced to hand over the Koh-i-Noor to the British as part of the Treaty of Lahore. However, Duleep Singh wasn't imprisoned or mistreated. He was feted by British society and became a favorite of Queen Victoria.

THE FINAL CUT

In 1851, Queen Victoria displayed the Koh-i-Noor to the British public. However, the 186-carat diamond hadn't been changed since the Borgio bungling two hundred years before, and it looked ugly and dull, not the brilliant cut the people expected.

After great debate, Prince Albert hired a lapidary named Coster from Amsterdam to cut the stone again. When Coster was finished, the Koh-i-Noor was radiant with dazzling light. However, the diamond was now a mere 105 carats.

The British have been very careful not to test the curse, and only the women of the Royal Family wear the diamond. The Koh-i-Noor was originally made into a brooch for Queen Victoria, then found its way into crowns for Queen Alexandra and Queen Mary before it came to rest in its current home, the centerpiece of the queen mother's crown. It can be seen in the Tower of London.

In my story, Parliament has enacted a temporary law allowing the queen mother's crown to travel to the United States to be the centerpiece of the *Jewel of the Lion* exhibit at the Metropolitan Museum of Art in New York City.

Given what happened, it is highly doubtful the British will ever again allow the prized Koh-i-Noor to leave their shores.

Keep reading for an excerpt from
the next Brit in the FBI novel
by Catherine Coulter and J. T. Ellison

THE LOST KEY

Coming soon in hardcover
from G. P. Putnam's Sons

1

FBI New York Field Office
26 Federal Plaza
7:25 a.m.

What in bloody hell have I done?

Nicholas Drummond reported for duty at the FBI's New York headquarters smartly at 7:00 a.m., as instructed. After twenty minutes with human resources, he felt a bit like a schoolboy: stand here, walk there, smile for your photograph, here's your pass, don't lose it. It was worse than the FBI Academy, and with their strict rules, the uniforms, the endless drills, more like his training at Hendon Police College with Hamish Penderley and his team.

The administrative realities of moving from New Scotland Yard to the FBI in New York were decidedly less romantic that the initial prospect had been. Three months earlier, Dillon Savich, head of the Criminal Apprehension Unit at FBI Headquarters in Washington, D.C., had encouraged Nicholas to make a new home in the FBI, and he'd accepted. It was now May, with graduation from Quantico and the FBI Academy two weeks in the past, and he was officially an FBI *Special Agent*, and technically at the bottom of the food chain.

Again.

Twice he'd done this. The first time he'd left the Foreign Office to work for the Metropolitan Police in London. He'd survived those days and he'd survive these too.

And even better, you don't have Hamish Penderley to ride you now, making you do tactical drills at 5:00 a.m. Zachery's a very different sort. So buck up.

Nicholas knew he should have started out in a small Bureau office in the Midwest, gotten his feet wet, but Dillon Savich had gotten him assigned to the New York Field Office, as promised, working directly for Supervisory Special Agent Milo Zachery, a man Nicholas knew and trusted, with Special Agent Michaela Caine as his partner.

When at last they issued him his service weapon, he felt complete, the heavy weight of the Glock on his hip comforting, familiar.

Freshly laminated and now armed, he'd been walked to the twenty-third floor, led through the maze of the cube farm, and ushered into a small space, blue-walled with some sort of fuzzy fabric, the kind Velcro would adhere to, with a brown slab of wood-grained Formica as a desktop. There was a computer, several hard drives, two file trays labeled *In* and *Out*, and a chair.

The cubicle was so small, he could easily touch each side with his arms outstretched, and that allowed the tiniest bit of claustrophobia to sneak in. He needed more monitors and more shelving, and maybe he'd soon feel at home. Once in the zone on his computers, the close quarters wouldn't be a problem.

He dropped his briefcase on the floor next to the chair, stashed a small black go bag in his bottom drawer, and took a seat. He spun the chair around in a circle, legs drawn up to avoid crashing. Small, yes, but it would do. He didn't plan to spend much time sitting here anyway. Part of the deal he'd made with Savich meant Nicholas would be working ad hoc with him at times, running forensic point on cases in Washington. From what he'd experienced four months ago working with Savich and Sherlock and Mike Caine, he was in for a ride.

A low, throaty voice said near his ear, "Needs a bit of sprucing up, don't you think? I know, how about your photo of the queen, front and center?"

Speak of the devil.

"The queen is hanging happily over my bed in my new digs." He bent his head back to see Agent Mike Caine looking down at him, smiling widely. She was wearing her signature black jeans and motorcycle boots, her blond hair pulled back in a ponytail. Her badge hung on a lanyard around her neck, and her black-rimmed reading glasses were tucked into her blouse pocket.

"I wonder why I didn't smell you first." And he leaned up, sniffed. "Ah, there it is, that lovely jasmine, like my mum. Hi, Mike, long time no see."

"Yeah, yeah, all of two weeks since your graduation. You all settled into your new place? By the way, where is your new place?"

He didn't want to tell her, didn't want to tell anyone, it was too embarrassing. Fact was, he'd lost a big argument with his grandfather about the location of his new home. He shrugged, looked over her shoulder at several agents walking by. "All settled in. A fairly nice bed in an okay place over there," and he waved his hand vaguely toward the east.

She cocked her head at him, and he said quickly, "You look pretty good after being on your own for four months. When can we get out of here?"

"Champing at the bit for a case already, Special Agent Drummond? You've only been here fifteen minutes. We haven't even had time to go over the coffee schedule and introduce you around. Are we calling you Nick or Nicholas these days?"

"You know what they say about rolling stones and moss. Nicholas will do fine."

She looked at her watch. "We can get out of here right about now, Nicholas. You're in luck. We've caught a murder."

He felt the punch of adrenaline. "A murder? Is it terrorism related?"

"I don't think so. I heard about it two minutes ago. It's time to get briefed."

SAC Milo Zachery joined them in the hall. In his tailored gray suit, white shirt, and purple-and-black-striped tie, Nicholas thought he looked a lot snazzier than Penderley ever had. Slick clothes, fresh haircut. He looked like a big-dog federal agent all the way down to his highly polished wing tips. Nicholas knew Zachery was focused, smart, and willing to let his agents use their brains with only subtle hands on the reins.

Nicholas shook his new boss's hand.

"Good to see you, Drummond. I'll handle your briefing myself. Walk with me."

Mike gave him a manic grin, her adrenaline on a level with his, and he was reminded of that night in Paris several months earlier, Mike barely upright, leaning against the overturned couch, bleeding from a gunshot to the arm, her face beat up, and smiling. He thanked the good Lord she was here and whole and ready to kick butt.

Nicholas smiled back and gestured for her to go first.

"Such lovely manners from the first Brit in the FBI. I could get used to this."

"Still cheeky, are we? It's good to see that some things haven't changed."

"Come on, you two." Zachery walked them past his office, down the blue-carpeted senior management hallway, straight out the door and to the elevators. As he punched the down button, he said, "You're headed to 26 Wall Street. Stabbing. The NYPD called us since it's on federal land, so it's our case. I thought it would be a good idea to get Drummond here liaising with the locals as soon as possible. And aren't you two lucky? Someone managed to get themselves dead on your first morning. Go on down there and figure out what happened."

The elevator doors opened and Zachery waved them in. "Drummond, I know you're going to be our big cyber-crime/computer-terrorism guy, but we also need to teach you to drive on the right side of the road, get your boots dirty on the ground first." He smiled and clapped Nicholas on the shoulder. "Glad you're with us, Drummond. Welcome to the FBI. Good hunting." He turned and said over his shoulder, "Oh, yes, Mike, keep him in line."

2

Mike's black Crown Vic waited for them in the garage. She jangled the car keys at him, then drew them back. "Maybe I should drive, even though you need the practice. Wall Street's pretty crazy."

"Contrary to popular belief, I do know how to manage the streets of New York. I have American blood, too, you know."

She laughed and got behind the wheel. Once they were out of the garage, she said, "Next time out, you'll drive. It's a requirement that you know all the streets. But not today. So tell me, did you really live up to Savich's lofty standards at the academy? And Sherlock's?"

"I tried my pitiful best, Agent Caine." He watched her come within an inch of a lane-cutting taxi without blinking an eye.

"What have you been doing here in New York for the last two weeks?"

He never looked away from the pedestrian zigzagging in front of the Crown Vic. "Oh, a bit of this and that, getting set up. That's about it." *Not to mention I shopped for furniture until I nearly cut my own wrists, fought with Nigel on where all the bloody furniture should go, and was forced to have dinner with my ex at a French place big on presentation and light on food. In short, I haven't used my brain for two bloody weeks.* But he didn't tell her any of that.

She sped through a yellow light. "I've missed having you around. Come on, now, tell me about your place."

Not in this lifetime. "Nothing much to tell, really. It's livable, that's all."

Nicholas's grandfather, in a magnanimous show of support for his grandson's decision to move to America, had purchased him a brownstone. No matter how hard Nicholas had protested, the Baron—and his parents, he suspected—refused to allow Nicholas his wish, an anonymous flat somewhere in Chelsea.

He was now saddled with a behemoth town house on East 70th Street, much to his butler Nigel's delight. Five floors, five bedrooms. Oh, yes, this sort of opulence was just the ticket for fitting in with the rest of the agents in the New York Field Office.

Mike slowly turned onto a street packed with pedestrians. "I can't wait to see it. Invite me over for a beer later, all right?"

And again he thought, *Not in this lifetime.* He said, "Where is our crime scene?"

"Off Wall Street. Right there."

Mike threaded through dozens of people across to Pine Street, not far from Federal Hall. He saw the yellow saw-horse barrier with NYPD on it, three blue-and-whites, lights revolving, flashing the stone buildings.

They badged the NYPD cop at the barrier, signed in to the scene, and were led to the small side street. It was going to be a beautiful day, he saw, already warming nicely. Considering the number of crime scenes he'd handled in the pouring rain in London, this was certainly preferable.

"What do we have here?" he asked the young NYPD officer standing inside the tape. His badge read F WILSON, and he looked barely old enough to vote, much less be a cop. Even though Nicholas knew he couldn't be more than five years older than the cop, he felt ancient, until Wilson spoke like the seasoned professional he was.

"Stabbing," Wilson said. "It's right there on your land. Another five feet and it would be ours. But, no, this guy decides to get himself dead and make it all yours. I hear it's your first day on the job. Welcome to New York."

"Thank you."

Wilson grinned. "We've been canvassing, got a small group of people held aside who were nearby when it happened. Most say the suspect was a Caucasian male, brown hair, medium height, wearing jeans and a white hoodie."

Nicholas looked over at the small knot of people at the street corner, gaping at the scene, some recording everything with their phones, others standing quietly, obviously shell-shocked. He said, "Rather a detailed description, that."

"I know, right? Amazing, really, since most witnesses

can rarely agree on the sex of the suspect. Talk about lucking out—from the statements so far, there were two men arguing, then a struggle, then one guy turned away and the other guy stabbed him from behind and took off, running."

Mike said, "Hold everyone here, Officer Wilson. We'll want to speak to them as well. We need to get a look at the body, then we'll be right back."

Wilson saluted her and moved away from the tape to let them in.

Nicholas took his time walking toward the dead man, noticed Mike was taking in everything as well. Special Agent Louisa Barry, one of their crime scene techs, was snapping on nitrile gloves, ready to get to work. Nicholas smiled at her, then went down on his haunches beside a man who was seriously dead. He was in his late forties to early fifties, his brown eyes staring sightlessly into the sky, salt-and-pepper hair combed slightly to the side to cover the beginnings of a receding hairline, his suit rumpled and creased. From the angle of his body on the pavement, and the way his arms were flung out from his body, Nicholas thought he'd fallen to his knees, then onto his back, and died. The blood pooled beneath him, dark and thick, but it was disturbed, like a child's finger painting, swirls and whorls whipping across the sidewalk. *What were you arguing about? Why'd he stab you in the back?*

"See anything interesting?" Mike asked, studying the blood pool.

"It's what I'm *not* seeing that's interesting," Nicholas said. "No murder weapon. The guy stabbed him, then pulled out the knife and took off. I wonder if any of the witnesses saw the killer do that."

Mike said, "He still has his wallet, isn't that right, Louisa?" Nicholas looked up at her, holding the man's belongings.

"Right here."

Nicholas asked, "What's his name?" He hated calling a once-living, once-breathing man a corpse. He deserved more than that.

"Jonathan Charles Pearce. Lives on the Upper East Side. Money and cards left in the wallet. His cell's a Black-Berry Touch, and here's a nice old watch and a set of keys. Cell is password-protected, I can't access it without my tools."

Nicholas said, "Do you carry a UFED in the field, perchance?"

"Is that British for 'universal forensic extraction device'?" And she grinned. "Yeah, so happens I have a Touch Ultimate on the truck. Hang on a minute."

"Good," he said. "Are there any cameras around?"

Louisa said, "Nothing that points directly to this spot, but there's a traffic cam at the intersection of Pine and William, and the building itself has a camera on the corner. Might have something from one of those."

"Excellent, Louisa, thank you."

"By the way, Nicholas, it's good to have you on board. Welcome to New York."

"It's good to be here."

In the next instant, Louisa was headed to the mobile command unit.

Mike said, "Glad she brought it. With the UFED, we'll get the passcode broken and access the data in no time. So, Nicholas, it doesn't appear Mr. Pearce was the victim of a robbery."

"No, it would seem not. A fight between two men. But about what?"

"Whatever it was, the killer lost it and stabbed Mr. Pearce in the back with a dozen people looking on."

M14G0610